LINDSAY McKENNA

HIGH COUNTRY
REBEL

ISBN-978-1-62490-802-6

HIGH COUNTRY REBEL

Dear Reader,

Former Navy SEAL Talon Holt knows all about loss. He lost both his father and stepfather and, later, his best friend. Now, his mother is sick and he is needed at home. Fresh from a veteran hospital and suffering from post-traumatic stress disorder, Talon finds his way home to Wyoming, his loyal dog, Zeke, by his side. Love is the last thing on Talon's mind.

Cat Edwin, paramedic and firefighter, drives through a blizzard and discovers a man and dog near death. Little does she realize that her compassionate act will change her life. From the beginning, Cat is powerfully drawn to this rugged soldier, though she fights it. Her history with relationships is rocky at best, especially since her last boyfriend is now stalking her.

With a little help, Talon gets back on his feet to be the loving son his mother needs. What he doesn't expect, however, is to find love for himself. The struggles of coming home could weaken a lesser man, but Talon calls on his years as a SEAL. He needs everything he's learned to protect Cat from a lethal element in her past. When Cat is surrounded by danger, all Talon can think is that, once again, he will lose someone he loves. And that just can't happen again....

I hope you enjoy this story! To stay up with my latest books, run over to www.lindsaymckenna.com.

Lindsay McKenna

To the many men and women volunteers
of Operation Gratitude.

To Carolyn Blashek, whose vision has created this
wonderful charity that supports our brave and
courageous military men and women.

To Linda Landau, who works for this charity
and who I get to call a friend.

Please join me and many others
on December 7, 2013, in Van Nuys, California,
as we all celebrate the one millionth box being sent
overseas to military personnel, who always treasure
a thoughtful gift from this charity.

For more information, visit
www.opgrat.wordpress.com/2013/02/26/save-the-
date-one-million-care-packages-and-counting/

CHAPTER ONE

TALON HOLT KNEW he was going to die. It was just a question of time. He slogged through the foot of snow quickly piling up on Highway 191 to the Bar H outside of Jackson Hole, Wyoming. Zeke, his U.S. Navy SEAL combat assault dog, a Belgian Malinois, walked at his side, looking up, a worried expression on his black face.

As he gripped the leather leash, Talon gasped for air. They were at five thousand feet in the middle of a late-May blizzard, no less. He could barely see the Snake River hundreds of feet below and to his right. On his right was a rocky, craggy mountain rising 6,200 feet, hidden by the blizzard.

He wiped his mouth, head down, the wind howling and gusting, beating against his wet, cold body. Miles earlier, it had rained. He and Zeke were drenched as they slogged alongside the muddy berm of the highway.

Talon had been born in this area so he knew he was in trouble. Few cars or trucks were on the road because of the unexpected blizzard.

What made his problem worse: the PTSD symptoms acquired during his tenure as a Navy SEAL. Talon couldn't just hop on a plane, ride in a bus or be inside any enclosed area if a panic attack hit him. When medically and honorably discharged from the SEALs, he had to walk from Coronado on the West Coast back home to Jackson Hole. He knew the journey would get dicey.

Lucky for him now, he wore his Navy camo coat and he had gloves. He took the wool blanket out of his sixty-five-pound rucksack and wrapped it around Zeke. The Belgian Malinois, who was often mistaken for a German shepherd, was not prepared for a blizzard, either. Zeke was short-haired and needed the protection. Talon tried his best to keep his loyal dog dry and warm.

He was so close to getting home. God, hadn't he suffered enough? Done enough for his country? Ever since the Taliban had captured him and Hayden, his SEAL partner, his life had disintegrated before him. They had been jumped by the enemy and Zeke had escaped and taken off. The dog had run thirty miles over rough, mountainous terrain to Camp Bravo, a forward operating base in Afghanistan.

He wouldn't be alive today if Zeke hadn't done what he did. After regaining consciousness in the hospital at Bagram Air Base near Kabul, he learned that Zeke had barked furiously, getting the SEALs' attention at Bravo. Zeke had led a six-man SEAL team back to where he and Hayden had been captured and were being tortured. During the firefight, Zeke had taken a bullet in the shoulder, nearly died himself.

Talon tried to shake off the memory of the torture. His gut churned with cramps from not eating for three days. He had to get home. He *had* to make it to the Bar H.

But would he survive? With every short, shallow breath that tore out of his mouth, Talon wheezed. His lungs were filling up with fluid, and he desperately needed antibiotics and pure oxygen. He cursed his bad

luck. In his soggy mind, the fever making him halluci-
nate, Talon figured he had about a mile to go.

He was either going to die of pneumonia out in this
storm or he was going to die of hypothermia. How
ironic was that? He'd survived gunshot wounds and
torture only to freeze to death out in this damn blizzard? If Talon hadn't been so exhausted, he'd be pissed.

The sky was a dark, gunmetal gray. He knew it was
probably around seven in the morning, but it looked
like early dawn due to the heavy, dark clouds carrying
the brunt of the blizzard. Talon stumbled over his own
feet and fell hard on the berm. He threw out his hands,
releasing the leash. Zeke stopped, wagging his long
brushy tail, whining and licking the side of his face as
Talon struggled to sit up. The world whirled around him
and Talon cursed softly, tightly shutting his eyes. Come
on! Dammit, if he could survive BUD/S training to become a SEAL, he sure as hell could get through this!

Gasping, grunting, he used every last bit of his
strength and pushed himself unsteadily to his feet.

He leaned over, placing his gloved hand on Zeke's
strong back, which had carried so many loads for him
over in Afghanistan for three years. He groped for and
found the leash. Talon awkwardly patted his dog's head,
saw the worry in Zeke's large brown eyes. Zeke deserved a helluva lot better than being out in this deathly
blizzard.

Talon winced, lowering his head against the stinging
bits of ice and snow striking his face. Hayden's screams
of pain haunted him in his nightmares. He'd never get
his friend's cries out of his head. And it drained Talon's
will to live. Add to that his mother's battle with cancer.

Talon doggedly pushed forward. He felt Zeke's comforting weight against his knee. The dog was shepherding him along. Zeke was a bona fide hero. He had been awarded a Purple Heart and a Silver Star by the Navy for his heroic efforts to save his and Hayden's lives. Only, Hayden hadn't survived. Shit.

The past was overlaying the present. The fever had him in its grip and Talon wasn't sure if he was in a Wyoming blizzard or back in a snowstorm in the Hindu Kush Mountains of Afghanistan. And when the fever rolled out like a tide in his head, Talon would realize he was in Wyoming, trying to reach the Bar H. Trying to get close enough to home to ask for help, to let his mother know he was near.

Since his mother had contracted breast cancer, Talon had sent most of his paycheck to her because she couldn't afford the horrendous, mounting medical bills. He'd wanted to help her as much as he could. As a result, when he got wounded and discharged, he had no bank account except for five hundred dollars in a savings account to get him home to Jackson Hole. And that money was mostly gone as he walked across half of the United States to reach Wyoming.

Jesus, the fever was messing with his head. Talon's breath was ragged and fast. Dizziness struck him in waves. His lungs were drowning in fluid and he couldn't get the oxygen he needed. No oxygen, no strength. Only brute determination kept him going.

A blast of frigid air struck Talon. He slipped, lost his footing and went down. Hard. His head slammed into the snow and the berm below it. Darkness took him briefly.

He felt his dog's tongue licking his bearded cheek. As

he fumbled, tried to rise, the last of his strength ebbed. He was going to freeze to death out here.

Talon lay there gasping for air, feeling the bubbles of liquid in his lungs. Death stalked him. He closed his eyes, cheek pressed into the snow, feeling nothing because his flesh was numb. Something snapped deep within. Something so primal, so visceral, that all he could do was lie there, helpless. Just as he'd hung helplessly, strung up, his wrists tied with ropes over an overhead beam, toes barely touching the dirt floor. He was forced to watch Hayden being tortured. Oh, God...

Talon wanted death to take him. He was so very, very sorry he wouldn't be able to help his mother. She was a survivor. Grief and sadness wound through him like a cold, icy river flooding him. He was so dehydrated he couldn't even cry.

His SEAL team friends would find out sooner or later that he'd died of hypothermia on an unnamed highway somewhere in Wyoming during a freak blizzard. What a screwed-up ending.

Talon closed his eyes.

Well, it looked like the blizzard was going to kill him. It felt good to just rest. To lie on his side, the snow all around him.

Zeke whined and paced around him, licking his face, trying to get him up. A hoarse sound scraped out of his throat. It was as close to a sob as he would get under these circumstances. Talon wasn't afraid to die.

Zeke lay down next to him, his moist, hot breath across his face. In Afghanistan, in the cold mountains, Zeke was like a warm, living blanket to Talon. He would lie at his side, their bodies glued to each other, keeping one another warm through those icy, frigid nights.

He couldn't let Zeke stay out here. The dog would die in the blizzard, too.

And that was what forced Talon to try to get up. To move. Gasping, his breath noisy and ragged, he struggled to move his numb legs. They were weighted down, hard to move. For a moment, the fever receded and Talon's head cleared. His black lashes froze to his cheeks and he couldn't force open his eyes. Somehow, he managed to pull his hand up, scrub his face and force the lashes to break free. Blinking rapidly, Talon got them open. Up! He had to get up! Zeke couldn't freeze out here. Talon couldn't let that happen.

Just as Talon got to his feet, wobbling and staggering around, he saw headlights come out of the thick veil of snow. Blinking unsurely, he thought he was seeing things—hallucinations due to his high fever.

Zeke whined, placing his strong body against Talon's leg to help him remain upright.

Talon gasped for air, like a fish thrown out of the water. He jammed his hands down on his knees, head down, trying to stay upright as the big, black SUV appeared like an apparition out of the blinding blizzard. It stopped in front of him.

A car door opened and slammed shut.

Jesus, he had to be imagining this! No one in their right mind was out in a blizzard like this. Wyoming people knew to stay home to stay safe. Was this how death happened?

Zeke barked a warning.

There really *was* someone walking toward him! Zeke was in combat assault dog mode. Anyone making a move toward Talon was seen as the enemy. Zeke's growl rumbled warningly, and the hackles of fur stood up on his neck.

"Allow," Talon rasped to Zeke. The command to the dog meant not to attack, but allow that person to touch or be around him. Instantly, Zeke stopped growling and watched the person who was heavily bundled up in a coat.

Talon forced himself to stand. He was so dizzy he had to step back so that he wouldn't fall over. He tried to focus his eyes on the person coming around the SUV. Whoever it was, he or she wore a down black jacket, white knit cap, a thick muffler around their neck, hands positioned beneath their armpits.

And then the apparition spoke.

"Hey, climb in. No one should be out in this blizzard."

A woman's voice. Husky. Filled with concern. She eyed him worriedly, her blue eyes warm. The snowflakes were landing on strands of her black hair peeking out from beneath her white knit cap.

"Hey?" she called. "Are you all right?"

Her hand came to rest around his upper arm, steadying him. *Jesus, she's real!* His mind shorted out. He couldn't talk. He knew he looked like what he was: a homeless military vet. He hadn't bathed in ten days. His hair was long by military standards. He hadn't shaved in God knew how long.

She saw the dog, suddenly becoming wary.

"Won't hurt you," Talon forced out, his voice rough and barely intelligible.

"Good to know. I'm Cat Edwin. Come on, I need to get you inside my SUV."

Her hand became firmer on his arm as he tried to

take a step toward it. Everything whirled and he halted, shutting his eyes. "Pneumonia," he muttered.

"Yeah, I hear it. You need medical attention pronto." Cat slid her arm around his waist and pulled his one arm across her shoulder. "I'll help you into my SUV. What's your name?" He looked awfully familiar, but she couldn't place him. Right now, she didn't have time to figure out why.

Cat slowly guided him toward the passenger side of her SUV. The man could barely keep his feet beneath him, his knees continuing to collapse beneath him.

"Talon," he managed, his feet barely working. In the next breath, he rasped, "Holt."

Cat gasped. Now she knew who he was. Sandy Holt's son! "Okay, Talon Holt, hang on." Cat reached for the handle and pulled open the door. "Let's get you inside. You're wet and freezing."

He hesitated. "My dog..."

"He's coming along, too," she reassured him.

Talon grunted and worked to climb into the SUV. He had a helluva time getting into the seat and she practically shoved him into the SUV. Zeke jumped into the front, sitting on the floorboards between his legs, facing him.

The door slammed shut. He could feel heat in the SUV. It felt wonderful. Talon lay back, closing his eyes, gasping for air, his lungs hurting with each wheezing breath.

Cat climbed in and shut the door. "I'm going to the Bar H. It's about a mile up the road. The roads are closed beyond that. I'll get you to the ranch and try to help you there."

He had to be dreaming. Talon couldn't answer, too

weak to speak. He felt Zeke's warm, wet tongue licking his hand. Just as she put the SUV into motion, his last memory was of Cat Edwin's face. She was attractive, slightly curled strands of black hair across her broad brow. He liked her large, readable blue eyes. Talon had seen every emotion in them. Her face was oval with wide cheekbones. Her nose was clean with slightly flared nostrils. He especially liked that wide, soft mouth of hers. If Talon had been healthy, he sure as hell would have wanted to know her a lot better. And with that last thought, he sank into unconsciousness.

CHAPTER TWO

CAT FELT A sense of urgency. As a fire department paramedic, she took one look at an unconscious Talon Holt
and knew he was in serious shape. The snow was dump-
ing in buckets and she could barely see ten feet in front
of her SUV as she drove slowly through the foot-and-
a-half snow on the highway. If it weren't for the snow
poles placed every tenth of a mile, she might literally
drive off the road and slide down the rocky slope and
into the churning Snake River below. Not what she
wanted to do.

Blindly, she reached out for the fire department radio
she had installed in her SUV. She needed to call the
Bar H and let them know she was coming in with a
sick passenger.

"Hey, anyone awake at the Bar H? This is Cat. Over."
Her heart was pounding a little harder in her chest. The
man, who lay slumped, his head tipped back, touched
her for some reason. Cat had taken care of hundreds
of sick and dying people over the years. What was it
about this man that moved her emotionally? Cat had no
answer. His beard was scraggly, his hair longish, dirty
and unkempt. And that dog of his, Zeke. The animal's
large, intelligent brown eyes never left his master's wan
face. She swore the dog looked as worried as she felt.

"Cat? Don't tell me you're out in this godforsaken blizzard?"

A smile twitched at her lips. "Hey, Miss Gus. I figured you'd be up by now." Gus was eighty-five years old and the matriarch of the Bar H.

Gus snorted. "I was just cooking breakfast for Val and Griff. I didn't think you'd come in this morning with this blizzard."

"Yeah," Cat said with a chuckle, "but I really wanted to learn to can fruit and veggies with you and Val today."

"What a sucker for punishment you are, my dear," Gus cackled.

"Listen, I just picked up a man on this highway a few minutes ago," Cat told her. "He's in rough shape. I'm bringing him to you, Miss Gus. He needs to be in the E.R. but there's no way I can make it ten miles back to town in this blizzard. Can you get Griff to meet me out front? The guy is unconscious and has a bad case of pneumonia."

"Who on earth would be out in this weather?" Gus demanded.

Cat cast a quick glance over at the man. She could smell him. "He told me his name. Talon Holt."

"Lordy!" Miss Gus exploded. "Talon Holt? He's Sandy Holt's son!"

"One in the same." Cat gulped and felt a lump form in her throat. "That's right. I knew there was something familiar about him."

"Sandy said her son, who was a U.S. Navy SEAL, was wounded a year ago. She told me he was coming home, but didn't say when. Said he was coming with a dog. Is there a dog with him?"

"Yes," Cat said, driving carefully, feeling the SUV begin to slide a little. She eased off the gas. There was no way to hurry in this stuff. "I remember Sandy saying he was wounded."

"Yes. He got wounded a year ago on a black ops mission and Sandy said he was getting a medical discharge sometime soon. Didn't say when. Sandy told me the name of the dog but I can't recall it."

"Zeke?"

"Yes! That's it! Aside from the pneumonia, how bad off is Talon?"

"Really bad," Cat murmured, frowning. "Listen, we should use your bedroom downstairs. Can you get it ready for him? He's soaking wet, freezing and he's breathing pretty badly. I've got to get him someplace warm and dry. Griff's going to have to help me. I can't carry him into your house by myself."

"Griff's out in the barn. I'll give him a call to come in. Val and I will get my bedroom ready. About how long before you arrive?"

She grimaced. "I'm barely going ten miles an hour. Probably another twenty minutes if I don't slide off the mountain."

"We'll be waiting for you, Cat. Be careful getting here. There's a sheet of black ice on that pavement."

"Great, thanks. Out." Cat felt her emotions unraveling as she gripped the steering wheel, focusing on the slippery road. All around her were evergreens cloaked in heavy white snow. A black, wet, rocky cliff soared a thousand feet above the highway. On her right a skimpy guardrail was supposed to prevent a car from sliding into a hundred-foot rocky abyss below.

Focus on the road. Get him shelter.

Cat didn't want to feel anything about this man, this vet, but she did. Talon Holt was pale and unconscious, but she could see the toughness in his face, the kindness in the shape of his chiseled mouth. And yes, he *did* look a little like his mother.

She white-knuckled it as the SUV slid a little toward the guardrail. Cat didn't easily panic. As a firefighter, she'd seen just about everything in her twenty-seven years.

She glanced quickly toward Talon, who was frowning, regaining consciousness. Cat could hear his raw, shallow breaths. She turned again to the snow-covered highway. "Talon?" she asked. "Are you awake? Can you hear me?"

Talon heard her husky voice. Weakly, he raised his hand and forced his eyes open. Every breath he took was a labored effort, as if he had an elephant on his chest. He heard Zeke whine, felt his pink tongue laving his hand.

"It's okay, Zeke," he rasped, opening his eyes. He'd never been so damned weak. Not even when he'd been wounded in the field had he felt like this.

"Talon?"

The woman's voice again. He barely turned his head in the direction of the sound. "Yeah?"

"How are you doing?" Cat demanded, guiding the SUV around the last curved corner that would lead to the Bar H.

"I'm not dead, yet," he rasped.

A good sign, Cat thought. As sick as he was, Talon was being a smart-ass. "I'm taking you to the Bar H. Miss Gus remembers you. I can't get you to the hospital where you belong. I'm a paramedic. Miss Gus is going to let you stay in her bedroom and I'll do what I can to help you. Okay?" Cat gave him a quick glance. His eyes were red rimmed, the gray color glowing with fever, his black pupils large. His face bathed in sweat.

"Miss Gus?" His mind wobbled.

"Yes. She remembers you. You're Sandy Holt's son?"

"Yeah, I am," he managed. Barely able to lift his fingers, he grazed Zeke's wet, damp head. "Look," he choked out, struggling to breathe, "you need to know about Zeke, here. He's a combat assault dog. He'll bite anyone who gets near me. You need to give the command 'allow' to Zeke. Then he'll consider them as a friend instead of an enemy. I can't have him biting Miss Gus or anyone else…."

Cat nodded. "Okay, I can do that for you. You just rest, Mr. Holt. You're in good hands."

Talon heard the sudden emotion in her voice. "What's your name again?"

"Cat. Cat Edwin."

Nice name. Cat. Yeah, with those slightly tilted blue eyes of hers, she looked like a cat. Maybe more a lithe, strong, lean beautiful cougar. Closing his eyes, Talon felt the darkness pulling him down again. "I…" And he lost consciousness.

Cat licked her lower lip, worried. The man's skin had a gray tint now. It meant he wasn't getting enough oxygen. A very bad sign. God, Sandy Holt couldn't lose her son, not when she was fighting for her own life. Cat's heart pounded anxiously.

She could see the entrance to the Bar H through the thickly falling snow. Wind gusts were pushing the snow sideways. Blizzards took no prisoners.

As Cat drove down the long, graveled driveway now covered with a foot and a half of snow, she saw the enormous main two-story log house appear out of the white stuff. Griff McPherson, now owner of the Bar H, stood in the driveway next to the house. Standing around six foot one, he was bundled up in a sheepskin coat, red knit muffler around his neck, cowboy hat and jeans. He had dark hair and green eyes. Val McPherson, his wife, stood on the porch, the screen door open, a worried look on her face.

Cat pulled up as close as she could. She climbed out, calling, "Griff, don't open that door!"

Griff halted halfway around her SUV, a puzzled look on his face. "Why?"

Cat hurried through the snow and came up to him. "Talon has a combat assault dog with him. I have to open the door myself or he'll attack you."

Grimacing, Griff's brow rose. "How do we get Talon out of there, then?"

Cat clumped through the snow and struggled over to the passenger-side door. "Come and stand over here, behind me. I'll open the door and give the dog a command. It's supposed to make Zeke think you're a friend instead of an enemy."

Griff nodded. "Okay," he said, worried.

Cat opened the door. Zeke immediately growled, his gaze fastened on Griff. "Zeke, allow," she told the dog in a firm voice. To her relief, she saw the Belgian Malinois relax. She turned to Griff. "I'm getting the dog out of here first so we can pull Talon out."

"Will Zeke attack Val?" he demanded.

Cat scowled. She noticed a leash trailing off Zeke's collar. "Probably. Hang on, I'm going to grab his leash and keep him with me so he can't go anywhere."

Griff nodded and walked around the SUV, calling to

his wife, telling her to stay in the kitchen with Miss Gus because the dog would bite. His wife nodded, closed the porch door and disappeared inside.

"Okay," he said, "bring the dog out."

Cat was hoping like hell the military-trained dog wouldn't chew off her arm as she reached for the leash. Zeke thumped his tail, looking at her with a happy expression, pink tongue lolling outside of his black muzzle.

So far so good. Cat tugged on the leash and Zeke lifted his front legs, leaped over Talon's thigh and landed in a snowbank.

"Good boy," she murmured, patting Zeke's head. Wrapping the leash around her fist several times, Cat pulled the dog aside so Griff could get in there to help Talon.

"Your turn," she told Griff, moving back from the opened door.

Griff moved in and hauled Talon out. He grunted as he took the man's full weight. Cat quickly got involved, heaving one of Talon's long arms across her shoulders. Between them, they dragged him up the porch stairs and into the house.

The warmth of the woodstove hit Cat. Zeke obediently walked at her side, his head swiveling toward the kitchen as they passed it.

And then Cat saw Miss Gus, her silver hair like a halo around her head. The woman was at the kitchen sink. Val stood next to her in a protective gesture, partially in front of her, a concerned look on her oval face.

"The bedroom's ready," Miss Gus hollered.

"Great," Cat grunted. "Thanks…" Talon Holt was

heavy and two inches taller than Griff. Together, they got him into the room.

Griff maneuvered him to the bed. "Cat, can you get that door shut?"

Cat released Talon and quickly did as Griff ordered. He didn't want Zeke out wandering around. "Got it," she said, breathing hard. She took Zeke aside and said, "Sit." The dog did. "Stay," she ordered, hoping he knew the command. He did, fortunately.

"Damn, he's soaking wet," Griff muttered, getting Talon's long legs straightened out across the bed.

"He's in bad shape," Cat agreed, breathing raggedly. "Listen, can you get my medical bag out of the Cherokee? It's on the backseat."

Standing upright, Griff took off his gray Stetson, hitting it against his thigh. "Yeah. Be right back."

The door closed. Cat gave one look at Zeke, who was sitting, fawn-colored ears with black tips up, alert. He hadn't moved, which was good. She quickly went to work, shucking the wet clothes off Talon's body. Her fingers were shaky as she moved Talon around to haul off his jacket. Griff came back with the medical bag.

Zeke thumped his tail. Griff gave the Malinois a narrowed-eyed look as he set the bag on the bed. "Need some help stripping him?"

"I do," Cat huffed. "He's heavy."

"He's a big man," Griff muttered. He got out of his sheepskin coat and threw it and his hat on a nearby overstuffed chair.

Together, they stripped Talon of every article of wet clothing. Cat had seen a lot of naked people in her time and tried not to look too closely at Talon. His flesh was cold and nearly gray. She got out of her jacket and dropped it onto the floor, grabbing her medical bag. As Griff layered several blankets over him, she listened to his lungs through the stethoscope.

"Damn," she muttered. "Griff? Get at least six pillows and pile them under his shoulders and head? He's got so much fluid in his lungs that he needs to get his upper body lifted up or he'll drown in this shit."

"Got it." Griff left and closed the door.

Cat heard the thunk of his cowboy boots along the wooden floor. She listened closely to both of Talon's lungs, trying to ignore the powerful breadth of his chest. She ran her fingers gently across his naked shoulder. He was hypothermic. Her heart twinged as she saw his ribs. He was pathetically thin for his height and body build. Why was he starving? When she pulled some skin between her thumb and index finger from his tightly muscled forearm, the skin stood up. It didn't immediately snap back down, which meant he was severely dehydrated. How long had Talon gone without food and water? She took his temperature and it was a 105°F, an indication his body was fighting hard to survive the infection. His pulse was pounding erratically, his blood pressure too high. All indicators of major war for survival taking place within his body.

Zeke whined.

Cat looked up as she looped the stethoscope around her shoulders. "He's in bad shape, boy."

Zeke whined again.

"But we're going to wage a battle to bring him back," she promised the dog. Getting up, Cat dug into her pack. In no time, she had an IV going into his right arm, full bore, to start flooding his body with much needed vital liquid.

The door opened.

Zeke growled. And then he recognized Griff with six pillows in his arms and stopped.

"That dog is dangerous," Griff muttered, keeping one eye on him as he shut the door and brought the pillows over.

"He's okay," Cat soothed. She stood and Griff lifted Talon's upper body forward so she could place the pillows beneath him.

"That's better," Cat murmured. With Talon slightly elevated, it would help him breathe easier. "Can you get my large oxygen canister from the truck and bring it in?"

"Yeah," Griff said, "no problem. Be right back."

Cat pulled out a bottle of antibiotics and a syringe and sucked up a maximum load. She put it into the IV port so it would quickly go into Talon's bloodstream, where it would do the most good. She listened to his shallow, raspy breathing. Without thinking, she slid her fingers across his wrinkled brow, feeling the cold, clammy sweat. His hair was matted, filthy, and he so badly needed a shower. Worse, Cat saw a lot of scars on his back and across his shoulders. What the hell had happened to him?

After tucking Talon in with the heavy wool blankets, she moved down and felt his toes. They were chalk-white and cold. She sat down and placed her hands over one foot and then the other, trying to warm them up, bring circulation back into them. Cat *liked* touching this man. Her heart went out to him. Clearly, he had suffered terribly. No military vet should be found sick along a highway like she'd found Talon. He was due better treatment than that.

Griff came back with a large canister of oxygen. Cat covered up Talon's feet, tucked the wool in around them and stood.

"Thanks, Griff."

"How's he doing?" he asked, watching Cat quickly place a cannula around Talon's head, the oxygen moving directly into his nostrils.

"Not good," she murmured.

"There's no way we can get him to the hospital in this blizzard," Griff muttered, pushing damp, black strands of hair off his brow as he stood watching Cat work over the man.

"I know."

"Good thing you came along when you did. I'm no doctor, but he looks in rough shape."

"He'd have died of hypothermia out there," Cat said, checking the oxygen tank and twisting the dial a little. Talon needed as much pure oxygen as he could get, but she only had four canisters in her SUV. And that wouldn't last long.

Griff studied Zeke. "I wonder if he's hungry?"

"Probably. Can you bring in some food and water for him?" Cat didn't want to leave Talon's side. She sat down on the bed, facing him, picking up his limp wrist. His pulse thudded like cannonballs through his arteries, indicating how much harder his heart was laboring without the necessary oxygen to push the blood through his body.

"Yeah." Griff smiled a little. "How about you? Miss Gus is out there making scrambled eggs, hash and toast for breakfast. Want me to bring you in a plate?"

Cat gave him a warm look. "That would be great. I'm starving to death."

Smiling a little, Griff said, "Coming up. I'll be back...."

Silence settled in the large, spacious room. Cat continued to hold Talon's large, callused hand between hers. She wanted to touch him. He might be unconscious, but she knew the value of a healing touch. Only, there was pleasure connected to touching this man, too. Cat moved her long, spare fingers lightly across his forearm. There were so many new, pink scars, along with older white ones, across his flesh. She knew little about SEALs, but his body was proof he'd gone through major combat many times.

Her gaze moved to Talon's slack face. He had a beautiful mouth. His nose was strong and had been broken a few times from what she could tell. Talon had a square face, a lean, hard jaw most likely, but the beard covered it up, so she couldn't really tell. Her lower body clenched. Surprised, Cat had never felt that reaction before. She felt her womb flooding with heat and it made her feel achy. Needy. Talon Holt was ruggedly handsome. She remembered briefly meeting his gray eyes that, despite the fever, contained hard intelligence. Even as sick as he was, Cat had felt the intensity of his eyes upon her. It excited her and scared the hell out of her.

She moved her fingers gently down Talon's slack forearm, which was lightly dusted with dark hair. For whatever crazy reason, Cat wondered what his hand would feel like exploring her. It was such a ridiculous response that her breath hitched. *Get a grip,* she ordered herself.

Cat unlooped her stethoscope from around her neck and once more listened to his lungs. She tried to ignore the sexual reaction she had to touching him. His shoulders were broad and his chest massive and well sprung. A dusting of black hair across his chest narrowed downward toward his blanket-covered waist. He was a powerful man, physically speaking, even if he was sicker than a dog right now. Listening intently, Cat could tell the extra oxygen, in addition to him being levered up into a Fowler's position, was putting less stress on Talon's lungs. A little relief fled through her. The antibiotics should kick in shortly.

"Hey," Griff called from the door. "Safe to come in?" he teased.

Cat headed toward the door. "Yeah, it's safe. Come on in."

"Miss Gus is asking to see Talon."

"Oh." Cat quickly went to Zeke, grabbing a hold of the dog's leash. "Okay, I got him."

Griff opened the door.

"Well," Miss Gus said, holding a bowl of water in her hands, "can you make friends with Zeke for me?"

Zeke was looking at the silver-haired woman, suddenly tense and alert.

"Zeke, allow," Cat told the dog firmly.

Instantly, Zeke thumped his tail and began to pant.

"Good doggie," Miss Gus murmured, coming forward with a slight limp. "I got water for you, boy. You should be glad to see me."

Cat held on to the leash, worried Zeke might do something. But as Miss Gus slowly bent over and set the bowl of water down in front of the dog, he thumped his tail in a friendly fashion and whined.

"Good boy," Gus praised, reaching out with her parchment-thin hand and gently patting the dog's head. "Now, you need to drink."

Cat was amazed when the dog instantly dipped his head, eagerly lapping up the water. She grinned at Gus. "You have a way with animals."

"I have a way with everyone!" Gus snorted, putting her hands on her hips, grinning widely.

Cat chuckled and released the leash, allowing it to fall beside Zeke. Gus was dressed in a long-sleeved red blouse with a blue apron around her tiny waist. She always wore black wool slacks because of the chill of the long winter in Wyoming.

"That you do," Cat warmly agreed. Even though Cat's grandparents were dead, Miss Gus had taken her under her wing and treated her like a granddaughter.

Gus turned, looking over at Talon. "How's he doing, honey?"

"A tiny bit better. The oxygen is helping him a lot."

"Come around yet?"

Cat shook her head. "He was very dehydrated, Miss Gus. And he's got a really bad case of pneumonia. He'll eventually become conscious, but I don't know when."

Patting Cat's arm, Gus said, "If anyone can pull him through, you can."

A fierce love for the old woman flowed through her. "He's going to need a lot of prayers, too, Miss Gus."

"We can do that." She crinkled her face and looked up at Cat. "Hungry?"

Groaning, Cat said, "Yes, I'm starving."

"Go on out to the kitchen. I got a plate of vittles waitin' for you. I'll stay with Talon until you get back."

Griff set a bowl of kibble down in front of Zeke. "Val's got the coffee poured for you, Cat."

Cat hesitated, not wanting to leave Talon. It was a

silly, emotional reaction. Zeke dived into the bowl of kibble as if starved. "Okay. I'll be back as soon as I finish."

VAL MET CAT out in the kitchen.

"How's Talon doing?"

Cat sat down and told her. She grabbed the cup of coffee and took a sip. "This is great. Thanks, Val." The red-haired woman sat down opposite her. Val's hair was pulled back in a long ponytail. She wore a heavy cream-colored fisherman knit sweater, jeans and boots.

"Someone should call Sandy Holt," Cat said between bites.

"I'll do it," Val said. She frowned. "Sandy's not in good shape. Should we tell her how bad Talon is?"

Cat shook her head. "Just tell Sandy that Talon's here and a little under the weather."

"She'll want to know when Talon can see her."

"Sandy's immune system is really down," Cat warned. "As long as he's sick, he can't visit her or she could contract the pneumonia. It might finish her off."

Val nodded and picked up her cup of coffee. "That's what I was thinking. Maybe we need to tell her he's got pneumonia and she'll understand why her son can't see her right now?"

"Yeah, maybe you're right," Cat said. "But say it in such a way that she doesn't worry. The poor woman has enough stress."

"I know," Val said softly. "I feel helpless."

"Me, too." Cat knew Val had left her career as an Air Force officer to come home to help Gus keep the Bar H alive. She wasn't a woman who scared easily at all. And once a week, Gus and Val went to visit Sandy

Holt. Talon's mother was destitute, having lost her job at Mo's Ice Cream Parlor two months ago because the cancer had come back and was twice as virulent as before. Cat made a point of dropping in to read to her and stay with her for at least a couple of hours once a week. Gwen Garner, who owned the quilting store, had a number of quilters who came over to visit weekly with Sandy and help her where and when they could. Cat felt her heart twinge. Now her son was in dire need of help himself. But that was what a small community did—it rallied those who were weak, sick or in need of help.

"Do you think Talon can talk to her directly?"

Shaking her head, Cat said, "He's unconscious. And he's got major trouble breathing. I'm hoping—" and she held up crossed fingers "—that he responds to the antibiotic. Maybe in a couple of days he can talk to her."

"It sounds like Talon should be in the hospital."

"Really. But it's going to take two days to clear the roads after this blizzard leaves," Cat griped unhappily. She finished everything on her plate and took a sip of her coffee.

Val frowned. "That bad?"

"Yeah. I'm sure they'd put him in the ICU if we could get him to the hospital."

"Could he die?" Val asked, worried.

"I don't think he will," Cat said. "He's young and he's strong, although, he's terribly underweight and dehydrated."

"Gus said Talon was wounded a year ago. Bad wound, whatever that meant. He might have just gotten out of the hospital?"

"I saw a *lot* of scars on his back and shoulders." Again, Cat's heart ached for Talon. Thanks to an abusive father, she was usually wary of men. Inexplicably, Talon had worked through the protective walls she had up against men in general—he'd gotten to her—and that was disconcerting. But she couldn't dwell on this right now.

Val stood. "God, the guy has been through his own hell," she muttered, going to the coffeepot and pouring herself another cup.

"You were in the military," Cat said, watching her come back and sit down. "What do you know about SEALs?"

"They're Navy black ops. I worked with them on some missions over in Iraq when I was stationed in the Middle East. I was an intelligence officer in the Air Force and, sometimes, we'd have joint missions with them, Army Special Forces and Air Force PJs." She sipped her coffee. "Those guys go where angels fear to tread, Cat. They're the best of the best at black ops. And they take the fight to the enemy. No fear."

"Assertive?"

Val smiled a little. "For sure. Type-A personalities with egos just as big. They're used to working as a team. Even though SEALs are U.S. Navy, they are found globally on sea, air and land. Talon was with SEAL Team 3 from what his mother told me. He was a shooter. A guy who was out with a rifle fighting Taliban and al Qaeda over in Afghanistan."

"I know nothing about the military," Cat admitted. And then she brightened and grinned over at Val. "With the exception of you, of course."

"I'm a cowgirl now," Val said, smiling.

Cat nodded. "And you met Griff in the process."

Val's eyes grew warm with love for her husband.

They had been married a year and worked hard to bring the Bar H back from being a total loss. "He's made it easy to come back." Val looked around the warm, quiet kitchen. "This place held a lot of really bad memories for me. When Gus broke her hip and I came home to help her, I was really bitter about it at first. But I love her very much. She's my grandmother and she was so important in my life when I was sixteen and she moved back here to the Bar H. I owed her, so I came back."

"And Griff made the difference." Cat knew they were deeply in love with each other. How often had she fantasized about meeting a man she could trust instead of fear?

Val wrapped her fingers around the mug. "Oh, yes, a big difference."

"I overheard Miss Gus say you were trying to get pregnant?"

Val flushed. "I think I am, Cat. I got a feeling about it."

"Have you tested for it yet?" she asked, thrilled. Cat loved babies and she'd delivered her fair share.

"No, and say nothing, okay? I haven't missed a period, but I just feel different. It's strange," she said, shrugging. "I can't put words to it. A new kind of happiness…"

"Fingers crossed," Cat said. "Your secret's safe with me, but do let me know."

"I promise," Val said, touching her arm.

"Hey," Gus called from down the hall. "Cat? Talon's waking up."

Quickly, Cat pushed the chair back and stood up. "Be right there," she said, and a new kind of excitement surged through her.

CHAPTER THREE

CAT SHOOED EVERYONE out of the room. Someone in Talon's shape would easily become confused, with his mental faculties close to hallucinations due to his temperature. Zeke came over to his bedside as she sat down facing Talon, eyes bright and on his master. Talon's skin appeared less gray and she took a cloth from the nearby bed stand. She gently sponged away the sweat on his brow, pale cheeks and thick, corded neck. Emotions swirled through her. How could one man have such a profound effect on her—and so fast? She watched his lids quiver. Yes, he was beginning to surface.

Setting the cloth aside, she listened to his lungs through her stethoscope. The antibiotics were starting to take a hold. Relief sizzled through her. She heard less crackling in his lungs. The fluids were slowly being reabsorbed by the body. Looping the stethoscope over her neck, she placed two fingers on the inside of his wrist. More relief. Talon's pulse was no longer bounding. She picked up her thermometer, placing it inside his ear. Looking at it, she saw why he was becoming conscious. The fever was now down to 102°F.

"You're one lucky guy," she told him.

His lashes barely lifted.

Cat placed her hand on his. "Talon? Can you hear me? It's Cat. You're at the Bar H."

A woman's voice cut through the confusion rush-ing across Talon's closed eyes. *Weak.* He felt so damn weak it was pitiful. Yet, when her warm, dry fingers curved over his sweaty wrist, the anxiety stopped. Her voice was low, intimate, and even his pounding heart responded to it.

God, he was thirsty.

It was the thirst that forced Talon to struggle might-ily to raise his lids. When he did, his vision was blurred and all he saw was the color red in front of him. Blink-ing, the red turned out to be a red flannel shirt someone was wearing. It took every ounce of his strength to lift his gaze upward. When he did, he saw an incredibly beautiful woman with exotic blue eyes somberly study-ing him, her lush mouth pursed with concentration. And when her fingers curved more surely against his large hand, he felt her soft, maternal touch.

"Talon?"

His brow wrinkled. She knew his name. How? His mind wasn't functioning. It pissed him off because as a SEAL, weakness wasn't a word that existed in his universe. He forced his lips to open. Only a harsh sound escaped. Had he died? For sure he wasn't going to heaven. Not in this lifetime. So was she an angel? His mind rolled around like a loose bowling ball with no boundaries.

She was pretty. Her black hair was slightly curled around her shoulders and framed her oval face. There was hidden strength in her face. A patient face. Her eyebrows were arched over those incredible blue eyes. Talon thought he saw her smile. Maybe he *wanted* her to smile because she looked so damn serious. Why?

And then his fevered mind put two and two together.

The woman at his side, leaning forward, was also holding his hand. He liked her hand around his. Her skin was velvet, yet strong, like her. He became aware of the strength in her face. She couldn't be more than twenty-five or so. And he saw redness around the left side of her slender neck, most of it hidden beneath the red flannel shirt she wore. Why? Was her skin burned from some tragedy?

"Talon?"

Her voice made him think of warm honey drizzled over his flesh. Talon almost wanted to laugh. As weak and sick as he was, he was thinking about sex. With her. He didn't even have the energy to smile, much less entertain other things. She certainly inspired his imagination, even if his body couldn't keep pace with the fantasy he was having about her in his arms, loving her, exploring her, kissing each square inch of that sweet-smelling skin of hers. He saw her lean away, and when she placed a warm, damp cloth against his brow and cheeks, it felt heavenly. He finally realized he was no longer freezing. The warmth of a blanket beneath him radiated heat. He could feel his fingers and toes once again.

Zeke whined.

Blinking slowly, Talon carefully turned his head and focused on his dog. Zeke panted and whined, his big ears up and his eyes dancing with happiness, his hot breath moist across his face. Talon wanted to speak, to pat his dog, but he could do neither. The woman laughed softly.

"Zeke's been waiting for you to become conscious, too."

Swallowing hard, his throat dry, Talon closed his

eyes, fighting to put one word together. He didn't want her to stop moving that warm washcloth against his neck and shoulders. God, it felt good.

Talon clung to her warm gaze. Her face was less than a foot away from his, studying him. Was she a doctor? He finally realized that black thing hanging around her shoulders was a stethoscope. Though he wanted to tunnel his fingers through that thick, shining mass of gleaming black hair that softly framed her face, he could barely move one finger.

"W-water…" His voice sounded like the croak of a bullfrog. The woman reached up and then adjusted the IV in his arm. SEALs were trained in giving a team member an IV when they were shot and losing a lot of blood.

How he enjoyed her profile as she turned and busied herself. It was clean. Beautiful. He laughed to himself. Somewhere in his mind, he remembered her name was Cat, appropriate because of her slightly tilted blue eyes. She wore no makeup. And when he flared his nostrils, he picked up her woman's scent, a special fragrance that was only her. It felt like life to Talon. Hope. Maybe he wasn't going to die after all?

"Water?" she asked him, looking into his barely opened eyes. They felt cloudy with fever.

"P-please?" he asked. Talon smelled the sweat and filth of his own body. He stank. Yet, this woman didn't seem to care or mind as she left his side. Where did she go? Talon didn't have the strength to move his head to find out. The warmth of the blankets felt incredibly good to him. He hated the cold.

And then she came back. Talon heard her tell Zeke to move and she sat down at his shoulder, her hip brushing his arm. Closing his eyes, he savored her warm, dry arm sliding behind his neck and shoulders.

"Okay, up you go," she urged.

Her breath was sweet and moist as she leaned down, her face very close to his. Talon couldn't even help her, too weak to sit up by himself. Yet, amazingly, she levered him up and held him with her woman's strength. She placed the lip of a glass to his mouth. The water was tepid, but it tasted like heaven. He drank thirstily, some of the water leaking out the sides of his mouth, soaking into his beard. In no time, he'd drained the contents.

Talon closed his eyes, feeling the water inside him, feeling less thirsty. He regretted her lowering him down against the soft, fluffy pillows once more, her arm sliding out from beneath his neck and shoulders. He was a big man, and yet, she'd had the strength to lift him. That amazed him. Granted, she appeared to be almost six feet tall, was medium boned, but she was still all woman. Starving for her touch once more, Talon closed his eyes, feeling better but missing contact with her. Better to imagine it for now. The fever still had him in its grip and his mind bounced around. What would it be like to kiss that mouth of hers? It was a soft mouth, full and wide. The kind a man could drown himself in, explore and make his own. He'd kissed his share of women over his time as a SEAL but her mouth intrigued him more than any other. Would her skin, those faintly flushed pink cheeks of hers, feel like warm velvet beneath his exploring fingertips? Would her hair feel warm and silky as he sifted them through those strands? Talon bet they would.

Cat continued to study him in the silence. The whole scene settled the anxiety that had hovered about him these past few months—maybe years. She gave him peace when he no longer had any himself. Made him feel safe in a world he knew was unsafe. All of this from just her gaze.

"Your fever has just broken," she said, touching his forehead.

Just keep on touching me. It feels so damn good. Talon greedily absorbed the feel of her fingers sliding lightly up and down his arm in slow, gentle motions. Did she realize how good it made him feel? How long had it been since he'd felt this kind of peace?

His dog. Talon barely opened his eyes. "Zeke?"

She smiled. "He's right here. We gave him food and water. He's okay."

Relief zigzagged through Talon. Zeke was being looked after. Gratefulness embraced him. He couldn't keep his eyes open any longer, exhausted.

The last thing Talon knew, her long fingers gently stroked his lower arm, as if to reassure him that everything would be all right. His mind began shutting down. This respite was like heaven to him.

Cat didn't want to stop skimming her fingers across Talon's arm. As she saw him sink into sleep, she remained at his side. Zeke had lain down parallel to the bed, his paws touching her booted feet. Cat swore she no longer saw worry in the dog's huge brown eyes that glittered with such fierce intelligence.

She had to stop stroking his arm or else she'd be in big trouble. She fussed with the covers, making sure Talon was snug and warm. Once again, she gazed upon his sleeping features. She wondered again what kind of weight this man carried on his shoulders. Why was he walking out in that miserable blizzard? Did he not have any money?

Cat stood and walked over to the pile of his wet, smelly clothes. She picked up his jeans and went through the pockets. She found a wallet and sat down on the edge of the bed to take a look. He had a driver's license, a military ID and about twenty dollars. And that was it. No credit cards. She set the wallet down on the bed stand and turned her attention to the dog. Moving her fingers slowly across Zeke's long, powerful body, she noted he was thin but not starved like his master. Talon must have fed Zeke before himself. He cared about Zeke, but not himself as much. Cat reached out without thinking, sliding her hand gently down Talon's forearm. His skin was no longer moist. Instead, she could feel the fever ebbing.

Cat sat there, couldn't bring herself to move. She felt an odd peace sitting here, witnessing Talon in sleep. She was rarely at peace with a man around. Oh, the guys that she worked with at the fire department were all known quantities and, over the years, had finally accepted that a woman could do as good as a man in that vocation. She treated them like the brothers she'd never had. And she was no longer threatened by any of them.

But a new man like this one? Well, she'd usually go into threat-and-defense mode. Her past taught her not to trust a man's intentions toward her. *Ever.* She'd blundered in and made some hellacious mistakes with men who'd encouraged her to let down her defenses. Beau Magee had been her last mistake. And now she was paying a heavy emotional price for her poor choice. She couldn't blame herself for not trusting, but then, why did Talon seem so...unthreatening?

Maybe he was the worst kind of man—the one who seemed kind on the outside but was a predator on the inside. And yet, she saw humor and kindness in Talon's expression. Plus, he treated his dog with love and respect. There had to be goodness in Talon.

Finally, Cat roused herself and reluctantly got up and left. Quietly closing the door, she walked into the warm, bright yellow kitchen. Val, Griff and Gus were sitting at the table having coffee.

"How's he doin'?" Gus asked.

"Much better," Cat murmured, pouring herself coffee and sitting down next to Gus. "Fever's broken and that's good. He drank a glass of water."

Gus nodded, eyeing Cat. "He has you to thank for saving his hide."

Cat took a sip of the coffee. "Helping people is the reward in itself."

Val smiled across the table at Cat. "You're always so humble, Cat."

Gus moved her hand across Cat's shoulders. "She's just built that way, Val."

"Talon owes his life to you and I'm sure he'll be grateful," Griff said.

Cat always felt uncomfortable when people praised her. "Hey, did someone call Sandy Holt?"

"I did," Val said. "She's thrilled Talon is here but worried sick about him having pneumonia. I told her that he'd be okay and would call her soon." Standing, Val went to the counter to start cleaning up the breakfast dishes.

Cat turned and looked out the windows. "That blizzard isn't letting up, is it?"

"No," Griff muttered. "It's not going to stop until late tonight, from what the radio said."

Val patted her husband's shoulder. "It's a stay-in-and-work day."

"Are you still going to show us how to can today?" Cat flashed Gus a hopeful look.

"Of course," Gus said, grinning. "You have to stay near if Talon needs you, anyway."

The suggestion filled Cat with warmth. She wanted to be near Talon. It was more than a patient-paramedic relationship and she knew it. But she wasn't willing to share that awareness with them. It was embarrassing that she wanted to touch him. How could she be drawn so powerfully to him, out of the blue like this?

"Well," Griff said, and sighed, "I'm going out to the barn. Got to tinker with the tractor engine. And I've got plenty of work to fill this day." He slowly rose and picked up his empty coffee mug to bring to the dishwasher. "You learn the art of canning today. I'll brave that weather and work out in the barn. I'll see you at lunch."

Cat watched the tender glances between Val and Griff. How many times had she wished she had that kind of intimacy and love with a man? She had to be cursed. That was all there was to it.

Gus slowly rose from her chair and Cat turned toward the elder.

"Are you really up for teaching us today, Gus?" Cat knew she had arthritis in the hip she'd broken a year earlier and was moving a lot slower. Weather affected it, too, and today she was walking stiffly.

"Of course," Gus said, smoothing down the blue

apron across her thighs. "I'm going to show you how to can corn, beans and tomatoes."

Griff sauntered out of the kitchen, threw on his cowboy hat, shrugged into his sheepskin coat and pulled the gloves out of the pocket. "See you ladies at noon." He grinned and caught Gus's attention. "What's for lunch?"

"I'm gonna make a big pot of chicken soup," she said. "Talon's gonna need something good and filling to eat and the rest of us can use a hearty soup on a day like this."

Griff leaned against the entrance, pulling on the gloves. "Miss Gus? Any chance you're going to make homemade biscuits to go with that soup?"

Gus grinned. "Just for you, Griff, I'll make a batch."

"Thank you," he called. "See you ladies later…."

Val straightened and turned toward Gus. "He loves your biscuits. I wish I could bake them the way you do."

Gus patted Val's arm. "Not to worry. I intend to be around until I'm at least a hundred. Griff will get lots of biscuits between now and then," she said, and chortled.

Cat laughed, finishing off her coffee. She loved being a part of the Hunter and McPherson families. And she was grateful to be hired as a part-time wrangler on her days off to help out Val and Griff. "Make *lots,* Miss Gus. I love hot, homemade biscuits with butter and honey on them, too."

Gus shook her head and gave Val a look. "We got a bunch of biscuit eaters on our hands, don't we, Val?"

"Yes," Val said, smiling, "we do. I have a hunch when Talon gets better, he's going to eat a *lot* of food. He's so thin."

Cat washed out her mug in the sink. "He's way underweight. I looked in his wallet and all he had was a twenty-dollar bill on him. That's nothing."

Gus snorted. "He was makin' sure Zeke was eating and he cheated himself in the process."

Cat rested her hips against the counter. "Why doesn't he have more money?"

Val shut the dishwasher. "Because he's been sending most of his paychecks home to his mother, Cat. And when he got wounded and then discharged from the Navy, his source of income dried up. He's out of work. Poor guy was probably trying to make it home before he ran out of whatever savings he had."

"Twenty dollars," Gus grumbled. "That's paltry. And why was he walking out in that consarned blizzard?" She shook her silver head. "Makes no good sense to me."

Val sighed. "Gus, he probably has post-traumatic stress disorder. Talon was in black ops. Those guys are bound to have it big-time."

Cat frowned. "And that means he couldn't ride in a bus? Or fly in a plane?"

Val shrugged. "He's got a combat assault dog at his side. I'd imagine the plane or bus people wouldn't want the dog on board. My guess is he's hitched and walked to get back home."

Cat said nothing, but felt even more deeply for Talon. "And his mother has no money to loan him to get him from the hospital to here. Rough deal."

Val grimaced. "Being in the military is always tough, Cat. And Talon's going to have his hands full once he gets back on his feet. Sandy's in bad shape and the chemo is really taking her down. I worry...."

Because she was a paramedic, Cat knew what chemo

did, understood it took a poison to kill a poison, but the person suffered horrendously during the process. "I wish we could do more for Sandy."

Val picked up some of the mason jars from a box on the floor and started lining them up on the counter. "Talon is coming home at a terrible time. I'm worried he won't be able to handle it all."

Cat bent down and put the last of the canning jars on the counter. She picked up the box and got it out of the way. "No one goes through life alone. Maybe Talon's going to need support himself."

Val pulled open a drawer and drew out two aprons, handing one to Cat. "We all need help from time to time. He should go see Jordana. She's an expert on PTSD and helped a lot of vets in this county."

Gus pulled out a huge kettle and set it in the sink to fill it with water. "Well, that young man has a job here at the Bar H. He's a hard worker. And once he gets well, Griff is going to need a full-time wrangler to help him. Talon grew up on the Triple H, which was next to our ranch, and then Curt Downing stole it from under Sandy Holt's nose for a song."

Cat remembered that Curt Downing was dead, shot by an escaped convict on a trail up in the Tetons. All his holdings, according to his will, went to a nephew by the name of Chuck Harper, who sold the ranch to an Easterner. And he was an even worse person that Downing had been. "I wonder if he'll sell the Triple H?"

Gus snorted. "I'm having Griff look into it. We need more land and it makes sense to buy it. The present owner did nothing with it except try to put condos on it. Thank the good Lord that the mayor said no to his plan."

Gus had made a lot of money off the sale of her

own ranch on the other side of Wyoming decades earlier. She didn't know exactly how much, but Griff had an MBA from Harvard and was now taking care of the woman's money for her. Gus had told her one time that Griff was making her a lot of interest and she was very happy to have her son-in-law handle the finances. "If you could buy the Triple H, that would make Sandy and Talon happy."

Gus nodded, then became sad. "It was such a shame Sandy's second husband, Bradley, died in that auto accident. He was in the process of expanding the ranch, doing good things with it. But Sandy wasn't up to dealing with the ranch after his death. And then, suddenly, there was the cancer. Griff's going over to see about the ranch after the blizzard is done blowing through. I'd really like to buy the Triple H. Fingers crossed."

Cat smiled to herself. Gus was a big thinker and dreamer. But she had the money, the smarts and Griff helping her to make her vision come true. Gus was unstoppable when she wanted something.

Cat heard Zeke urgently begin to bark.

"Uh-oh," Gus muttered, peering toward the hallway. "That dog's barking. Wonder what's wrong?"

"I'll go see," Cat said, hurrying out of the kitchen. Her heart amped up a little as she opened the door. Zeke instantly whined, wagging his tail at the doorway. He turned around and hurried to the bed.

Cat frowned and quietly shut the door. Talon Holt was sitting up, his long legs hanging over the edge of the bed, most of the covers pulled aside. His maleness struck her. He was naked, his body massive and powerful even though he was underweight. His head was hanging almost on his chest, his large hands gripping the mattress to stay upright. Only a few blankets lay across his hard, thick thighs. His feet were large, his legs spaced apart as if to stop him from keeling forward and falling off the bed. She heard his labored, rasping breaths. Her eyes widened as she saw he'd yanked the IV out of his right arm, bright red blood streaming down his forearm. No wonder Zeke was barking.

"Talon?" she asked, keeping her voice low and soothing as she walked toward him.

He barely raised his head, his eyes slits as he regarded her.

Cat felt sudden alarm. Talon was pale, breathing hard, his eyes glassy looking. She crouched down in front of him to make eye contact. "Did you take your IV out?" Did she dare touch him? He was different when he was awake. He'd been so approachable in sleep. Now he trembled, as if it took every last bit of his strength for him to remain upright.

"Yeah," he managed with a croak.

"I need to stop the bleeding," Cat said softly. She slowly reached out, placing her fingers on his right hand. His fingers dug deeply into the mattress. When she touched him, he winced. Instantly, she withdrew her hand. Something was wrong. She sensed it.

"Talon, you're safe. You're here at the Bar H. My name is Cat Edwin and I'm a paramedic. I'm here to help you. Will you let me touch you?"

He scowled, staring sightlessly past her, his attention on something else she couldn't fathom. Was he hallucinating? The way his naked shoulders were bunched, Cat felt in danger herself. Maybe it was overreaction from her past, from her childhood. And then she saw him lift his chin and look directly at her.

"Blue?"

Cat stared, her lips parting. "Blue? Who's Blue?" she asked softly. And then tears came into his murky gray eyes. He seemed to fight them back. He swallowed convulsively several times.

Talon had to be hallucinating. Cat eyed the dark red blood still leaking from the IV wound. He must have ripped it out of his arm, because the flesh looked torn and ragged. She had to stop the bleeding and get him to see and hear her instead of whatever held him prisoner.

Slowly getting up, she called Zeke over. She guided the dog over to Talon.

"Talon? This is your dog, Zeke. He needs you to pet him. He's worried about you."

Zeke began licking the blood off Talon's arm, whining and anxious.

Holding her breath, Cat watched Talon slowly blink a few times. His mouth opened and then closed. His eyes became harder and more focused on the dog sitting between his legs. The dog was thumping his tail against the pine floor, the only sound in the room. Talon slowly released the fingers of one hand from the mattress and he laid his hand on the dog's broad skull. A little fear left her and she slowly unwound from her crouched position.

"Talon? I'm going to fix your arm. Is it okay if I touch you?" Cat stood uncertainly, her own senses telling her that if he wasn't yet here with her and Zeke and if she touched him again, he might lash out at her. She had no experience with soldiers or anyone with PTSD. Druggies, yeah. But not this. And she knew enough to go slow, to allow Talon to process her request.

Zeke whined, reaching up, licking Talon's bearded cheek.

"Yeah…go ahead," he rasped thickly, his gaze fixed on his dog.

Relief sped through Cat. She went to her medical bag, drew out items and then walked to his side. Putting on a pair of gloves, she cleaned the area inside his right arm and quickly patched it up, halting the bleeding. There was a bowl of water on the dresser and she took the washcloth and wiped away the blood left on his arm and hand. When she crouched down to gently pry his fingers out of the mattress, she felt the heat of his stare on her. Her skin prickled and her heart took off in an unsteady beat. He turned his large hand over for her and she saw the many calluses across his fingers and palm. After wiping his hand free of blood, she placed Talon's hand back on the mattress.

"You okay?" she asked, meeting his eyes. There was clarity now in them. Huge gray eyes with large black pupils staring intently at her. For a second, Cat's imagination took off. He was the hunter. She was the prey. Oddly, she didn't feel threatened. Instead, she felt her womb contract. Felt the heat of his intense stare, the utter masculinity of him, the power of him as a man. It excited her and simultaneously scared her.

No man had ever made her feel hot, needy and achy in her lower body. But Talon did. In spades. Gulping, Cat stood up and quickly moved to the dresser to rinse out the bloody washcloth. What the hell was going on with her? Licking her lip nervously, Cat cast a glance over her shoulder. Talon had lain back down, drawing the blankets haphazardly across his lower body. His eyes were closed.

Zeke lay down by his bed.

Watching the dog helped Cat understand what was going on with Talon Holt. He'd also ripped off the cannula that had given him extra oxygen and it lay on the floor next to the broken IV line. She picked them both up and shut off the IV. Did she dare sit down beside him as she had before? No, she couldn't. Her throat went tight and she found it hard to breathe for a moment.

As she worked near the bed, she felt his eyes open and focus on her again. Looking up, he was watching her. Cat muttered, "I'm cleaning up."

He barely nodded his head.

Her hands were shaky. Cat removed the IV and placed it in her medical bag. She wrapped up other equipment.

"I remember you."

Cat froze for moment. Talon's voice was deep and hoarse. But he was awake and alert. Considering his medical condition, she was stunned by the strength of his tone and the clarity in his eyes. "What do you remember?" she asked.

"How beautiful your eyes were after you stopped to help me and Zeke."

CHAPTER FOUR

CAT WAS BRINGING Zeke back from a potty break an hour later. She pushed open the bedroom door. Talon jerked and suddenly sat up, tense, breathing harshly. His hands were curled into fists, raised as if ready to strike. Surprised, Cat anchored just inside the entrance. The man's narrowed eyes went black. Instantly, her heart started to pound. What was going on?

"Talon? It's me, Cat. It's all right," she managed, her fingers tightening around Zeke's leather collar. The dog whined, his gaze riveted upon his master.

Talon stared hard at her. His breath came in gasps, his chest heaving with sudden exertion. Slowly, he lowered his hands and unfisted them. "What the hell are you doing?" he snarled.

Stung and shocked, Cat kept her anger closeted. "I just took your dog out."

Talon wiped his face and uttered a curse under his breath. It was a bad idea to wake him suddenly, as if he were still in the middle of a nightmare. "Yeah…okay… thanks," he muttered and lay down on the bed, throwing his arm across his closed eyes.

What had just happened?

Shaken, Cat released Zeke. The dog instantly trotted over to the bed, wagging his tail. She quietly closed the door, her heart banging away in her tightened throat.

The expression on Talon's face scared the hell out of her. He looked savage. Lethal.

As she moved closer to his bedside, she could see that Talon's color was better. He dragged his arm off his face, opened his eyes and stared grumpily up at her.

"I need to listen to your lungs and take your temperature," she offered by way of explanation.

"Do it," he rasped, closing his eyes again, his mouth a single line.

Zeke whined and then sat down next to the bed. Cat gathered the equipment from her medical bag at the end of the bed. She hesitantly sat down, her hip brushing against his. His eyes snapped open, a fierce look in them. She recognized an adrenaline surge when she saw one. Cat felt badly. The man didn't need any more shock or trauma than he presently had.

"I'm sorry I startled you," she murmured, holding his dark, turbulent-looking gaze. Even his nostrils were flared, and he was still dragging in and releasing short, sharp breaths. Yeah, she was no stranger to adrenaline, understood its effects from her firefighting duties.

"Whatever you do from now on," Talon growled, "don't ever come over and touch me while I'm sleeping." He dug into her gaze. "I could hurt you very badly, Cat, and that's the last thing I want to do."

She chewed on her lower lip, regarding his warning, searching his eyes. "Is this because you were a SEAL?"

"Yes," he said. Talon held up his hands. "I know how to kill a person fourteen different ways with these. They are considered lethal weapons here by U.S. law enforcement. Please—" and his voice lowered with emotion "—no surprises. If you need me awake, stay at the door and call my name. I'll come up in a hurry, like I did just now."

Her heart contracted with pain. "Got it." As she pulled the blanket down to expose his chest, she saw more than anxiety in his narrowed eyes. Maybe fear? She wasn't sure. Talon was still breathing hard. Labored. Cat warmed the stethoscope between her palms so it wouldn't feel so startlingly cold to his flesh. Gently, she placed the stethoscope against his chest, listening. She tried not to be influenced by his warm, hard flesh. As she grazed him, his skin tightened, the muscles leaping beneath. The man's chest was powerful.

"Can you move your head to one side? I need to put my ThermoScan into your ear for a moment and take your temperature," she said.

He nodded and turned his head slightly so she had easy access.

Cat felt shaky inside. Talon was a sensual, dark, dangerous and exciting man. She wasn't used to feeling this way.

She looked at the ThermoScan. "Thanks. Your temperature is really going down. It's a hundred degrees now. That's good news."

"How about my lungs?" he asked. "I feel like an elephant's sitting on my chest."

Cat gave him a sympathetic look. "I know. There's still crackling in them. That means a lot of fluid remains in them. I'm going to give you another shot of antibiotics." She got up.

Talon watched her move. Cat was medium boned, had flesh on her, but she was clearly athletically fit. Her red flannel shirt barely outlined her breasts. They were full breasts, the kind a man could hold in the palms of his hands. She was long in the torso and her hips flared. His gaze roamed the longest pair of legs he'd ever seen on a woman. He liked a woman's legs and fantasized just how taut and curved her thighs were beneath the material of her jeans. He could feel himself hardening. Cursing mentally, Talon forced his body to not react to her. When Cat turned around, he feasted on her oval face, those so-soft lips of hers, wondering how she would taste beneath his exploration.

Cat sat down and rubbed an area of his upper arm with an alcohol swab. "This is going to hurt," she warned him. His biceps was huge.

"That's nothing," Talon said. Her eyes focused and he barely felt the sting of the needle into his arm. She was good as a paramedic, no question. As she leaned forward, her slightly curled black hair slid off her shoulders and swung forward, bracketing her face. Talon itched to lift and sift the ebony strands through his fingers. He'd probably startle the hell out of Cat if he gave in to the desire, and he didn't want to scare her. Sometimes, Talon saw fear banked in her eyes. Fear of him? Well, after he came up swinging, yeah, she'd be scared. But there was more to it. At some point, he'd find out the truth because he wanted to know her a helluva lot better.

Cat placed a small piece of gauze over the shot area and quickly wrapped it in some latex. Just getting to slide her fingers around his arm gave her secret pleasure. Talon's muscles tensed automatically wherever her fingertips brushed against his flesh. Worse, she felt turned-on, a dampness between her thighs. No man had ever elicited that kind of response from her. Ever. Cat had no reasonable explanation for her body's reaction, as if it acted independently from her mind. And her contact with Talon created dark, intense and unreadable emotions in his eyes. Cat impulsively reached out, touching his wrinkled brow. His skin was warm and drier than before. His eyes instantly narrowed upon her. Her womb contracted. Pulling her hand away, Cat quickly stood and put her equipment into the medical bag. She wiped her damp palms against her jeans and turned.

"Your skin is drier. That's a good sign, too. Can I get you anything to eat or drink?"

"Water," he growled. Talon saw her reaction to his rough tone. For a moment, Cat looked confused. Her black hair was mussed around her shoulders. He wanted to thank her for taking care of Zeke. And he felt like hell for snarling at her when she'd awakened him out of a dead sleep. *Dammit.* The last thing he wanted to do was ever hurt her.

Talon watched Cat walk to the bed stand and pour him a glass of water. He struggled to sit up, the covers pooling around his hips and lean waist. When she turned, he reached out, his fingers wrapping around the glass, accidentally grazing her fingers. The moment sizzled between them, warmth flowing up his hand. God knew, he wanted to touch Cat all over. Her lips parted, as if she was wildly aware their touch had created a firestorm between them.

"Thanks," Talon said gruffly, taking the glass. He tipped his head back, gulping it down.

"More?"

"Please." He pushed the pillows against the headboard and relaxed against them, watching her. Cat was tall. And solidly built. She was all grace in motion. Her hands were long, slender and beautiful. Talon saw a number of scars across them and he wondered how she got them. "I'm sorry I scared you earlier."

Cat handed him the second glass, her body feeling hot and needy. There was regret in his rough voice as he took the glass. "It's okay. I've dealt with combative, injured or sick people before." *But I've never seen the reaction I just saw in you.* Standing there, unsure, Cat watched him tip back his head, the strong column of his throat exposed, his Adam's apple bobbing. *Masculine.* He was so blatantly, sexually male that it shook her. And his dark sexuality called to her whether she wanted it to or not. Talon's shoulders were incredibly broad, the muscles taut. His arms were ropy with lean muscle. There was nothing weak about this man and Cat tried to still her stunned reaction to him: he was pure sex. Her mouth went dry, and she took the emptied glass, needing a glass herself.

"More?" she managed, her voice husky.

Talon shook his head, regretting the anxiety in her eyes. "No...thanks. Look, I'm not going to bite you. I'm sorry I went into combat mode when you opened that door." His mouth thinned. "I can't help it." Talon wished he could.

"It's all right," Cat said softly, setting the glass down. "You know where you are, right? You've had a high fever since I picked you and Zeke up this morning."

Talon rubbed his face. "Yeah, I'm here at the Bar H. Right?" His hand fell away and he stared up at Cat. Those eyes of hers made him long to dive deep into them and never resurface. They reminded him of the color of the Indian Ocean he'd swum in as a SEAL. Deep blue. Mysterious. Amazing. He'd like to be deep in her. Buried up to the hilt. The thought was searing.

Talon felt himself respond. Great, he was going to get
an erection. Not a good idea.

"Yes."

"And your name is Cat Edwin and you're a paramedic."

Shocked at how well he remembered things, she nodded. "Right."

"I think I remember Miss Gus was in here one time,
but I'm not sure. Sometimes, I was hallucinating." Talon
felt filthy and he smelled sour, his body unwashed for
weeks. It wasn't a pretty smell, unlike Cat. She smelled
sweet, her hair holding a cinnamon scent and that of
cold, winter air. Talon closed his eyes, getting a grip on
himself. Yeah, he was horny. No, it wasn't a good idea
to be that way right now. He'd been in and out of the
Naval Hospital at San Diego for almost six months. The
nurses were nice. Some drop-dead gorgeous, but in the
state he was in, sex was the last thing on his mind. His
body, mind and soul were struggling to heal.

Until now.

Until *her*.

Dammit, he was in so much trouble. Pushing his
hands along the blankets over him, Talon scowled.

"Do you work for the Bar H?" he demanded.

Cat pulled up a chair and sat facing him. She folded
her hands in her lap. "I work here part-time."

"Is that why you were driving on that road this morning?" Talon saw a clock on the dresser. It was 3:30 p.m.
He remembered looking at the watch on his wrist this
morning. It had read 7:10 a.m.

Cat nodded. She could see his gray eyes were sharply
focused. "My full-time job is as a firefighter with the

Jackson Hole Fire Department. On my days off, I come out here and I'm a wrangler."

He stared at her. "You're a wrangler?"

She grinned. "What? A woman can't herd cattle? Fix fence? Tangle with a bull?" She saw color settle briefly in his cheeks. Was Talon Holt blushing? Laughing softly, she said, "It's a gender-neutral job as far as I know."

Talon had the good grace to manage a partial, apologetic smile. "You're right," he acknowledged. Did Cat know how hot her mouth was? How sexy she would look if she didn't wear those loose clothes? Oh, why the *hell* was he noticing her this way? This woman had just saved his sorry ass. He should be feeling grateful, not aching in pain from an erection he kept hidden deep beneath the covers.

"Are you hungry, Mr. Holt? Miss Gus made some chicken soup for you. I could bring you a bowl?"

He looked over at her. "Call me Talon. It's the least I can do to thank you for saving me and Zeke this morning." He began to cough. It was a deep, ragged cough and he pressed his hand hard against his chest, trying to catch his breath. When he finally stopped coughing and could breathe, he saw Cat's concerned look. "Yeah, I could eat a little something."

She stood. "You're really underweight."

Talon gave her a flat look, saying nothing. He wasn't about to go into why he was underweight with anyone. "I need some clothes to wear."

Cat walked over to the dresser and brought over some folded men's clothes and set them next to him. "Griff McPherson is the owner of the Bar H with his wife, Val. He's about your height and he gave me these for you. Your, uh, other clothes...well...they're pretty done for." Cat didn't want to embarrass him by telling him they were ratty, thin, smelled horrible and that they belonged in the trash. She watched as his large, scarred hand took the jeans, dark blue flannel shirt, boxer shorts and socks out of her hands.

"Thanks," Talon said, his voice hoarse after the coughing. "While you get me that soup, I'm going to the head, get a shower and put on these clean clothes. Where are my boots?"

"Out by the woodstove in the living room. They should be pretty dry by now. I'll bring them in with me when I bring in the soup. There are towels, washcloth and soap in the bathroom for you, too."

Talon nodded. "Okay. I'll see you in about half an hour?" What he didn't want was to be strutting naked across the room when she came in unannounced. That would not be a good idea. Talon saw her smile a little. Damn, her mouth was a magnet. Soft, full and that lower lip slightly fuller than the upper one, this side of being pouty, just begging to be kissed, nipped and taken.

"Deal," Cat murmured, heading for the door. "And next time, I'll knock first."

One corner of his mouth quirked upward. She was a fast learner.

Talon had forgotten the sheer luxury of a hot, steamy shower and soap rubbing the sour smell off his flesh. He spent nearly twenty minutes in there scrubbing his dirty hair and beard free of how many weeks of accumulated crud? He was weak, his legs shaky, but he used the glass shower wall to keep himself upright. The softness of the thick terry-cloth towel felt incredibly lush over his flesh. He climbed into Griff's clothes, found a comb to tame his long hair. He discovered a razor in a drawer. It was a woman's razor, but it would do. In no time, he'd gotten rid of the damned beard, his face free of the hair. In Afghanistan, as a SEAL, he always wore the beard to fit into the Muslim culture. In reality, Talon preferred his hair military short, his face beardless.

Rubbing his hand across his jaw, he noticed that he'd nicked himself pretty good a couple of times. He used a tissue to blot the blood away, putting pressure on those places to stop them from bleeding. He took a smaller towel to wipe the steam off the mirror. God, he looked gaunt, like a damn skeleton. Dark circles rested beneath his eyes and his skin was stretched tight across his wide cheekbones. Talon forced his hair back into a small ponytail behind his neck after spotting a stray rubber band on the counter.

Talon didn't look closely into his eyes. He knew what was in there, hoping no one else could read him. His sixth sense, honed by years of combat and saving his and the lives of his men, told him Cat Edwin saw *everything* about him. He sensed she could look into his soul and that made him nervous.

He wiped his face free of the dampness caused by the steam of the shower and dropped the towel on the counter. Opening the door, he saw Zeke standing by the bed.

"Come," he called to his dog.

Instantly, Zeke bounded into his opened arms after he crouched down. It was important to have playtime with his Belgian Malinois. Zeke's black muzzle, dark ears and fawn-colored body was wriggling with excitement. He danced around in Talon's opened arms, whining and playful.

There was a knock.

"Come in," Talon called.

The door opened.

Talon told Zeke to sit and he did. He rose as Cat entered with a large tray in both hands. In her fingers beneath it dangled his dried leather boots. He walked over and gently retrieved his boots from them.

"Thanks," he told her. Her eyes widened and she almost halted, staring up at him.

"Y-you look so different," she stammered. Talon was so ruggedly good-looking that Cat nearly lost her grip on the tray. His eyes were clearer. There was much less tension swirling around him, too. His mouth was relaxed. Cat felt a sweet, building heat bubble up inside her. The man's mouth without that scraggly beard was so kissable. Chiseled and strong, like him.

Talon closed the door behind her. "Can you set the tray on the bed?" he suggested, going to the chair and sitting down. He pulled on his hardened leather boots, knowing they'd need some softening work with leather soap. *Another day.* His legs were weak.

Talon sat down on the edge of the bed. Cat placed the tray across his lap.

"Miss Gus made some of her world-famous biscuits for you," she said, straightening. Cat couldn't stop her reaction to the coiled tension swirling around Talon once again. It was dangerous. Exciting. Taking a few steps away, she watched as he looked longingly at the bowl of steaming chicken soup. Miss Gus had put several sizable chunks of breast meat in it along with oodles of noodles.

Talon shook his head. "No…this will be fine. Thank her for me." He glanced up at Cat. The expression on her face startled him. Was that desire that he saw? Something was going on between them. It was like a living, organic connection simmering and popping between them.

He didn't dare think about it.

Talon scowled and picked up the large soupspoon. There was a pink linen napkin beside the bowl and nearby salt and pepper shakers.

"Okay," Cat murmured. "I'll let you eat in peace." Because if she stayed, she'd start asking Talon a hundred questions and he didn't need that right now.

Nodding, Talon watched her leave. The sway of those sweet hips beneath the loose-fitting jeans made him go hard again. Damn, the woman was really riling up his body. It wasn't her fault, Talon realized as the door quietly closed. Cat was not flirting with him. He didn't see a ring on her left finger, either. But nowadays, that meant nothing one way or another. She was probably hooked up with one lucky bastard who was privy to that luscious body of hers. He grew harder. Cursing softly beneath his breath, Talon took a first, tentative sip of the soup.

His stomach growled loudly. How long had it been since he'd last eaten? Three days, maybe? Walking the plains of Wyoming, the towns so far apart there was no way to get food. He always kept enough kibble for Zeke in his rucksack, which lay across the room, propped up against the wall. And he'd run out of protein bars, which were good but too damned expensive for him to buy.

The soup tasted delicious and he ate slowly, reintroducing food to his shrunken stomach. The silence settled around them. Zeke appeared happy, his brown eyes alight with joy. Talon could read his dog just as well as Zeke could read him. They'd been together a long time and knew each other like few animals and humans ever would. He smiled at Zeke and then picked up a noodle, blew on it to cool it and then gave it to his dog. Zeke gobbled it down, licking his muzzle on both sides and then giving Talon a pleading look for more.

Outside the window, Talon could see the blizzard was still in full force. It looked like another six inches had accumulated since Cat had rescued their sorry asses off that highway this morning. His hand shook badly as he brought the spoon to his lips, spilling half of it into the bowl and the rest around the tray. Cursing softly, Talon set the spoon aside, curved his hands around the bowl and lifted it to his lips, instead.

Talon wiped his mouth with the linen napkin afterward, thinking he'd died and gone to heaven. A warm room. He was dry. He wasn't freezing anymore. His teeth weren't chattering. He could feel his toes and fingers. Life was good. All thanks to Cat stopping and the generosity of Miss Gus and the McPhersons. He had a lot to thank them for and he would once he got some strength back.

Cat Edwin. He sat there, mentally repeating her name, scowling. Maybe he was frustrated because of nearly a year without a woman. As a SEAL coming back off deployment, it was easy to hook up with a woman, no strings attached. SEALs were always a hot commodity. Talon shook his head. Cat interested him on that level, for sure. But there was something more to her that he itched to explore. And then Talon grunted and shook his head. He was penniless, needing a job and he had responsibilities for his mother. Getting involved with Cat wasn't in the cards right now. *Maybe later. Probably never.* For all Talon knew, she could be married and have a bunch of kids. Still, he owed her. Big-time.

TALON WAS DOZING when he heard a soft knock at the door. Cat called through the door. Instantly, he sat up.

"Come in," he called, his voice rough.

"You look better," Cat observed. That was an understatement. Talon was stunningly handsome. He could be a model, that rock-hard, clean jaw of his. His large, well-spaced eyes missed nothing. She felt the heat of his gaze on her face, drifting south, to her breasts. Instantly, her nipples hardened. Thank God she wore a heavy flannel shirt. Cat wanted to cross her arms, hide from him. His look triggered threat within her. It brought back memories of her father looking at her in much the same way and it scared her for a moment. The mature woman in her understood it was a man appreciating a woman. But the little wounded girl inside her cringed in terror. Of possibly being hurt. She swallowed hard and forced herself to walk in, regardless of his inspection.

"I feel better," Talon said, watching her progress. Jesus, he felt like a starved wolf wanting to claim his mate. Cat was in good physical condition. He could tell just by the way she walked, the way she carried herself. There was no excess on this woman's body except in all the right places. He sensed trepidation in her—and he was the cause. He had the laserlike focus any SEAL would have. Their sudden intensity scared people or made them uncomfortable. But it was an ability that had saved his and his team members many times before.

"Miss Gus would love to come in and visit you," Cat said, picking up the tray and facing him. Zeke sidled up to Talon, and the man gently petted his dog with his large hand. Her flesh rippled with possibility. She wondered what it would feel like for Talon to graze her flesh in just such a way. Despite his height and his size, his touch on Zeke was clearly tender with love. Her heart melted. Though Talon was a rugged and big man, he could be gentle. That reduced the threat level markedly as she stood beneath his warm appraisal.

"Sure," Talon said, clearing his throat. "But if I could get someone's cell phone? I need to call my mother first. She needs to know I'm all right." He had a cell phone but couldn't pay the bill, so it wasn't working. Not something he wanted to admit to anyone. Talon felt ashamed that he was destitute, relying on the goodwill of others to help him scrape through this harsh period in his life.

"I'll tell Miss Gus. She's got a cell she can loan you."

Talon watched Cat turn and leave. Man, the sway of her hips, that very nicely defined butt of hers and his fantasy of wrapping his hands, grabbing—

"Talon!"

He lifted his head, seeing Miss Gus limp into the room. "Hey, Miss Gus, good to see you," he rasped.

Gus grinned and stopped in front of him. "Talon, you look awful."

"Thank you, I think." And then he lost his smile, slid his hand into hers and squeezed it gently. "Thanks for giving me room and board."

Snorting, Gus leaned over and kissed his recently shaven face. "Welcome home, Talon. You know you're always welcome here." She released his hand and sat down in the wooden chair near the bed, intently studying him. "Cat said you're doing better. Your fever's down but not gone."

Talon nodded and lay on the bed, his back against the headboard. "Whatever she's doing is helping me a lot."

"Cat's the best. Thank the good Lord she found you out there this morning or a snowplow would've discovered your frozen body tomorrow morning on that highway."

Grimly, Talon sighed. "It was a close call, Miss Gus."

"Well, you weren't meant to die just yet."

Flinching inwardly, memories of Hayden and him strung up, being tortured, slammed into Talon. Hayden did die. Talon had almost died but clung to life until Zeke brought help and he had been rescued, a hairbreadth from death himself. His throat tightened and he croaked, "Yeah, it wasn't my time."

"The soup good?"

"Wonderful," Talon admitted, suddenly emotional. "I remember you making me those chocolate-chip cookies when I was a kid, Miss Gus. I knew your chicken soup would be good." Tears pricked the backs of his eyes and Talon quickly willed them away. "You and your family have been very kind to me and I appreciate it." Shame flowed through him. He wanted to tell Miss Gus why he'd sunk to such an all-time low, a homeless vet, without money, without any support, but he couldn't go there. At least, not yet. His focus was on his mother, Sandy, not himself or trying to explain why he was in this predicament.

Gus pulled out her cell phone and handed it to him. "Listen, you call Sandy. Lord knows, she's on tenterhooks waiting for your call." She waved her finger at him. "But you can't go see her, Talon. You could give her your bacterial pneumonia and she's on chemo right now. If she caught your pneumonia, she could die. Okay?"

He nodded, opening the cell phone, seeing that Gus had put his mother's number up on the screen. "Got it," he rasped.

Gus stood up. "Okay, you call her. And oh, tell her that once you're well, you're a full-time wrangler at the Bar H." Her eyes gleamed with pleasure. "We need help here, Talon. And I can't think of hiring anyone better than you. Are you agreeable?"

Agreeable? Hell, he was downright grateful. Tears burned in his eyes. Again, Talon shoved them deep down inside himself. Into what SEALs referred to as their kill box. That's where all their unwanted emotions, good or bad, were shoved. Never to see the light of day again. That way, he could continue to function, continue to be a warrior on the front lines, not distracted by human feelings. Clearing his throat, he said, "Yes, that's agreeable, Miss Gus. Thank you."

"Good. Now, I'm having Cat fix up a small bedroom down the hall from my room here. Cat always takes the room next to yours. She's getting yours ready for you right now. After calling Sandy, if you feel up to it, we'll move you to your permanent room here in the house until you're well. Will that work?"

Talon's mouth pulled into a grin. "That will work, Miss Gus. Thank you."

She limped to the door. "My granddaughter, Val, and her husband, Griff, agreed to hire you. It wasn't just me who wanted you. I told them you'd grown up next door and were pushing cattle around and mending fences since you were a kid. We'll all be happy you're here with us, Talon." She waved a finger at him. "Come out to the kitchen when you're done speakin' to your mom if you're up to it. You are so skinny it's scary. You need to eat some of my freshly made biscuits with some strawberry jam I made last August."

Talon felt new warmth flow into his heart. Hope, maybe. He had a job, thank God. It was the one thing he desperately needed. Talon tried not to think about everything, focusing in on calling his mother. His heart wrenched as he punched in her phone number. He tried to shore up his emotions. How he wanted to be with her, hug and hold her. A phone call was going to have to do for right now. He was just grateful he was alive to give her a call in the first place. Talon didn't want her to know how close he'd come to dying this morning. Or before that, either. He wanted her focusing on herself.

CHAPTER FIVE

TALON SQUEEZED HIS eyes shut, desperately trying to stop
the tears after he finished the emotional phone call to
his mother. He gripped the cell phone so hard he thought
he might destroy it. Finally, he dropped it on the bed
beside him.

Zeke came over, whining. Blindly, Talon reached out,
rubbing the dog's dark ears, something he enjoyed. It
felt as if there were a bunch of writhing, angry snakes
in his tight gut. Unconsciously, Talon rubbed the area,
still fighting back the tears that wanted to fall.

His mother sounded like she was dying. As if she'd
given up. Talon understood it better than most. He'd
given up this morning out on that highway.

Lifting his head, Talon blinked back the tears, angrily stuffed them into his kill box and glared around
the bedroom. A sense of suffocating helplessness over-
came him. His shoulders sagged and he leaned over,
pressing his brow against Zeke's broad head. The dog
whined and pressed his seventy-five-pound body in
between his legs, always a sign of affection and care
toward his master.

Chest tight, his throat aching, Talon ran his long
hands across Zeke's soft, dry fur. "What the hell am
I going to do, Zeke?" His voice cracked. "What?" It
felt comforting to have his dog pressed against his leg.

How many times in Afghanistan had Zeke done this? Known when he was upset, needing a doggy hug? *So damn many times.* This dog had saved his life so many times that Talon had lost count.

Lifting his head, Talon shoved the tears away. He glanced at the clock on the dresser. Four-thirty. Dinner would be at six. Miss Gus had asked him to come to the kitchen but, dammit, he didn't want to. The thought of talking to anyone right now, with the exception of Cat, rubbed him raw.

Talon needed her. He yearned for Cat's quiet sense of stability, her husky, honeyed voice soothing his rough, jagged and exposed edges. Every time Cat touched him, he felt a moment's peace. She gave him a corner of quiet in a violent, stress-filled world of combat that lived and raged inside him nonstop. Six months in a hospital had done nothing but agitate him. The only thing that had healed was his physical body. God, he needed Cat. She was like a battle dressing around his bleeding heart. Talon felt as if he were hemorrhaging emotionally.

His mother was dying.

Just then a soft knock came at the door. Talon scrambled to control his feelings. The only person he wanted to see was Cat. Anyone else, and he'd send them away, telling them he was too sick to get out of bed. It was the truth.

"Who is it?" he called, his voice harsh.

The door opened. Cat peered in. "It's just me. Do you need anything?"

As he stared at her, his heart started to pound. "Come in," he said. Relief flowed deep and strong through him as she quietly entered and closed the door behind her.

"You talk to your mom?" Cat asked hesitantly, stand-

ing uncertainly by the end of his bed. Talon looked pale.
His eyes were dark and anguished. No doubt, he was
upset. Zeke sat between his opened legs, Talon's long
fingers stroking the dog's head and ears. The way his
mouth was pursed, Cat knew what Talon knew: Sandy
Holt was slowly dying. Her heart wrenched with grief
for Talon. All she wanted to do was slide her arms
around his shoulders. Talon really needed it. But Cat
was unsure he'd accept her embrace.

"Yeah, I just got done talking to her." The words
came out hard-edged, laden with emotion. Talon looked
over and patted the bed next to him. "Come and sit
down." He searched her blue eyes, silently pleading
for her nearness.

"Sure," she whispered, walking over. Cat sat down,
leaving a foot between them. She remembered him
warning her not to touch him. But what would Talon
do if she suddenly embraced him? He needed touch,
kind words. "How are you doing?" she ventured, looking and holding his tormented gaze.

"Not good," Talon said roughly. "My mom's dying."

Cat rubbed her hands slowly between her thighs.
"She's fought so long, so hard, Talon. Sandy's tired…."

Savagely rubbing his face, he wanted to cry. Cat's
subdued voice was a healing balm to his ravaged
heart. Talon had no way to stop the grief awakened in
him once again. He had thought that in the year since
Hayden had died, the grief would recede. Now it was
there again at the same intensity, glaring at him, raking
his heart over cut glass once more. Talon wasn't sure he
could take another personal death. Hayden had been a
brother to him, and his mother, whom he loved deeply,
was now slipping away.

Cat took a huge risk and reached out, slid her hand across his shoulder. She felt his skin tighten beneath her fingertips, felt his muscles leap. "I'm so sorry, Talon. So sorry…"

Her touch broke something wide-open. He made a sound, maybe a sob, maybe a cry for help that had never been released. Raggedly whispering her name, Talon swept Cat into his arms. He buried his head against her shoulder and jaw, his breath uneven, his heart raw. Talon held her so tight he thought he might be squeezing the life out of her. He could smell the sweet scent of Cat's skin beneath her shirt. She smelled of fragrant almond. The silken strands of hair trapped between his cheek and her shoulder reminded him of an apple pie cooking in the oven, the hint of cinnamon encircling his flared nostrils.

A soft gasp tore from Cat as Talon turned and inexplicably hauled her into his arms, crushing her against him. It was so unexpected, but so right and so wonderful. Without thinking, Cat curved her arms around his tense shoulders, tightening them, holding him near. She closed her eyes, feeling his ragged, moist breath against her shoulder, his need for human contact. Talon trembled in her arms, and Cat could feel him fighting back tears, struggling to stop so many awful emotions from erupting.

"It's going to be okay, Talon," she whispered. "Just breathe. Take this one minute at a time. I'll help you get through it." Cat was shocked at the words tearing unthinkingly out of her mouth. She couldn't stop them. Cat soothed him with her hand, her fingers skimming across his back, smoothing the flannel shirt here and there. Gradually, she felt him begin to relax in her arms. Begin to give over his steel control to her. She'd seen this re-action before in traumatic car crashes, the shock start-ing to wear off the survivors, their need for comfort.

"It's a path you have to walk, but you don't have to walk it alone. I'll be here for you. Gus, Val and Griff will be here, too. It's going to be hard, but you'll sur-vive." Tears jammed into Cat's eyes as she haltingly spoke the words. Talon's response was to hold her even tighter, crushing her against him, clinging to her as if she were his only anchor in his world of chaos and if he released her, he'd be lost. Closing her eyes, Cat re-laxed completely in his grip. She felt the hard thud of his heart against her. Felt her breasts pressed against his chest wall.

And when Cat threaded her fingers through his clean, silky hair, he trembled violently. How long had Talon gone without care? She continued her ministra-tions because she felt Talon relax in her arms, loosen his grip around her. She smiled to herself, grateful for all her experience as a paramedic to know what to do. She knew all about dying and death. She'd grown up in a household where she was unsure from one day to the next whether she'd be breathing.

Her fingers moved from his hair to the nape of his strong neck. Cat thought she heard Talon groan but, then, figured she was making it up. There was such se-cret pleasure in exploring his flesh. All this had done was fuel a hunger she'd never experienced before. She was shocked by her body's response to him. This had nothing to do with her mind—it had to do with his being so damn sensual. Being around him made her feel needy.

Talon knew he had to release Cat. It was the last

thing he wanted to do. God, she was strong and soft at the same time. He absorbed her warmth like a famished man. She was relaxed in his grip, surrendering to him. Trusting him. Talon felt like a thief. Cat gave herself to him freely and without reservation, holding him, stroking him and feeding him in so many invisible ways.

And all Talon could think about was pulling Cat down on the bed, kissing her senseless, taking her, filling her, running from all those dirty emotions that were eating away at him right now. If he could just bury himself into her soft, wet confines, the world would go away for a while. Sex was the greatest mindblower of them all. It stopped him from thinking. His feelings were channeled into pleasuring the woman, pleasuring himself and the powerful emotions of lust that would ripple through his body. It would erase all the grief. The terror. The anxiety. *Everything.* It was the most powerful medication in the world. Oh, God, he ached to take Cat, make her his woman, make her his.

Reason started creeping back into Talon's brain. Cat must have had a significant other or she was married. That made his heart cringe with renewed grief. He'd never met a woman like her. She was a healer. She could heal him, he just knew it. Sensed it to the black depths of his fractured soul. Now he had to release her. He didn't dare kiss her. Because if he ever touched that mouth of hers, he would be lost. And he'd want her like he'd never wanted anything so badly in his life.

Talon had to let Cat go. Finally, he eased his arms from around her and lifted his head from her shoulder. As he looked up into her eyes, his heart crashed. He wanted to cry. Her eyes burned with love and care for him. Just for him. And her mouth, damn, her lips were parted and tears streamed down her cheeks, nestling into the corners of her mouth. She was crying for his sorry-assed soul.

Shaken, Talon stared at her in the thickening silence. No one had cried for him before, except his mother when he was a young child. And Cat was crying for him, for the coming loss of his mother, who meant the world to him. He'd already lost his father. Then he'd lost Hayden. Now…oh, God, now his mother was leaving him, too.

The loneliness gutted him wide-open. The emotional rawness was tempered only by Cat's arms still loosely placed around his shoulders as she stared without apology for the tears in her eyes. He made a sound in his throat, lifted his hands and used his thumbs to remove her tears.

"Don't cry for me," he growled. He wasn't worthy of her tears. His life was a train wreck. He didn't deserve this kind of care.…

Closing her eyes, Cat felt his callused thumbs brush the tears from her cheeks. Her throat tightened, the lump growing. She wanted to burst out into sobs for him, for what she felt around him that he'd never released. She lifted her lashes as his hands fell away from her face. How she missed his touch! Sniffing, Cat eased her arms from around his shoulders. With trembling fingers, she wiped the tears from her lashes.

"It's okay to cry, Talon," she whispered, her voice unsteady. "It's good for the soul." Seeing the look in his stormy eyes, Cat knew he wasn't accepting her whispered words at all. "Think of crying as a way to discharge the infection, the toxins, the awful emotions you're carrying around inside of you, cleaning you out.

That's a good thing." Cat reached out, trailing her fingers tenderly across his cheek.

Talon placed a steel hold on himself. Never mind he had an erection pressing painfully against his jeans. Never mind what he saw in Cat's half-closed, drowsy blue eyes as she'd grazed his cheek. One part of him said she'd touched his cheek out of compassion. *Care.* The other part, the dark, male part of him, the sexual hunter who wanted her, read her touch as a way to let him know she wanted him.

Talon felt like a mess. He was still sicker than a dog, still had a fever, wasn't breathing all that well and he'd just talked to his dying mother. No way in hell could he sort out Cat's response to him. And he cared enough about her not to try. Cat sat there looking so innocent, the compassion clear in her gaze. Getting a grip on himself, Talon forced himself to put his hands on his thighs, not on her.

"Your mom is a fighter, Talon," Cat said, her voice raspy. "I came to Jackson Hole seven years ago and met her right after she'd gotten cancer the first time. I'd met her at Mo's Ice Cream Parlor where she worked as a waitress. We became really good friends and when I saw her looking bad one day, I asked her what was wrong." Cat stared down at her clasped hands in her lap. "I told her I'd be there for her and I have been ever since. Your mom loves books, and when the chemo really got her down and she was too weak to work, I'd go over on my lunch hour when I had the shift at the fire department, and read to her. She loves her books so much." Cat managed a small smile, holding his flat, dark look. "Maybe…if things work out, you might support her by going over to read to her every once in a while. I know she'd love that. She loves you so much."

Talon hung his head, grappling with the knowledge. "Yeah," he rasped, "I know she does. She used to read to me as a kid. I always looked forward to her coming into my bedroom every night and she'd read a chapter from a book." The memory was sweet. Filled with love. Talon had always looked forward to that special time with his mother.

"Sandy told me," Cat admitted softly. "Over the years, she brought out all her photo albums." She gave him a tender look. "I guess you might say I got to know you from the time you born. Sandy is so proud of you, Talon. I knew you were in the Navy, went into the SEALs and she really didn't have much in the photo album from recent times except for the few pictures you sent back to her when you were in Afghanistan."

Wincing internally, Talon remembered those photos he'd sent her. They were all of Hayden and him or Zeke. His mother loved animals and he could email her about Zeke. He could never tell her about his missions or anything that had happened on them, but she loved his stories about Zeke. His heart clenched with renewed grief. Cat had seen photos of him and Hayden together, their arms across one another's shoulders, their M-4 rifles propped on their hips, grinning like fools into the camera after a twelve-hour patrol. He dragged in a shallow breath, the pneumonia still not allowing him to take a deep one.

"I'm glad you've been here for my mom," he admitted, giving her a quick look of sincere thanks. His heart contracted. There were still tears in her eyes. Cat was too easily touched. He felt helpless to fix this.

"Sandy's a wonderful person," Cat said quietly. "And I can see so much of her in you. She has been such a strong member of our community. She did a lot of volunteer work before she got sick. Now all those people she's helped over the years have turned around to help her. You need to know your mom is greatly loved, Talon. Gwen Garner, who owns the quilting store, has her club members see Sandy weekly. In fact, it's Gwen who gave all of us a monthly visiting schedule. Your mom gets lots of company every day. Gus fixes her a dinner once a week and I drive it over to her. A lot of the quilters make her breakfast or lunch." The darkness in Talon's eyes lightened, some of the tension around his hard, thinned mouth dissolved. "About fifty people volunteer to help Sandy. I don't want you to think your mom has been abandoned. We've embraced her and she's as happy as she can be. And now you're home." Cat's voice grew stronger with feeling. "I know how much she's been looking forward to this. You'll give her a level of hope and care none of us ever could. This is the time when she needs you at her side."

Nodding, he stared down at Zeke, who had laid his head on his thigh. "She sounds so damned weak." And it scared the hell out of him to realize how close she was to dying. When he'd call her from the Naval Hospital, about once a week, she was always cheerful, upbeat and hopeful. *Not now.*

Cat placed her hand lightly on his shoulder. "She is weak. It's the chemo. And I know you're feeling pretty weak yourself right now. It's going to take about two weeks for you to throw off this pneumonia and begin feeling halfway human. Did Sandy understand you couldn't see her right away?"

"Yeah, I lied a little." Talon absorbed Cat's touch, desperate for more contact with her. He'd wanted to kiss her. Make love to her. How she sensed his needs was beyond him, but he was grateful anyway. "I made light of my pneumonia because I didn't want her to worry. She knows I can't be sick and visit her or it could impact her lowered immune system in a major way."

"I think calling her daily will be a huge emotional boost for her," Cat murmured, smiling a little. She couldn't keep her hands off Talon. Just simply moving her fingers across his shoulder sent heated signals to her lower body. Wanting. *Just him. Just Talon.* Cat removed her hand. There was so much uncharted emotional territory with this man and she couldn't trust herself.

"I can at least do that," Talon agreed, his voice gravelly. His flesh was tingling, heat radiating from where her fingertips had rested. Did Cat know her power over him? That she gently held his heart between her workworn hands? That any contact with her made him grow hard? The innocence in her expression stunned him. She was old enough to understand a woman's ability to inflame a man. Talon wanted to know everything about Cat. His finely honed sixth sense told him her innocence was real, that she wasn't worldly.

Something…God, he knew something terrible or traumatic had happened to Cat to make her this way. And his sexual response to her was like that of a hungry wolf. She'd saved his life, brought him back from the brink of death. She sure as hell deserved a helluva lot more than him stalking her like a selfish bastard. Talon moved his hands slowly up and down his thighs, scowling. Unhappy with himself.

"I need to check your lungs and get your temperature," Cat told him, forcing herself to move. A chance to touch him again, but this time, it really was about checking Talon's temperature and making sure he stayed on the road to recovery. "Can you lie down?"

"Yeah," Talon grunted, easing Zeke from between his legs and then lying down on the bed. He watched Cat through half-closed eyes. When she looped the stethoscope around her neck, he couldn't help saying, "Whoever the guy is in your life, he's one lucky bastard."

Cat's eyebrows moved up and she froze for a moment. She stared at Talon on the bed. He was a big man and his hands were tucked behind his head, his expression curious. She managed a short laugh. "There's no one in my life." She reached down into her bag and retrieved the handheld Braun ThermoScan thermometer.

"Why?" Talon cursed himself for his bluntness. Pain flashed across Cat's face as she sat down on the bed.

"I have bad luck with men in general," she admitted. Opening his shirt and folding it open, she listened to his lungs.

Talon stared up at her. Cat had problems with men? He watched her closely as she listened intently through her stethoscope. When she was finished, he asked, "So, you're not seeing anyone presently?"

She picked up the ThermoScan and eased it into his ear. "That's right." Shame flowed through Cat. Her latest bad choice involved Beau Magee, a truck driver with Ace Trucking. As she removed the thermometer, she murmured, "Good, your temp is ninety-nine degrees." She smiled down into his troubled-looking eyes. "That antibiotic is really taking hold."

"And my lungs? How do they sound?" He absorbed her every move, her every expression. That smile of hers was like sunlight piercing the heavy darkness of his mangled heart and broken soul.

"Improving. Still crackling sounds, but less so." She patted his hand. "You're really going to have to rest for two weeks, Talon. If you overdo it, you'll relapse."

"I'm not the type to sit around."

"Yeah," Cat said, and chuckled, getting up and walking to her medical bag. "I got that. You're a man of action."

"Being a SEAL, you're on the move all the time. I get antsy if I have to stay anywhere for more than fifteen minutes."

As she leaned down to put her equipment away, he truly appreciated her rear, those generous hips. It was too bad she didn't wear clothes that fit her a little better. Everything Cat wore hung on her, as if she were hiding her body within the folds of the fabric. She should be proud of it, showing it off.

Straightening, Cat turned and grinned at him. "Well, you'd best give yourself a talking-to about that, because as bad a case of pneumonia as you have, enforced rest is mandatory."

"So, do you play any card games?" he teased. Talon liked the way her mouth curved upward.

"No, but I like Scrabble. I'm always trying to improve my vocabulary." Because in grade school she nearly flunked out of reading. But then with her father stalking her, abusing her, Cat's mind wasn't really focused on learning the alphabet, phonetics or reading. She was focused on surviving. "Actually, your mom got me into it. I would read to her and stumble over words I couldn't pronounce, so we played Scrabble."

Warmth filled Talon's heart. His mother was a good

and kind person. "Okay, Scrabble. You can teach me how to play it. Otherwise, I'll go crazy if I have to stay in a room for two weeks. Maybe I could move around outside a little." Talon touched Zeke's head. "And my dog absolutely needs to get outside, play and run around."

"Like his master?" Cat teased. "When I'm here at the ranch, I'll make sure to drop by for a game of Scrabble. Right now, Griff is starting spring cleanup and getting all the leather, saddles and mechanical equipment up and running again. Once this snow clears, he's going to have me out mending a lot of fence that has been destroyed by the winter."

"And as soon as I can, I'll be helping Griff and you."

She smiled. "Gus told me they hired you as a full-time wrangler. That's wonderful. I'm really happy for you, Talon."

Talon was happy about a lot of things. Mostly, happy that he'd see Cat at least a few times a week. *Precious time.* Food for his heart, his body and soul, but he said nothing. "Listen, I'm not going to make it out to the dinner table tonight."

Cat nodded and walked toward the door. "No worries, Gus will understand. Do you feel like eating some solid food, though? Gus made rump roast, boiled new red potatoes, steamed broccoli with cheese sauce and a rhubarb pie for dessert. Interested?"

He didn't want her to leave just yet. "Maybe a little of everything." Powerful emotions raced through him as she brightened. Her cheeks flushed. Cat cared about him. He could see it. But she might just see him as another patient—and not as a man. There was always a gold glint in the depths of her blue eyes when she was close to him, touching him. As if she enjoyed the contact as much as he did.

"Okay," Cat called over her shoulder, opening the door. "I'll bring in a tray at six."

CHAPTER SIX

"TELL ME ABOUT yourself." Talon sat on the edge of his bed, Zeke nearby. He picked up his knife and fork to cut into the roast. The food smelled heavenly and his stomach growled.

Cat sat in the chair, a tray across her lap. She didn't want Talon eating alone at dinnertime. It had been Gus who suggested she keep him company. Of course, she couldn't argue.

"Not much to tell," she murmured. Zeke thumped his tail as Talon gave him a piece of cooled meat. The smile that came to Talon's face made her melt. He looked so different from the hard, focused man she had seen before. When he lifted his chin, those gray eyes focused on her, Cat felt that pull, that euphoria. It was as if she were wrapped in light, held, loved. *Loved?* Cat slowly set her flatware on her tray, confused by her senses.

"Where were you born?" Talon saw her cheeks flush and she avoided direct eye contact. Why?

Zeke whined.

Talon pulled his gaze off Cat and patted the dog's head.

"I was born near Cheyenne, Wyoming," she said simply.

Talon sampled the beef, closing his eyes and savoring the hot, delicious food. It had been two months of walking from San Diego to Wyoming, on foot with Zeke, to reach home. He hadn't eaten well but had made sure Zeke was properly fed. The meal on his lap was a banquet. A feast of unimaginable proportions. And it all smelled so good.

"What did your parents do?" he asked casually, hoping to defuse the wariness in her eyes.

Cat frowned and pushed her food around on the plate. From the quiet way Talon asked the question, she could tell he cared. But it was like stirring up a toxic waste dump from her past, the last place she wanted to go. She'd spent the past ten years of her life distancing herself from it, from him, her father. She never wanted to go back to that time. Now Talon was forcing her to and she was resistant.

"My father worked as a wrangler on a ranch," she mumbled.

"Your mom?"

"She died when I was ten." She glanced up and gave him a sympathetic look. "Breast cancer."

Talon scowled. "I'm sorry." He could see the tension on her face. "Listen, if I'm being too nosy just tell me to back off." Because he had no desire to bring pain to Cat. God knew he carried enough in him.

Cat shrugged. "My childhood wasn't pretty and I don't like talking about it."

Okay...well, that answered some of his questions. "How did you get interested in being a firefighter and paramedic?" he asked instead. Maybe that was safer ground for Cat. Some of the fear left her eyes. She started eating again.

"I always wanted to be one since I could remember. I went to college in Cheyenne and took Fire Science."

She didn't want to tell him how much she struggled with reading. Or the nights spent with a teacher who helped her catch up. "When I graduated, I came here, to Jackson Hole, and got a job."

Talon nodded, enjoying her as she relaxed. "Are there any other women on the fire department?"

"I'm the only one."

"You picked a tough career."

"No man is going to tell me what I can or can't do in my life."

Talon heard the steel grit behind her words. She was frowning, paying attention to eating, not looking up at him. Yeah, he'd sensed a toughness in her, like Kevlar plate armor. It wasn't that obvious, because he'd been privy to her paramedic side, the healer—not the firefighter. "I imagine some of the men didn't want you in their ranks, thought you couldn't perform the physical work."

"That's for sure," Cat said. "Lieutenant Matt Sinclaire, though, gave me a chance. Half the department didn't want me. The other half was okay with it. I'd taken all the physical tests and passed them with flying colors." Cat smiled a little and held Talon's interested gaze. "I'm not exactly petite, as you can see. I'm five foot ten inches tall and strong. I can pull a two-and-a-half inch hose filled with water just as well as any man. I'm not even the smallest firefighter, either. Steve, who is twenty-seven and near my age, is a few inches shorter and definitely weighs less."

"I'll bet you two are best friends?"

She caught the amusement in Talon's eyes. "Yes. From the get-go we were tight. Maybe misery loves company, although the guys at the fire department never made it tough on Steve like they did to me."

"But you had paramedic skills. That must have helped convince them."

"It did. But it was Matt who stood by me. He fought for me and, fortunately, I was good at my job."

"And how many years ago was that?"

"Seven," Cat said, feeling the tension dissolve. She didn't mind talking about her life from eighteen years old onward.

"Now are you fully accepted?"

"I am."

"And why are you working out here at the Bar H on your days off?"

"Because I want to buy a house."

He grinned. "What's your dream house look like?"

She laughed a little, finishing off the vegetables. "You'll laugh."

"Try me."

"Why do you want to know?" she challenged.

"Because I care." He held her mutinous look. Cat really didn't want anyone within those walls she had erected. He added gently, "Because you saved our lives this morning. I'd like to know more about you as a person." That was the truth, but Talon didn't add that he was attracted to her. If he admitted that, Cat might disappear.

Cat looked down. "I'm a very private person, Talon."

He said nothing and resumed eating. Cat wasn't someone to be pushed into a corner. She'd shut down, just as she had right now. There was definitely some baggage in her life.

"In some ways, you're a shadow warrior like me," he admitted.

"Is that what SEALs are? Shadow warriors?"

"Black ops always works in the shadows," he told her. Talon handed Zeke another morsel of beef. The dog's eyes were alight with happiness.

"Why did you join the SEALs?"

Talon studied Cat for a moment, trying to decide if she really wanted to know or if she was turning the tables on him and deflecting more questions. He decided she was genuine in her curiosity. "I wanted to make a difference."

"You could have done that any number of ways. You didn't have to be a SEAL to protect the country or do your patriotic duty."

"I liked what they did," Talon said. "I grew up hunting and tracking and felt my skills could be best used in that way." His stomach tensed. They were going into forbidden territory. He didn't want to talk too much about his work, his past.

"Sandy always loved getting your emails. She said there was a lot you couldn't tell her."

Nodding, Talon said, "My military life is top secret. I can never talk about it."

"She said you're a hero."

Talon cringed inwardly. He didn't feel like a hero. More like a failure. He'd failed to rescue Hayden. His mouth flexed. "I'm not."

Cat regarded him for a moment, sensing his pain. Maybe it was in the sudden tightening of his face or the way his fork and knife hesitated over the food. "She said you'd earned two Silver Stars, a Bronze Star and two Purple Hearts. In my world, that makes you a hero even if we never know what you did to earn them."

"They're just medals," he growled. "They mean nothing."

Cat remained silent and cleaned up the rest of the food on her plate. She risked a look at him. His mouth was hard. Zeke was watching his master intently, as if sensing his withdrawal.

Standing, Cat said, "Do you want some dessert? Coffee? I'm going out to get mine."

Talon shook his head and gave her his unfinished tray. "No…thanks. Tell Miss Gus it tasted good. I'm just not up to eating that much right now."

There was misery in his expression. She ached for him. "After we're done with dinner, are you up to walking down the hall to your room? I've got it ready for you."

He nodded. "Yeah. I just need to rest a little bit." Because he felt the weight of the world on his shoulders, Hayden's death. His inability to save him.

"Sure," Cat murmured, taking the tray and putting it on top of hers. "I'll be back later."

Talon stretched out on the bed. Outside, it was dark. "Could you turn the light off when you leave?" he asked.

"Will do."

"HOW IS TALON?" Gus asked as Cat sat down with her rhubarb pie with vanilla ice cream.

"He's tired. His fever is lower, but he's really underweight, and pneumonia can fell the strongest of men."

"I had pneumonia once as a kid," Griff said. "Miserable stuff. Took me almost a month to recover fully from it."

"It's nothing to mess with," Gus agreed, grim. She looked over at Cat. "How's Talon really doing?"

"I think he's on an emotional roller coaster. He talked to Sandy and he's upset," Cat said.

"Anyone would be," Val offered, giving Cat a gentle look. "How are *you* doing, Cat? You're on the front lines with Talon. He's got PTSD."

"He sure does," she admitted, enjoying the tart, sweet rhubarb pie. "I accidentally walked in and woke him up earlier. He sat up in the bed, his fists cocked, and the look in his eyes scared the hell out of me."

Gus shook her head.

Val reached over and touched Gus's arm. "Talon just left the hospital. He'd been wounded. I'm sure he's reliving all the hell he went through." She looked pointedly at Cat. "And you have to be careful with him. Those black ops guys, when they're wounded, they pose a threat to the nurses and doctors. They're taught how to kill with their hands and if you get too close to them accidentally, they can take you out. If you have to wake him, just stay by the door and call his name. That way, you're not within arm's reach."

"That's what he told me afterward," Cat admitted. "Val, you've never talked much about your Air Force service or being an intelligence officer. How do you know so much about what Talon did?"

"Because from time to time, as an intelligence officer, I went out with black ops groups into the field. It was dangerous, clandestine work."

Griff studied his wife. "And I'm glad you're no longer doing it."

"Makes two of us," Val assured him. "I'm glad I came home."

"Makes three of us," Gus said. "The Bar H is coming back to life under your and Griff's guidance." She grinned and rubbed her hands together. "And now, with Talon agreeing to work for us full-time, that's going to help us with the plans we've got on the back burner for the ranch."

Cat smiled, always enjoying Gus and her fiery personality. "Don't expect him to start doing much of anything for about two weeks."

"Don't worry," Griff assured her, picking up his coffee mug. "May is always testy and we get more snow than spring sunshine. I'll go easy on him."

"Good," Cat murmured, "because he's really underweight, Griff. He's lost forty or fifty pounds from what I can tell."

"Why so much?" Gus demanded, scowling.

"Maybe six months in the hospital did it," she suggested. "He doesn't talk much about himself and he didn't like my questions when I asked him."

Val nodded. "Just give Talon time. Don't press him too much, okay? Chances are him getting wounded has something to do with it. He's probably going through a lot of emotional trauma he can't share with anyone."

"That must be tough," Gus muttered, "not being able to talk about it to anyone."

Val put her empty pie plate aside and slid her fingers around the coffee mug. "It's being caught between a rock and a hard place, Gus."

Griff sat back, watching his wife with concern. "And that's why after we got married, on some nights, you'd wake up screaming."

Val sighed. "Yes. I still get them, but not as much as

before." She reached over and touched his cheek. "Because I have you, I feel safe now."

Cat tilted her head. "So, you have PTSD, too." It shouldn't have surprised her, but it did, because Val seemed so calm and collected.

"Yes. I'm sure not one-tenth as bad as Talon has it. He was out on the front lines against the enemy all the time. My work was off and on for a couple of years over in Iraq. Still, when your life is on the line, it affects you." Her voice lowered and she held Cat's gaze. "Talon has probably seen terrible things, Cat. He's jumpy and he's been finely trained until his reactions are all based on muscle memory. He doesn't think about his defensive moves—they are a part of him. That's why you can't be near him when he suddenly jolts awake for whatever reason."

Griff nodded. "I remember the first time you sat up screaming in bed shortly after we got married. You scared the living hell out of me. I thought you were hurt."

Val smiled sadly. "Yes, I remember that night. That dream."

"What did you do to help her, Griff?" Cat wondered.

"When I realized she wasn't hurt, I just held her."

"Love always heals," Gus uttered, eyeing the couple with tenderness. She reached out, patting Val's arm. "I wish you'd told me this before."

"It's hard for military vets to open up, Gus," Val said. "Man or woman, it doesn't matter. We carry so much toxic crap inside us, we're afraid to release it." She glanced over at her husband. "I guess that's why we have nightmares and maybe we're working it out in the landscape of our mind. So much of it is top secret and we can't speak about it to our spouse or friends. We're like time bombs."

Cat sat back, digesting Val's admissions. She'd known the woman for a year, since she'd left the Air Force to come home to help Gus after she broke her hip. "Can you give me any advice on how to deal with Talon?"

"Just be there for him." Val smiled a little and took a sip of her coffee. "I think he likes you, Cat. And if that's so, then he's going to trust you just a little bit more than anyone else. Getting a vet's trust is ground zero. It anchors them in the here and now." She looked at Griff, her voice warm. "Just being around Griff helped me so much, whether he knew it or not."

"I didn't know," Griff said.

"Sometimes a vet can't put how he or she feels into words," Val admitted. "You helped me because you loved me, Griff. You didn't realize when you touched me, held me or were just around helping me, that you were making a huge difference emotionally in me."

"Healing takes many forms," Gus said. She narrowed her eyes on Cat. "That young man likes you a lot. I saw it in his eyes when I went in to visit him earlier today. The way he looked at you."

Stunned, Cat said, "He does?"

Val grinned across the table at Cat. "You weren't aware?"

Embarrassed, Cat muttered, "No...not really. I mean, I'm a paramedic, my focus is elsewhere."

"Don't feel bad, Cat," Griff said.

Cat stared at Val. "How can I help Talon, then?"

"Just be your wonderful self," Val murmured, smiling. "You're a healer, Cat. You've always been one.

The value of your touch can never be underestimated. Especially with someone like Talon. I know that when Griff would touch my shoulder, my hand or hold me, it made a huge difference for me."

"But," Cat stumbled, "I don't love him!"

Gus snorted. "Blind as a bat."

Eyebrows raising, Cat stared at the elder. "What does that mean?" She was beginning to feel panic. Did they see something she didn't between her and Talon? Was she *that* blind?

Gus patted her hand. "Dearie, you just continue to be yourself. Talon's getting better because you're around him. Aren't healing and love entwined?" Gus gave her a hard, searching look.

"Well," Cat sputtered, "I guess in a way they are. I mean, I love being a paramedic." Surely, that was what Gus was talking about, her compassion and care for others.

Gus glanced over at Val. "She doesn't know."

Val grinned. "Give her time, Gus. We're not as all seeing and knowing as you are."

The table broke into warm laughter. Cat wasn't laughing, however, feeling an outsider to a secret they all knew but she didn't. Confused, she shrugged and finished off her warm pie. What wasn't she seeing that they saw? She felt Gus pat her arm.

"Child, you are a wonderful person, so don't let us razzing you upset you, okay?"

"I guess I am blind, Gus."

"It's all right. You're young and that's the reason why."

Young and stupid. Cat railed against her lack of experience with men. She'd give anything for what Griff and Val had. They were so clearly in love with each other. Cat couldn't seem to pick men who loved her, much less respected her. Her father had never respected her, either. Not as a human being. Not as a child. Not as a little girl. Cat forced a smile she didn't feel because she didn't want to hurt Gus's feelings. The elder had done so much for her.

"Young and dumb," Cat teased her.

"No, you're not dumb," Gus said. "You're innocent. There's a huge difference."

Innocent? Her? Hardly. But Cat said nothing. She automatically shoved away memories of her childhood. Only Val knew what she'd endured. Cat was just too guilt ridden to tell anyone else. "All I want to do is be of help to Talon, Gus. He looks like he needs a friend."

"You're doing fine dealing with Talon. And I feel he's beginning to trust you, Cat. That's good for him. Maybe for you, too." Her eyes grew kind as she held Cat's gaze.

Val gave her grandmother a sweet smile. "Gus, you just go watch your favorite TV programs." She looked at her watch. "Cat and I will get your room back in order. We know how you like it."

Cat grinned. "You go enjoy the rest of your night, Gus. We'll take care of the details."

"Oh," Gus muttered. "I guess I can."

Moments later, Cat and Val gazed around her grandmother's bedroom.

"There," Val said, pleased. She and Cat had just finished putting clean sheets on her bed and moving the furniture around. She glanced at Cat.

Lowering her voice, "Do you have any experience as a paramedic with PTSD?"

"No. I've seen trauma but not the lasting effects."

"You already know it's nothing to mess with," Val said grimly. "Now, Talon's down the hall. And there's a door between your bedrooms." Her mouth thinned. "I'll bet you anything Talon has horrible nightmares. You might get woken up on any night from his screaming. But you can't go to him, Cat. He's imprisoned in the event. And if you run into his room to try and help him, he will likely see you as the enemy and try to kill you."

"He told me." Cat gulped. She felt sudden pain for Talon. His suffering went beyond what she normally saw. And, yes, her first instinct would be to run into his room and try to help him. She stared at Val for a long time. "What happens to a guy who's married and comes back home? Does his wife get beat up? Killed by him?"

"It can happen," Val said. "That's why I'm warning you off right now, Cat. Let Talon alone. He'll handle it."

"But—"

Val held up her hand. "No buts. He'll be okay. He's got Zeke. That dog, I'm sure, has seen him through all of his nightmares. The dog may even help and give him comfort."

"We need to tell Gus about this."

"Already did. I told her if she wakes up hearing Talon screaming, to stay in her room. She got it."

"And Griff knows?"

"Griff knows."

"Is there anything we can do to help Talon?"

Val shook her head. "Not right now. I'm hoping that, as he mends and starts working as a wrangler, I can persuade him to go see Jordana. She said a lot of the nightmares stem from high cortisol in his bloodstream. And she's got a method to reduce the cortisol permanently. It doesn't cure PTSD, but it does level out the playing field and it will help Talon sleep at night. Insomnia is one of the signs of PTSD."

"I really need to get up on those symptoms," Cat muttered.

"Talk to Jordana. She's got all kinds of literature in her office on it. Take advantage of her coming over this Sunday." Val slid her arm around Cat's waist and gave her a quick hug. "Just understand, Talon isn't doing this on purpose. He can't help it. It's his psyche's way of trying to off-load the horror he experienced. If you play Scrabble with him, that's a safe outlet for Talon. He'll trust you more and more over time."

Trust. Well, that was a word Cat knew well. "Maybe I have PTSD, too. I don't trust anyone. I have problems sleeping at night."

"You don't trust men because your father hurt you and he was a man. You trust women. They never hurt you. Talon's trust issue is different. He's steeped in top-secret stuff he can never reveal to anyone. And he's trying to heal without ever talking about it. Sometimes, other things can come along in his life to bleed off this toxicity he carries. Over time, he'll honestly start healing from it."

"Scrabble will do that?" Cat demanded, unsure.

Val gave her an evil grin. "Scrabble is the focus. It's *you,* your being with him, that's the key."

"I'm not a touchstone for anyone, Val. That's been proven too many times. I just feel so messed up inside when it comes to men."

Val pat her shoulder. "Trust me, you're *good* for Talon. And he might be good for you."

Cat straightened. "You're giving me your blessing?"

"Absolutely. He's wounded, Cat, but he's a good man.

I can spot one a mile away. And I kind of think you like Talon, too."

Cat nodded, more to herself. "I liked him the instant I saw him. And nothing's changed my feelings about him from that moment to this one."

Val gave her a loving look. "You have a heart of gold and you do so much for so many. It's time you met someone of your own caliber. And you have."

CHAPTER SEVEN

TALON WATCHED FROM his bedroom window as Cat and Val slogged along a newly shoveled path through the snow from the house to the barn. He rubbed his face tiredly. Dammit, he wanted to be well. Five days into this pneumonia thing and his nerves were frayed.

Zeke whined, standing at his side, his body pressed against Talon's leg. Absently petting his war dog, Talon yearned to get outside and breathe in fresh air. Every day, he'd improved. And every day, he waited, anticipating Cat's touch, her smile, her warmth, which lifted him up, like light.

A knock on his door made him turn.

"Come in," he called.

Gus poked her head around the door. "Don't you think it's about time you joined the land of the living, Talon?"

He managed a sour grin. "Yes, ma'am," he said, turning.

"Come on, I got everyone breakfast. Your turn."

Talon felt warmth in his chest toward Gus. He walked to the door and opened it for the slight, spare woman with challenge in her squinted eyes. "You look like you're on a mission this morning, Miss Gus."

Gus cackled, turned and limped down the hall.

"Come on, we need to put some meat on those bones of yours."

In the warm, cheery kitchen, Gus pointed to the large pine table. "Take a seat, son. What do you feel like eating?"

"Whatever you're fixing," he murmured, pouring himself a cup of coffee and sitting down. Gus was in a bright red sweater and a pair of heavy black wool slacks, her blue apron wrapped around her tiny waist.

"I'm not picky," he added, sitting down and noticing the flatware in front of him.

"Okay, how about three scrambled eggs, some diced ham and sprinkled with cheese?"

"Sounds good," Talon murmured, grateful. "Snow's melted enough that everyone's out working?" he asked.

"Yep. That darned blizzard dumped three feet of snow across the area. Taken five days to get it melted enough so we can move cars and trucks on the highway. Hate these late-spring storms," she muttered, whipping up the eggs with the ham in a bowl near the stove. She lifted her chin, narrowing her eyes on him. "How are you doing?"

"Better," Talon admitted. For the past four nights he'd slept solidly. No one was relieved more than him because, normally, he woke up screaming from the nightmares. So far so good. Maybe he'd get well enough and not wake up the household.

"Cat checked you out earlier," Gus said, pouring the mixture into the big, black skillet. "Said you have no fever this morning. That's a good sign."

"Tell me about it," Talon said, sipping the coffee.

Gus popped in some bread to make toast. "Cat's goin' into town today. I told her I wanted you to go see

Dr. Jordana McPherson. You need to get checked out
by a doctor and she's Griff's sister-in-law. A real nice
lady. You met her at the Sunday dinner."

Talon remembered Sunday dinner. He hadn't felt like
coming out to join everyone, so Jordana had popped in
to see him. She and Cat had examined his lungs once
again and they'd talked medicalese about his condition.
He liked Jordana and she really didn't seem like a doctor, rather a warm, caring person. He roused himself.
"Is there anything I can do for you or the ranch while
I'm in town?" Talon asked. He was looking forward to
getting out, moving around.

"Nope. Cat's gonna drop you off at Jordana's office.
She's going over to the Horse Emporium. Andy, the
owner, has a load of horse feed for us. About a thousand pounds' worth of feed."

"Maybe I could help her?"

Gus eyed him darkly as she stirred the contents in
the skillet. "Young man, you're still sick."

Talon smiled, saying nothing, and sipped his coffee.
You didn't want to pick a fight with Gus.

"When Cat's done pickin' up the feed, she'll swing
by and get you."

"It will be nice to get out, get some fresh air," Talon
admitted.

Gus picked up the skillet and put the eggs into a
bowl. The toast popped. "I see that look in your eyes,
Talon. You're restless and you want to get to work, but
I'm not going to let you."

Talon thanked Gus as she brought the bowl over and
set it in front of his plate with a large spoon. She put the
toast on his plate for him to butter.

"And you know this about me how?" he asked as

she sat down at his elbow after pouring herself a cup of coffee.

"Sandy told me. And I saw that in you as you grew up," Gus said. "Cat's just afraid you'll relapse."

"I like hard, physical work, Miss Gus."

"That's a given when you work on a ranch as a wrangler. But I do want you to take it easy, listen to what Jordana says." She tapped his arm smartly with her index finger. "Oh, I know you're going stir-crazy in here. Once Cat drops you off here, she's driving back into town. She's got a forty-eight-hour shift at the fire department starting at three this afternoon."

Talon frowned. He'd gotten used to Cat being part and parcel of his life. Now she'd be gone for two days. "When will she be back here?"

"Two days. You'll hang in there." Gus hooked a thumb over her small shoulder. "I had Griff take that huge room down the hall and make two smaller bedrooms out of it. We were still building the bunkhouse at the time. And really, Cat is like family, so we don't mind if she stays with us."

"She's a good person," Talon said, enjoying the tangy breakfast.

Gus gave him a narrowed look. "You like her."

Talon swallowed and cut a glance in her direction. "There's nothing to dislike about her, Miss Gus."

"Humph."

Talon wasn't about to go there. It wouldn't be wise to admit his feelings for Cat. He was about to work for Gus and he wasn't sure she'd be happy with her wranglers getting together. He was concerned more for Cat's sake than his own, although Talon figured that she was like family to the people here.

"Once Jordana gives you an okay that you're well, I do want you to see your mother. And I'm loaning you our white Ford pickup truck. You need wheels, Talon."

His gratitude ran deep. "Has anyone ever accused you of being a fairy godmother?"

Gus had the good grace to flush.

"Only to certain people," she admonished, patting his forearm. "We all get knocked down to our knees from time to time. I've been there, too. It's always nice to get a helping hand."

"Really, you're a guardian angel, Miss Gus." And she was. During his formative years, Miss Gus had always been kind to him. Talon owed her. Big-time.

"That's not generally what people see or think when they hear my name."

Chuckling, Talon finished off his food. This morning, he was eating normally. Cat had told him earlier that he'd turned the corner on the fight with the pneumonia. "I always will."

"That's because I baked you cookies, young man."

Talon smiled. "And I never forgot your goodness, Miss Gus."

She frowned. "Do you want to get a haircut today?" She motioned toward his short ponytail.

"If I can, yes. I don't like my hair long."

"Of course you don't," Gus said. She pulled out some money from her apron pocket and set it next to his plate. "Here's two weeks' worth of your money you'll earn, Talon. You need some decent work clothes, gear, a haircut and some good work boots. Griff takes care of the accounting books and I asked him to take a small portion out of your coming paychecks for this loan to you today. You all right with that?"

Was he? *Absolutely.* Talon took the money and shoved it into the pocket of his jeans. "I'm more than fine with that, Miss Gus. Thank you."

"Well," she grumped, finishing off her coffee, "we can't have you lookin' like a bum."

He couldn't help but laugh before he heard the sound of the front door opening and closing. Someone was stomping their snow-covered boots on a special rug in the porch area. Within moments, Cat appeared at the entrance. She wore her heavy nylon coat, her hands in a pair of thick sheepskin gloves, the red knit muffler wrapped around her neck and a cap of the same color over her black hair. She had the longest legs he'd ever seen and those jeans did nothing but showcase them. Her face was flushed, her blue eyes dancing with happiness.

"Hey, are you ready to go?" she called, taking off her work gloves.

"I am," Talon replied, rising. He carried his plate and flatware over to the sink where Gus was cleaning up.

"Talon, Griff is loaning you his other sheepskin coat," Gus said, pointing to the coat hanging on one of the wooden pegs in the hallway. "If Cat has time, you two might do a little clothes shopping after Jordana gives you a good bill of health."

"No problem," Cat said, tucking the gloves in her pockets. "They've got sales on winter gear over at the Horse Emporium. Andy has good wrangler gear. We can drive over there after you're done being checked out by Jordana."

Talon approached her, eager for closeness. "I'll need to put Zeke in my room. He'll be fine there while I'm gone."

Nodding, Cat tried not to stare blatantly at Talon. Today, more than any other, he looked healthy. His skin was no longer pasty, his eyes dark with fever. It was amazing how quickly he'd rebounded. But then, he was young and strong, not to mention terribly handsome and easy on her eyes.

"Take him to the barber," Gus told her. "Then get him some clothes to wear."

"Will do," Cat told Gus.

Talon passed Cat, caught her eyes and saw her smile up at him. Damn, but her mouth was beautiful. He could almost taste it beneath his. The better he felt, the more he wanted her. And he was going to miss her presence in the house the next two days.

As Cat drove the gray Ford pickup, she pointed out where she'd picked up Talon and Zeke. He scanned the area and shook his head. "It was a close call," he admitted.

"Too close." She gave him a quick glance, noticing his pensive expression. Talon had shaved before they left the ranch house. She would swear that he'd gained some weight, too.

"Gus said you have to work today?"

"Yeah, my shift starts later this afternoon."

Talon looked at all the slushy snow piled up on either side of the wet asphalt highway. The sky was a piercing blue, the sun bright. He'd taken his dark glasses and worn them along with his black baseball cap. Cat's black hair peeked out from beneath her red knit cap. She had no idea how much she affected him. The sunshine, the first in five days, seemed to invigorate her and she was chattier than usual, laughing more and her eyes shining with happiness. Talon wanted her to see *him* like that.

Wanted her eyes to shine with desire toward him. Was it possible? Talon was going to find out sooner or later.

"So," he said, "are you going to miss our daily Scrabble games?" He tried to sound light.

"I will," she admitted, giving him a smile. "Is Gus going to let you do a little work around the place if Jordana says you can handle some light duties?"

"Yes. And I'm going to do light duty whether she says I'm up to it or not. I'm just not telling her."

Cat nodded. "I understand. It's tough being cooped up and sick. You're an outdoor guy."

"You're pretty perceptive, you know that?"

Cat kept her focus on her driving. The mountain curves had straightened out and they were in the valley, the road straight and four lanes, leading into Jackson Hole. "Thanks."

"You have good insights into people, Cat." Hell, he was sleeping like a baby, no nightmares, and Talon found that shocking. He never slept through a night. Maybe because some part of him knew Cat was nearby, just a door away, was the reason he was sleeping so well. Talon was starting to feel human and his depression was lifting, as well. Was it all due to her? His gut told him yes.

"Thanks." She licked her lower lip, feeling a little shy in Talon's presence. He was getting well and he no longer needed her care as before. She would miss their intimacy. Now he seemed completely at ease in his world, no questions, no hesitation. He knew his mind and she could see the set in his well-shaped mouth and the gleam in his gray eyes. Even more, she wanted to kiss him, wanted to know how his mouth felt against hers. The man's sensuality had only grown as he'd recovered.

Their daily Scrabble games had revealed softer, more thoughtful sides to him, and Cat had found herself starved for those precious hours spent in his company. She'd never felt happier. More fulfilled. Hopeful. And when he smiled that slow smile of his, her whole body responded, powerfully.

"I appreciate you making these stops for me today," he said, meaning it.

"I'm happy to do it," Cat said.

Talon watched the sunlight touching the snow-clad evergreens. A lot of the snow was melting and then falling off in clumps, creating sudden snow showers, the sun dazzling and almost rainbowlike through the crystals. "Is what you do dangerous, Cat?"

"Firefighting?" She opened and closed her hands against the steering wheel, slowing down as they entered Jackson Hole. "It can be. You just have to know what you're doing."

"I noticed you have some red burn marks on the side of your neck."

Cat's heart fell for a moment. Talon missed nothing. "Every firefighter gets that," she said. "When we're entering a burning structure, our necks and ears are the most exposed and least protected at times." She unconsciously touched the nape of her neck. "Guess you could say it's the mark of a firefighter."

"Your skin is too beautiful to be marred like that."

"Thanks…" The sincerity in his voice shook Cat. She suddenly felt very feminine beneath his hooded inspection. He wasn't coming on to her necessarily. He wasn't a man with pickup lines, unlike other past boyfriends. She sensed Talon was trying to understand her, observe her in a benign kind of way, not to discover a way to control her.

There was silence and she got the feeling he might be a little shy.

"Do you want me to help you load those grain bags?" he asked.

"Naw. Andy has guys who work for him at the Horse Emporium. They'll stack them in the rear of the pickup. And Griff will carry them into the barn when we get home. No worries."

"Okay," he murmured. "What kinds of things happen when you're on duty at the fire department?"

Cat smiled a little, hearing concern in his tone. "Oh, anything from a run with the ambulance to fighting a structure fire. We get more fires in the winter because so many people have woodstoves in their homes. Some folks don't get their chimneys cleaned out regularly and chimney fires are very common calls."

"Isn't that dangerous? Don't you have to put a ladder up on an icy roof to get to the chimney stack?"

"Better believe it," Cat said. She slowed down as the light turned red. There was a lot of traffic in the town. Given that the roads had been impassable for nearly four days, everyone was out and about getting supplies. "You want to know something funny?" She turned briefly, meeting and drowning in his gray gaze. Her womb clenched, her mouth went dry. The look in Talon's eyes was predatory. Not in a bad way, but it served to tell her once more, he desired her.

"Sure."

Cat tried to sound normal, although her breasts tightened beneath his heated look. "I used to have a fear of heights. I got over that real quick out here in Jackson Hole. Some roofs were two or three stories high. That's when I just bit the bullet and climbed and worked through my fear to put out the chimney fire."

Grunting, Talon muttered, "That's a damn dangerous situation. You could fall off the roof and get killed." He didn't like the idea of Cat being in that kind of unstable line of work. He was becoming protective of her, as if she were already his woman, someone to take care of, keep out of harm's way. Yet, when he heard her laugh softly and shake her head, Talon realized she wasn't going to give in to his idea of safety for her.

"Been doing it for seven years and so far—knock on wood—I've never fallen off a roof."

Talon grunted again, his brows drawing downward. "Where did you get this desire to throw yourself into fires?"

She grinned and looked at him for a moment. "What is this? The pot calling the kettle black? Like your work as a SEAL wasn't even more dangerous than my work?"

"You're too smart for your own good, Cat."

She laughed. "Yeah. Right. I'm not some fragile little girl, you know? I'm good at what I do. I love being a firefighter."

"You're a warrior princess."

"I like that. Thank you."

"I'm going to miss our daily Scrabble tournament."

"So am I." Cat turned down another street that would lead to Jordana's medical office. "You're a fast learner, Talon."

In his job as a SEAL, he had to be, but he didn't say that. "I've got a good teacher." Talon saw her cheeks grow pink. Cat was so easily touched by compliments.

She wasn't capable of the usual games women played with men, he was discovering. There was a rock-solid honesty to her. Cat didn't try to hide how she felt, but at the same time, if she was grumpy, Talon had noticed she didn't take it out on others. She was refreshing to him in so many ways, not jaded by life. Talon didn't like women who played games, who manipulated. He'd had too many relationships in his past where he'd had to deal with it.

Talon had always appreciated honesty but found it harder to come by in women. Maybe he was just drawing the wrong kind of woman to him? Most likely. But he'd always been honest with them. He hadn't wanted strings attached, no long-term commitment. It was about sex, enjoyment in the moment, and then he'd be leaving, going back into training. It wasn't a good life for a woman and Talon had known that from the outset. SEALs had a 90 percent divorce rate and he had no wish to travel that road. Best to be honest up front.

Cat pulled the truck to the curb and pointed to a single-story brick house with a neat yard and white porch. "This is Jordana's office. It'll probably take about an hour before I come back, so if you get done, just wait inside for me."

Talon nodded and opened the door. He glanced at his watch. It was 9:00 a.m. "Got it. See you later."

Cat watched him ease out of the truck. His shoulders were broad beneath Griff's sheepskin coat. When he turned to shut the door, she met his eyes. A shiver of need coursed through her, hot and sweet. She hadn't been mistaken about the look in Talon's eyes: he definitely wanted her.

As she drove away, Cat gulped unsteadily, feeling a

bunch of different emotions. Talon was so personable that all he had to do was give her that disarming smile and she was putty in his hands, whether he knew it or not. And Cat suspected he *did* know. But he hadn't made a single move on her. She was grateful, since she was still getting over the debacle with Beau Magee.

Shivering, she hoped she didn't meet him over at the Horse Emporium. It wasn't likely to happen because he worked as a driver at Ace Trucking. Still, Cat did not want to meet him. Why hadn't she seen his violent streak earlier? It wasn't as if Talon lacked violence, but he had a gentle soul. She knew she was safe with him. Maybe Talon wasn't the only one who needed to talk to Jordana....

CHAPTER EIGHT

BY THE TIME Cat drove back to Jordana's office, later than she'd anticipated, Talon was waiting for her outside. She gulped at how good he looked, having just gotten a haircut. As he emerged from the shadow of the porch and into the morning sunshine, she got a quick glimpse of his military-short hair before he put on his baseball cap. Talon stood tall, his shoulders broad and pulled back with natural pride. At six foot three inches tall, he was devastatingly handsome. Now she was seeing the SEAL in him, that clean, unyielding line of his jaw, his mouth firm, his gray eyes hard and alert. To say he was ruggedly good-looking was an understatement. He was powerful.

Their eyes locked as he casually walked toward her. Shaken, Cat tried to calm herself, her fingers tightening around the steering wheel. This was not the man she had picked up in the snowstorm. Talon oozed that kind of raw, sexual, alpha-male energy. Her mouth went dry.

"You got a lot done while I was picking up grain," she managed as he entered the cab and pulled on the seat belt. Talon's profile was like granite—a tough, lean face, strong and resolute.

Talon slipped on his wraparound sunglasses, a SEAL staple and something he'd always wear. "No problem." He closed the door. "I walked a few blocks and found a barbershop and—" he held up his cell phone "—found a store that would turn on my phone."

He felt pretty damn good having some money in his pocket to do the small things. As he watched Cat, he could see she was in some kind of shock. Her cheeks were flushed a deep rose. Damn, she looked good to him.

"That's great. You sure look different with your hair cut short."

"I like it short. Stays out of the way."

Cat managed a weak smile. Her body was on fire. She had to force herself not to stare too much. "What did Jordana say?"

He grinned a little. "Light duty. Said my lungs are pretty much clear, and in another five days, she wants me back. She thinks I can do serious wrangler work after that." He lost his smile and added, "Then I can go see my mother."

Cat noticed the sudden sorrow in his eyes. "I know she's looking forward to seeing you, too, Talon."

He didn't want to pursue it. "So what now?" He looked at the watch on his wrist. It was ten o'clock and he was keeping in mind Cat had duty at three this afternoon at the fire department. She had taken off her cap and her shining black hair was mussed around her shoulders. Talon itched to slide his fingers through it, discover how silky and strong it was, like her.

"Andy's got lots of great sales on winter clothes and gear at the Horse Emporium. Thought I'd drive us back there."

"Sure," Talon said, looking around. He never stopped checking out his surroundings. It was a natural part of being a SEAL: knowing your territory, knowing where the humans were. Just part of the wary security since it could save his life. Not that there was danger in Jackson Hole, but Talon knew he'd never stop being watchful.

As they drove through Jackson Hole to get to the Horse Emporium, Talon asked her, "Should we get the grain?"

"Yes. They were still mixing it in a hopper and that's why I was later than I thought I'd be."

"I made good use of the time," Talon assured her, seeing she was anxious. "No worries, okay?"

Trying to relax, Cat gave him a nervous smile. He filled up the cab of the pickup truck. And she swore she could feel the heat of his body rolling off him. It wasn't upsetting, just…well…sexual…sensual. And her body was doing somersaults inside. She'd never reacted to a man like this. It made her edgy. What made it more frightening was the way Talon returned her look, as a man who desired his woman. There was blatant interest. And she liked it. A lot. She simply had no experience with an alpha-male wolf like him.

"Did Jordana change your antibiotic?"

"No. Said what you put me on was doing the job." Talon absorbed her profile, his gaze resting on her full, soft lips. Cat really had no clue as to how sexy she really was. Talon intended to change that if she gave him a chance.

"Oh, good," she whispered, relieved.

"You're a paramedic. You're good at what you do."

Warmth flowed through Cat as Talon's growling words blanketed her. She moved her fingers nervously on the steering wheel. "Jordana's a wonderful doctor and she knows her stuff, too." Cat gave him a quick glance. "You do know she's a PTSD expert?"

Talon nodded. He was feeling too good, happy, even. His life had turned around in a heartbeat and he didn't want to spoil the new tendrils for Cat growing in his heart. "Yeah, we talked a little about it at Sunday dinner."

"Are you going to see her about it?" She was thinking of his nightmares, although he hadn't had any that she knew of since he'd come to the ranch house.

"In time," he murmured. "I want to focus on my mother's care and being a good wrangler for Griff and Val."

Cat got the message. She could feel that tightly wound tension around Talon. This was new. Was he like that all the time? As he became well, was he going to become more like his old, military SEAL self? She didn't know. The energy around him, though, was palpable. And it made her feel…well…cared for. She risked a quick glance at him after she'd turned the corner and saw the Horse Emporium. Was he aware of this? Was he doing it on purpose? She knew little about SEALs. And she had a million questions for him but wasn't sure he'd answer any of them.

Once inside the store, Talon made quick work of buying eight pairs of Levi's, the same number of long-sleeved chambray work shirts, a pair of decent work gloves and other gear he'd need. He knew Andy and it was good to shake his hand and see him once again. Best of all, Talon could pay for his purchases. Cat had shadowed him but said little. She seemed happy to carry some of his clothes to the counter for him.

Andy smiled. "Glad you're back home, Talon," the man said, putting the purchases into a big paper bag.

"I imagine you'll be taking over for Cat in coming here for feed and supplies?"

"Most likely," Talon said, handing him the money.

"Ah, come on, Andy, I'm not disappearing on you," Cat protested with a grin.

"Miss Cat, you are like a beautiful flower gracing my humble store," Andy said, serious. "I'd hate to lose the sunshine you bring in with you. You always make my day when you show up."

Talon noticed how Cat suddenly turned shy, lowered her lashes, her cheeks red. He was beginning to see more facets of her. Hell, she was a confident and competent paramedic, yet, when Andy, who obviously loved her like a long-lost daughter, gave her a compliment, she didn't know how to handle it. This was one more piece of the puzzle of Cat Edwin.

"Hey, Mo's Ice Cream Parlor has some really great pecan pie for lunch today," Andy told them, handing Talon the huge sack.

Talon looked over at Cat. It was almost noon. "Want to drive over and grab lunch?"

"Well...sure," she answered. She hadn't thought about eating in town. Normally, she swung by her condo to eat lunch.

"I'm buying," Talon assured her.

"Okay," she murmured, taking the second big sack from Andy.

"See you later," Andy called, raising his hand.

In the truck, Talon turned to her. "You okay with going to Mo's for lunch? We can do something different if you want."

She shrugged and started the truck. "No...that's okay. I keep forgetting you haven't been home for a long time and you'd probably like to visit your old haunts. Usually, I make lunch at my condo."

Talon nodded. "Saving money for that house, right?"

She backed the truck out and put it in Drive. "Right." She gave him a quick smile and drove back onto the street that would lead them to Mo's, which sat on the main plaza in downtown Jackson Hole.

Talon wasn't sure about Mo's, either, but he said nothing. On a good day, he could handle noise and crowds. He knew Mo's was the most popular restaurant for locals. Today, he felt he could handle it. Besides, it meant quality, private time with Cat, which he would seek out any chance he got, PTSD or not.

They arrived at eleven and Mo's wasn't crowded. Talon chose a booth in the rear of the restaurant, near the exit. He was positioned so that he had a full view of the restaurant and he could see who was coming. Plus, Talon could see through the huge windows that faced the two streets. Cat had given him a strange look as he directed the waitress to a seat in the rear. There were plenty of booths up front along the windows.

Sitting down, Cat shrugged out of her coat and set it beside her with her purse. She watched as Talon took off his sunglasses and hat. Looking around, she swung her gaze back to him.

"Why did you want this particular booth?" She opened the menu, wildly aware of the man opposite her. He looked like a huge cougar just sitting with coiled, tense energy around him, his alertness always present.

Talon picked up the menu and smiled a little. "SEAL habits, Cat."

She tilted her head. "Teach me."

He met her curious blue gaze. Her black hair was

mussed and he watched as she tamed it with her long, tapered fingers. "Security stuff," he explained. "You never sit in front of windows. You're a target. If someone is watching you, you will be found."

"And sitting by this exit?"

He grinned. "Very astute. SEALs never sit in a place where they can't leave in a hurry. If the bad guys are coming in the front door, you can go out the rear exit door."

"Survival?"

"Yes."

"When we're at a structure fire, I always want to know the entrance/exit points, too, in case we get into trouble inside."

"See?" he teased, laying the menu aside, "you're more like a SEAL than you realized."

She grinned and felt heat surge into her cheeks. When Talon gave her that smoldering, intense look, she felt it all the way down to her toes. Never mind the dampness between her thighs. "But I'm not being hunted by a bad guy, just the fire."

"Both can kill you," Talon said, frowning. He worried for her.

"No doubt," she said.

The waitress came over and took their orders, filling their coffee cups before she left. Talon folded his hands, absorbing Cat. She wore a dark purple long-sleeved tee with a denim vest. The color reflected the hue of her large eyes. She seemed uncomfortable.

"Are you okay?" he asked.

Cat shrugged. "Yes. Fine." Oh, the lies! What? Go tell Talon that every time he looked at her, she felt he was invisibly touching her? That she thought about

sex—all the time? *Right.* The man was certifiably, sin-
fully delicious. There were the fine lines at the corners of his eyes, the deeper lines that appeared when
he smiled at her. His flesh was weathered by years as
a SEAL. She saw the scars on his hands, heavy scarring on his back. He'd led a very hard, dangerous life,
her instincts told her.

"Do I make you nervous by looking at you?"

She stared down at her clasped hands resting on
the table. Her mouth went dry as she struggled to find
words.

He reached over, laying his hand over hers. "Look
at me, Cat."

The instant he touched her, his long, callused fingers
curving across hers, Cat jumped inwardly. She stared
into those gray eyes "What?" she managed, her voice
off-key. She wanted to pull her hands away. This kind of
contact with Talon was really making her feel too much.

"Why are you so uncomfortable with me looking
at you? You're a beautiful woman and you should feel
good about it. Not…" He hesitated, casting around for
the right word. "Not scared. I see fear in your eyes every
time I look at you. I'm not going to hurt you, Cat." And
Talon lifted his hand from hers because he saw panic.

Cat sat back, tucking her hands beneath the table.
"It's a long story," she whispered.

Talon gave a shrug and a gentle look. "I've got the
time if you do."

"I'm really ashamed to even talk about it, Talon,"
she muttered, refusing to meet his eyes.

"Okay," he said. "Do you mind if I tell you what I
think?"

Cat lifted her chin and held his gaze. "No." She felt

his protection suddenly cloaking her. How did he do this? No man had ever given her that sense.

He lowered his voice so no one could over hear them. "I think you're afraid of men in general because your father or a male relative or friend probably did something to you when you were a little girl. I've found that we're all branded, one way or another, by our parents. Sometimes in good, positive and supportive ways." Talon's voice grew concerned as he held her unsure gaze. "And sometimes, parents can harm a child in so many ways—physically, mentally or emotionally." He opened his hands around the cup of coffee he held between them. "Maybe all of the above."

The silence thickened between them.

Cat gulped. How could he have possibly known? "You know, Val and I, when we met one another for the first time, we instantly got along like sisters." She forced herself to look at Talon. His face was normally unreadable. Maybe his game face. Right now, he was open, vulnerable to her, and that shook Cat. It made her feel less threatened. "We...uh...discovered pretty quickly that we sort of shared the same rotten childhood. Val's father, Buck, was a drunk and he physically abused his wife, Cheryl, and Val. Cheryl was so beaten down after living years with Buck, that she never protected Val like she should have." Cat hitched one shoulder, her voice growing painful. "When we discovered we had a similar past with our fathers, we just clicked." Her voice dropped into a whisper. "We understood one another, our crazy quirks, maybe eccentricities...."

Talon wanted to get up, slide into the seat where Cat was sitting, sweep her into his arms and hold her. Hold her and give her the protection she had never gotten as an innocent child. The need was so powerful he had to literally stop himself from doing exactly that. Her face had gone pale, her eyes haunted. She bit on her lower lip as if to stop from crying.

"I'm sorry, Cat. I didn't mean to make you feel bad...." Talon would do anything to remove the anguish he saw in her eyes.

"I-it's not something I want to talk about, Talon." Cat shifted, feeling anxious. "I try not to remember. Every time I think about it, I get scared, upset and anxious, like right now. I'm sorry. I'm not exactly whole."

"I'm not, either," he admitted wearily. "No one is perfect, Cat. We all carry invisible scars of one sort or another." He saw a hint of tears in her eyes. Oh, hell! She couldn't cry. Not here. Not now. A sense of utter helplessness spread quickly through him. "I like you just the way you are."

Cat glanced out over the restaurant that was getting more and more customers in for lunch. "Jordana said I had PTSD. We, uh, talked about it after Sunday dinner. I'm going in for treatment once I'm back in town. Maybe someday I'll be able to trust men again." She tapped her head. "In here, mentally, I know all men aren't my father. But when a man looks at me and I pick up on his intentions toward me, emotionally, I get scared."

Talon's mouth tightened. "Because you see your father stalking you? Hunting you down?" He wanted to kill the bastard. What father would *ever* hurt his child? Staring at Cat, how beautiful she was, how much she helped others with her kindness and compassion, Talon felt rage tunnel through him toward her father.

"Yes," she whispered. "You look at me and it just

triggers my reflex, Talon." She leaned forward, her voice hoarse. "I *know* you don't intend me harm. My head knows that. But…God, I'm so oversensitized to men that I pick up their intentions, like an invisible radar. Jordana has helped me to understand that when it happens, I have to mentally separate out what I'm feeling. It isn't like every man is stalking me. It's that I pick up their interest in me and the message gets twisted inside me, my feelings… And instead of being able to accept their compliment, I realize I interpret it as stalking me."

Talon sat back, digesting her words. Even though Cat had nothing to feel humiliated about, Talon understood a little more about her reaction. "You're still trapped in the emotions of when you were a child."

"Not that I'm proud of it," Cat admitted wryly, one corner of her mouth hooking upward in a twist. "I'm twenty-seven years old. Jordana said that often, when a child is traumatized like that, the emotions don't grow and mature as they should. It's sort of like being stuck. She's really helped me see this, Talon. When you look at me and it triggers me, I stop and tell myself you're not my father. You're not out to hurt me." Cat tilted her head, seeing his face go dark with an unknown emotion. "I know you wouldn't hurt me," she admitted, her voice soft. "You're a good person."

Watching Cat struggle made him want to cry for her. For the pain she lived with daily. Her sick, abusive father had stolen so much from her.

"Look," he began, spreading his hands out in front of him, "maybe we need to reset how you see me? Would you react the same if I were your friend?" Not a lover, which was what he wanted to be.

Cat sat back and digested his question. Talon had never been a friend to a woman. Didn't have a friggin' clue how to be one. But he'd do anything to win Cat's trust, and maybe, just maybe, offering her friendship was the safe place to start.

"I don't know, Talon."

He nodded in understanding. "I want your trust, Cat." That wasn't a lie. That was the whole, unvarnished truth. Without trust between a man and a woman, nothing was going to happen.

The waitress brought over their plates and refilled their coffee cups and left.

Cat wasn't hungry, but she knew she had to eat. Going on shift, she had to eat or else. A structure fire could go on for hours, half a day, and Cat would have no chance to eat at all. She had to keep her strength. She felt Talon's eyes on her, but for whatever reason, it didn't trigger her anxiety. Right now, she experienced his gentle side. Oh, she'd seen his gentleness with Zeke. And at those times, Cat had wanted his hands on her. How would it feel to be stroked with his long, large-knuckled fingers? She waited until the waitress was out of earshot to answer him.

"I'm weird, Talon."

"So am I. It's a fit."

She frowned. "I have my moments. You've seen the paramedic side to me. Not…when I'm down…" *Or scared or threatened,* but the words were left unsaid. She sought out his gaze, the kindness in his eyes. Maybe Val was right: Talon was good for her. And God knew, she wanted him in her life.

"Well, you've seen some of my moments. Did it scare you off?"

She smiled a little, putting salt and pepper on her hamburger. "No."

"You know I have PTSD, that you can't wake me up or I'm liable to hit you out of reflex. That didn't scare you off."

Cat shook her head, watching a slow, lazy smile tug at his gorgeous, kissable mouth. If Talon could read her mind she'd be in such trouble. "Val knows about PTSD. She said it's muscle memory, something you can't help."

"I'm glad you talked to her about it," he said.

"She's like a sister to me. And she's helped me understand my own PTSD from childhood."

Talon wondered if most people who came out of a dysfunctional and abusive home didn't have some form of PTSD. "Sometimes it's easier being around a person with similar eccentricities," he told her, slight amusement in his tone. "We'll be able to understand. We won't be confused about it. And we'll give each other a lot of latitude when it hits us."

Cat cut her huge hamburger in half. "It all makes sense, Talon."

"But does it make enough sense so that we can become friends over time?" He dug into her unsure blue gaze, seeing the indecision there. He also saw attraction. He knew without a doubt Cat desired him. Man to woman. Sex. He didn't challenge her on it. If he did, he knew she'd run and never look back.

"Definitely," Cat admitted, picking up a French fry.

"Want to try it?" Never had Talon wanted something quite so badly as this.

Cat raised her eyes to the ceiling for a moment. And then she smiled a silly smile. "The guys at the fire department are men and they're my good friends. I'm not afraid or threatened by them."

That's because they don't want to take you to bed. And I do. Talon nodded, compressing his lips. "This should be easy for you, then."

She laughed, embarrassed by her hesitation. The glitter in Talon's eyes made her go hot with longing. An invisible heat naturally sprung to life between them. It wasn't something she could explain away. It was simply there.

"Sure, we can be friends."

Talon sat back and picked up the bottle of ketchup, spreading it across his fries. "Good." Happiness flowed through him, sweet and strong. Finally, he didn't see anxiety in Cat's eyes as she munched away on her hamburger. She was eating with enjoyment, finally relaxed. *One word. Friendship.* Well, he was going to have to figure out how to be a friend, not a lover constantly wanting her.

CHAPTER NINE

CAT WAS HURRYING to get ready for her firefighting shift when there was a loud banging on her condo door. Scowling, she hurried out of her bedroom and through the living room. As she looked through the peephole, her heart dropped.

It was Beau Magee.

Fear suddenly raged through her. She hesitated, her pulse beating strong in her throat. Finally, she got herself under control and opened the door.

"What do you want?" Cat asked, standing with one hand on the doorknob, the other on the door frame, blocking the path so he couldn't just waltz in.

He was dressed in his driver's uniform. Automatically, she didn't like the way his brown eyes assessed her.

"Now, is that any way to greet your boyfriend?" he teased.

Her nostrils flared with anger. "Beau, come on. We're done. You knew that a year ago."

His thin mouth curved, but to her, it was frightening, like evil personified. She glanced down at his large hands, which were curling into fists. Yeah, she remembered getting shoved by those fists. He was sorry afterward, but she wasn't going to hang around with someone like her father.

"Saw you walking with your new boyfriend outta Mo's earlier today," he sneered, anger in his voice.

Her throat went dry. "My personal life is none of your business, Beau. Now leave. I don't know why I even opened the door." She glared up at him. He was about two inches shorter than Talon, but just as big, more heavily muscled. Magee was not a small man. Cat again wondered why she'd *ever* been attracted to him. Looking at Magee now in comparison to Talon, there was a world of difference. Starting with the fact Beau did not respect her. At all. His brown eyes flared with rage. She went on guard, wanting to slam the door to protect herself from him. Beau had a hair-trigger temper, she'd found out too late.

"Ah, come on Cat. What we had was good."

She snorted. "Yeah, maybe for you. Sure as hell not for me. Please leave, Beau. I'll call the police."

"Yeah, yeah. So who's this new guy? I ain't seen him around before."

Something froze inside of Cat. Jealousy flared in Beau's slitted eyes. "None of your business. I'm going to be late for my shift. Don't bother coming around again, Beau."

She shut the door and quickly locked it, her heart thundering in her chest. Half-afraid Beau would fly into a rage and try to beat the door down, Cat hurried to the bedroom where she was going to change her clothes. Right now, she wished Talon was around. He gave her that sense of protection. He'd make sure Beau left her alone.

After a few moments of silence, Cat figured Beau had left and shimmied out of her civilian clothes. She quickly threw on the light blue shirt with all her firefighting patches and her silver badge denoting she was a firefighter. She pulled on a newly pressed pair of dark blue gabardine trousers. Finally, she slipped on special black boots that had steel in the soles to prevent nails from jamming up inside them at a fire scene.

Breathing unevenly, Cat hurried out of the bedroom, her "go bag," in hand. Before moving to the kitchen, she peered at the door. Had Beau left? She didn't trust the bastard. Why had she ever gotten hooked up with him?

She opened the fridge and got out sliced turkey, mustard and a loaf of bread.

Okay, she could be honest. She'd been lonely when Beau came into her life. She'd sworn off men, endured a long dry spell. Then Beau showed up at a winter armory dance. He'd been well dressed and incredibly charming.

Snorting softly, her hands moving quickly, Cat made three sandwiches to put into her go bag. Beau was good-looking, there was no question. And he'd been the perfect gentleman at the dance. And she loved to dance. Maybe that was where she'd made her mistake.

She put the items back into the fridge, then plopped the sandwiches into a Ziploc bag.

Being with Talon was a different experience. When she first saw his face, she felt as if she'd been struck. Her heart had squeezed powerfully with emotions. Ever since, there was a living, sizzling connection that throbbed wildly between them.

Cat frowned. She had no experience with that kind of feeling. She had other things she felt more qualified for, like helping people. Maybe, when she got her hour for dinner tonight, providing there were no fire calls, she'd drive over to see Sandy. Cat always valued the woman's wisdom.

Miss Gus hobbled out to the tack room in the barn near noon the next day.

"Ah," she crowed, "thought I'd find you out here, Talon." She rubbed her gloved hands together and walked into the large room that smelled like leather.

Talon was sitting on a stool and looked up, a bridle between his hands, cleaning it with neat's-foot oil. "Hey, Miss Gus. What happened? Did they unlock you from that prison of a house?" Talon grinned. He quickly got up and pulled an old wooden chair from the corner and set it in front of her. Val kept trying to egg Gus into getting a power chair so she could get around, but Gus always put it off.

"Thanks," Gus said, glad to sit down.

Talon walked over and shut the door. "Does Val know you escaped?" he asked.

"No, she don't." Gus grinned and took off her bright yellow knit cap and dropped it into her lap. "I just needed to get out and get some fresh air. Mighty nice outside. Blue sky. Sunshine. Two things we only see in late spring through late summer."

"Yeah," Talon said, going back to work. "Eight months of winter in this area is no fun."

"You should know," Gus griped good-naturedly. She studied him closely. "How are you feelin' this morning?"

Talon wanted to say he missed having Cat around but thought better. "Okay." SEALs said okay to everything, whether they were in pain, suffering or otherwise. He heard Gus snort.

"My lungs feel clear," he said.

"That's good," Gus said. She looked around the large tack room that held bridles, harnesses, blankets and saddles. Inhaling deeply, she said, "There's nothing like the good smell of a tack room."

Talon nodded. "Best smell in the world," he agreed.

"I just heard on the police scanner that the fire department is answering a house fire."

Instantly, Talon's head snapped up. His eyes narrowed. "Cat's crew?"

"Yup. I kinda thought you might want to know."

Talon's hands stilled on the bridle in his lap. "Is it a bad house fire? Do you know?" Because he'd like to drive into Jackson Hole, make sure she was safe. Damn, he was really getting protective about her.

"Dunno. You never know until afterward. She'll be okay, Talon. Cat's a fine firefighter."

Scowling, he forced himself to work on the leather. "I don't like her doing that kind of work."

"Kinda thought you'd feel like that."

Glancing up, he noted the twinkle in Gus's eyes. "And you know this how?"

"I see the way you look at her, young man. It's not lost on me."

Talon felt himself flush, something new. "Busted."

Gus chuckled. "Well, it will be our secret. Although, Val's kinda aware of it, too."

"Great," Talon grunted. Where the hell was top secret when you needed it?

"She's a wonderful person, Talon. She'd do right by you."

Talon studied the woman's wrinkled face and heard the warmth in her voice. "I wanted to talk to you about Cat."

"Okay," Gus said, "what do you want to know, son?"

Though he felt a little embarrassed, Talon needed to

understand Cat's background. "We had lunch the other day and when I tried to find out about her family, she locked up. Something about her father." He drilled a look into Gus's eyes. "Am I right?"

"Yes." Gus shook her head. "She and Val suffered the same fate—bad, abusive fathers. When Val was sixteen, I left my own ranch and came to live here at the Bar H. I knew Buck was abusive to my daughter, Cheryl, and my grandchild, Val. I warned Buck if he ever laid a hand on them again, he'd deal with me. By moving in, I broke the cycle of violence. Buck never touched them again," she said, satisfaction in her tone.

"But what about Cat?"

"Chuck Edwin was hell on earth. Cat's mom died of breast cancer when she was young. Chuck worked on the Rocking L ranch outside of Cheyenne. He was one of their top wranglers. Cat grew up around men and learned wrangling from fourteen years old onward. That's probably why she's in a man's career now as a firefighter, would be my guess. Anyway, Chuck was a mean son of a bitch. He was well-known to abuse his wife, Cindy. They had a small house on the Rocking L. I'd heard about him through local gossip because me and my husband's ranch butted up against the Rocking L's property line."

"Did you know Cat then?"

"I did. Sometimes when they were repairing fence up against our property, I'd see her. She was a pretty little thing." Gus frowned. "I was out with my husband one morning and she and another wrangler were repairing a post when we rode by. I noticed a lot of bruises on her lower right arm, just above her work glove. I asked her how she got them. She lied and told me she fell off her horse." Gus became grim. "Wasn't the last time I saw bruises on her."

Talon tried to rein in his anger. "Is that son of a bitch alive?"

Gus snorted. "No, thank the good Lord. Cat was a smart young woman. She left a day after graduating from high school for college. Left Chuck high and dry. Just deserts, I'd say. Six months later, he died of a heart attack. Left her penniless. Cat never had a scholarship. She worked odd jobs to pay for her tuition." Gus rubbed her thighs slowly and added, "She's a special person, Talon. Like another granddaughter to me. Cat has no family here. Her grandparents are dead and gone. We're her family now and I've gotta say, a much better one than the one she came from."

Talon rubbed the leather, afraid to lift his head because he knew Gus would see the rage in his eyes. "She is special," he muttered.

"You like her, don't you?"

When he finally looked up, he could see Gus was grinning. His mouth curved ruefully. "What isn't there to like, Miss Gus?"

Chuckling, Gus waved her hand in the air. "Oh, I dunno. Saving your butt for starters, maybe?"

"There is that," he agreed.

"I was talkin' less in generalities and more specifics."

Talon applied oil to the leather, slowly rubbing it in with the cloth. Gus knew damn well that he liked her. Wanted her. Badly.

"Well?" Gus prodded.

"If I say yes, is that going to change me working on the Bar H?"

"Heavens, no!" Gus slapped her hands on her thighs. "You'd think I'd fire you for likin' Cat?"

Talon shrugged. "I didn't know if you'd approve of it or not. We'll be working together, wrangling, from time to time."

Snorting, Gus stood up, shaking her head. "So long as you kiss her on breaks or lunch, I could care less."

What a feisty, testy old woman she was. "You put my commander to shame, Miss Gus. Sure you haven't served in the military?"

Grinning, Gus pulled the knit cap onto her silver hair. "What would your commander do in a situation like this?"

"If he's a good officer, he'd have handled it like you're doing," Talon said.

"Well, only thing I'm concerned about is that you understand Cat. She's a good person. She's got problems with men. Can't read 'em right. I just want you to be gentle."

Gus stood there, spine as straight as a broom, her hands imperiously on her hips, giving him a hard look of warning.

"Not to worry, Miss Gus," Talon said seriously. "My focus is on my mother. She's first in my life. This job is second. Anything left over...well...if I can get to first base with Cat, is for her."

"You got your priorities straight," Gus said. "And I'm here if you need to talk, need a shoulder to cry on, but I got a hunch Cat will take over those duties." And she left the tack room.

Talon sat there thinking about their conversation after Gus left. He continued rubbing the neat's-foot oil into the leather, softening it between his fingers. Cat wanted a friend. Not a lover. His brow wrinkled. And right now, she was on a fire call. His conscience ate at him and he worried for her. Damn, he barely knew the woman and he was behaving as if he was already in love with her.

That thought made him lift his chin and stare at the dark, rough wall at the other end of the room. Love? Hell, he didn't know what love was. Sex, he knew about. Good sex. Great sex. Mind-blowing sex. But love? No. That was a land far, far away from his reality.

Talon sighed in frustration. He felt trapped in a new and different way. He wanted Cat, but she didn't want to be caught. Gus wanted him and Cat to be together, but not just for sex. *Great.* He was old enough to realize time would sort things out provided he remained patient. And Talon had to admit, he was good at just that. Besides, Cat was worth waiting for. He just wasn't sure yet, what category of his life she fit in, if at all....

CHAPTER TEN

TALON TRIED TO still his urgency to see Cat once again. It was nearly dark when he and Griff walked into the ranch house. They hung up their coats and hats on pegs near the hallway. Inhaling, he could smell lamb in the air along with Mediterranean spices. Val and Gus were in the kitchen, preparing the coming meal for all of them.

Where was Cat? He knew she had gotten off duty at three this afternoon, but all day he'd been down at the six cabins near Long Lake that the family rented out to fishermen. He and Griff were getting them ready for their first visitors come June first.

Heading straight to the bathroom at the end of the hall, he noticed Cat's door to her bedroom was closed. He sensed something was wrong but couldn't pinpoint what.

"Dinner's in five minutes, everyone!" Gus called down the hall.

Just time enough to wash up. Talon took off his damp red bandanna from around his neck and laid it on the counter. He'd worked up a sweat even though the May temperature was only in the forties and snow stubbornly stayed around. It felt good to start working, stretching his muscles, sweating and getting out of bed and the stuffy house. He doubted Jordana would consider what he did today "light" work, but Talon was more than ready to get busy instead of sitting around waiting for the last dredges of the pneumonia to leave.

Keeping one ear keyed toward the hallway, Talon heard everyone's voices, the laughter, but Cat's. Was she here? He'd seen Cat's truck parked in the driveway. Worried, he quickly washed up, dried his hands and arms and walked down the hall toward the kitchen, rolling up the sleeves on his shirt.

Gus had just sat down at the head of the trestle table and Val was bringing over the last of the dishes as he entered the busy kitchen. Talon didn't see Cat as he sat down. Val and Griff sat on one side of the table, he on the other. Cat's seat was empty.

"Where's Cat?" he asked Gus.

"She's not feelin' well," she said, picking up the bowl of mashed potatoes that had large gobs of yellow butter floating in the center.

Val leaned over Talon and handed him the bowl of steamed green beans with pearl onions and slivered almonds. "She had a really bad ambulance call today, Talon. When it happens, Cat needs some alone time."

Talon's heart clenched. He took the bowl and thanked Val. She moved around the table, slid her hand across her grandmother's small shoulders and squeezed her gently and then sat down next to Griff.

He said nothing, noting the silent worry on all their faces. Generally, dinner was a happy, chatty affair. This time, they made some conversation but it was tense.

AFTER DINNER, VAL made up a dinner tray for Talon to take to Cat. The woman seemed to know how much he wanted to see her.

"Just go down the hall, knock on her door." Val gave him a warm look. "I'm pretty sure she'll let you in."

As Talon nodded and took the tray down the hall he wondered if everyone knew he liked Cat. Seemed that way. He halted at her door and knocked gently.

"Cat? It's Talon." His heart rate amped up. He was torn between worry and anxiety. He'd missed her so much the past two days, he'd been miserable. The work around the ranch kept him busy and took the edge off his loneliness, but it didn't stop his heart from pining away for her.

Cat opened the door. "Hey," she murmured. "Sorry I didn't join you for dinner."

"Don't worry about it. Val said you might eat a little." Talon held the tray forward. He didn't like the look in Cat's murky blue eyes. She seemed utterly devastated, her shoulders slumped.

"I'm not really hungry, Talon. But come on in." She stepped aside. His presence just automatically lifted her spirit and made her feel better.

Talon entered her room, which was furnished exactly like his room. There was a flowery, tufted couch in one corner along with an overstuffed chair. "Where do you want the tray?" he asked.

Cat shrugged. "Just put it on the dresser."

The pain in her eyes tore at him. He placed the tray on the dresser, watching as she pushed her fingers distractedly through her loose hair. He said to hell with it and walked over to her, placing his hands gently on her shoulders.

"What happened?" he demanded in a low tone, searching her face. Inwardly, Talon groaned as tears glimmered in her eyes. "Talk to me," he rasped.

Cat tried to pull away, but he wouldn't let her go. She was going to cry and she hated crying in front of anyone. The concerned look in Talon's narrowed eyes, the set of his mouth, tore at her. All Cat wanted to do was be held. Talon was so tall and strong, quiet and calm compared to how she felt right now. Grief mixed with anger and frustration.

"I—I don't cry in front of others," she whispered brokenly, turning away from his burning look.

"I don't, either," he growled. "But sometimes it's good to let someone who cares for you hold you, Cat." His voice grew firm. "Let me at least do that for you."

Someone who cares for you. The words shocked her, warmed her. They scared the hell out of her. But his thickly spoken words beckoned to her, too. Cat was unable to sort through the avalanche of feelings that came simply because Talon was here. In front of her. His hands large and warm, comforting on her shoulders. Did he know he made her feel less alone? She could see his sincerity. Talon really *did* care about her.

Finally, she surrendered. As soon as her cheek brushed the rough weave of his chambray shirt, she closed her eyes. His arms came around her, warm, comforting and strong, but not hurting. She felt him rest his chin gently against her head. This was exactly what she needed, she realized, her arms automatically sliding around his narrow waist. And then the hot tears spilled out of her eyes. Cat pressed her face into his chest, feeling the strength of his muscles beneath the fabric, felt them tense. The moment he slid his fingers through her hair, it broke her, because the gesture was one of him comforting her, not taking something away from her.

Talon tried to prepare himself for Cat's sobs. She

clung to him as if she was in an emotional free fall, needing him as an anchor. Her face was pressed against his chest, the sounds tearing out of her ripping him up. He had absolutely no way to shield himself from Cat's weeping. Talon's mouth tightened, and he held her tightly, feeling her entire body shake with each deep, clawing sob. The sounds were filled with so much anguish that he cursed to himself. And yet, a new tenderness unfolded and flowed through Talon toward her. This wasn't about sex. About wanting her in his bed, he discovered. It was about protecting Cat, supporting her when she was hurting. All of this was new to Talon. He knew that he'd move heaven and hell not to ever hear her sob like this again.

Finally, the sobs lessened. Cat leaned heavily against Talon and he could feel her knees weakening as he took more of her weight. "Come on," he whispered roughly against her ear. "Let's sit you down."

Talon guided her over to the couch. He chose a corner and eased her down beside him. She clung to him, sniffing and hiccuping, her hand pressed against her face, as if ashamed she'd cried in front of him. Talon knew that one. Men never cried in front of anyone, either. Maybe out of embarrassment that someone would call them weak. As Cat nestled against him, Talon steeled himself. She was all curves against his angles, but she fit against him perfectly in every way. He felt his body harden, respond swiftly to the way she rested against him. Her breasts were pressed to the wall of his chest, her long, spare hand resting there, his skin smarting, tightening beneath her fingers. Jesus, did she realize what she was doing to him? No. Talon closed his eyes and slowly dragged in a breath, struggling to control his sexual reaction to Cat. She was seeking a safe harbor, not sex. Talon wanted her so badly. He was dying to feel her soft mouth beneath his. Trapped within so many emotions, her tears shattering him in ways he'd never had to deal with before, Talon gritted his teeth. He could feel the dampness of her spent tears on his shirt, his skin moist beneath the fabric. Tears of pain. He was so screwed.

Sliding his fingers through her hair was a secret pleasure that made him throb. Talon hoped like hell Cat didn't nestle closer, because she'd become very aware of his erection very quickly. Her hair tickled his jaw and chin. The scent of cinnamon. It reminded Talon of his mother's kitchen as she baked an apple pie. He couldn't help himself, finding deep enjoyment in his fingers as they moved across those silky ebony strands.

Cat began to relax against him with each gentle stroke, as if he were taming a skittish, wild horse with his touch. A sudden realization humbled him. Cat *trusted* him. He kept up his light ministrations, his fingers brushing her shoulders and upper back.

And then he did the unthinkable, driven by his need to heal her from whatever she'd just experienced. Talon pressed a light kiss on her hair, inhaling her scent. It drove him mad to kiss her again, this time, along her hairline. He wasn't thinking. He was reacting emotionally, wanting to protect Cat, ease her pain. Sliding his hand beneath her jaw, he eased her chin upward until his mouth curved tentatively against her lips. He was lost. Driven. The sweetness of her lips, their natural lushness, overwhelmed his mind and Talon was hungry, wanting Cat in every way. He tasted the salt of her tears on her lips and it did something to his heart. Something good and clean, and then he was lost. So lost.

Cat closed her eyes as Talon slid his mouth lightly across her lips in invitation. It seemed so right that she didn't freeze or try to pull away. Talon's male scent filled her, driving her to increase the pressure of her mouth against his. She'd wanted to kiss this man from the second she saw him. She heard him groan, his large, callused hand sliding against her jaw, holding her in place, his mouth deepening their unexpected but, oh, so wonderful kiss. Heat unraveled within her like a lava flow suddenly springing to life from deep within. As his mouth touched her, worshipping her lips, Cat quivered inwardly. This man knew how to kiss. Her body erupted with fire, need and hunger. Dampness suddenly gathered slickly between her thighs. His mouth was coaxing, asking her to meet him halfway, to dance fearlessly, to take and give.

Her world stopped spinning as she slid her hand up across his chest, fingers caressing his thick, corded neck. Cat inhaled his unique male fragrance, part sweat, part fresh evergreen and the rest cold Wyoming air. She'd never been kissed like this, the man *asking* her to participate, not just taking from her. His tongue moved skillfully with hers, creating electric jolts inside, tightening her breasts, making her nipples hard and needy. Her mind unraveled beneath his moist breath flowing across her nose and cheek, the roughness of his hand against her skin eliciting even more erotic sensations. Talon's scalding kiss erased her grief. She found herself feeling her body as never before, as if he were awakening it with just his slow, deep exploration of her lips, her mouth. A gnawing ache built rapidly between her legs. Cat pressed her hips against his, and when her hip met the hardness of his erection, it didn't scare her. Just the opposite.

Talon dragged his mouth from hers, breathing unevenly. He opened his eyes, staring down into hers. God, she was just as hungry as he was. His brain wasn't working, his body hard, painful and aching for her. He had to get a grip. Her face was flushed, and her eyes glistening with arousal damn near dissolved his control. Without thinking, he grazed her cheek, his thumb moving across that pouty lower lip of hers.

"I—" His voice was rough. "I didn't mean to kiss you, Cat. I'm sorry." Friends didn't kiss. Wasn't that the argument he'd pitched to her a couple days ago because she was afraid of intimacy with a man? Afraid of men, period?

Cat laid her head on his shoulder. "I'm not sorry," she whispered unsteadily. Because she needed exactly what Talon had given. Right now, all she could do was feel her lower body behaving as if fireworks were going off within her. Talon's kiss had opened up a treasure chest of sensations she'd never, ever experienced with any man. And she felt safe.

"Neither am I," he admitted thickly.

"It's okay," Cat managed, her voice wispy. All she wanted was for this moment to never end. Talon was so tall, strong and caring. She felt weak. At least, emotionally. And he'd unerringly realized what would heal her. Even now, her mouth tingled in memory of his branding kiss. Cat had never experienced this kind of heat. *Until now.* Cat worried that maybe her body was different. Because of her childhood. Her fear of men. But her friends had reassured her that she was all woman and that the right man would make her feel exactly as she was feeling right now in Talon's arms.

Talon relaxed against the corner of the couch, gratefully absorbing Cat against him. He couldn't stop touching her, feeling the silky strength of her hair sliding across his fingers, her hand soft against his chest, her palm over his thudding heart. She remained relaxed against him and he breathed a deep sigh of relief. His kiss hadn't destroyed the new trust that was silently strung between them. His mind told him he shouldn't have kissed her at all, but dammit, he had lived too long on his instincts. Kissing Cat was the most right thing in the world for her in that moment. He wanted to ease her tears, absorb her anguish.

He didn't know how long they lay in each other's arms, time dissolving into only awareness of Cat's softened breathing, the rise and fall of her breasts against his chest, her arm around his waist, content. Hell, he was equally content. For the first time in Talon's life, he hadn't made a move to get a woman into his bed. For whatever reasons, Cat was bringing out another side of him as a man. Contentment wasn't something he'd necessarily equate with bed, woman and sex. Right now, it felt wonderful. And it was all Cat, he realized. Whatever magic resided from the moment he'd opened his eyes and seen her looking down at him with that caring blue gaze of hers, it had triggered openings into his heart that he'd never realized existed. Until now. Right now.

Did he want to love Cat? *Hell yes.* But was it the right thing for her? Funny, Talon mused, that he was even considering what she needed versus his needs. Before, women had been plentiful at the Coronado base. He never wanted for female companionship. All he had to do was walk into one of the SEAL bars on Coronado Island, and there they were, eyeing him, telling him they wanted him in bed. It had been that easy.

So what had changed? Maybe he had. Since the capture and torture. Hayden dying. Grief scored Talon as he thought of his best friend. And just as quickly, the warmth of the woman in his arms eased that anguish. Just her soft breath across his chest soothed his grief. Just her trust. Talon swallowed hard, caught up in such a foreign feeling. Cat brought out all of his protectiveness. All his need to care for her, make her happy, see her smile. He ached to see her lustrous blue eyes shining with joy. He *wanted* to make Cat happy. She came first in his life, not second.

Cat stirred. She reluctantly eased from Talon's arms and sat up, wiping the dampness from her cheeks. The silence weighed between them as she looked at Talon, really looked at him. His eyes were clear and he wasn't hiding how he felt. At all. Her pulse quickened because she sensed his powerful protection and care and that, yes, he wanted her. No question. To her surprise, Cat wanted him just as much. Talon lifted his hand and moved it along her shoulders, a gesture of caring. Not sex.

"How are you doing?" His voice was thick with emotions he still didn't understand. A bolt of need went through him as she watched him. He knew in that instant he could take Cat to bed, love her, make her feel incredible pleasure. He could give her that gift. And God help him, he'd never wanted to pleasure a woman more than Cat. Her innocence felled him. Made him breathless.

"Better," Cat admitted softly. "You're good medicine for me, Talon." She reached out shyly, her fingertips barely grazing his sandpapery cheek. He'd shaved this morning, but his beard had grown enough to emphasize the hard lines of his face. It made him dangerous looking. Exciting. Frightening. Her body, however, was completely trusting of Talon, his mouth taking her lips with heat and promise, his touch upon her making her flesh contract and skitter with fire.

"Do you want to talk about it?" he asked her, tucking a few strands behind her ear. Talon couldn't…didn't… want to keep his hands off Cat. She was okay with his contact and, God knew, he wanted to touch her.

Everywhere.

Cat sat back, folding her hands in her lap. She stared down at them. "I'm just not used to talking about stuff."

He grunted. "Yeah, I know that one."

She eyed him coyly. "We're a lot alike."

Talon nodded, moving his fingers across her shoulders. "Like Miss Gus would probably say—two peas from the same pod."

Cat chuckled, nervously knitting her fingers. "I've never cried in front of anyone until now."

His heart turned to mush. Powerful, aching new emotions flooded Talon as he held her unsure gaze, her eyes moist. "I don't cry in front of anyone, either, if it makes you feel better."

"You want the truth?"

Talon's hand stilled on her shoulder, and his voice dropped with emotion. "I always want to know what you're thinking, Cat." He saw a flush move across her cheeks and she tucked her lower lip between her teeth for a moment. Heat soared through his lower body. He'd kissed that lush mouth of hers, tasted her inner sweetness, felt her shy, hot response.

Cat forced herself to look at Talon because he deserved her courage, not her fear. "It felt good to be held by you... I felt safe." And wonderfully kissed, but she couldn't go there. At least, not yet. For Cat to even admit this was monumental.

Talon lifted his arm away from her shoulders, sat up and turned toward her. He framed her face with his hands. "Babe, you deserve to be held, to be protected." His voice grew husky. "There's something good between us. And I want to explore it with you, Cat. At your pace. What feels right for you." *Because I need you. I need to crawl into your arms and be held when I have a bad nightmare. I know you can heal me. I know that in the depths of my miserable, fractured soul.*

Talon stared hard at her, saw the shock register in her Cat's glistening eyes. At the same time, felt her warm, damp fingers curve around his forearms.

"That's more than being friends," she managed in a choked voice.

"Yeah, I know it. Are you game?"

The words leaped of her mouth before Cat could even think. "I need time...."

CHAPTER ELEVEN

TALON KNEW HE had to be patient but couldn't help feeling some disappointment over Cat's response. She was going to think about them. He didn't want to scare her off.

Cat stood up, pacing the bedroom, turmoil in her eyes. He sat there forcing himself to understand that they had just kissed. Already, they were more than friends. And she'd kissed him back. That would definitely confuse her.

"Can you tell me what happened out there today?" he asked.

Cat turned and studied Talon. He seemed at peace with the fact that they'd kissed. Her whole body still felt hot and hungry. His gaze never left hers. He leaned forward, clasping his hands between his opened thighs. How could he look so calm, cool and collected after that life-altering kiss? She felt anything but! Licking her lower lip, Cat swore she could taste Talon on her mouth.

"It was a bad rollover accident out on the main highway," she muttered. "I have a real soft spot for children." Her voice dropped to an aching whisper. "The husband was driving drunk. The wife was holding her two-year-old in the front seat when he drove off on the berm and the car flipped. None of them were wearing a seat belt. By the time we arrived, the mother was dead, the child dying."

She went to sit on the other end of the couch. Cat rested her elbows on her thighs, hands clasped. As she leaned forward, her black hair partially hid her profile from him, but there was no mistaking how she felt.

"I was the first paramedic on the scene with my guys. The child died in my arms." Cat's mouth quirked, her voice dropping with anguish. "Such a waste of a young life…"

The silence turned up in volume in the room. Talon pushed his hands slowly down his thighs as he straightened. "I'm sorry," he said, seeing the tension in her.

"We were all upset. It wasn't just me. Most of the guys at the fire department are married and they have kids of their own." She pushed her fingers through her hair and sat up, looking up at the ceiling. "It's just so tough on some days…."

Talon sat back, observing Cat. "How did the guys react?"

"Well, they certainly didn't cry. They just jammed the pain deep down inside themselves. They're fooling themselves, though. You can't keep that kind of horror and trauma quiet within you forever."

Talon winced, thinking about Hayden. His torture. His death, and Talon surviving the horror. "Maybe some of that stuff needs to never see the light of day," Talon countered.

Cat lifted her chin and studied Talon. There was darkness in his eyes, a terror banked in them she'd not seen before. What was he hiding? Clearly, he was carrying trauma. "That's why I cry." She added wearily, "I go somewhere and hide and cry. I don't do it front of others. But at least I know how important it is to discharge the awful stuff I see on days like this. I don't want to carry that emotional crap inside me."

Talon wondered if she'd cried as a little girl after her father abused her. Or had she run off to a closet or outside where no one could hear her sobbing the way she'd just cried in his arms? His heart contracted with pain for her. There were so many times when he felt how alone Cat was. Now Talon was beginning to understand why he was feeling it around her. No mother. A mean father. Running and hiding from him, from the pain he'd given her. He gentled his voice and said, "I'm glad you trusted me enough to hold you while you got it out of your system."

Cat watched him with sudden serenity. "You're the first." Though she wanted to tell him how grateful she was, Cat was still flustered over their kiss.

The expression on his face was pure caring. "I'm here for you, Cat. Anytime you want to be held, I'm more than happy to do it." And so much more, but Talon realized he had a long road to walk with Cat. She wasn't like all the other women in the past who had orbited his structure. If anything, she was already rethinking their kiss, her crying in his arms. He wanted to say so much more but held off.

Cat got up, unable to remain still any longer. Talon's voice was like him skimming his hand across her skin. It felt good. Wonderful, even. And she could see the sincerity burning in his thoughtful gray eyes. "All I did was get your shirt wet."

Talon stood up and gave her a faint smile. "It's okay." He touched the dark splotch where she'd cried on his chambray shirt. "You're worth it."

She stood by the window, tense. "I just need some time alone, Talon. I hope you understand? Thank Val for the food, but I'm really not hungry. Maybe later."

TALON COULDN'T SLEEP. The clock on the dresser read 2:00 a.m. Cat was on the other side of the door. He ached to walk in there and be with her, the kiss still lingering hotly in his mind, heart and body. Finally, he said to hell with it and quietly got up and went out to the kitchen for a glass of water.

Cat started when Talon walked into the kitchen. Zeke was at his side. She gave a little gasp, her hand flying to her chest. "God, you scared the hell out of me!"

Talon stood there looking at her dressed in a pair of lavender-flowered flannel pajama bottoms and a loose, long-sleeved lavender tee. Her hair was mussed and she still had remnants of a sleepy look on her face despite the fact that he'd just scared the hell out of her. Cat was at the stove stirring something in a pan.

"Sorry," Talon muttered. "Couldn't sleep, either?" He walked into the warm kitchen and went to the cabinet and found a glass.

"I was hungry," she admitted. Cat felt her heart pounding in her chest. She frowned and tried not to be swayed by the fact he wore only a pair of light blue pajama bottoms, his upper body naked. The man was terribly good-looking. And Cat could see his ribs were not as pronounced as the morning she'd discovered him on the highway. Talon had a wide, clean set of shoulders, the muscles thick and tight, his chest dusted with dark hair. Just the way he moved, Cat knew he was in good shape. Once again, she noticed the scarring on his back as he turned and took the glass of water to the table and sat down.

Zeke came over to her, his wet, cold nose pushing against her thigh in greeting. She smiled at the dog and petted him. Zeke then went over to his master and sat next to his chair, watching her.

The kitchen was silent and warm. Talon wished he'd put on a T-shirt or something. He didn't want Cat seeing the scars on his back, although he was sure she knew they were there, anyway. He just didn't want her asking about them just yet.

Sipping the water, he absorbed her tall, lithe figure at the stove. There was something vulnerable about Cat in her flowery flannel pj's. He smiled a little, feeling his body stir to life. She looked so young, not the serious paramedic he knew she was. Talon forced himself to stop remembering Cat in his arms. And that hot, hungry kiss they'd shared. The woman was certifiably sexy and sensual. She just didn't know it.

"Hungry? What are you making?" he asked.

"Hot chocolate." Cat smiled at him. "It cures everything. Didn't you know?"

He grinned, moving the glass between his hands on the table. "So you say."

"Well," she said archly, "if you drink a cup before you go to bed, don't you sleep better?"

"So far, that's true." Gus had needled him into drinking some every night before bedtime. Tonight, he'd forgotten.

"Did you have a cup tonight before you went to bed?"

"No."

"See?"

Talon wasn't about to tell her their kiss had kept him

tossing and turning all night. He watched as Cat poured the mixture into her favorite mug. She had the bag of marshmallows on the counter and was dropping lots of them into the cup.

Zeke whined, his tail thumping as he eagerly watched Cat with the marshmallows.

"You know you're spoiling him?" Talon drawled. *Like you're spoiling me.*

Cat grinned once again, brought over her mug and sat down at his elbow. Zeke's large brown eyes were zeroed in on her. He got up and walked around the chair between them, his large black ears up and his face in begging mode. "One marshmallow? Come on, Talon, you can't be that mean to your best friend, can you?" Cat picked one of her marshmallows out of her cup and made sure it wouldn't burn Zeke's tongue before she offered it to the dog.

With his long black muzzle, Zeke delicately took the small marshmallow from between her fingers.

Talon watched his combat dog chew enthusiastically on the tiny marshmallow, an unwilling grin tugging at the corners of Talon's mouth. Zeke licked his chops, his long pink tongue relishing the sides of his muzzle.

"Traitor," he told his dog.

Cat chuckled and held the mug between her hands, slowly sipping the steaming chocolate. Talon seemed much more relaxed, and her heart beat a little harder in her chest. The only light in the kitchen was coming from over the sink area, throwing deep shadows across the area. It made his face look even more lethal. She wondered what he was like in combat and decided she would never want to run into Talon if she were an enemy. It was the glint in his shadowed gray eyes that made her realize Talon's constant alertness.

"Are you feeling better?" he asked, holding her softened gaze.

Cat set down the mug. She licked her lips and felt some of the foam on the corner of her mouth, wiping it away with her fingers. "Better," she said. "I couldn't sleep. Kept seeing the accident." She shrugged. "Just another way to work out the trauma."

"Crying some more?" He gripped the glass a little tighter between his large hands.

"That, too. It takes me days to get over something like this."

"Does it happen often in your line of work?"

"Thank God, no." Cat gave him a wry look. "You know how much of a softy I am. If my paramedic work was nothing but auto accidents like this type, I couldn't stay in the career. I…just can't take the emotional hits. Other paramedics get distance on it, but I never could."

"You're human. You have feelings," Talon said.

She slid him a glance. "How did you survive what you did in the SEALs? Val said the kind of work you guys do is all about trauma."

"We're trained for it," Talon replied gruffly, looking down at the glass.

Snorting softly, Cat sipped her hot chocolate. "Well, I'm trained, too, but some days are worse than others."

He shrugged. "I can't talk about it, anyway. It's all top secret."

Cat said nothing, enjoying the rich taste of the warm chocolate. Zeke whined and thumped his tail. The dog gave her a pleading look, begging for a second marshmallow.

She grinned down at him. "You are a real heart stealer. You know that, Zeke?"

"He doesn't need another one," Talon said.

"Meanie."

Zeke whined, as if understanding English, and gave Talon a look that spoke volumes.

Talon shook his head. "Sugar is bad for you, big guy."

Zeke glanced over at Cat. His tail thumped harder and he whined.

"He's got your number," Talon warned her, smiling a little.

Cat reached out, petting Zeke's broad brown-and-black head. "Sorry, Zeke. Your master says no. But you are so beautiful." *Like his owner.* Talon would probably not like to be described with that word, but he was a gorgeous male specimen. Cat had to stop herself from staring at him. The man could set her on fire with just a look. Or a kiss. "Do you think Jordana will deem you fit for duty tomorrow?" she asked, sliding her hand around her mug.

"I hope so," Talon said. "My coughing is gone and I feel strong. Felt good to really work hard yesterday."

Cat saw some concern deep in Talon's eyes. "You can go see Sandy, then."

Talon's gut clenched. He was looking forward to seeing his mother. But he also dreaded it because it meant he had to face the fact she was probably dying. "Yeah," he said, scowling, not wanting to look into her eyes. Cat was just as highly intuitive as he was. She felt a lot but said little about it to anyone. She was a paramedic. He was a warrior. They both lived in dangerous worlds where bad things happened all around them. The huskiness in her voice just brought up a lot of old grief, as if she understood that his journey with his mother from here on out would be bittersweet at best.

"I saw her yesterday," Cat said, regarding him warmly. "I dropped over at noon and read to her on my lunch hour. She was counting the hours until Jordana declares your health good enough for you to visit her. I haven't seen her this happy or hopeful in a long time."

Talon nodded, his lips compressed.

Cat sensed his trepidation. "Sandy said you lost your father when you were ten. I imagine this brings up a lot of bad memories for you."

"Yes and no. When you're ten years old and your father is suddenly not there in the blink of an eye, it's shocking. Hard to take. Hard to understand." At least his father didn't suffer and for that, Talon was grateful. A quick, fast death was better than a slow one in his world.

Without thinking, Cat reached out, laying her fingers across his lower arm. Instantly, his flesh tightened and she felt the muscles leap beneath them. Touch had such healing power. "Listen, you're going to need some help. I'm here for you, Talon. Your mom and I are close and maybe I can help fill in the blanks for you in the years you weren't here while she was sick."

Talon wanted to pick up her hand, kiss it, draw Cat into his arms, but he quickly squashed all those thoughts. The look in her eyes was one of sympathy. Not lust. "Thanks," he rasped. "There's a lot I don't know. It was tough getting leave to come and visit her. My life in black ops pretty much keeps me either in training or deployment overseas." He called at least every couple of weeks when he was stateside.

Overseas, he managed a few emails to her, but that was all. And trying to get leave was next to impossible for him. Talon had wanted to visit his mother, but because he was single, the married SEALs got first dibs on leave while training. He didn't like it, but there was nothing he could do about it. Hayden had been in a similar situation and they would bitch to one another about the unfairness of it all. He said they should get married to get leave, but Talon wanted nothing to do with that idea.

Cat heard the sadness in his voice, saw guilt in his expression. He had not been there when Sandy needed him the most. "Well," she soothed, "maybe with the way things have worked out, you'll be here for her now. That's all she needs at this moment."

When she removed her hand, Talon missed her touch. "Yeah, that's what I was thinking the other day."

Cat frowned. Nervously, she said, "This is probably none of my business, but have you ever dealt with dying and death? I don't know that much about black ops or the SEALs." She was worried he might not understand the journey that dying often took with a person who had a slow-moving disease.

His eyebrows drew down. "Yeah, I'm just a little familiar with death and dying, Cat."

She winced inwardly over the harsh sound in his voice. His eyes had gone flat and hard. And just as quickly, he looked away. The sense of insurmountable grief around Talon bludgeoned her like an invisible sledgehammer. Reeling from the sensation, she sat back, trying to absorb the anguish and grief she suddenly felt around him. The warning look he gave her told her to not ask one word about it. Not one.

"Sorry," he said gruffly, finishing off his glass of water and standing up. More than anything, Cat understood the loss of both parents at an early age. And God knew, he *wanted* to hide in her arms, her body and find solace from the unremitting pain from the past overlaying the present. Hell, he hadn't even begun to work through the loss of Hayden and now, his mother dying was weighing on him even more. He felt as if his shoulders were weighted with Abrams tanks. Rubbing his bearded jaw, he put the glass on the counter.

"See you tomorrow morning," he said abruptly, leaving the kitchen. Zeke followed him.

"Good night...."

The kitchen fell silent. The larger-than-life energy of Talon left the kitchen. Cat missed him. She knew he was upset. How badly she'd wanted to get up, stand behind his chair and wrap her arms around his shoulders and just hold him. He had looked so desolate and lost during their conversation about Sandy. She felt it. Something terrible had happened to Talon and it hadn't been that long ago. All she had to do was see the freshness of the vertical scars across his back and she knew he was carrying a horrific load of trauma within him. Would Talon reach out to her in moments of need or not? Cat wasn't sure. But she wasn't going to be put off by his snarling warnings, either. She could help Talon get through this. If he'd let her.

TALON GIRDED HIMSELF emotionally as he knocked lightly on his mother's apartment door. Jordana had given him approval to see her, his pneumonia completely gone. Val had told him to take the rest of the day off for this visit. He was grateful to the McPhersons. As a wrangler, they could have insisted he work his eight hours today instead of visiting his mother.

Talon knew from talking with Cat that the door to her apartment was locked, but there was always a key beneath the doormat, which he had in hand. He heard his mother's voice through the door and, with trembling hands, he unlocked and opened it. The apartment building was three stories high and worn looking. He knew living in Jackson Hole was tough for people like his mother, which was why most of his paycheck had gone to her. Talon didn't begrudge his mother at all. She'd grown up on a ranch just outside of town. All her friends and support group were here.

Talon wasn't prepared to see his mother in a wheelchair. Tears slammed into Talon's eyes as he closed the door and turned to see her sitting in the living room in such a weakened state. His mother had been a strong, vibrant ranching woman when he was growing up. She was about five foot eight inches tall and sturdy. Talon could recall her during branding season easily hefting young calves off the ground and turning them on their backs. Those calves weighed a goodly amount and Sandy had no trouble with them. She had always been the strength and core of their family in every way.

Until now.

Ruthlessly, Talon shoved his tears back. He forced a smile he didn't feel, trying to deal with the shock over her gaunt condition, her skin sallow looking, and the scarf wrapped around her head, her hair gone.

"Hey, Mom," he murmured, coming over to her.

"Tal!" Sandy cried, pushing herself out of the wheelchair. She stood uncertainly, her arms open to her son. "Thank God, you're home!" She swept her thin arms around his broad shoulders, holding him with all her strength.

Talon held his mother as if she were a fragile, breakable egg. She buried her face against his shoulder and sobbed. Closing his eyes tightly, fighting not to cry with her, Talon held her. God, tears from two women he cared deeply about in less than twenty-four hours. Talon wasn't sure he could handle the excessive emotions. He awkwardly patted her gently on the back. He could feel how bony her spine and ribs felt beneath his fingers. It tore him up. Tears squeezed out of his eyes.

Finally, Sandy released him, patting him weakly on his shoulder. She smiled brokenly up into her son's hard face. Seeing the tears in his gray eyes, she slid her hand against his cheek. "You look so good, Tal. I'm glad you're here. Thank you… I love you so much."

Talon nodded, his throat tight, a lump growing larger by the second. "I love you, too, Mom. Come on, you need to sit down." He guided her to the wheelchair. Once she was sitting, he picked up the edges of her blue robe and drew them across the white flannel nightgown she wore. He tried to keep the shock out of his face over her deteriorated condition.

"Sit down," she whispered, her long, graceful hand pointing to the couch next to her wheelchair. "Can I get you anything to drink? Have you eaten lunch yet?"

Talon smiled and sat down. He put his hand over hers. "I'm fine. Have you eaten?"

"Yes, Gwen Garner just brought over lunch." She motioned toward the small table near the kitchen. Wrinkling her nose, she added, "I'm just not hungry, Talon. I'm so appreciative of what everyone does… The chemo kills your appetite."

He looked into her cloudy hazel eyes. "You need to eat, Mom. If I bring it over, will you try?" He had to get some weight on her. She was literally skin and bones. Talon was blown away by how gaunt his mother had become. "No," Sandy murmured, giving him a sad look. "If I eat, I throw it up later. I just don't want to go there."

A sense of helplessness clawed at him. He was a SEAL. He was used to fixing things. Making them right. "How about some water? Are you drinking enough?"

She smiled weakly. "Cat is always on me about not drinking enough water."

His heart broke in half as he realized that his mother had given up. Shock and grief rolled through him, smothering him, making him feel as if he couldn't draw a breath into his body. "Cat's right."

"Isn't she something?" Sandy said, staring at her son.

Talon nodded. "She's a decent person, Mom. Does right by others."

Sighing, Sandy squeezed her son's hand. "You know, I often wondered, if you ever came home and met her, whether you two wouldn't like one another."

"She's a good person, Mom."

"Do you like her?" she asked.

He smiled, seeing the anxious look in her eyes. "Yeah, I do." His mother's face radiated with happiness and he found he'd do anything to see the light come to her eyes.

"Oh, good," Sandy murmured. "I was telling Gwen Garner that I thought you two would make a wonderful couple. Cat is so beautiful." And then she reached over, patting Talon's cheek. "And you are drop-dead handsome, Talon. You look like your father. You're so handsome and strong."

He felt himself blush beneath his mother's sudden

enthusiasm and joy. "Listen," he told her in a thickened tone, holding her gaze. "My only priority is you right now. Okay? Everything else in my life comes second."

Tears sprang to Sandy's eyes. She pressed her other hand across her eyes. "I'm so sorry it's come to this, Talon."

Wrestling with his grief of losing her sometime in the future, Talon squeezed her hand. "Listen to me," he insisted, getting her to look at him. "I love you. I'm not leaving you, Mom. We'll take this walk together, wherever it leads us. I'm in for the long haul." *Because I couldn't be with you the first time you got this damned cancer.* Talon felt terrible he couldn't be here for when she went through radiation and chemotherapy before. Now life had seen fit to give him a second chance.

Sniffing, Sandy released Talon's hand and dug into the pocket of her robe for a tissue. "You always say and do the right thing, Talon. I never doubted for a moment you wouldn't be here at some point." She wiped her eyes and nose. "How are *you* doing? You spent six months in rehab."

Talon kept his face carefully arranged. His mother was not going to know one damn thing about what had happened or why he was in the hospital. "I'm fine now," he assured her. "Let's not talk about me. Let's talk about you."

CHAPTER TWELVE

CAT WAS IN the darkened living room, a cup of hot chocolate in her hands. It had been good to hear that Talon had visited with his mother. She heard a door quietly open and close down the hall. It was one-thirty in the morning and she couldn't sleep. She wondered if it was Gus who was up. Sometimes, the elder didn't sleep well at night. And sometimes, Cat would make her a cup of hot chocolate and they'd talk at the kitchen table.

As she looked to her left, she saw Talon appear out of the hall barefoot, heading into the kitchen. The open concept of the kitchen and living room made it easy for her to see him. This time, he was wearing a dark green T-shirt with his pajamas. Her heart took off in an aching beat of need for him. Talon's short hair was mussed and he looked drowsy. There was something vulnerable and appealing to her about him with his large, bare feet.

"Couldn't sleep?" she called softly.

Talon hesitated, rubbing his eyes. He heard Cat's voice from the living room. As he glanced through the grayness from the light at the kitchen sink, he noticed her shadowy figure at one end of the couch. "Yeah, something like that," he said.

"Join me."

"In a minute. Getting a glass of water."

Zeke came and sat down next to Cat, thumping his tail in welcome.

"You know I have marshmallows," she accused him with a grin, reaching out and petting him. "I'm going to have to ask your master if you can have one."

Talon appeared silently and sat down at the other end of the couch, leaning into the corner and stretching out his long legs across it. "Now he's going to think every time I get up to get water you're going to be out here with marshmallows," he accused, his voice thick with sleep. He pushed a few strands off his brow and sipped the water. Cat's profile was clean. His gaze automatically went to that lush mouth of hers. He'd kissed that mouth. And he wanted to taste her again. She'd been so warm and willing in his arms. Would she ever be again?

"What are you doing up?" he demanded.

Cat nestled her back into the corner of the couch, drawing her legs up against her body. "I get nights like this."

"Still chewing on that accident?"

"Yes." Cat felt the raw masculine power around Talon. "You seem at ease." Because that normal tightly sprung tension didn't exist around him right now.

"I am." Because he was near her, but Talon didn't dare say that. Cat looked relaxed, too. And if he could, he ventured to think she might be happy. Happy he was here with her?

"I'm glad Sandy ate today. I've been worried about her. She's been getting so thin...."

"I couldn't believe how gaunt she looked when I saw her," Talon muttered, sipping the water. "Scared the hell out of me."

"I'm sure it was a shock."

"I grew up seeing my mother as young, strong and full of life." His voice fell. "I didn't know how far down she'd gone. I wish...I wish I'd gotten home more often."

Cat could tell how guilty he felt. It showed in the dark set of his face. "I learned a long time ago that you do the best you can. Sandy has never once complained to me about you. She has many wonderful stories about you growing up, so don't feel bad. I know you did the best you could, Talon."

How easy it was to say, he thought. And how hard it was to reconcile her simple truth within him. Few people understood black ops, precisely because it was top secret. His life wasn't really his own. Had he worried about his mother after she got breast cancer? Absolutely. But his job required intense, uninterrupted focus and he couldn't be thinking about her for days or weeks, sometimes months, depending upon the mission. "I like the way you see life."

"I've made so many mistakes," Cat confessed, shaking her head. "That's all we humans do is mess up. And many times, it's not our fault. We all get caught up in things that may or may not be of our own making."

Talon thought about her as a child growing up with an abusive father, her inability to escape, to cry out for help. She had no mother to protect her. "Still, I like your live-and-let-live policy," he teased gently. Because, despite the terror Talon was sure she experienced quite often as a vulnerable child, Cat had grown up to be a good person. He had never seen her abusive toward anyone else, so her father's sins had not rubbed off on her, thank God.

Cat gave him a thoughtful look. "What's the choice? Blame everyone for the mistakes they make?" Cat hitched her shoulder. "We learn from our mistakes." And then she added wryly, "Usually…" She thought about the three men in her life she'd drawn. All abusers. She hadn't learned. Thank God, she had friends around her.

"Mistakes in my business can get you killed," Talon said. "But I do understand what you're saying."

"Not all mistakes cost a person their life."

Talon wondered how much of Cat's life had been destroyed by her father. Did the man ever understand what he'd done to his daughter? How it had shortchanged her? Made her mistrust all men? Talon grew angry because he knew Cat still hadn't separated him out from his father. He'd never touched a woman except to love her, make her feel good. His own father had held his mother in deep, abiding respect. And that had rubbed off on Talon, as well.

"I'll bet you got Sandy to laugh."

"Yeah, we shared a few laughs," Talon admitted, smiling a little, feeling good about it. His mother's eyes had lit up and that was when he'd seen life come back into them.

Cat's hair was softly tangled around her face. Talon watched her continue to softly stroke Zeke's head. His dog was in complete adoration of her, his huge, intelligent brown eyes worshipful.

"What happened that she decided to fight the cancer?" Cat asked.

"I don't know. We talked about her therapy, what the doctors said and what her goals were in regards to it."

"Humph," Cat muttered. "Sandy refused to talk to anyone about it. She'd told Gwen Garner she was stopping the chemo treatments a couple of weeks ago."

"That's changed," he said. Now Talon hoped she wouldn't change her mind.

"You've given her a reason to live," Cat confided softly, catching and holding his gaze. "You're good for her, Talon. I know coming home meant leaving a job you loved, but you're giving her back her life. That's pretty powerful."

"I did like being a SEAL," he admitted quietly.

"The work or the guys you worked with?"

Her insight was startling. Hayden's square face, the cockeyed smile that was always on his mouth, appeared in his mind. Talon's heart ached with grief. He took a deep drink of the water. Wiping his mouth with the back of his hand, he said, "It was both." For whatever reason, Talon almost started telling her about his best friend. Hayden was like the brother he'd never had but had always wanted. He'd been a single child in his family. Hayden filled a void in him, and now that he was dead, Talon knew the emptiness would remain.

Cat regarded him in the silence. "It's very hard to leave a way of life," she whispered. "You gave almost a decade of your life to the SEALs. I don't know what I'd do or how I'd feel if someone told me I could never be a paramedic again. I think I'd feel lost."

He was. Completely. "Yeah, it's tough making the changes." He wanted to share that she was helping him to find himself whether she knew it or not. And he did have focus on his mother. He had his priorities clear, but that didn't mean he didn't miss his friends in Bravo Platoon.

"But you can never go back to the SEALs?"

"No."

"Because of your wounds?"

Talon could feel the tightness of the many scars on his back. "Yeah, because of that." He hoped she wouldn't pursue this. Coming home was something he'd had to do. And while his heart was in seeing his mother and helping her, Talon had felt depressed about everything else. Until Cat appeared unexpectedly in his life.

"Val said she had a rocky landing coming home from the Air Force," Cat mused. "Gus had broken her leg and Val was her only relative. She was forced to take a medical-leave discharge, which she didn't want to do."

"It's not easy," he said.

"She said the first six months was rough." Cat smiled fondly. "But I guess when Gus hired Griff McPherson, he kind of grew on Val in a nice way."

"So that's how they fell in love."

"Yes." Cat sighed and sipped her hot chocolate. "Val and Griff had a rough start, but he was determined to win her love. And he did. I just love when they look at one another at the table. There's such a fierce love shared between them."

"You're a romantic like my mother," Talon said, his voice low but not accusing. Like the fierce emotions he held secretly for Cat. Only he didn't know what to call them. He was afraid to use the word *love* because he'd never really loved a woman. Absently, Talon rubbed his chest, feeling his heart yearning for her, wanting her in every possible way.

"Your mom had two happy marriages. I think that's rare, but I also feel her attitude gave her many years of happiness."

"My mother was lost without my father after he died," Talon said, remembering that terrible time in their lives. "Looking back on that time, it seems like providence that Brad walked into her life nine months after that."

"Did you get along with your stepfather?"

"I did. I missed my father, but Brad worked hard to earn my trust. He treated me like a son and he helped raise me to be what I am today." There was a good feeling in his heart for Brad. It was too bad he died. His mother was diagnosed with breast cancer shortly after his death. Talon often wondered if the shock and loss of the two men she loved had pushed her body toward a disease. It was a sense, nothing else, but Talon had seen some of his SEAL friends lose their loved ones and they were never the same afterward. Another reason never to fall in love. Yet, his mother had successfully negotiated that cliff and met Brad, who had loved her with a passion Talon had seen every day growing up. Brad had worshipped her. And both had felt blessed to have been given a second chance at love.

"You were lucky," Cat said, moving the cup slowly between her hands.

"I know that now," Talon admitted. "At the time I felt Brad's love and his care for my mother. He was a big man with a big heart."

"I wish I'd been so lucky," Cat grumped.

Talon held her gaze. "If I could change anything in the world, I'd have wished you had father like Bradley. He never lifted a hand to me. His voice, yes, but never did he threaten or hit me."

Cat shrugged. "It was a long time ago, Talon."

"Might be, but you're still working your way out of it, Cat."

Chewing on her lower lip, she nodded. "I know."

The pain in those two words scored his heart. "Not

every man was like your father. You know that, don't you?"

"I do. Just on some days, I see my father in all of them. I don't want to, but sometimes, it happens."

"Well," he said, "try not to paint me with that brush?"

She compressed her lips. "No, I won't do that with you."

"Why?"

"Because of our kiss." And she looked straight at him, her chin lifted, confidence in her expression. He smiled slowly, his eyes gleaming with humor. No one kissed like Talon. "I mean," she stumbled, "it felt good and wonderful…"

Even in the grayness he could see a blush staining Cat's cheeks. "I liked it, too," he admitted in a rasp, seeing her eyes flare with surprise and then happiness.

"I'm not very experienced," Cat said, almost in apology.

Talon's heart opened with yearning for Cat. Right now, she looked so damned vulnerable and beautiful to him. His arms ached to hold her. His body was hardening. If he said her kiss was one of the best he'd ever had, it would probably scare her off. Instead, he said, "Experience has nothing to do with the heart."

"Maybe you're right," Cat murmured. "But your priority is your mom. I'm so glad you got her to eat some food."

"I told her I'd already buried one parent and that I didn't want to bury her."

"Well, that's one way to put it. Brutal honesty sometimes shocks the person out of depression."

"Was she depressed?"

"Of course. Very. I tried to get her to take some antidepressants, but your mom hates drugs in general. She said she was fine." Her voice dropped. "But she wasn't. I couldn't convince her otherwise."

"My mother likes alternative medicine. I was raised on herbs, not drugs," Talon said wryly.

"So, that's why she didn't want the chemo?"

He nodded. "Yeah. But I persuaded her differently." Because he wanted his mother around. Wanted to give her a better life than she had now. Granted, as a wrangler he wasn't going to make a lot of money, but Talon wanted her out of that ratty, small apartment. She deserved a helluva lot better.

"I'm glad," Cat said, her voice soft with emotion. "Your mother is a wonderful person, a fighter." *Like you.* She could see the stubbornness in Talon's face, the set of his jaw, the tender look in his eyes when talking about his mother.

"Makes two of us."

"Did she promise to start eating her meals?"

He nodded.

Cat sipped her hot chocolate. Zeke was eyeing her intently. She felt sorry for him but wasn't going to give him a treat unless Talon authorized it.

"How about you?" Talon asked, holding her gaze. "How are you doing?"

A special warmth embraced her, as if Talon were touching her. It made Cat feel loved. Loved? Where did *that* word come from? "Okay."

"Now you sound like a SEAL," he said.

"Oh?" She saw his mouth lift.

"We say we're good even if we've got a broken arm or leg. If we've been shot and are bleeding out."

"So, 'good' in SEAL vernacular means I may be

hurting like hell itself but I'm not going to admit it to anyone?"

His smile grew even wider. "You got it."

She held his dark gray gaze, felt her flesh rifle with pleasure, remembering his hand skimming her shoulders and back. It felt so good. As if in some unspoken way, Talon was claiming her as his woman. Cat finally said, "I couldn't sleep because every time I closed my eyes, I saw the rollover accident."

"Yeah," Talon grunted, "that's what happens in trauma."

"How do you handle it? I struggle all the time." She hitched up one shoulder, her voice low. "I never completely forget anything that's affected me strongly as a paramedic. It loosens its power over me in time, but I never, ever quite forget it. I wish I could."

"You never forget, Cat. If a sound doesn't bring it back to you, a smell will, or…" He scowled.

Cat studied him in the shadowy grayness, seeing anguish come to his face. Talon might be able to hide how he felt, but sometimes, when he was relaxed, she could see his real emotions. "That's pretty tragic, then," she said.

Zeke whined and thumped his tail, a pleading look on his face.

Cat looked at Talon.

"Okay, you can give him one," he muttered, shaking his head. His combat assault dog was becoming too attached to Cat. He didn't blame Zeke. He wanted to be close to her, too. For a moment, Talon wished he was Zeke. The glint in her eyes, the way her luscious mouth curved upward as she picked out one of the marshmallows from her cup, sent heat streaking down through him. God, he was getting hard and there was no place to hide it. Grimacing, Talon stood up and walked toward the kitchen.

"I'll see you tomorrow," he growled.

Zeke mouthed the marshmallow, his eyes shining as he licked his chops afterward.

Cat glanced up toward the kitchen. She wanted Talon to stay. He always made her feel good and protected. "Good night," she called softly, not wanting to wake up Gus. Talon disappeared like a ghost down the hall. Zeke quickly got up and trotted after his master.

Silence cloaked her once again. She ached to be in Talon's arms, to share another kiss with him. His mind and heart were on his mother, where they should be. As for her, she could have feelings for Talon and knew that he had touched her wounded soul. Lifting her chin, she felt a sudden chill move through her. Beau Magee had shown up again at the fire department yesterday. He'd been leaning against her truck, arms across his chest, waiting for her to get off her shift. The bastard had the balls to invite her out to dinner. Shaking her head, Cat wondered what made some men so damned stupid. She'd told him in no uncertain terms she was done with him. But he hung around, ambushing her at times when she never expected it. Why the hell didn't he know the meaning of the word *no?* He had to want something from her; otherwise, why show up now? She didn't even want to dwell on it.

CHAPTER THIRTEEN

TALON SAT AT the dinner table that evening with the family. Cat seemed quieter than usual. He'd dropped over at lunch to be with his mother and make sure she ate everything on her tray. Cat had gotten off her shift at three o'clock, and he'd seen her truck parked at the sheriff's office as he drove a load of hay back to the ranch. Why was she at the sheriff's office? He decided not to bring it up at the dinner table.

The fried chicken Gus had made disappeared quickly. So did the corn slathered with butter, the mashed potatoes and white gravy. Cat got up and helped Val serve a chocolate cake Gus had made earlier in the day.

As they sat around the huge table, Gus, who sat at the end of it, gave Cat a hard look.

"You're awful quiet tonight, Cat. Did you have an upsetting shift?"

Cat roused herself. "No. It was quiet. Took care of a little girl who had skinned her knee when she fell off her bike, but that was about it," she said.

"You didn't eat much."

Cat wanted to cringe and disappear. She forced a smile and picked up her fork. "I'll make up for it by eating your cake."

"Humph." Her gaze moved to Talon. He had washed

up, the sleeves of his shirt rolled up to just below his elbows. "How's Sandy?"

"Good," Talon told her. "She's eating a lot."

"That's important," Val murmured. "How many more rounds of chemo does she have, Talon?"

"Four more weeks, twice a week," he said.

"Is she still weak?" Gus asked.

Talon nodded sadly. "It's worse right now. Most of the time, she uses the wheelchair."

"That will pass," Cat assured him, catching his glance. She could feel the heat radiating off him. It wasn't physical, but she sensed his interest in her. Even if she was avoiding him for the most part. Her heart didn't want to avoid him at all, but her life was a convoluted mess right now. Still, when she met his warm gaze, her whole body went hot and needy. He had a beautiful mouth, chiseled, strong. Cat felt shaky inside and it wasn't from fear. It was from sexual desire for Talon.

After dessert, Cat got up and poured coffee for everyone. She noticed Val seemed animated about something, as if she were bursting with a secret.

"We have an announcement to make," Val told everyone, smiling.

Gus tilted her head, cup in her hands. "Oh? What's going on?"

Griff grinned widely. "Val's pregnant."

Cat gasped, her smile instantaneous.

Gus clapped her hands and gave a whoop of joy.

Val held her husband's hand. "You all know we've been trying for some time. We're three months along now."

Gus cackled and gripped Val's hand. "I'm gonna be a great-grandmother. How about that?"

Cat grinned. "That's so wonderful, Val!" She knew they had wanted children. The look of radiant joy on both their faces said everything.

"Congratulations," Talon murmured, smiling.

"See?" Gus said primly, one eyebrow raised as she looked at all of them. "Good things happen. Dreams *do* come true."

The love in Griff's face for his wife was real. And Val's cheeks were suffused with a rose color. Cat had never seen her so soft, so vulnerable, as right now.

"Wow," Cat murmured. "This calls for a celebration."

"Definitely, we'll be celebrating. But this news also means that Val's not going to be riding or wrangling for a while," Griff said. "She needs to stay here and take good care of herself and our baby."

Cat smiled, loving Griff's sudden protectiveness toward independent Val. "Not to worry, Talon and I can handle the spring start-up around here," she told Val and Griff. Most of it would fall on Talon and Griff, but she was a third hand who would pick up the slack and make a difference. Val was always in the saddle, always out walking the fence line, making sure cattle or moose weren't tearing down their barbed wire.

Val laughed softly and patted Griff's hand on the table. "My riding days are over for now," she agreed.

Gus rubbed her hands, glee in her face. "This is just the best news, Val. I'll make sure you take care of yourself."

Cat had no doubts. Even at eighty-five, Gus was almost as active as they were. She no longer rode a horse, but that didn't stop her from fixing three meals a day, keeping the house clean, doing laundry for all of them, either. Gus wasn't one to retire.

Talon felt Cat's happiness over the announcement. He saw the gleam in her eyes and wondered what she would be like as a mother. Probably a damned good one. And then his mind wandered into forbidden territory. What if she was carrying his child? The thought took him by surprise. He hadn't ever thought about marriage. Or love. Or having a family. *Of all things.* Uncomfortable, he sipped his coffee, listening to the excited chatter between all of them.

His life was in utter turmoil, having turned from being an operator out on the front lines of combat to becoming a wrangler, looking after his mother. Talon wasn't sorry to be home to take care of his mother. The rest of it? He missed his team. He missed his friends, who were closer and thicker than blood. And they'd all spilled blood for one another over time. And yet, he'd met Cat. She filled a hole the size of the U.S. in his heart. Damned if he could figure out all the twists and turns his life was taking.

As Talon sipped his coffee, listened to Cat's enthusiastic and husky voice, he wanted her in the worst damned way. Sure, he was plotting on how to get her back into his arms. Had his kiss done more harm than good? Since the kiss, she had been avoiding him. Talon could feel it even if he didn't have actual proof. And she seemed distracted. His mind turned to the fact her truck had been at the sheriff's department. Why? Maybe, if he got lucky, she might wake up and come out to the living room tonight. Talon had trouble sleeping himself and they seemed to meet more often out there than anywhere else. He'd come to look forward to their talks late in the night when the household was asleep. He needed them. Talon didn't lie to himself. The raw truth was that he needed Cat.

CAT WAS NURSING her hot chocolate, sitting with her legs against her in the corner of the couch when she heard a door quietly open and close down the hall. It was three in the morning. Her heart bounded a little as she saw Talon move silently out of the darkness and wander into the kitchen. Zeke came over and sat next to her, his head tilted, eyes on the prize: the cup she held. He wanted his marshmallow.

Cat said nothing, simply enjoying watching Talon putter around in the kitchen. He wore a black T-shirt that fit him to perfection. His feet were bare beneath his light green pajama bottoms. It made her smile softly because Talon didn't look as powerful in bare feet. She instinctively knew he was aware of her presence in the living room. A warmth flowed through her, sweet and gentle. She looked forward to meeting Talon like this. And he seemed to like it, too, although he had never really said.

Talon wandered into the living room, hot chocolate in hand. He saw Cat's face was shadowed, her eyes watching him as he approached the couch. Her hair was unruly and she had thrown an afghan over her lower body, hiding her legs beneath. The air was a bit chilly. He sat down at the other end of the couch, stretching out his legs.

Zeke thumped his tail.

"Did you give him one?" Talon asked, his voice drowsy.

"No. I was waiting to see what you thought about it."

He snorted softly. "Zeke, you're hopeless," he told his dog.

Zeke thumped his tail and whined, giving Cat a pleading look.

She laughed softly. "Well?"

"Go ahead," Talon groaned.

Zeke eagerly took the marshmallow, making big chewing sounds as he wrestled with it in his mouth.

Cat gave Talon a grin. "Has Zeke always liked sweets?"

"No. As a combat assault dog, his diet was severely limited." But the dog's life, like his own, had taken a 180 degree turn in a new direction. Talon wondered if Zeke wasn't rolling with the changes better than he was.

"His work was dangerous? Like yours?"

"Always." Talon sipped his hot chocolate, not wanting the spotlight on himself. He felt compelled to change the subject. "I was driving back to the ranch yesterday afternoon and saw your truck at the sheriff's office."

Cat lowered her lashes, paying attention to her cup in her hands. "Oh."

"Is everything all right?" Talon saw her push her fingers through her hair in that nervous gesture. Something was up. He sensed it. And he was worried. Cat's shadowed face became tense. She didn't want to make eye contact.

"Everything's fine," Cat muttered, resting the cup on her drawn-up knees. A niggle of fear went through her because she could see Talon's eyes narrow upon her. She just felt scared because she wanted no one to know what she'd done. She was ashamed she hadn't been able to grapple with the situation earlier, before it started oozing like an infection into her workplace.

"Something's bothering you, Cat." Talon held her unsure gaze, felt terror around her. *Why?* "I care enough to ask." That was the truth.

"It's nothing," she muttered, frowning at him, wanting him to stop asking questions.

The silence thickened between them and Talon sensed she was ready to bolt. He drank his hot chocolate, letting the tension slowly ebb. She was in some kind of trouble. He could sense it like he could sense an awaiting Taliban ambush. Zeke was studying her with his own intelligence. No longer was he friendly and wagging his tail. No, Zeke was alert, watching her closely. He sensed something wrong, too.

Talon cast around for another way to approach her. "How's work going for you?"

"Okay. Busy as usual. Nothing new."

Her clipped, cool answers raised a red flag.

"Did Matt Sinclaire ask you to go over to the sheriff's office for something?" He liked the fire captain. Matt was a quiet man with highly intelligent eyes. Talon had accidentally met him at the Horse Emporium last week. He was picking up a new dog collar for his yellow Lab when he had run into him. Matt had offered his hand to him, welcoming him back to Jackson Hole. Gossip in the small town moved fast, Talon had discovered. They'd talked a few minutes and Cat had come up in the conversation. Matt had praised her as a paramedic and firefighter. Talon wasn't surprised to hear that. Cat was good at anything she set her mind and heart to.

"No."

Talon nodded and decided to stop pushing her, because Cat was going to get up and leave if he didn't stop asking her questions. Tomorrow, he'd go to the sheriff's department and talk to Cade Garner. He liked the deputy sheriff. He was Gwen Garner's son and Talon had discovered she knew more about the town's residents than anyone else. Maybe he should go talk to Gwen first. The idea had legs.

GWEN GARNER SMILED as Talon walked up to the counter where she was cutting fabric for a customer.

"Talon Holt. This is a pleasure."

Talon removed his black baseball cap. "It's good to meet you, Mrs. Garner."

"Call me Gwen. Hate being called Mrs. Garner." She smiled, quickly folding up the fabric. She wrote down the price on a ticket and handed it over to the woman customer who then left. Gwen said, "And you're here why? I don't think you're a quilter, are you?"

"No, ma'am, I'm not," Talon said with a slight smile.

"Come with me," she said, crooking her finger and then heading off to a quieter part of the busy quilting store.

Talon followed her, cap in hand. He'd heard about Gwen's reputation as being the go-to gal for legitimate information, not gossip, about someone or a situation. Her son was a deputy sheriff, but Talon doubted he shared information with her. Still, as he gazed around, there must have been fifteen or twenty women in the large quilt store. And where women gathered, women talked. Maybe Gwen might have some intel on Cat.

"So," Gwen said, moving along a row of fabric and straightening the bolts here and there, "how can I help you, Talon?"

"Well," he began, keeping his voice low, "I just wanted to come by and thank you for all the help you've been giving my mom over the years. I really appreciate everything you've done." And he did.

Gwen nodded. "Sandy is an important part of so many of our lives, Talon. She's a good person and circling the wagons to help her in her time of need is something Westerners do."

Talon held her smiling eyes. Gwen exuded energy and vitality, much like Gus. "I owe you. If there's anything I can do to help you, you just let me know."

"Thank you, Talon. I appreciate your offer." She tilted her head and looked up at him. "Something tells me you're here for a second reason, too."

He had the good grace to blush as he moved the cap between his fingers. "Yes, ma'am, I was wondering if you could help me with Cat Edwin. I've grown to like her a lot and I know there's something bothering her, but she's not talking." He lifted his chin and looked down at Gwen. "Might you know what it is?"

Gwen put her hands on her hips, frowning. "Now, Talon, you know I don't gossip. If someone approaches me with something, then I can say yes or no. Or, maybe give them some facts, not gossip, about it. Do you have something you want to ask me about her?"

Talon thought for a moment before telling her about seeing Cat's car at the sheriff's office. "I'm worried, Gwen. She's hiding something."

"Did you approach her about it?"

"Yes. She refused to talk about it."

Gwen scowled, her hands dropping to her sides. "I don't ordinarily talk about a person's private life, Talon."

"I understand."

"But you *like* her? Is that it?"

"I like her a lot." *But she doesn't trust me....*

"You haven't been here long," she said.

"Not long," Talon agreed. "But I'm staying. My mother needs me and I have a job as a wrangler at the Bar H."

"Yes, I knew that."

So what else did Gwen Garner know? Talon felt as if he were walking through a minefield with the quilter. She was sizing him up. "Is Cat in some kind of legal trouble?" he pressed.

Gwen rubbed her chin, eyeing him. "No, she isn't."

"Look," Talon said, speaking quietly, "I used to be a SEAL. I've lived eight years on my gut hunches and my intuition. It's saved my butt more times than I can count. My sense—" he stressed the word, holding her stare "—is that Cat is in danger of some kind. I tried to ask her last night about it, but she got nervous and refused to say anything. I *care* for her, Gwen. And I'm worried. Is there anything you could say that would help me to help her?"

"Well, your intuition is bang on," Gwen said. "But I'm really torn about saying more, Talon. If you care that much for Cat, you'll find a way to approach her and get the story out of her firsthand."

Standing there, Talon gazed around the store and then looked back at her. "Okay, I'll see what I can do." He settled the baseball cap on his head. "I appreciate your help, Gwen. Thank you."

Just as he turned, Gwen gripped his lower arm. "Listen, Talon, this place isn't the same as when you lived here. There are a lot of dangerous elements out there.

I'm sure you hear gossip over at the Horse Emporium, but you need to be careful. And if I were you, I'd use that SEAL knowledge and sensing ability, because Cat needs some protection. Okay?"

Alarms went off inside Talon as he stared down at the woman. She released his arm and stepped back, frowning. Gwen was worried about Cat. His gut clenched. Just what the hell was Cat into? Or mixed up in? His mouth thinned. "Okay. Thanks...."

CHAPTER FOURTEEN

CAT'S HORSE SUDDENLY looked up, its ears pricked forward. Cat frowned and looked across the saddle, toward the slope of a hill they'd crossed earlier.

The early July morning was warming up fast. There, coming up the hill on his new gray horse, was Talon. Zeke was loping along beside him, tongue hanging out. Her heart picked up in beat. Talon was riding at a long, ground-eating trot up the hill, his face intent. He wore his black baseball cap and a red neckerchief around his strong neck. The chambray shirt outlined his broad shoulders. Cat smiled a little to herself, glad to see him. Of late, they had passed one another, more or less, like ships in the night.

The fire department had changed her shifts for the next three months and she no longer got to sit down with the McPherson family for dinner. Cat missed it and knew her shifts would change in another three months and that she could be back on her old schedule. That way, no group of firefighters was saddled permanently with night duty.

Talon looked at ease on the big gray horse that was half mustang. He knew how to ride and she enjoyed watching them breast the hill. Talon wore heavy chaps just as she did. He smiled a hello at her as he rode up.

"Hey, Miss Gus said you were out riding fence line,"

he said, pulling the gray to a halt. Talon hadn't seen Cat in nearly a week with her new shift schedule. Zeke trotted over and nuzzled Cat's gloved hand in hello. Gazing down into Cat's upturned face, Talon felt his heart swell with silent joy. His lower body reacted just as quickly to her smile. Controlling the reaction, Talon drowned in her warm, returning smile, her eyes shining with happiness.

"I thought Griff was coming out later," Cat said, pulling the tools out of the saddlebag.

Talon dismounted and dropped the reins on his steel-gray gelding. "I told him I'd do it." *Because I want alone time with you.*

Cat felt a skitter of pleasure thread through her heart as he walked around her horse. She tried to sound casual even though she didn't feel that way. "That was nice of you."

Talon pushed up his baseball cap, studying her. "I haven't seen you for a week."

"I got the graveyard shift for the next three months."

"I've missed you at dinner."

Her heart squeezed. "I've missed it, too," she admitted softly. She looked up into his narrowing eyes, saw desire in them. As time had gone on, Talon didn't try to hide how he felt toward her. It was a shift in their relationship. Not that it *was* a relationship, but Cat could not forget their one and only kiss. And damn, she ached to kiss that well-shaped mouth of his even now.

She dropped the pliers into the wet grass, nervous beneath his warm inspection. Talon had placed his hand on the horn of the saddle, too close to her. She could feel the male heat of his body. In fact, she unconsciously inhaled his scent. It was so familiar to her. It always sent licks of fire straight through her body, making her achy and needy for him. Again.

"I'll get them," Talon said, leaning down and picking up the tool.

Stepping away from him, she muttered, "Someone's deliberately cut the fence. Take a look." She was desperate to break the sizzling connection between them. Her heart was thudding in her breast and Cat wondered if he could hear it. SEALs seemed to have the eyes and ears and nose of a wolf. And one time, Talon had jokingly referred to SEALs in general as male alpha wolves. She believed it.

Talon walked over to the curled strands of barbed wire that had been cut. He scowled and checked them out. "What's this all about?" he asked, holding up one strand, the end cleanly sliced off.

Cat stood at the opposite fence post. "Yeah, that's what I want to know." She pointed toward the tire tracks. "These go all the way down to that road along Long Lake on the forest service side."

Dropping the wire, Talon walked over the crest of the hill near the tire tracks. He studied everything and turned back, walking over to where she was prepping the wire to restring them. "You have any ideas about it?"

New wire would have to be attached to one end of the strands and then looped and tightened on the other side of the cut wire to bring it together. He held the first strand so Cat could quickly and expertly wrap the new wire around the old. She was fast and he watched the concentration on her face.

"A year ago," she told him, "there was a Guatemalan drug ring that tried to set up shop here in Jackson Hole," she said. Pointing toward the lake, she said, "A plane carrying cocaine would land on Long Lake twice a week. It kept waking Val up at night because the plane flew directly over the ranch house. She and Griff, who was her wrangler at that time, eventually came down to the lake to check out one of those night flights."

Talon picked up the second strand and held it for Cat to rewrap. "Val was telling me about that the other day," he said. Cat was so close he could smell her unique womanly fragrance. She liked using a soap that had ginger in it. Nostrils flaring, he inhaled it. Her scent made him go hot with longing. Talon wanted to kiss her, take her to his bed, love her. Every night, he had dreams about Cat, and it was a helluva lot better than the nightmares that usually stalked him. Talon saw how some of her black hair, caught up in a ponytail, moved gently in the morning breeze. A number of shorter tendrils softened her temples. There was a sheen of perspiration to her skin as she worked with focus and intensity.

Talon had never ridden fence with Cat before and he could see why Gus had hired her as a wrangler. She damn well knew what she was doing, was strong enough to wrestle with wire and thorough in her patching of the fence.

Frowning, Cat muttered, "I just wonder if that Guatemalan ring is back."

"Did you take photos of the tire treads?" He moved, his shoulder brushing hers as he moved beside her.

Cat felt the quiet strength of Talon beside her. He, too, knew how to fix fence and they worked well together. "Yes, I did. I thought I'd go in early before my shift tonight, drop by and see Cade at the sheriff's office. See what I can find out. Or, at least report it." She grimaced. "Probably some drunk local kids screwing around."

Talon walked over and picked up the lowest piece of cut wire and brought it to her so she could apply the splice. "Tell you what," he said, holding her gaze for a moment, "let me take you to an early dinner at Mo's late this afternoon. I'd like to go in with you and see what Cade has to say."

A frisson of joy moved through Cat. And fear. Her mouth tightened. Did she want to be in Talon's company? *All the time.* Still, she worried she wouldn't be able to control her desire for him. And God knew, he was a man's man in every possible way. He made Magee looked weak in comparison. "This isn't a date, Talon, if I go to dinner with you," she insisted.

He grinned and chuckled. "Okay." Seeing the warning in her eyes, he smiled into them. "Call it whatever makes you comfortable." Talon could feel Cat wanting him, wanting to kiss him. Yeah, he wanted it, too. That invisible connection was sizzling and popping between them right now as they struggled with the barbed-wire repair. Smiling to himself, Talon had the patience of Job when it came to her. Someday, he was going to make Cat his. He sensed she wanted him, but there was just so much fear from the past stopping her.

"I miss our nightly hot chocolate with one another," he told her, his voice gritty.

Cat tried to ignore his effect on her as she put the second splice in place. They were working together like a well-oiled team, their bodies brushing one another as they did so. "I imagine Zeke is longing for his marshmallows." She wasn't about to admit she missed having

Talon so close to her and their conversations. He was eye candy. *Look but don't touch.*

Talon smiled, watching the sheen of perspiration make her skin glow in the morning sun. "Yeah, he is. I'm an ogre. I never give him sweets."

She had her white cowboy shirtsleeves rolled up to just below her elbows. He could see the taut play of muscles in her lower arms. Cat was in top shape. He knew she also worked out at the gym at the fire station to stay strong. Entertaining the thought of those strong arms around him made him grow even harder.

"You're hardly an ogre," Cat muttered, hauling hard against the wire, tightening it. *Anything but.*

Talon picked up the top wire. Cat made swift work of it, and in no time the fence had been repaired. He walked the line, making sure the U-shaped nails were solid in the fence post, running the fingers of his gloved hands over each strand to check them. Often, when wire was torn and ripped, the nails needed to be replaced. But not this time. This time, someone had deliberately driven up here, got out of their vehicle and calmly used a pair of wire cutters to open up the fence line. He wondered who would do this.

Cat was checking the post at the other end, her gaze on the nails for each strand. Talon watched her, absorbed her tall, graceful body. She was voluptuous, her hips shapely, breasts full. The kind of woman Talon saw in the old masters' paintings from the Renaissance. There was a natural softness, beautiful curves that inspired him, made him hard as hell to explore all of her with his hands, lips and body.

Cat lifted her chin, looking over at Talon. She felt the burn of his gaze on her. On her breasts, her belly and hips. For a moment, a skittering desire flamed to life within her lower body. The look on his face was nothing but naked, raw desire. For her. There was no mistake in it and he made no effort to hide it. Mouth quirking, Cat moved toward her horse and put the tools away in the saddlebags, her hands trembling. She hoped he didn't see it.

"I'm going to continue to ride the line," she told him, pulling the straps closed on the saddlebag. Her throat ached with tension. Her heart had galloped off wildly beneath his silent, intense perusal. Groaning inwardly, Cat grabbed the reins on her horse and mounted up.

"Lead on," he said, swinging with sheer male grace into the saddle. Cat decided that the years in the SEALs had given Talon's body tightness, hard muscle and a grace she'd rarely seen in a man until now. He walked silently, like a cougar on the prowl. She never heard him coming or going. Without another thought, she nudged her heels into the flanks of her horse.

A noisy blue jay swooped down in front of them, landing in a tree down in the center of the pasture below them. Talon brought his horse alongside hers, their boots occasionally touching one another as the horses swayed from side to side.

"How are you getting along on the graveyard shift?"

Cat shrugged. "I hate it, but it's just part of twenty-four-hour duty at a fire station." She was on from midnight until eight in the morning.

"Do you get fire calls every night?"

"No, thank God, we don't." She briefly turned and met his gaze. "Most of the time, especially in the summer, we can sleep the night through, which is nice."

"Miss Gus is grumbling that you aren't there for breakfast or dinner."

Cat smiled. "I know. I don't like it either."

"You stay at your condo most of the time." Talon didn't like that at all. He couldn't see her, which was why he'd decided to ask her out to lunch. He'd felt triumphant when she said yes, but far be it for him to call it a date.

"I have to. But I'm out here at the ranch on my days off. Then I can eat lunch with the family."

Nodding, Talon watched as they crested another hill, his eyes always on the fence line. "Everyone misses you." He, more than any of them.

"I know," Cat admitted softly. "They're family to me."

"I miss you, too." Talon made a point of watching for her reaction. She tensed a little, her mouth going tight before relaxing again. "So does Zeke." His dog was his secret weapon to getting to her and Talon knew it. Maybe it wasn't fair, but he was searching for ways to get inside her walls, to get her to relax and accept he was going to be in her life.

"I like Zeke." Cat ignored the rest of his statement, seeing a faint smile play across his lips.

"It's good he's around people, a family," Talon said. They began to ride down the gentle slope of the next grassy hill. The sun felt good on his back, the temperature beginning to climb, taking the chill off the air.

"You said he was a combat assault dog? What does that mean?" Cat found it infinitely safer to talk about Zeke rather than them.

"He was trained to go after the bad guys," Talon said. "I trained with him at Lackland Air Force Base in Texas. SEAL dogs have a specific kind of work they do. When they assigned Zeke to me, we got along in an instant."

"How did you use Zeke?" Cat wondered. She saw Talon's mouth tense.

"If we were on a patrol, often Zeke and I were at point. He could smell or hear the Taliban before we'd ever get close to them. He protected us many times and we avoided being trapped by the enemy as a result."

"Does he bite the enemy?"

"Yes. But he won't do it unless I give him the command. And once he has the guy down, he'll hold him until I can get there. Then I'll give another command and he'll release the guy."

"Isn't that dangerous for Zeke? Couldn't the Taliban see him coming and shoot him?"

Nodding, Talon said, "Zeke always wore a bullet-proof vest. These dogs are highly trained and we don't want to lose them in a firefight."

Cat shook her head. "How much duty has Zeke seen?"

"Three years with me." His voice grew warm. "Zeke is a real hero. He saved my life and the life of my team so many times, I lost count." But he hadn't been able to save Hayden. Talon blamed himself for that.

"Was he ever shot at?"

"Yes."

Cat made a sound and shook her head. "And he's alive."

"He got wounded once," Talon said. "That's why he was released from military service." Zeke had been wounded charging into that house where he and Hayden were held and being tortured. His brave dog hadn't waited for the SEAL team to arrive. Instead, Zeke had burst through a window, shattering the glass, lunging at the man who was torturing him, and took him down. Another Taliban in the room had shot Zeke. By that time, the SEAL team had arrived and shot them. After being cut down, Talon didn't even have the strength to help his brave dog.

Another SEAL had done what he could to patch Zeke up, stop the bleeding and then carried the dog a mile to where they were all picked up by an MH-47 Chinook helo and choppered back to Bagram.

Talon had lost consciousness en route, his last word was his dog's name on his lips. Zeke had been shipped out to Germany, to a military vet hospital at Landstuhl medical center, where he underwent lifesaving surgery. When Talon woke up two days later after extensive surgery himself, he'd found out Zeke was alive but would never work again for the military. Neither would he.

"You're both very brave. Both heroes," Cat told him softly, holding his dark gaze.

Talon said nothing. It wasn't a place he wanted to go, but Cat's observation made him feel good. Better to be a hero than a coward. In his case, he was neither. Zeke, on the other hand, had been awarded a Silver Star for his heroism and it was well deserved and earned. But no one outside the SEAL community of those who had rescued him and Hayden would ever know the particulars. It was top secret. Like his life.

"Do you stay in touch with your friends who are SEALs?"

"I try," Talon admitted, "but they're so damned busy training constantly or being deployed that it's tough to keep up communications."

"It sounds like they were on 24/7/365."

"You could say that."

"That's why Sandy said it was tough for you to find time to get home to visit her."

"Yes," he admitted, his voice heavy. "Now, looking back on it, I wish I'd have pushed back with my master chief and demanded the time off. I just never realized what chemo and radiation did to a person."

Hearing the regret in his voice, Cat reached out, briefly touching his upper arm for a moment. "Sandy understood."

His skin burned beneath her unexpected touch. Talon told himself it was her paramedic side expressing itself. Not the woman wanting to touch her man. How he wished it was reversed. The sympathy in her expression told the real story. "My mother's very quick to forgive someone like me."

Cat laughed quietly. "Well, you *are* her son, after all. She loves you, Talon. Do you think she wouldn't forgive you?"

"I've made a lot of mistakes in my life, Cat." *Ones that will haunt me until the day I die.*

"Like you're the Lone Ranger?" She chuckled and shook her head. "God, I've made so many mistakes, too. I don't see why anyone would like me."

Talon gave her a dark, assessing look. "That doesn't diminish who you are, Cat. You care. You've saved lives." *And I've taken so many lives I've lost count. Big difference between you and me.*

She snorted. "I'm talking personally, Talon." And then, without thinking, she admitted, "I have such lousy taste in men that it's pitiful."

His eyes narrowed. And he saw Cat gulp, suddenly realizing what she'd let slip. "What do you mean?"

She took a deep breath. "I choose guys who don't respect women. I wish I could stop or go back and fix my mistakes."

Talon digested her comment, seeing how uncomfortable she'd become. "What do you mean, lack of respect?"

"I don't want you to think less of me," she blurted. "But the guys in the past were…well…abusive toward me." She saw his eyes instantly harden. She felt his anger. "I mean, I didn't stay with them. The moment they laid a hand on me, I was gone."

His throat tightened and Talon forced his rage into his kill box. Because he wasn't angry with Cat. There was real shame in her eyes. He could hear it when she talked, as if feeling she had to apologize. "Your father abused you," he rasped. "That's all you knew."

She couldn't even look at Talon. "Yeah, that's what Casey Sinclaire said. She's really smart and my best friend. She's seen the guys I chose over the last seven years. Not that there were that many…. And she pointed out the pattern. I didn't even see it but I do now." She rolled her shoulders and forced herself to look over at Talon. "I'm not about to get tangled up with another guy like that ever again."

"We all have a pattern," Talon acknowledged. He kept his tone sympathetic and without incrimination. "If no one showed you growing up that a man was supposed to respect a woman, Cat, you wouldn't know it. You wouldn't realize there are men out there that would respect you."

Talon felt his heart squeeze with pain for her. It made

sense that she was so gun-shy of him. She probably wondered if he was capable of abusing her like the other men. Of course, he would never lay a hand on her in anger. For a moment, Talon felt as if trying to reach Cat, get her trust, was hopeless. But one glance into her tender-looking eyes and Talon was resolved to prove to her a man could love her, not hurt her.

She really didn't know what real love between a man and a woman could be like, Talon realized. And then he gave himself an internal shake. He knew what good sex could be between a man and a woman. He'd studiously avoided love for all the right reasons, being a SEAL. Whatever the feelings he held for Cat, they kept getting stronger every day. Sex was easy. But love? He hadn't a clue. And he didn't want to go there, either. His mother was his priority right now, not his personal life.

The horses walked down into the swale, a lower hill in front of them. Cat knew that on the other side of that hill was the boundary fence line with the Triple H. Once Talon's family ranch. She wondered how he felt about the loss of a ranch that had been in his family for nearly a hundred years. Sandy had had to sell it after she got sick since she wasn't able to keep it up.

"Well," she said more grimly, "Casey helped me see the pattern. That's one mistake I'm never going to make again." Cat felt the resolve. And glancing quickly at Talon, she saw he was upset. Maybe he thought she was dumb for making the same stupid mistakes. There was some shame involved, Cat realized, and she really did care what Talon thought of her. And somehow, this affected her so deeply she didn't even have words to express it.

CHAPTER FIFTEEN

CAT HID HER smile as Talon asked the hostess at Mo's Ice Cream Parlor for the same corner booth they'd sat in before. The place was getting busy with the lunch-time crowd. Cat took her baseball cap off and slid into the booth. They'd left their chaps and gloves back at the Bar H. Miss Gus had come out before they left in the truck and handed them a list of items she needed from the grocery store.

Talon watched as Cat sat down. Her hair was wind-blown and she moved her fingers through the strands to tame them back into place. The waitress handed them the menus and took their drink order.

"Why are you giving me that look?" he asked, picking up the menu.

"Just smiling about you choosing the same booth again. I guess it's your SEAL training coming out again?" Her back was mostly toward the restaurant, but Talon had a clear view of all people coming and going.

Nodding, he said, "Some habits will never die and this is one of them." Heat sheeted down through his body as she smiled. Their serious discussion while rid-ing the fence line earlier had made her tense. Talon wished he knew Casey Sinclaire. She sounded like a good person, someone who knew psychology and who was helping Cat figure her way out of her bleak childhood. He could hardly stand knowing a man had physically hurt Cat. He wanted to kill the bastard.

The waitress came back with their cups of coffee. Talon ordered a half-pound hamburger and Cat ordered a Reuben sandwich. She seemed more relaxed. Getting precious time with her meant a lot to him.

"You're saving money to buy a house?" he asked, wanting to know more about her dreams.

Cat slid her hands around the heavy mug and nodded. "Yes. I'm tired of seeing my money going out on a yearly lease for a condo."

"Is that your dream? Owning a house?"

She nodded. "Yes."

"Where do you think you'll find this house?" Talon knew prices of homes in Jackson Hole were ridiculously high. This place was considered the Palm Desert of the West. Movie stars lived here. So did Fortune 500 CEOs. It was an expensive watering hole for working people.

"I really don't know," she said. "I keep hoping as I build my nest-egg down payment, that some small house on the outskirts will be for sale. People who live here tend to stay here until they die. So, not many houses come on the market."

"They're building a lot of condos west of Jackson Hole, near the Idaho border. What about one of them?"

"I don't want a condo, Talon. I hate them. Well," she amended, "I don't hate them. I'm tired of hearing footsteps above my ceiling all the time. Or loud music drifting in when I'm trying to sleep before a shift."

"You'd like to wake up to a rooster crowing at dawn?" He smiled a little, watching her. The light coming in through the large windows of the restaurant emphasized her high cheekbones and flawless blue eyes.

His gaze automatically dropped to her soft, luscious mouth. Talon gripped the mug a little tighter.

"I'd love that." Cat leaned forward, her voice low and animated. "I really want a place where I can have a couple of hens to lay eggs. Maybe a dog. I love animals but I can't have them at my condo."

"What else would you like if you could afford it all?"

Cat made a face. "Oh, well, if you're talking about my dreams instead of reality?" She laughed. "If I could have anything I wanted, I'd love to have a ranch like the Bar H. I love working outdoors and I'd have some cattle, definitely a chicken coop, at least one dog, flowers around the house because I love the wildflowers around here."

"What else?"

She shook her head. "The rest of what I want isn't grounded in reality."

"What are your dreams, Cat?"

"They're typical and boring, Talon."

"So, share them with me anyway."

"Well," she began, hesitant, "meeting the right guy. Getting married. I love kids and always thought that at some point I'd shift from being a firefighter to remaining a paramedic, instead. Getting pregnant, I couldn't do firefighting, anyway, nor would I want to."

"But if you were pregnant, would you continue your work?"

"At a certain point, no," Cat murmured. "If we're just talking fantasy here, I'd quit my job and be a full-time mother. I'd have the ranch, so I would want to devote my attention and heart to it, to my family and to my husband."

Talon could easily see Cat as a mother. His whole

lower body went hot with need. He suddenly felt more protective of her than normal. So, what the hell was this reaction? Maybe her softness, that maternal look in her expression, grabbed him.

"How many kids?"

"As many as we could afford. I don't believe in bringing a child into this world that you can't take care of, devote your attention to and…well…you know…" Cat looked away, embarrassed.

"You never got that chance growing up," he said, seeing the pain she was trying to hide. His intuition was highly developed and he knew instantly Cat had made a connection with her own miserable childhood. She had no mother. Just a father who most likely didn't want her around and beat her when she got in his way. He ached for Cat because she had turned out to be a beautiful, caring person despite her past. The scars she carried ran her life even now. Did that sick bastard father of hers even begin to realize how he'd wounded Cat?

Cat hitched one shoulder up, as if summoning her strength. "Listen, everyone has stories about their growing-up years. It's not an excuse. It's common."

Talon's mouth thinned. "Abuse is not common, Cat. My parents never laid a hand on me growing up. I know you'd love the hell out of your children, Cat." Talon knew it, saw it and sensed it. He wanted her to love him with the same kind of female fierceness that burned so brightly within her. Cat might have been abused but, as a woman, she was a warrior just like him. Fighting fires wasn't something many wanted to do, man or woman. To him, it was another kind of war, only there weren't bullets being shot. It was fire stalking them, trying to kill those who fought it.

The waitress came with their platters, refilled their cups and left. Talon could see that Cat was upset. He reached over and captured her hand. "Hey, stop being so hard on yourself, will you? You're a good person, Cat. You do right by others. You didn't do anything wrong to deserve what happened to you."

Shocked at his unexpected touch, Cat felt her mouth go dry. She stared at Talon, who had such compassion etched on his face. The low, vibrating warmth of his voice soothed her senses...and made her want him even more. She craved Talon. His touch. His attention. His care. And it was care he was giving her right now. She reluctantly pulled her hand away.

"Sometimes I am too hard on myself," she admitted. "My friend Casey says the same thing."

Talon withdrew his hand, forced himself to reach for the ketchup bottle instead. What Cat needed right now was a little care and support. He could offer all those things for her. "Probably because you believed you're no good inside, Cat. You took your father's beatings as evidence that you're unlovable. And that's why he beat you—because you weren't worthy of being loved. The truth is, the beatings weren't about you. They were about your father. You did nothing wrong, Cat. Children are innocent and you need to get that and believe it." God, how he wanted her to believe it.

"Have you been talking to Casey about me?" she asked curiously.

He laughed. "No. I've never met her. But I'd like to. She sounds like a good friend to you."

Cat picked up half her Reuben. "I'd swear to God you sound just like her. We had a similar conversation once, a long time ago. She said when children were beaten, they carried the silent message inside them that they were no good. Otherwise, why was the parent beating them in the first place. Right?"

Talon cut his burger in half. "Precisely."

"So, how did you get so smart about psychology?" she challenged, eating.

"You learn it from real life. Observation. I haven't had any formal training."

Cat studied him, the silence growing between them. "There's a lot more to you than you let people realize, Talon."

He gave her a wry grin. "Yeah, I 'spose that's true."

"Is it because of your job as a SEAL? You don't show who you are?"

"Only to the enemy," he told her.

"Oh," she muttered defiantly. "Like you're an open book to the friendlies?"

He nearly choked on the burger. Wiping his mouth with a napkin, he managed, "Not exactly. When you live in a black ops world, which is all top secret, you tend to play your cards close to your chest as a survival mechanism with everyone. Enemy or friend."

Cat eyed him. "Do you feel like you're in survival mode with me?"

How he ached that she sincerely wanted to understand why he was so closed up. "I'm not in survival mode with you, Cat. You saved my life."

"And that means you're an open book to me?"

"Not exactly."

"But I'm being dirt honest with you. Why can't you do the same toward me, Talon?"

Hearing the frustration in her low voice, he realized the connection between them was serious. And deep.

And continuing to develop. Was that what he wanted? Talon had no experience with what was happening between them right now. Cat's gaze dug into his. Talon felt her care, felt her wanting a helluva lot more from him than he'd ever given another woman.

"Is that what you want from me, Cat? Because I've been honest with you at every turn." Yet, Talon inwardly crumpled, his gut tight, because he never could tell her about his SEAL life. At least, not in details. Maybe in broader terms. He could feel Cat's frustration. And her need to know him on a more personal level. Most surprising, Talon wanted to give her access to him.

"Yes," Cat muttered, "I'd like to know you better." She wanted to add that she loved the kiss they'd shared. Wanted more of him touching her because something in her heart told her Talon would be an incredible lover. And he'd never threaten her. Cat felt safe with him. And she'd never felt safe with any other man before. Most of all, right now, she wanted his kiss. The thought was molten and filled with such promise that Cat felt her lower body simmering close to a boil with hunger. The man absolutely incited an inner riot within her with just that lazy, hooded look as he studied her.

"What do you want to know?"

She searched his turbulent eyes. "Why did you go into the SEALs?"

"Because they're warriors. And I grew up wanting to be one myself."

"But joining the military, SEALs or not, made you a warrior, didn't it?"

He smiled a little. Cat's ability to lift the layers beneath him made him see her depths. But he already knew that. "I liked the water. I liked the fact SEALs had to be multiskilled in a lot of areas. I liked the idea of fighting behind the scenes. I guess I'm one of those people who doesn't need fanfare or to have others recognize or know what I do."

"You're confident enough in yourself that you don't need others to tell you that you're good at what you do?"

Talon held her gaze. The woman had a shovel and was going to dig much deeper into his psyche, no doubt. "Right."

Cat tilted her head, wondering aloud. "Was that because your parents never hit you? That you kept that part of yourself intact? That you never questioned what you were capable of doing?"

Whoa. He grinned a little. "You've been taking psychology courses at a local college?"

Flustered, Cat muttered, "Well, honestly, I did, but that was because years earlier, I met Casey. I was so screwed up and she started helping me understand myself. And she had a minor in psychology, so it got me interested in why people are the way they are. I took a couple of courses. It was a huge help to me because I wanted to be free of the abuse. I wanted to know who I really was."

"Well," he said gently, "you've come a long way." He was proud of her grit, her courage to look at herself, see where changes needed to be made and then make them. Not everyone had that drive or capacity in them and Talon knew it.

Feeling suddenly shy, she wished she could disappear. "Did you take courses in psychology to become a SEAL?"

"No." Talon picked up a French fry. He saw her flush,

her cheeks a bright pink. Cat was easily touched by a sincere compliment. "Life just gave it to me, I guess."

"Maybe you should be a psychologist instead of a wrangler," she said wryly. "Because you sure see into me."

He smiled a little. "I want to understand you, Cat."

"Why?"

Talon sat up. He wasn't expecting *that* question. Yet, as he held Cat's gaze, he saw she wasn't playing games with him. She was honest, Talon realized, in a way his past experience with women had never been. "Because you interest me, that's why."

Interest? Cat stared hard at him. She remembered their kiss. Was that an "interested" kiss? "What does *that* mean exactly, Talon? *Interested* as in a specimen?" And why was it so important to her? Not that any of her prior relationships had contained meaty conversation.

"*Interest* means I'm very attracted to you, Cat. But I'm the kind of man who wants to understand why."

"I'm not sure that was a compliment or an insult."

Talon did grin. "It was a compliment, Cat."

"And you're interested because I saved your life? Is this your way of paying me back? Taking me to lunch?" *Kissing me?* She was afraid to go there, didn't have the guts to ask him that question. Not yet.

Talon wished they were alone, not in a crowded, busy restaurant at noon. He pushed the half-eaten platter of food to one side and folded his hands, holding her confused stare. She'd opened up to him earlier, admitted she had poor relationships in the past with men who had abused her. And he could see her struggling to understand their connection. Was she trying to figure out if he would abuse her, too? Was that where these ques-

tions were coming from? Because Talon understood
Cat didn't trust her own senses regarding a man. And,
maybe, her questions, blunt as they were, were a way
for her to try to get to the heart of why she was attracted
to him. This was messy, but he cared enough for her to
see it through. Talon didn't ask himself why.

"You did save my sorry ass," he told her. "And am
I doing this because of that? No. I find you refreshing,
Cat. You're honest and you don't play games."

So she was *refreshing*. Whatever the hell that meant.
Cat could tell he was sincere. She chewed on her lower
lip, unsure of where to go with this. With him. "As you
can tell, I don't have much experience with relationships," she muttered by way of apology.

"I like you just the way you are." And he did. Cat
didn't see herself. She had no mirror to reflect back the
goodness that was inherently a part of herself.

"Okay," Cat murmured, picking up the other half of
her sandwich, "I just didn't want you doing this because
you owed me, was all."

Talon wanted to grab her, sweep her into his arms
and kiss the hell out of her until she melted like hot
honey all over him. His voice became guttural, intimate. "What I feel for you, Cat, has nothing to do with
me owing you anything."

Her flesh reacted to his husky admittance. The burning look of desire in his gray eyes put her on warning
in such a way that, for a moment, she couldn't breathe.
It was as if he'd reached out and stroked her cheek,
touched her lower lip. The sensation was so real it startled her. With just one intense, heated look! That's all
he'd given her! His eyes glittered and were focused

solely on her. She whispered, "Any relationship I have from now on has to be more than just about sex."

"I understand." And Talon felt damned guilty because that's what he'd wanted from her originally. Their burgeoning relationship was morphing into something else Talon couldn't yet identify or name. Men used women. Hell, he was one of them, but he'd been up front about it every time. God knew how bad he wanted to love Cat. He could give her the pleasure she deserved.

Cat quivered inwardly with that hot look he shared with her. Is that what she wanted? Sex with Talon? For sure, but Cat wanted a lot more than that. Did that make Talon like the rest of the men who had stalked her just to get her into bed?

The waitress came over. Cat asked for a to-go box to save the rest of her Reuben sandwich. She glanced at her watch and said, "We need to get going."

"I'm buying," Talon said, taking the bill from the waitress. He watched Cat closing up on him. As if shielding herself from the world around her. He wanted to protect her so she never had to go there again. A good feeling moved through him.

"Thanks. I'll pick it up if there's a next time," she teased, sliding out of the booth with her foam box.

He gave her a lazy grin. "Oh, there will be."

"See you at the truck." Cat turned and left.

It was a pleasure just watching the soft sway of Cat's hips as she walked toward the front door. She seemed oblivious to her sensuality, how sexy she was. As he slowly stood up, digging into his pocket for his wallet, he thought about the fact Cat never had a mother. Without one, who was to teach her about being a woman?

No one. That explained why she was so unaware of her beauty. *Or the impact it has on me.*

Cat had just gotten to the truck when she heard Beau Magee's voice behind her.

"Hey, Cat, how you doin'? Been a while."

Her breath jammed as she whirled around, facing him. Beau was big. And tall. Instantly, adrenaline flooded her bloodstream. He gave her an angry look. Magee was walking toward her in his one-piece black Ace Trucking uniform, his head bare, a pair of gloves sticking out of one of his pockets.

"Get the hell away from me!" she snarled.

Beau came to a halt six feet from her. "Now, is that any way to treat an old friend?"

Everything in her told her to run. Cat looked around. No one was in the parking lot. There was an empty space next to where the truck was parked. Nostrils flaring, she gritted out, "We're done, Beau. I've told you that a hundred times. Now, please just leave me alone." She turned to jerk the door of the pickup open.

The next thing she knew, her foam box flew into the air and she felt Beau's large hand grab her by the upper arm. He spun her around, slamming her into the side of the pickup.

"You bitch!" he thundered.

Cat screamed. She tried to twist out of his hands, which gripped her, holding her against the truck. Pain reared up her arms as his fingers sank like claws into her shoulders. His fingers dug painfully into her flesh as he leered down at her, his lip lifting in a snarl. The odor of onions assailed her and she grunted, trying to kick out at him to escape. Her boot nicked his shinbone and he cursed.

The moment his hands loosened as he winced in pain, Cat jerked free. She stumbled against the truck, her knee hitting the ground. Breathing erratically, she bounded back to her feet, trying to run away from him.

"No, you don't!" Magee yelled, lunging after her.

Cat whirled around to face her attacker. Her eyes widened when she glanced across her shoulder as she got to her feet. Magee had his hand in a fist, cocked back to strike her. His face was red with rage, his eyes small and angry. Off balance, she hit the side of the truck with her shoulder, twisting, trying to avoid the oncoming fist aimed at her face.

Cat felt the power of his fist graze her jaw, flinging her down on the ground. She slammed into the dirt, a cry ripping out of her. The next second, she heard Magee grunt. And as she looked up, she witnessed Talon throwing a punch directly into the man's face, hearing the crunch of bone. At the same time, a black Tahoe with Sheriff written on the side pulled up. Barely able to think, Cat pushed herself up into a sitting position. Talon dropped Magee with one punch, the man crumpling like an ox to the earth.

Cade Garner, the deputy sheriff, leaped out of the Tahoe, gun drawn. Talon stood over Magee, a murderous rage in his expression, his fist cocked back, waiting.

"Talon?" Cade called, trotting around the end of the Tahoe and seeing Magee unconscious on the ground. And then he noticed Cat nearby.

"Get that son of a bitch out of here or I'll finish him off," Talon snarled. "He hit Cat. I saw it."

Quickly holstering his weapon, Cade maneuvered Magee onto his back, checking his pulse along his neck.

He pulled out his radio and made a call for an ambulance.

Cat blinked, feeling dizzy as Talon turned those thunderous gray eyes in her direction. He looked as if he wanted to kill Magee. Gasping for breath, she tried to get up. Instantly, he was at her side, his hand gentle on her shoulder.

"Stay where you are, Cat. You're hurt."

Talon's voice was oddly soothing to her. A cold, calm tone. She felt his hand on her shoulder, steadying her. She remained sitting, stunned by the sudden attack.

"Where are you hurt?" he asked.

"Uh…he hit me," she managed, lifting her hand to her aching jaw.

"He did more than that," Talon growled, pulling off her neckerchief and putting it in her hand. "Your nose is bleeding." He helped guide her hand upward. "Keep it pressed against your nose for a few minutes."

Cat saw Magee come around. He grunted and cursed as he got to his hands and knees, blood pouring out of his nose. Cade Garner told him he was under arrest and he cuffed him as he read him his rights.

Talon crouched down, worriedly studying her eyes. Cat was in shock. Her knee was bloodied, her jeans ripped and torn open. As he carefully moved his hands from her neck, down across her shoulders to her upper arms, she winced.

"Hurt?" he asked.

"Yeah," Cat muttered, closing her eyes. "He grabbed me. I—I was opening the door on the truck and he came up behind me." She bowed her head, feeling suddenly spent.

Talon opened up the cuff on her shirtsleeve and

rolled it up until he could look at her upper arm. There were four deep, purple bruises starting to appear on her skin. Rage tunneled through him. "Bruises," he told her. "Is it the same on your other arm?"

"Y-yes. I—I'll be all right, Talon. I just need a few minutes…."

He moved his hands down her back, then the sides of her rib cage, looking for more injury. "You'll be okay," he rasped. "Let me keep checking you. All right?"

His hands felt steadying. "F-fine." Cat wanted to cry and she squeezed her eyes shut. She heard the scream of a siren. The ambulance pulled in behind their truck and soon Magee was put onto a gurney, the two paramedics working on him. "You really hit him," she muttered through the neckerchief.

"I wanted to kill him," Talon breathed softly. He finished his examination of Cat and placed a hand on her shoulder. "How are you feeling now?"

"Like a fool," she confessed sadly. "I should have been more aware. I wasn't thinking…."

Mouth twitching, Talon watched as they took Magee to the ambulance. "Stop blaming yourself. He attacked you. Is this the guy you left?"

"Yes. A year ago. I told him it was over. But he keeps bothering me, Talon. He thinks I want him back." She shivered. "I don't. I never did."

"Okay," Talon whispered, "it's all right. Do you think you can stand if I help you up? We need to get you to the E.R. to be checked out."

Cade Garner walked over. He lent a hand and they both brought Cat to her feet. Concern was etched on the deputy sheriff's face as Talon opened the door to the pickup.

"Cat? You okay? Do you need to see a doctor?" Cade asked, helping her into the cab.

Sitting felt good. Cat lifted the neckerchief away since her nose had quit bleeding. "I'm just shook up, Cade. She rubbed the side of her swelling jaw. Nothing's broken. Just bruises."

Cade nodded, giving her a hard look. "Do you feel like telling me what happened?"

Talon stood next to Cat, listening to her story. Why the hell hadn't he escorted her out to the parking lot? He didn't know Magee was stalking her. If he had, he wouldn't have let Cat out of his sight. Talk about holding secrets. He grimaced. She had her own and was just as bad as he was, never discussing them. *Damn.* Talon couldn't stop the terror in his heart for her. Who knew what Magee could have done to her if he hadn't walked around the corner and seen it? A cold chill worked through him.

Cade was taking notes and nodded. "Okay, why don't you get home and take care of yourself? If you feel like it, can you come in tomorrow morning and I can get any other details you might remember. Magee will be put in jail on assault charges, Cat. Do you want to press charges?"

Talon tensed. Cat had been abused as a child. And this bastard had abused her. Would she do it? Or would she be like so many other victims and not? He couldn't tell her what to do, and he watched Cat close her eyes for a moment, her lower lip trembling. When she reopened them, she stared down at Cade.

"Yes."

Talon gave her a crooked grin and a nod. All he

wanted to do was get her to her condo and take care of her.

"C-could you call Matt Sinclaire? I'm supposed to go on duty later today."

Cade closed the notebook and said, "No problem. I'll handle it."

"Thanks, Cade."

"Cat? You're doing the right thing." And Cade nailed her with a look that spoke volumes. "Magee needs to be put away."

She grimaced, feeling her whole body begin to stiffen from being knocked around. "I'll testify against him, Cade. I'm not changing my mind."

"Okay," he said, then looked over at Talon. "Can you take her home?"

"Of course," Talon answered.

Cat slid over to the passenger side of the truck, happy not to drive. Her jaw was aching and when she slid her fingers along the left side, it was badly swollen. A couple of her teeth felt loose. She hated to think what would have happened if Magee had connected with her face. A shiver wound through her. She tipped her head back, closing her eyes as Talon backed the truck out of the parking lot.

"How are you doing?" he asked, pulling out onto the highway that would lead to her condo.

"I feel whipped," she admitted tiredly.

He slid his hand over her thigh for a moment, giving it a pat. "Hang on. I'll get you home and take care of you, babe."

CHAPTER SIXTEEN

ON THE WAY to Cat's condo, Talon made a call to his mother, telling her he wouldn't see her today. Getting a hold of Val, he asked permission for the rest of the day off from work and tomorrow, as well. He filled her in on Cat's condition so no one at the Bar H would be worried. Val told him to take whatever time he and Cat needed. By the time he pulled into the driveway of her condo, Talon saw Cat had grown paler. Maybe he should have taken her to the E.R. to be examined. Relying on his SEAL medical training, Talon decided he would make that decision once he got her home. Cat might be a paramedic, but she was in shock and not in the best space to determine the extent of her own injuries, but he would be. Talon kept his hand beneath her elbow as she slowly walked up the stairs to the master bathroom located within her bedroom.

"I'll be okay," she reassured him, hesitating at the entrance.

Talon took off his hat. "Let me check you over, Cat. It won't take but a minute. Let's go into the bathroom."

She frowned, no doubt feeling emotionally raw. "You're not a doctor."

Talon tried to be patient, gently guiding her to the master bathroom. "No, but I've had extensive combat medical training." He could see the wariness in her darkened eyes, felt her wanting to trust him, unsure if she should or not. He kept his voice low and persuasive as he pulled out a chair and guided her to it. He added teasingly, "I haven't killed anyone yet with my medical knowledge, so you'll probably survive me, too."

"Oh…" Cat wanted to cry but fought it. It was the shock playing havoc on her emotions. But not now. And especially not with Talon.

Talon set his baseball cap on the counter and opened up the medicine cabinet, pulling several articles from it and lining them up. "You're in shock, Cat. You know what shock does to people," he murmured, turning around and meeting her gaze.

Nodding, Cat felt her shoulders stiffening up from the fall. Her knee was throbbing. "I don't want to go to the E.R. I'm all right." She was ashamed she'd allowed Magee to injure her. *Again.* And it was so hard to look into Talon's worried gaze. He was being incredibly gentle toward her, something she hadn't thought a man could be.

"Will you let me look at your injuries?" Talon pointed to the bloody, torn fabric on the right knee of her Levi's. "I'm going to roll up your pant leg and take a look at it." He crouched down in front of her.

She could smell the sweat on him, the dust and the special male scent that made her feel so hungry for him. How could that be? She watched as he carefully folded her Levi's trouser leg up and over her bloody, torn-up knee. Her skin singed with fire as his roughened fingertips brushed her thigh, anchoring the trouser leg into place.

"It's just a scrape," she muttered. Preparing herself for the touch of his hands around her knee, Cat closed her eyes. His hands were callused and rough from work and her skin skittered with pleasure as his fingers wrapped gently around her knee to support it.

"You got a lot of dirt in it," Talon said, examining it closely. Yeah, he liked any excuse to touch Cat. Her skin was velvet, her flesh firm. He felt her stiffen as he gently moved the knee joint one way and then another, looking for more serious injury.

"Hurt?"

"A little."

Talon stood up, washed his hands with soap and water in the basin. "It's bruised but usable. I'm going to have to clean out that wound, Cat. You okay with that?" Now he was in SEAL mode. They always carried a blowout kit on them and other medical supplies that could save their lives. He twisted a look over his shoulder at her to get her agreement.

Cat seemed unsure. Hesitant.

"Will you trust me to do this?" Because trust was their issue. Hers, more specifically, but if Cat couldn't trust him, Talon was going to bundle her up and take her to the E.R. That knee abrasion was ugly and Talon knew if it wasn't cleaned up properly, she'd have a roaring infection within forty-eight hours.

"I do trust you," she whispered, avoiding his sharpened gaze.

Talon retrieved more supplies from her medicine cabinet. "You got a pair of latex gloves around here?"

"Yes." Cat pointed out toward the bedroom. "I have my paramedic bag in the closet, over there. Just bring it in here. I can help you get the right articles to clean up my knee."

Talon nodded. Something changed between them. He

could feel it. Cat had gone from distrust to trust. Maybe because he'd sold her on his confidence and ability as a field medic? Talon didn't know. He brought in the large bag and placed it next to where she sat. He opened it up so she could dig around to locate the items. In minutes, he had everything he needed. Crouching down, gloves on, he warned her, "This is going to hurt."

Cat shook her head and muttered, "It doesn't hurt one tenth as much as me letting Magee hit me again."

Giving her a sharpened look, Talon's mouth thinned. He busied himself. "What happened the first time?"

Dammit. Cat swallowed painfully and watched as he took a large square of gauze and squirted it with sterile water. "I broke it off with Beau a year ago," she whispered, watching him work to clean out her torn-up flesh. Somehow, the agony of admitting how embarrassed she was overrode the pain of him scrubbing out the laceration. "Beau hid his drug habit from me and I didn't know it for about a month into our relationship. He was jealous when he was coked up. He started accusing me of going out with one of the guys at the fire department."

Talon focused on her knee, but he listened carefully to everything she said. "Were you?"

Cat snorted, "Hell no. I wouldn't do that! Beau is an addict. He was insanely jealous of me working with the guys on my shift. One day, he shoved me into a wall, calling me a liar, accusing me of sleeping around."

Talon glanced up, cleaning off the dried blood at the edges of the injury. He felt rage toward Magee. "And you left him?"

Her throat tightened. "Yes. For good."

"But he doesn't want to let you go?"

Cat shook her head. "No. I wish… God, why didn't I see Magee's drug habit? What in me is so damaged that I don't see a guy who's an abuser?"

Talon heard the self-incrimination and strain in her voice and he lifted his chin. Tears glimmered in her eyes, tears of shame. "If someone who has secrets wants to keep it that way, Cat, you won't know. Stop blaming yourself for choosing him. You couldn't have known he was jealous or an abuser."

Cat felt the sting of the iodine as he swabbed it across her flesh. The pain wasn't near the level of how she felt about today's debacle and the serrating humiliation she felt afterward. Talon's touch was gentle as he focused on what he was doing. His hands felt good on her and she almost told him that when he touched her, she felt no pain in her knee. "I'm sure you think I'm an idiot."

Talon shook his head and smiled. "And who among us hasn't chosen a bad partner?" He met and held her moist gaze. Her lower lip trembled and Talon almost lost his professionalism. Damn, Cat needed to be held. Needed to know she was safe.

"I wish," Cat said raggedly, "I knew how to fight. I'm sick and tired of him stalking me."

"Well," Talon said mildly, "that's one thing I can teach you how to do. When you feel like it in a week or so, I'll show you some CQD maneuvers."

"What's that?"

"Acronym for Close Quarters Defense." He looked up. "All SEALs are taught how to fight and kill with their hands in a small area like a room or a tight space you'd find on a ship. I can teach you some moves that will guarantee no man will ever take you down like Magee did today. Okay?" Hope flared in her eyes.

"Really?"

"Yes," he murmured, easing the Levi's pant leg down and over her knee after bandaging the injury. "Really." And then Talon gave her a boyish smile. "You could even use it against me if I get too frisky with you."

His teasing always lifted her. Made her feel better. Warmth sheeted through Cat as she watched him unwind like a lithe cougar and stand. This was a side of Talon she'd never known existed. A man who cared for her. He had a wonderful bedside manner and he really was a medic. She swallowed hard. "You saved me out there today."

"Cade Garner was pulling up just as I came around the corner to see what was happening to you, Cat. If I hadn't been there, Cade would sure as hell have taken Magee down."

He was humble. Cat watched as he gestured to her swollen jaw. He crouched down beside her and placed his hands near her left jawline, carefully examining the area. His touch was electric. Comforting. She sat very still, breath held for a moment as he skimmed the area where Magee had hit her.

"Any loose teeth?"

"Just one," she managed, closing her eyes, hungrily absorbing his touch. Her lower body began to ache with just one brief touch. "It will tighten up in a few days," she managed.

"An ice pack on the area will reduce the swelling," he told her, rising. "What about your arms where he grabbed you?"

"Just bruises. No big deal."

They were to Talon. He pulled off the gloves and dropped them in the wastebasket, turning toward her.

There was more color in her cheeks now, more life in her eyes. Talon knew it was because he'd made her feel safe and cared for. He rested his hands on his hips, studying her. "Can I draw you a hot bath? You've got to be feeling pretty stiff from the fall by now."

She managed a smile and shook her head. "I'm going to take a hot shower."

"Okay. I'll be downstairs if you need me."

"Are you staying?"

"Yes." Because Talon knew Cat needed someone around right now. He could give her a sense of safety. He'd seen the panic in her eyes earlier. And the panic had dissolved as he'd tended to her injuries. "I want to stay around just in case you need anything."

Cat felt her emotions wildly seesawing. So much of her wanted to be in Talon's arms right now because she felt threatened. She'd thought she would die out there in that parking lot today. She knew Magee was in jail. Knew he wasn't going to come over and stalk her like he had before. The grave look on Talon's face and the concern burning in his eyes gave her the courage to whisper, "Y-yes. I'd like that. There's a spare bedroom down the hall on the right you can have." She knew Talon was giving up his time for her and it made her feel good, but guilty. He was supposed to see his mother this afternoon and Cat never wanted to stand in the way of Sandy seeing her son.

Talon leaned down, tucking errant strands of her hair behind her ear. "I'll check it out later. I'll be downstairs if you need anything."

Her ear tingled wildly. Cat closed her eyes, starving for his attention. *Trust.* She trusted Talon. It was such a foreign emotion to her, and yet, he'd proved he was trustworthy over time and incidents. She looked up as he walked toward the entrance. "Talon?"

He turned. "Yes?"

"Th-thanks...for everything...." She frowned, her voice cracking. "You didn't have to do this...."

He smiled lazily. "You're worth it, Cat." Talon turned and left, because if he didn't, he was going to haul her into his arms, carry her off to her bed and hold her. This wasn't about sex. It was about him knowing what she needed in order to stop the shock from tumbling through her, skewing her emotions and making her feel so terribly vulnerable. Talon almost hesitated. Almost turned around. But he forced himself to leave because he didn't want to break that tenuous trust he'd just built with Cat.

Cat felt drugged after her long, hot shower, no doubt a reaction to the assault. Pulling on a lavender silk nightgown that fell to her knees, she crawled into bed, just wanting to rest. And as soon as her head hit the pillow, Cat spiraled into sleep because, for once, she felt safe. Talon was downstairs. He wouldn't let anything happen to her. She didn't have to worry about Magee banging on her door at odd hours, waking her. For once, she could honestly relax and allow sleep to heal her.

Talon checked up on Cat later. Her bedroom door was ajar and he saw her sleeping, the sheet bunched up around her waist. The lavender gown made him want to move closer, but to do so wouldn't be right. He had no business going into her bedroom uninvited. Talon moved down the carpeted hall and quietly opened the door to his bedroom and checked it out.

It was two in the afternoon. He ached to go back to Cat's bedroom, slide into bed next to her and hold her.

That's all he wanted to do. Talon laughed to himself, shaking his head ruefully as he looked around the large bedroom. Hell, in the past, if he held a woman it was to make love with her. Not to comfort her.

Rubbing his jaw in thought, he left the room and checked on Cat one more time. She was sleeping deeply and that was good. He then went downstairs. He wanted to call Cade Garner to get an update on Magee. And then he'd call his mother and Val to let them know how Cat was doing.

Everything in Cat's condo reflected her. The kitchen was pristine, clean, and it was evident from the contents of her refrigerator, she obviously preferred healthy food. Talon searched for something to make for their dinner. Sooner or later, Cat would wake up, and she needed to eat.

The living room had an ivory couch and stuffed chair along with a large television on the wall. The carpet was beige. Colorful purple, red and gold pillows were thrown on the furniture. She had a number of photos on one wall and they were present-day, not any of her family. On one wall hung a photo of a brilliant rainbow in what look like the Hawaiian Islands. It was obvious that Cat liked color.

Talon had discovered a number of magazines she subscribed to. It was amazing to him how much a person revealed about themselves by something so seemingly innocuous. There were two magazines on travel. He wondered if she wanted to travel but never had. Another was on organic gardening and he remembered her dream house would have a garden. There was another on wildflowers. And a real estate magazine of houses for sale in Wyoming.

Talon made himself some coffee, called a few people and then leafed through those magazines trying to discover more about Cat. On some pages, the corners were turned down. On others, she'd underlined articles or made notes out in the margin. In the real estate magazine she had circled a couple of homes for sale. She had all kinds of notes in it and by the time he was finished going through it, Talon smiled a little. There was something poignant about Cat. She had such a strong, confident demeanor out in the world. A real warrior woman as a firefighter. Still, from looking inside these magazines, there lurked someone with unfulfilled but hopeful dreams. The feminine side of herself, Talon supposed. He liked getting to know her inner world of her secret self. Getting to discover Cat was like opening a treasure chest to Talon, and no woman had ever intrigued him like that before.

He set the magazine aside and noticed it was nearly five o'clock. Getting up, he went to the kitchen to make dinner. He was going to let Cat sleep until she woke up on her own. And if she slept right through the evening, that was fine with him, too. Talon knew the healing power of a deep, long and uninterrupted sleep.

As he made a salad on the counter, he couldn't shake the look on Cat's face when Magee had pinned her against the truck. In that instant, he'd seen a terrified child. It had torn his heart apart. He'd leaped off the wooden walkway and sprinted toward Magee, who had cocked his fist to strike Cat. He'd seen the helpless fright emerge in her expression. It was then that Talon realized the depths of the wounds her father had given her. How many times had Cat looked like that as a child growing up around her abuser? She'd lived in terror all the time.

And yet, she'd become a strong, independent warrior. He put the salad in the fridge and drew out two chicken breasts he found in the freezer. He cooked rice and mixed it with raisins and walnuts. He sprinkled Middle Eastern spices on the meat, placed foil over it and slid it into the oven to bake.

No matter what he did to busy himself, Talon could not wipe out that childlike terror he'd seen in Cat's eyes as she tried to fight back and free herself from Magee. His knuckles were skinned, bruised and swollen from striking the son of a bitch. He took private satisfaction that he'd purposely broken Magee's nose. SEALs were trained to kill with their hands and Talon had come very close to doing just that with this bastard who had hurt Cat. Magee had made her life miserable.

How must she feel about the bastard stalking her? Like a hunted animal, most likely. Anger simmered in Talon as he found a chocolate-cake mix in another cabinet and located a can of white frosting. No wonder Cat didn't trust men, with someone like Magee shadowing her every move. But how much was Magee tailing her? Talon didn't know, but he was going to find out—he wanted to put that bastard into prison for a long, long time. He wanted Magee out of Cat's life. *Permanently.* And every protective instinct in him was oriented toward guarding Cat, keeping her safe. Giving her a place where she no longer felt constantly threatened. And his heart was ripped up by what had happened to her as a child.

As he worked on the cake, Talon shook his head, confused. Hell, he wanted Cat in his bed, wanted to be in her, love her, take her to places of intense pleasure and satisfaction she probably hadn't discovered yet. But he wanted more. It was unnamed, but a new hunger was making him crave her company, her smile, her laughter and the way she saw her world. He wanted to discover her facets and so much more.

As Talon worked quietly in her kitchen, he felt a new kind of peacefulness cloak him. A lot of the anxiety that was always with him dissolved. Cat's condo was like a sanctuary, a place where she dreamed and made notes in the edges of magazines. Talon found himself wanting to share her dreams, to be a part of them. So what did that make him? Was he wanting, for the first time in life, a serious relationship with a woman? Yeah, for sure. Now he was in uncharted territory and it scared him, but it also called to him like a siren. And as uncomfortable as he was, Talon had learned as a SEAL to work through the fear and keep moving toward the objective. In this case, it was Cat.

Once Talon finished his dinner duties, he washed his hands one last time and dried them on a towel. His heart centered on Cat. He felt things for her he'd never felt for another woman. And he hadn't even taken her to bed. That was the hell of it. Something about her, just as she was, fulfilled him. Expanded his heart, made him feel a happiness that had been foreign to him up until now. Talon had no explanation for it. He was grappling with his feelings and unsure of what would happen between them.

Dragging in a ragged breath, Talon moved to the dining room and set it for dinner, hoping Cat would awaken and join him later.

Cat made him feel complete. Talon stood, plate in

hand as he considered the realization. He'd been so lost since Hayden had died, the guilt so heavy and grinding, shredding his heart. Depression was all Talon had known since Hayden's death. And when Cat entered his life, Talon felt hope again. It had occurred quietly, over time. But with each moment spent near her, his feelings for her deepened and widened. And happiness was always a part of it, moving in the background beyond the grief he carried daily for his fallen brother. Cat was healing to him. Talon frowned, halting and closing his eyes, following that feeling. God, he'd been so deeply wounded by the torture and Hayden's death. How was it possible a person could help him out of that pit of despair? Ease his grief? Erase his depression? Yet, as Talon stood there looking at himself, remembering where he was at six months ago compared to now, he felt so much better. He wanted to live again. Cat had infused him with hope. Talon doubted she knew the powerful effects she had upon him. He'd never realized it until just now, himself. It shook him to his foundation.

Rubbing his chest where his heart lay, Talon finished setting the table. Stunned by the weight of his relationship with Cat, which was pretty desultory at best, she was still deeply affecting him in so many good ways. And today, he'd been made aware of it as never before. The hunger he felt in wanting to love her was driving him over an edge of a symbolic cliff he'd never known existed. Until right now.

"Hey," Cat called, her voice thick with sleep. The condo was filled with the odors of spices and chocolate. The fragrances had slowly awakened her from a deep sleep. She'd pulled on the lavender silk robe that fell to her ankles and slowly descended the carpeted stairs, barefoot. Feeling groggy, she saw Talon was busy in the kitchen. He wore a pair of oven mitts and was taking something that smelled very good out of the oven. When she halted at the granite island and caught his attention, a warmth flooded her. She wiped her eyes, barely awake. Talon straightened and saw her. His smile went straight to her heart and down to her lower body. How she wanted to be closer to him.

"Hey, yourself," Talon greeted, setting the Pyrex dish on a trivet on the dining room table. "How do you feel?" God, Cat looked like dessert to him, the silk lavender robe clinging softly to her, outlining her tall, shapely body. Her hair was tousled, her eyes drowsy with sleep and her mouth, soft and slightly parted. Groaning inwardly, Talon took off the mitts and set them on the counter.

"I'm really sleepy," Cat admitted. "But I smelled what you were cooking and realized I was a little bit hungry." Cat watched him move with animal grace, the Levi's accenting his narrow hips and his long, powerful thighs. He had the sleeves of his shirt rolled up to just below his elbows, his forearms dusted with dark hair. Swallowing, Cat noticed his beard had grown enough to give him a dark look that made her body yearn even more.

"I figured you might wake up," he murmured. Talon drew out a chair. "Have a seat? I'll get the rest of our meal on the table."

Cat sat down, gathering the folds of the robe across her legs. Outside, the sun was in the west, shafts coming in brightly through the front living room window. "What time is it?" she asked, picking up a glass of water.

Talon placed the bowl of salad on the table. "Six-thirty." He'd given Cat the seat at the head of the table and sat down at her left elbow. "Dig in," he invited. "Kind of a Middle Eastern banquet tonight."

"I didn't know you could cook," she said, spooning the fragrant raisin and walnut rice onto her plate.

"And I didn't know you were a firefighter. There are many facets we haven't explored yet, but I like getting to know you, Cat." Talon met her drowsy eyes, noticing they were less cloudy looking. Cat had slept off some of the shock, and that made him breathe a little easier. Talon watched her mouth curve over his comment. He placed a chicken breast on her plate.

"Thanks. Me, too," she said. Pushing her fingers through her hair, she tamed it away from her face and across her shoulders. "You have lots of layers, Talon. Like a torte cake."

"I've been called many things, but never a torte cake."

She smiled tentatively. "You are a man of many skills, I think. This smells wonderful."

"Hopefully, it will taste as good as it looks," he teased lightly, placing salad into the bowl near her plate. "Been a long time since I've taken on making a serious dinner." He saw a flush of pink come into her cheeks. Cat was incredibly open, her shields not present, and Talon tried not to be too assertive with her. Even picking up the fork and knife, her fingers long and tapered, there was grace in her movement. He wanted those hands exploring him. But he quelled his sexual appetite. The quiet and peace they shared right now was amazing and fed him.

"Mmm, this is really good," Cat murmured between

bites. She shared a look with him. Talon seemed bashful over her compliment. "Hey, you can say thank you."

"Thank you," he growled, finding he was starved. "How are you feeling?" He glanced up to see her reaction. She seemed more relaxed but not 100 percent.

"Still wrung out," she slowly admitted. Everything tasted delicious. For once it was nice to have a real meal that she hadn't had to make herself. She glanced at Talon. "Shock."

"Yeah, it is. You need a good night's sleep under your belt to get rid of the rest of it."

She stared at him for a moment. "There's so much more to you."

Talon smiled a little and held her gaze. "Funny, I was thinking the same thing about you."

Cat managed a twitch of her mouth. "Why?"

"You're an amazing person with hidden depths."

Cat frowned. "I don't see that."

"You're not supposed to. It's part of discovering who you are through my eyes." *And my heart.* And there was no longer any question that his heart wasn't involved.

Talon's voice was like rough velvet across her flesh. Cat held his genial gaze and felt her heart opening wider, with ribbons of happiness flowing through it. "I'm pretty simple and straightforward," she groused.

Talon laughed and shook his head. "No, you're highly complex. But that's a good thing in my book."

"I don't see that, either."

"It's tough for anyone to see themselves, don't you think?" Talon asked, picking up the salad dressing. Just getting to talk and explore Cat was another kind of dessert to him. She had no ability to play games. What you saw was what you got. And while Cat was open and maybe trusting toward him, she was far from simple.

"God knows I'm not good at seeing beneath a person's mask. I wish I was...." She frowned.

"You think all people wear masks?"

"Yes. The mask as I see it is the face everyone else sees out in public." She pointed toward the door. "But when a person goes home, the mask comes off and the real person appears." She shared a wry look with him. "I don't have the ability to see beneath a person's mask and I wish I did. I think you see beneath mine."

"So if you could ferret out who lived under that mask, you think it would stop you from making mistakes with men like Magee?"

"Yeah. Why didn't I see under his mask? If I had, I'd never have gotten involved with him."

He felt her frustration. "You're too hard on yourself, Cat. Look at us. We have a good relationship, don't we?"

"You're one of the men in my life that has been good for me."

"So, you've upgraded," he teased. A hesitant smile came to her eyes as she regarded him.

"You're too good for me, Talon."

His heart squeezed with pain. He scowled. "Why do you say that?"

Cat shook her head and stopped eating. "Sometimes, Talon, I think you're a dream come true for me. I've been floundering for years trying to understand and straighten myself out. I guess, to be honest, I felt like I wasn't worthy of much. I'm so screwed up inside. I couldn't see how any man would want me." The words were out and she saw Talon's eyes grow dark and focused on her. "You're very different from the other men

I chose." Her voice dropped. "That's why I think you're a dream…." And like a dream, she was afraid he'd disappear from her life.

There was such shyness in her face, in her voice, as if she were revealing a precious secret and uncertain about admitting something so deeply personal to him. He nodded, moved powerfully by her trust. And it *was* trust. She'd just handed him a great gift.

He held her gaze, his voice suddenly emotional. "Well, you're my dream come true, too…."

CHAPTER SEVENTEEN

CAT'S SCREAMS JOLTED Talon out of sleep. He woke up instantly, adrenaline pouring through his bloodstream as he threw off the covers and headed down the hall toward her room. Moonlight drifted around the edges of the front window. He had excellent night vision and as he reached Cat's opened bedroom door, he heard her sob. The sound ripped at his heart.

He pushed open the door. "Cat? What's wrong?"

She was sitting on the edge of the bed, the covers rumpled, half of them on the floor. She'd had a nightmare. Mouth tightening, he saw her head bent, hands covering her face, sobbing, her shoulders shaking. *Damn.*

He wore only a pair of boxer shorts. Crouching in front of her, unsure if she was still wrapped up in the nightmare, he called out softly, "Cat? Hey? Look at me. Are you okay?"

Talon wanted to reach out, touch her arm, but he knew what it was like to be caught up in a nightmare. It could scare her even more, deepen the trauma she was already experiencing, if he touched her unexpectedly.

"Cat?" he called more firmly. Barely able to stand her softened sobs, she was bent forward, as if to shield or protect herself.

Cat heard Talon's low, quiet voice break through the

terror of her nightmare. She lifted her wet hands to find him crouched in front of her, his face deeply shadowed and worried. It was his stormy gray eyes that told her he cared. Sitting up, she pushed her hair away from her face.

"Oh, God, I'm sorry I woke you," she rasped, feeling guilt.

Talon rose and smiled a little. He sat down next to her and slid his arm around her shoulders. "I'm glad you did," he told her roughly, a lot of emotions on the surface. "Come here, let me hold you for a bit."

To his surprise, Cat turned and pressed her face against his shoulder and neck, her hand covering her face. She was warm and he bit back a groan as she entrusted herself to him. He could feel her trembling and understood the depth of the nightmare's hold on her. Sliding his other arm around her waist, he held her gently, his body going into overdrive with need for her.

"Talk to me," Talon urged, resting his cheek against her hair.

With a shaking hand, Cat tried to wipe the tears away from her cheek. Talon felt incredibly warm, hard and powerful. She inhaled the male scent that was mixed with his evergreen soap. Her voice broke. "I— Oh, God, I just relived Magee attacking me in the parking lot."

Sliding his fingers through the tangled mass of her hair, slowly smoothing it out into strands, massaging her scalp, he said, "I thought so. It's going to be okay, babe. You're safe. Safe…"

His voice was like balm across her scattered, terrorized emotions. Her heart pounded wildly, her breath ragged and uneven. Cat felt her nipples harden against his chest wall. His fingers eased the tension in her scalp, tiny prickles of pleasure and fire sheeting down across her head, into her neck and flowing directly to her breasts. She placed her hand on his chest, the hair soft, feeling the slow thud of his heart beneath her palm. It soothed her. Talon's flesh tensed, the muscles leaping where her hand rested.

"I feel so stupid. I'm sorry I woke you up," she whispered, wanting the sense of protection he was affording her. Talon squeezed her reassuringly.

"You're not stupid, Cat. I get nightmares, too. And I wake up screaming. I'm always afraid I'll wake up everyone else in the house when it happens." He inhaled her sweet, spicy scent, aching to kiss her. Talon knew he could make Cat forget the nightmare and move into a world of scalding pleasure with him. He eased his hand down to her neck, gently massaging the tension. Feeling her relax more, sinking into him, allowing him to hold her weight, he smiled to himself. He skimmed his fingers down across her nightgown, and feeling how damp it was with sweat, his heart contracted. Yeah, she was having a wicked nightmare. Talon continued to stroke his hand lightly up and down her arm to soothe the remnants of the terror away from her. With each stroke, she sagged a little more trustingly into his embrace. He felt her moist breath across her neck and upper chest, felt her nuzzle her face more surely against him.

"Okay," she managed hoarsely, "now I don't feel so bad...." She sniffed, continuing to wipe the tears that still fell. Why couldn't she stop crying? Was it because Talon was holding her? A safe harbor in the storm of her life? It felt so good to be held like this. The aphrodisiac of his male scent entered her flaring nostrils, an unguent against the terror. With each intake of breath, a little more of the paralyzing fear dissolved. Cat almost moaned as his hand moved gently down her arm. Unconsciously, her fingers tangled in the soft hair of his chest. She could feel the powerful pulse in his neck beneath her cheek. Talon was so male, but for once, Cat wasn't afraid of it. Or him. She wanted his touch. Wanted to languish in his arms, needing whatever invisible care he was giving to her right now.

Talon felt his erection hardening to the point of pain. With her hip against his, Cat wasn't aware of his condition, thank God. It was the last thing he wanted her to discover right now. She sank fully against him and he felt her surrender to him for the first time. He sat there in the darkness, the muted moonlight giving the room just enough grayness so that he could see.

Her hair tickled his jaw. The moisture of her breath inflamed him. He wanted to kiss her. Did he dare? Would Cat see his action as taking advantage of her in this situation? The questions spun through Talon's mind. And yet, he felt her slowly beginning to explore his chest, her fingers sliding and making his skin scream for more contact. Was Cat doing this on purpose? Talon honestly didn't know and wasn't willing to assume a damn thing.

Finally, he felt her surrender to him. There was no more sniffing, no more of her wiping the tears from her face. Just…silence. And Cat in his arms. Talon knew he was the one responsible here for whatever actions he initiated. Was Cat ready to be loved by him? Was that what she wanted? If he hauled her onto the bed beside him, how would she react? Cat was different. And he felt differently toward her. He cared and he wanted her to voluntarily want the same things he wanted.

Easing Cat out of his arms, he placed his finger beneath her chin and gazed into her shadowed, moist eyes. "What do you want right now, Cat?"

She gulped over the burning desire in Talon's eyes. Felt the sensuality binding them silently. Talon wanted to kiss her. Her lower lip trembled as an unknown emotion washed over his face. "I want to kiss you," she managed. Feeling unsure, she watched as Talon's mouth curved faintly, his eyes narrowing upon hers.

"I want the same thing," he rasped, framing her face with his hands, leaning down, his mouth barely an inch from hers. "Cat," he whispered, his low voice uneven, "I not only want to kiss you, I want to love you. You're in charge here and I need to know how far you want me to go." Talon searched her upturned eyes, torn by the tears still glimmering in them. The last thing he wanted to do was hurt her. Cat had been hurt enough by men.

Talon's mouth was so close to hers. She could feel the hot moisture of his breath. "I—I don't know...." she choked. Shame wound through her. She didn't see what he saw in her. She didn't consider herself pretty. Worse, she worried what he'd discover about her body.

"Let's start with a kiss? See where it leads? All you have to do is tell me to stop, Cat, and I will." Talon searched her unsure gaze. He was on thin ice with Cat and it could break at any second. She seemed to wrestle with herself. "Tell me what you're feeling, Cat."

She shrugged, feeling unworthy of this man who was so incredibly masculine, ruggedly handsome and wanting her. "I just don't think I'm good enough for you," she admitted hoarsely.

Talon gave her a very male smile. "In my book, you're a ten."

"I like being a ten in your eyes."

He smoothed strands of hair away from her cheek.

She could feel Talon waiting, felt the throbbing power around him, felt his need of her. Yet, it was contained. No man had waited for her before. No man had ever told her she was in control. He was so different from her experience that it rendered her more uncertain. When she stared at his mouth, her body went from zero to a hundred in a split second. She remembered Talon's mouth on hers. She felt dampness collecting swiftly between her thighs. Tired of her indecision because it was based upon fear, Cat leaned that inch and pressed her mouth barely against his.

Talon felt heat sizzle through him as she initiated the shy kiss. Her lips barely grazed his mouth. He nudged his mouth against her upper lip, silently asking for entrance. And she willingly complied. His erection hardened and he drew in a deep breath, forcing the discomfort out of his mind, focusing on how soft and chaste her opening lips felt against his. Her breath was sweet and Talon angled her just enough to ask her lips to blossom fully beneath his urging. She moaned softly as he fully took her, deepening their connection, their contact with one another. He nearly lost it then, her trust implicit with him. Using his tongue, he slowly moved it from one delicious corner of her mouth to the other. Instantly, he felt Cat stiffen but the sexy sound in her throat told him everything he needed to know. She liked it. Emboldened, Talon moved his tongue gently against hers, inviting her to respond, to play with him. Her breath became ragged. Cat gripped his shoulders as their tongues wove into a sliding, sensuous dance with one another. She pressed herself against him, wanting, needing more contact with him. It was her fingers digging frantically into his bunched shoulders that told Talon she was fully committed.

Talon broke the kiss and watched her eyes barely open. He saw lust in them and smiled. "I want you on the bed, beside me."

His strength was surprising as he eased her onto her back and lay down beside her. The nightgown had hitched up above her knees. Talon moved his hand slowly upward across her covered thigh.

"Did anyone ever tell you how beautiful and strong you are?" Talon whispered against her lips. His hand stilled midway up her thigh. Her hair was like a black halo about her head, emphasizing her large blue eyes. Eyes that burned with arousal.

Talon leaned down, taking her mouth gently. He wanted her badly, but she was still shaken from the nightmare and he needed to approach her slowly. Tenderly. Her eyes shuttered closed, her hands wrapping around his shoulders as he glided his mouth against hers. Slipping his hand across her hip, he angled her onto her left side and drew her up against him. The gown was cut low in the back. As his fingers grazed her naked back, he stopped. What the hell was he feeling? Moving his fingers lightly, he felt ridges. *Scars?*

Cat froze.

Easing his mouth from hers, Talon raised his head and saw the fear in her expression.

"What are these?" he asked, gently moving his fingers across her back. There were scars maybe an inch to two inches long at least in five different places across her flesh. He saw the shame. Had her father done this to her? *Jesus.* Leaning down, he kissed her, trying to take away the pain. At first, Cat didn't respond, but Talon moved his mouth persuasively, focusing her on the natural heat that automatically seethed between them. And only then did he lessen his kiss, keeping his hand splayed out across her back.

Cat felt a lump in her throat as she lost herself in the heat and strength of Talon's mouth against her own. His eyes were questioning as his hand moved tenderly across her back, touching the scars from so long ago. He deserved to know.

"My father would beat me with a belt when I was a kid," she whispered raggedly, watching his reaction. She tried to prepare herself for him to be disgusted, as her two other lovers had been. His hand remained firmly on her back, a protective gesture that dissolved her shame.

"Can you turn over for me?" he urged her quietly.

Confused by his request, she allowed him to place her on her stomach. And then Cat felt him kiss every scar that had been inflicted upon her back. He would trace each one with the pad of his finger, kiss it softly and move on to the next one. She closed her eyes, never having felt such tenderness in all her life. His hand cupped her rib cage gently and Talon held her as his mouth moved across each scar. Cat swore she could feel the pain of the memories of each of those beatings vanish beneath his gentle kisses.

Talon eased his hand beneath the straps of her night-gown, pulling them aside, continuing to find scars here and there. He lightly kissed each of them. Tears jammed into Cat's tightly shut eyes as she realized his gesture, absorbing it and wanting to cry because of the loving act he was sharing with her. This wasn't about sex. It was about one human healing another. Hot tears leaked out of her eyes.

Talon held on to his rage. There were at least fifteen scars across Cat's back. The bastard must have used the belt buckle end because he saw the scars were deeper at one end than the other, indicating the metal had gouged deeply in one area as it first struck her soft, unprotected flesh. He wanted to kill him. He felt his heart shredding with anguish over what had been done to Cat. Her skin was velvet smooth, firm, and yet, in the grayness, he could see the raised and puckered scars. He ached for her. When he finished, Talon slid down beside her, resting his cheek against her bare shoulder, tucking her close to him, holding her. Talon wanted to will the deep, beautiful feelings he felt for her into every one of those scars. He wished he could take their memory away from Cat. He knew with his own scars, he remembered each and every one of them. He remembered how he'd gotten it and what had been going on at the time. Everything. It was no different for Cat.

"I'm sorry," he rasped thickly, kissing her shoulder. "I'm so sorry this was done to you. You never deserved it." He kissed her slender nape and slid his hand down her rib cage to her flared hip. It was then that he felt Cat shudder, and he knew she was crying. But, this time, they were healing tears. Talon murmured her name and turned her around so that he could gather her up into his arms and hold her.

The straps of the nightgown had fallen to her upper arms and he slid them back into place. Her eyes were tightly shut, her mouth drawn in anguish as he brought her tightly against him. Groaning, he felt her breasts press against his chest, felt her nipples hardening instantly as they grazed in the soft hair across his chest.

Her tears wet his chest and he closed his eyes, holding her, stroking her hair and shoulders. Talon crooned softly to her. It only made her cry harder, harsh sobs tearing out of her like a perfect storm. First, the assault, then the nightmare, and then he brought back the suffering from her childhood by discovering her scars. What he felt right now was something so deep, visceral and good, and yet, it had no name. He wanted to do so much more for Cat. Talon dragged in a breath, tucked his head against hers and held her tightly, trying to protect her from those terrible memories. Talon knew they would never go away. But, in time, maybe he could bring her peace in his arms. Eventually, her weeping abated and Talon eased Cat away just enough to kiss each of her cheeks, taste the salt of her spent tears and give her his tenderness. Studying her in the silence, he slipped his fingers through her thick black strands. "You have nothing to be ashamed of, Cat. You know that, don't you?" He searched her face.

"I was so afraid of what you would think of me when you found them."

He gave her a tender smile, cupping her cheek. "Babe, it only makes me more sure that you're one of the bravest women I've ever known. Each scar is a Purple Heart as far as I'm concerned."

Cat released a torn sigh. "I thought you'd find me ugly." Because her two lovers had. Her first had discovered them and refused to even touch them, disgusted. The second lover told her she looked ugly. The shame Cat had felt was intensified by their callous comments that she was damaged goods.

Shaking his head, Talon growled, "Ugly? Scars are anything but." He looked up at the ceiling for a moment and then shifted his gaze to Cat. "Listen to me, will you? You are so brave. You survived. I'm sorry there was no one to protect you growing up." Talon gave her a softened look. "Now I understand a little better why you were so hesitant to let me love you. Sooner or later, you knew I'd find them."

Cat's throat tightened and she barely nodded. Her heart was beating with a mix of fear, pain and hope. The look in Talon's eyes was one of understanding. Not pity. Not accusing. But…God, understanding. Talon had kissed her scars. Lovingly. With care. He hadn't been repulsed. Hadn't refused to touch them.

"Do you know what I want?" Talon asked her.

"What?"

"I want to sleep with you, Cat. I want to lie here with you in my arms. I'm not talking about sex. I want to hold you, make you feel safe so you won't have any more nightmares. What do you say?"

Cat closed her eyes, unable to hold his tender gaze. She could feel the power of Talon's desire, knew he wanted her. Yet, he was offering her something even more important: compassion. Opening her eyes, she searched his. "You wouldn't mind?"

Talon grazed her cheek. "I've been dreaming of touching you from the moment I saw you," he admitted, his voice rough with emotion.

His admission gave her the courage she needed. "I've wondered what it would be like, too." Cat could feel his erection pressed against her belly. Talon looked like a cougar in repose, nonetheless dangerous to her. She felt the slickness between her thighs, understanding her body wanted him. Her heart, however, felt pulverized, and as Talon pulled back the covers and gave Cat room for her to move over, she wanted nothing more.

Talon brought the covers up. Cat had come into his arms, laying her head on his shoulder, her arm spanning his torso. "Better?" he rasped against her hair.

"Much," she whispered. "I'm so tired, Talon."

"I know you are." He pressed a kiss to her hair. "Close your eyes? I'll just hold you the rest of the night. Only good dreams…"

CAT WASN'T SURE where her dream began or ended with Talon. Just having the strong, male warmth surrounding her, his arms holding her close, she was caught up in her dream of sliding her hand down across his chest, feeling the spanned hardness of the muscles beneath, the soft hair tangling between her fingertips. He felt so good. So alive. So sexy. There was nothing soft or forgiving around his body, however. His muscles tensed wherever she skimmed his chest, shoulder and upper arm. And when she felt herself laid upon her back, his mouth warmly sipping from her lips, she slowly opened her eyes.

"Is this what you want?" Talon asked in a low, rasping voice, holding her aroused gaze. He was afraid of survivor sex with Cat. People who were traumatized frequently turned to sex to reaffirm life. It would be taking advantage of Cat, something Talon refused to do. He wanted Cat to come to him when she honestly felt ready, not driven into his arms due to trauma.

She blinked once. "I—I thought it was a dream."

"You don't want this because of what happened yesterday?" he demanded, digging into her soft eyes.

"Oh," she muttered, "survivor sex?"

"Exactly."

"I've seen so much trauma, Talon, and I never once went looking for sex as a Band-Aid for my emotions. Does that answer your question?" Her mouth curved softly as she held his narrowed gray eyes, which burned with desire for her alone.

He smiled a little and shrugged, his hand grazing her cheek. "That's good to hear. Where do dreams end and reality begins?"

Cat realized it was dawn, the night chased away as she'd slept deeply and without nightmares in Talon's arms. She looked at the growth of his beard, how it emphasized his hollowed cheeks, the stormy look in his narrowed, hunterlike eyes as he leaned over her, intently watching her. "Talon," she whispered, "I want to love you. I've wanted to love you, I think, since I looked into your eyes out on that highway."

Utterly speechless, Talon leaned down, kissing her hairline, hearing a soft sound of surrender escape her lips. A sound of pure pleasure.

"Tell me what you want, what you like." He felt her tense and he lifted his chin, looking down at her. She seemed confused, which prompted him to add, "You let me know if you like or don't like something I'm doing, okay?" He traced her full lower lip with his thumb. "I want to make you feel good. That's all."

"It sounds wonderful," she admitted, her voice hoarse because the look he gave her sent scalding signals straight down to her lower body.

"I'm going to get a condom from my room. I'll be right back." Talon eased away from her, stood up and disappeared from her room. He came back and got rid of the boxer shorts. Her gaze moved over his taut, honed body. In the dawn light, the shadows emphasized the power of him and she felt her heart thud with anticipation. He was indeed a lithe, boneless cougar as he walked around the bed, coming to her side and sliding in next to her. The look on his face was one of focus—on her. It excited her. As Talon slid next to her, Cat felt an anticipation she'd never experienced as he cupped her cheek, angling her toward his mouth.

Her world spun like golden webs beaded with rainbow droplets of water, only each droplet was his kiss, his mouth teaching her how to kiss him in return, drowning her mind in fiery depths where she no longer thought, only felt. As he slid his hand beneath the hem of her silk nightgown, slowly working it upward across her thigh, gathering at her waist, her world began to melt. Talon's hand followed the curve of her taut thigh, slowly opening her, kissing the inside of her soft, sensitive flesh, moving toward her wet entrance. Feeling his mouth move closer and closer, her breath became uneven and she moaned with anticipation.

Talon moved slowly, testing Cat, teasing her, seeing where she was at. He wanted this first time to be good for her, not a disaster. Unsure of whether she'd ever been touched in her most secret of places, he lay above her, watching her expression, hearing the soft sounds caught in her slender throat, her eyes closing, pinkness flooding her cheeks. Yeah, she liked it, but he took his time, playing her, asking her to participate.

As Talon leaned down, his moist breath across her nipple hidden by the silk nightgown, she gasped softly. The next time, he settled his lips around that hardened nipple and she cried out, but it was a sound of pleasure.

And just as he slowly suckled her, he slid his finger into the soft, yielding folds, gauging her reaction. She was wet and slick, more than ready for him. The moment he began to tease that knot of nerves just inside her, she arched into his hand, groaning. Her eyes flew open and he smiled down into them, seeing nothing but surprise coupled with deep arousal. No fear. That was good, because Talon felt her body begin to tighten, begin to prepare for an orgasm.

Whispering her name across her lips, drinking her breath into him, Talon slid a second finger into her, slowly moving forward. She was incredibly small and tight. Instantly, she cried out, the raw sound drowning like sunlight into his mouth, her entire body convulsing. He felt her muscle tighten and grip him, her breath ragged and hoarse with small cries as the orgasm flowed through her. Sweet, hot fluid surrounded his fingers.

Panting, Cat's whole world turned hot and scalding, as if someone had hurled her off into some bright, floating, beautiful place she'd never been before. She heard Talon growl her name as her body rippled and gripped his fingers. A second orgasm filled with rich heat spread throughout her, pleasure flooding every sense she had. He moved his fingers within her, not allowing her to come down, rather, stimulating another, even more powerful orgasm that shattered her lower body. Cat could only sob his name, gripping his upper arm, her back arched tautly against him.

Talon watched the flush of orgasm sweep sweetly up across her straining body. He slowly removed his fingers, wanting her to rest for a bit, allow her to absorb all the pleasure he could see reflected in her skin.

As Cat dug deep into his thick biceps, he smiled. She barely opened her eyes. They were glazed with awe as she held his stare.

"Wh-what happened?" she whispered, her brow furrowing.

Talon kissed her swollen, wet lips. "Multiple orgasms. Feel good?" He pulled away just enough to see her luscious mouth curve into a delicious, satisfied smile.

"Good," she whispered. "So good." Cat closed her eyes.

"There's more to come," he promised thickly, pulling the straps of the nightgown off her shoulders. In a few pulls and nudges, the lavender silk ended up on the floor next to the bed. Now Talon could look at her naked. Cat was long, firm and sculpted from the workouts and firefighting she did for a living. Skimming her lower leg, knee and thigh, he settled his hand against her gently rounded belly. Talon captured the first nipple in his mouth. Cat was so sensitive, exquisitely so. Every touch, large or small, made her react in some way that told him she liked what he was doing with her. She nearly came apart between his hands as he lavished each nipple, suckling her and then moving one hand to between her thighs, feeling her slickness with his fingers, knowing she was more than ready for him. Talon felt her building toward another orgasm. He was so close to coming he had to get inside of her. He rolled on the condom.

Parting her thighs with his knees, Talon knelt before her, his hands on her curved thighs. She had wide hips, a long rib cage and full, perfect breasts. Her nipples were a rosy pink color, hard, and as he leaned down, he placed his throbbing erection at her slick, hot entrance. Talon saw Cat brace her back, her fists curling into the bedcovers. All good signs. She was small and tight. And Talon wasn't small at all. Covering her with his body, his elbows taking most of his weight off her, he eased just inside her, gauging her response.

A groan tore from her and Talon patiently waited. She was incredibly wet, and it felt as if a fist surrounded him. Very slowly, he moved in and out of her, rubbing that sweet knot. It took the tension out of her and he watched Cat sigh and become aroused. And when he pulled a nipple into his mouth, biting it lightly, just enough to reach that pleasure-pain point to focus her attention, she released a sweet moan and automatically arched her hips against his. Cat instinctively reacted, drew him more deeply into her. It was give and take, gentle, slow and burning him up alive. Talon could feel himself tighten and scream for release, but he wasn't going to cause Cat pain. He could handle his own hunger for all the right reasons.

Moving to her other breast, he blew his moist breath across the taut peak, heard her moan his name. Placing his teeth around it, he tugged on it just enough and she groaned, her hands releasing the covers, flying to his shoulders, digging frantically into his flesh. Talon thrust deeper into her and forced himself to wait. The time allowed her body to accommodate him until, finally, he could feel her muscled walls begin to relax around his erection. Talon then drew the nipple deep into his mouth, suckling strongly. Cat cried out, her hips bucking wildly against his hips and he thrust as deep as he could go into her, then forced himself to halt. Perspiration dotted his wrinkled brow.

Cat tensed, but the more he suckled her, the more she relaxed and she began to push her hips insistently against his. She was slick, hot honey around him, and Talon planted his elbows on either side of her head. Now he could rock her rhythmically, stimulate her and have her orgasm with him inside her this time.

Her fingers convulsively dug and released against his shoulders as Talon pulled out and then thrust slowly into her. All the way. He wanted to teach her about speed and rhythm, while watching her, feeling how her body responded to him. As he increased the swiftness of his thrusts, he heard her mewl, bucking against him, feeling the surge of another orgasm preparing to explode within her. Talon gritted his teeth, closing his eyes, moving hard into her, her fingers clawing into his tense, bunched shoulders. The slick dampness between them made it easy for him to pump into her and, seconds later, he felt the violent convulsion of the orgasm grip and surround him.

Cat sobbed his name as her orgasm exploded within her. He used his body to not only make it more powerful for her but prolong it to the point where she would go suddenly weak beneath him. And when she sank limply into the mattress, Talon lay very still within her, feeling her breasts heave against his chest, the harsh rasp of her breath against his neck, the rose flush covering her body beneath him.

Yeah, this was what it was all about: giving her absolute, mind-blowing pleasure. Cat's eyes were shut and a faint, almost mysterious smile of satisfaction curved her swollen lips. It made Talon feel powerful, like a man. As he pressed kisses against her hairline, her lids, cheeks, he allowed Cat to rest beneath him. She was so soft and curved against his unforgiving angular lines and hardness.

Now Talon was going to take pleasure for himself, but he wasn't content without her participation. Raising up on his knees, he settled his large hands around Cat's hips, drawing her tight against him. As he leaned over, her breasts were within easy reach of his mouth and hands. Sinking deep within her, Talon moved slowly, awakening her body once more. Curving his hands around her taut breasts, watching those nipples harden with just his touch, he smiled into her barely opened eyes.

"Come with me," he urged thickly. "One more time?"

She smiled. Her hands curved around his forearms. He felt the wetness collecting as he nudged. Talon smiled to himself. Yeah, she was so damned responsive, so sensitive…and then he set about taking her right up to that ultimate moment. Talon framed her face, took her mouth hard and plunged himself deep and repeatedly into her, triggering that incredible reflex within her body. The livid, scalding fire surged down his spine, ripping through him. Talon pulled her into his arms, holding her hard, fused with her, never wanting to let her go.

CHAPTER EIGHTEEN

CAT AWOKE SLOWLY, nuzzling into the pillow. Sunlight was bright around the curtained window in her bedroom. She was filled with a sense of quiet euphoria, a satisfaction humming through her body she'd never experienced before. She heard the door open and slowly opened her eyes.

"Hey," Talon said, smiling as he brought over a tray and set it on the dresser. Cat's face was drowsy, her eyes barely open, a faint smile curving her mouth, which made him go hot with longing for her again. She slowly turned onto her back and rubbed her eyes.

"What time is it?" she asked thickly.

"Nine o'clock." Cat was naked and as she sat up and the covers pooled around her hips, he absorbed her luscious body. Talon hoped she knew by this morning how beautiful, how sexy and sensual she was. Sitting down on the edge of the bed, he said, "I thought you might like a cup of coffee." He held the mug toward her after she dropped her hands into her lap.

Cat felt the heat of Talon's stare, felt her body effortlessly respond to his very male look. "Thanks," she said, her voice groggy. Their fingers touched and Cat held his slate-gray eyes, felt the unspoken warmth unfurling around her. "I had the most delicious, sexy dreams I've ever had last night." She put the cup to her lips, inhaling the fragrance of the coffee, watching him over the rim.

Talon was dressed in a white cowboy shirt, the sleeves rolled up, his jeans and boots. He had shaved and showered. She inhaled the scent of the evergreen soap he'd used earlier. The way his mouth quirked, the amusement dancing in his eyes, she smiled with him and then took a sip of the hot coffee.

"Funny thing," Talon offered, reaching out and taming some of her hair away from her cheek, "I had the very same dreams. Want to compare notes?" She looked satisfied and Talon could feel himself growing hard wanting Cat all over again. Her cheeks grew pink over his touch. Yes, she was easily affected by him, Talon realized. This morning, though, Cat looked like a woman who had been pleasured with the gifts a man could give her. That made him feel good.

His heart expanded with fierce emotion as she lowered the cup to her lap, both her long, graceful hands wrapped around it.

"This is a dream that seems to keep going even while I'm awake."

"It's a good dream. I like sharing it with you."

Talon seemed to become serious, his heated gaze on her. She was naked but she felt no discomfort or shyness. When his eyes moved from her face to her breasts, she felt them tighten, felt her nipples hardening. "I like our dream," she whispered, lifting the cup.

"So do I." Talon watched her slowly sip the coffee. He'd kissed that wide, full mouth, tasted her, loved her, and he wanted more. "How are you feeling this morning?" Talon was sure she was probably sore and achy. He leaned forward and brushed her pink cheek with his thumb. Her lashes lowered and she leaned into his palm. *Trust.* Cat trusted him.

The power of her gesture humbled him. He'd worried about the trust being broken between them, but if anything, it only grew stronger. The words *I love you* damn near tore out of his mouth. He was so shocked by it he lowered his hand, stunned. *Love?* Was this what love felt like? Because Talon couldn't remember a time when he'd awakened the next morning after having sex with a woman and feeling like this.

"I'm happy," Cat whispered. Her skin prickled pleasantly as he'd grazed her cheek. The intimacy between them was quiet and strong. She remembered his hands making her flesh sing last night, giving her priceless gifts of pleasure she'd never known existed until he'd walked into her life. And looking at him sitting near her, his hip against her blanketed thigh, Cat had never felt so happy. She could see the love shining in his eyes for her. And although she thought she knew what love was, she really hadn't until now. Because the gleam in his eyes held so many unspoken, good emotions in them for her alone.

"Sore?"

"Oh," she murmured, smiling a little shyly. "Well, some, but I'm okay."

"A hot bath will put you in good order." Talon wanted to take that cup out of her hands, lie down at her side and start to love Cat all over again. There was a new tenderness and openness to her this morning. His body was hard, wanting to teach her, show her so many intimate ways to fly with him on the wings of pleasure. "Want me to draw it for you?"

She gave him a sleepy smile. "You'd do that?"

He slid his hand down her blanketed thigh, remembering the sensitive flesh on the inner side, how she'd come apart beneath his fingers, how slickly wet she'd become. "Of course."

She tilted her head, the coffee halfway to her lips. "Am I in a dream?"

"When a man and woman have a good relationship, Cat, it flows into all the rest of the parts of their lives." And who was he to talk? Talon had never spent a morning after with a woman he'd had sex with. Ever. It had been an unbroken rule in his book of life. Until now. Until Cat. And he found himself wanting to please her, care for her, make her smile. Make her happy in large and small ways. Just the velvet look she gave him made his heart sing powerfully and joy tunneled through him. He rose and leaned down, kissing her brow. "I'll get the bath ready for you. And then I'll make us breakfast."

His lips on her sent a sheet of heat all the way from her breasts straight down to the simmering heat in her womb. She looked up into his eyes, feeling his need of her. "Thanks," she whispered. "You're absolutely spoiling me."

Talon stood for a moment and absorbed her half-awake expression, the happiness glinting in her eyes. "You deserve to be spoiled, babe."

Cat wasn't used to such kindness from a lover, much less having a bath drawn for her. As she dressed in a pair of khakis and a pale pink top, an invisible rapture kept bubbling up through her. She pulled a brush through her black hair and the ends curled naturally across her shoulders. Noticing her eyes, Cat stared into the mirror. There was new life in them. Talon had put it there. She bowed her head, hands on the counter, closing her eyes, feeling her lower body. He'd given her something so rare and exquisite. Cat placed the brush on the counter. What was this feeling? At times like this, Cat wished she had a mother she could talk to. Maybe Casey would know. Whatever it was, she'd never felt happier.

After brushing her teeth, she went downstairs, relishing the scent of salty bacon frying. Her step felt light, almost as if floating. Looking from the stairs toward the kitchen, she saw Talon working at the stove. A smile came to her mouth as she saw he'd already set the dining room table. All of a sudden, the condo felt like home to her. Was it because Talon was here? Cat descended the stairs and walked into the kitchen.

"Smells great," she said. She poured herself a second cup of coffee. "Want some?"

Talon took the bacon out of the skillet and set it in a bowl with paper towels in the bottom of it. "That would be great," he said, glancing over at Cat. Her pink tee matched the flush in her cheeks. "Bath feel good?"

"Mmm, the bath did wonders," she murmured. "Can I help out here?"

"No. Just tell me how many eggs you want."

"How about two."

"Over medium?"

"Please."

The toast popped up. Cat turned and put the slices on a nearby plate. They fell into an easy pattern of working with one another. In no time, Talon had their eggs on two plates next to the stove. She carried the bowl of bacon and the toast to the table.

Talon pulled out the chair for her.

"You are truly spoiling me."

"And why not?" he teased, sitting down at her elbow.

Cat shared a warm look with him as she picked three pieces of bacon from the bowl between them. "I'm just not used to it."

Talon gave her a dark look, smiled a little but said nothing. "We need to be over at the sheriff's office at ten-thirty. Cade called and asked if you felt up to the official interview and report on what happened yesterday. Are you?" He held her gaze. Talon could see fear enter her eyes but she quickly hid it.

"Sure."

"Are you having second thoughts about pressing charges against Magee?"

"No. I don't want him on the loose, Talon. I'm afraid he'll come after me again."

"Then you need to tell Cade that and you need to write it in your report. The judge will make a decision based upon what you tell Cade. Don't leave anything out."

Some of the happiness she felt dissipated. "Do you have to leave and go to work after breakfast?"

"No. I'm taking today off. I'd already told Val I'd be there at the ranch tomorrow morning." He slathered blueberry jam across his toast, watching Cat's expression. "I thought after we got done at the sheriff's office, we could pick up a to-go lunch at Mo's and take it over to my mother's apartment and share it with her?"

Heartened, Cat said, "I'd like that. I know you were going to see Sandy at noon yesterday before Magee attacked me."

"My mother was fine with me not showing up, Cat. She was more worried about you than missing a lunch with me." Talon was discovering Cat always put those she loved or cared for before herself. It was just a part of who she was, but he knew he needed to sometimes corral her intentions so she would take adequate care of herself first.

"I was worried it would impact Sandy. I know she's rallying, and she is getting much stronger, but…" Cat made a face.

Talon reached out, his hand covering hers, gently squeezing her fingers. "Right now, the focus is on you. Where it should be, Cat." Talon could see the swelling along her jaw. And he could see the bruising, a faint purple color along her left cheek and eye. He wanted to kill Magee for touching her. "Today, we do things that are as stress-free as we can make them for you."

Cat sighed and finished off her breakfast. She picked up her plate and took it to the sink. Her feelings were bright, happy, and yet, she felt fear. Why? Pouring them more coffee, she sat down at the table. Talon had made himself four eggs, eaten at least half a pound of bacon and four pieces of toast. The man knew how to tuck it away. Yet, he was lean and hard, not an ounce of fat anywhere on his body. She sat with her elbows on the table, coffee between her hands.

"Where are we going, Talon?"

He stared over at her. There was uncertainty in her eyes. "I don't know, Cat. I like what we have. Do you?" He had never lied to a woman and he wasn't about to lie to her. The word *love* kept swimming around in his head and he kept pushing it away. Talon didn't know what love was. And maybe these new, brilliant feelings rummaging around in his heart were love, but he honestly didn't know. He saw that Cat studied him in the gathering silence.

"I like it, too," she admitted, feeling the warmth and

care in his gaze. With a little shrug, she added, "I just don't know what to expect."

"Makes two of us. Let's take it one day at a time."

"Yes." Nodding, Cat thought about her other disastrous relationships. None had lasted long. And it was only about sex. And not about her pleasure at all. Not until last night. Neither of those men ever talked about the future. They came around when they wanted sex with her and that was it. And now, Cat knew it hadn't been good sex. Not like it could be, which was what Talon had shared with her last night.

Talon could sense her quandary and he wasn't sure how Cat was reacting to his statement. She appeared distracted. "Tell me what you want." He dug into her gaze. He wasn't one to assume anything, having learned ages ago that straight talk between two people was essential.

Cat shrugged. "I've never met anyone like you, Talon," she began in a low tone. "I don't know how to proceed, what to do or what you expect from me."

"I want to know what you need from me, Cat. It isn't my way. Or yours. Two of us are sitting here at this table. Talking it out is the only way to go."

She gave him a shy look and swallowed hard. "I don't have any experience with someone like you."

He reached out, covering her hand. Talon sensed her other relationships had all been one-way: what the man wanted and demanded. There was no consideration for Cat or her needs. "That's okay. Life is always about learning something new every day." He held her hand a little more firmly. And more than anything, Talon was aware of the fragile trust she'd just built with him. It would be insane to push what he wanted on her and end up destroying it and their relationship. He had to have her input, her needs and what she wanted from him.

"I want to be with you, Talon. I want to know more about you, what makes you the man you are." Cat turned her hand over, tangling her fingers between his, seeing the care burning in his eyes toward her. "Last night…" Her voice grew hoarse.

"Last night was so incredible for me, Talon. I—I'm ashamed to admit this, but I never knew that I could have so much pleasure before it happened." She avoided his sharpened look. "You made me feel things no man has ever given me." Cat forced herself to lift her eyes and meet his dark, turbulent gaze. "I liked it. I like you. I've always been drawn to you. And right now, I feel happy, like my heart is going to burst. You've given me so many new feelings, new experiences…."

Staggered by her bravery, he lifted her hand and pressed a kiss to the back of it. "I like what we have too, Cat. And I like making love with you." Talon felt adrift emotionally, afraid to put a name on what he felt for Cat. It was way too soon. They had to have time.

"I don't know the rules," she admitted.

"Rules?"

She licked her lower lip, nervous. "Between us."

Talon shook his head and gave her a gentle look. "We'll make them up as we go along, Cat. Are you okay with that?"

"Will you stay with me tonight?"

"Do you want me to?" Talon held her gaze, feeling her sense of inadequacy.

"Yes, I'd like that."

"Then I'll stay." Talon released her hand and cupped her cheek. "The rules between a man and a woman are their own, Cat. All you have to do is speak up, tell me what's on your mind, in your heart. I know this is new to you, but it's new to me, too."

Surprise flared in her eyes. "But…you're so worldly compared to me."

Talon grinned. "In some ways, yes, but in other ways, no, Cat." And if she knew he was wrestling with all these new, vibrant feelings deep within his crazy heart, it would only serve to confuse her more. Until Talon could understand what was going on within him, he couldn't give it adequate words. "What we need to do is be patient with one another. And honest."

She shrugged. "I don't know how to be otherwise."

"One of the many qualities I like about you, babe."

CAT FINISHED WRITING up her report and handed it to Cade Garner. They sat in his office at the sheriff's department. She felt better because Talon was there beside her.

"Just so you know," Cade told her, taking her signed report, "someone hired an expensive attorney out of San Francisco for Magee."

"What does that mean?"

Cade grimaced. "The guy is already making noises about getting him released until the trial."

"No way," Talon growled. "He'd start stalking Cat again."

"You and I know that," Cade said. "Cat's statement will help the judge decide."

Fear bolted through Cat. "But…he can't be freed."

Talon reached out, gripping her hand for a moment. "Let's take this a day at a time, Cat. Cade doesn't know what the judge will decide."

Cade stood. "Yeah, I'm hoping the judge assigned to Magee's case will slam the bastard's ass in jail and set the bail so damned high no one will pay it."

Frowning, Cat stood. "Okay, but you'll let us know?"

Cade held her worried gaze. "I'll give you a call as soon as I know, Cat. In the meantime, just relax. It's sunny outside. Go enjoy your day."

"Okay," she said. "Thank you for everything, Cade."

As she walked with Talon out to her truck, she was glad he held her hand. The morning sky was a medium blue, the sun bright, and she slid on her sunglasses. "This thing with Magee scares me," she confided to Talon.

He nodded and opened the truck door for Cat. "Let it go. There's no way a judge will let that bastard loose before trial."

Cat grimaced and said nothing. She fished the keys out of her vest pocket. Once Talon climbed in, they left for Mo's to pick up lunch for the three of them, although Cat had lost her appetite.

CHAPTER NINETEEN

CAT WANTED TO visit Gus and the McPhersons after they left Sandy's apartment. She wanted to at least let them know she was all right. Talon had nodded and given her a look of pride over her decision but said nothing. Gus was in the kitchen preparing dinner for the evening when they walked in.

"Well, look who the cat dragged in," Gus crowed, grinning.

Cat couldn't help but smile and walked over and carefully hugged the small woman. "I just wanted to show you that I'm alive and well," she joked.

Talon walked to the counter and pulled down three cups and filled them with coffee. While the two women hugged and talked, he placed the mugs on the table and sat down. Pretty soon, they came over. Gus was looking spiffy in a pair of bright red slacks and a white blouse. The dark green apron reminded Talon of Christmas, not spring. Her silver hair looked like a halo beneath the lamps suspended above the table.

Gus rubbed her pointed chin. "I was over at your old homestead last week." She gave him a one-eyebrow raised look.

"Oh?" And then Talon remembered that the place was up for sale and Gus had been interested in buying it, according to his mother.

"Yep. Still got that white picket fence around the house, Talon. Needs a coat of paint, for sure, but it's still there. Sandy says, from the pictures I took with my cell phone, it's pretty much what it looked like when you were there as a family. Just more run-down."

A lump started to form in his throat. He couldn't even speak. Talon could only imagine how much hurt, the memories, had been plowed up by seeing them.

Gus continued, "I told her the place was up for sale. You know, your ranch has gone through about five buyers since you left for the Navy?"

"No, I didn't know it."

"Anyone who bought the Triple H was an Easterner thinking they were gonna play Westerner." She snorted. "None of them had a clue how to run a ranch or take care of it. I watched it being bought and sold over and over again. Every once in a while, I'd drive over and see what was happening."

His heart wrung with pain. Talon remembered riding fence line with his father so many times. Gardner Holt had shown him how to repair downed barbed wire. He'd taught him everything he could up until the day before he died of the massive heart attack out in the barn. He missed his father. Wished many times he'd stayed alive. Gardner was an easy man to talk with, never judged anyone, always was a good listener and always had a smile for everyone. How his mother must have missed him. Glancing over at Cat, knowing how he felt about her, Talon now could understand the depth of devastation his mother suffered when his father had suddenly died. He couldn't even begin to imagine if Cat was suddenly torn out of his life. The loss was unimaginable to Talon.

"I've never been over to the Triple H," Cat admitted quietly, seeing the emotions in Talon's eyes. He was gripping the mug a little more tightly than usual. Judging from the look on Talon's face, the grief registering in his eyes, he must have had a wonderful relationship with his father. And she ached for his loss.

"Well, I make it my business to always be a good neighbor," Gus told them. "Every time it changed hands, I'd go over and introduce myself, tell them the Bar H butted up against their property. I'd always offer help or advice if they needed it. That way, I got to see what shape the ranch is in."

"How is it now?" Talon asked, almost afraid to hear her answer.

Gus grumbled, "It has fallen into a state of terrible disrepair, Talon. And of course all the previous owners thought they knew how to run a ranch." Gus snorted. "Not one of 'em called me and asked for advice or help. You can't just walk in, buy a ranch and expect it to run itself. You have to invest your heart and soul in it."

Pain rifled through Talon's heart. He frowned and stared down at his coffee cup, wrestling with dark emotions. "Does my mom know this?"

"She knows some from the pictures," Gus said. "But she had her album of photos when the place looked beautiful. I think she wanted to keep those dreams. I encouraged her to remember the property as it used to be."

Relief tunneled through Talon. "Thank you."

She patted his arm. "I wouldn't ever do anything to hurt Sandy. She needs every reason she can grasp hold of to fight and stay alive."

Cat thought she saw moisture in Talon's eyes for a split second. And then the look was gone. His mouth tightened up. She could tell he was holding back a lot of feelings he couldn't express. "Sandy told us the Triple H was up for sale and that you were looking at it?"

"Yep," Gus said. She sipped her coffee and grinned. "I was over there with the Realtor yesterday. The last owners have already run back East and the place is sittin' empty."

"Any cattle on it?" Talon asked.

"Nah, nothin' on it, son. Pretty much abandoned."

"Sandy said you were considering buying it?" Cat asked.

"I am." Gus took a deep breath and studied Talon. "I've been waitin' to see if the Triple H would come back on the market. And I was hoping like the devil it would, because your mother was really goin' downhill after her cancer came back. I wanted to buy the Triple H and give her something to hold on to, Talon. But the ranch didn't come up for sale when I wished it had and she was already slipping away from us with this second battle with cancer. And you were gone and no one knew where you were." She shrugged and stared off in the distance for a moment, the kitchen growing silent.

"Miss Gus, I couldn't tell anyone my whereabouts when I was deployed." Talon felt the gnawing pain grow wider in his heart. When his mother, who had lost two men she loved, was falling ill a second time, he was over in Afghanistan. *Again.* Always.

Gus patted his arm. "It's okay, son. I understand. So did Sandy. That's why I was holdin' my breath hopin' like the dickens that the ranch would come up for sale. But it never did, and she slid far and fast." She gave Talon a gentle look. "Call it what you want, but you getting wounded and sent back here to us was a godsend for Sandy. You fed her hope. Just by being near, you did that for her. I'm not wishing you got wounded, mind you, but in another way, you are giving your mother hope again. And she's respondin'."

Talon avoided her gaze. He didn't want to remember anything about his wounding, but it was impossible. Turning the mug around in his hands, he muttered, "At least something good came out of it."

Cat felt Talon withdraw. Felt his agony even though he wasn't showing it physically. There was an invisible tie between them, something profoundly beautiful and it made her grateful that she could pick up on it, because Talon rarely gave words to his feelings. Except in bed, loving her. And her body glowed warmly in the memory of last night.

"Listen, son, I've lived eighty-five years and seen it all. I can tell you that most often, the darkest night of our soul is a blessing in disguise. But it will take you a decade or longer to realize it." She gave him a kind look. "You and your mother have been through many rough times. And now you're on an upswing. She's gettin' better and so are you."

Talon smiled briefly. "You're an eternal optimist, Miss Gus."

"Well, I really don't like the other choice. Do you?" She drilled a hard look into his eyes. "What? Depression? Giving up? Hopelessness? Nah, not for me." She poked his arm with her index finger. "And not for you, either. You're Wyoming bred. Wyoming tough."

That drew a sour smile from Talon. "You're truly a force of nature, Miss Gus."

"Humph."

Cat laughed and shook her head. "Miss Gus, you should be doing YouTube videos on positive thinking."

"Not interested." She sipped her coffee. "Now, I dunno if Sandy told you, but I'm puttin' in a bid on the Triple H, Talon."

"She said you were looking at the possibility." He couldn't keep his heart from pounding a little harder in his chest. His home. He had been born in that ranch house. The memories were as sharp and clear as when he'd lived them. "Yep, I called my Realtor and put in an offer." She smiled slyly. "They're wantin' five million for that place. And it does have five hundred acres of good land but they've let the place go. It's in dire need of a lot of work to bring it back. The house, the barn, the corrals and outbuildings are in terrible shape. If they think I'm gonna pay for a run-down, shambles of a place, they got another think comin'."

Talon felt hope. If Miss Gus bought the Triple H, maybe he might be able to help fix it up. Get it back to the way it used to be when he grew up there. "If you get it, what are your plans?"

Gus scratched her chin. "Well, my first reason for buying it, Talon, was to get your mother installed back there. My feelin' is that if she can return home, she'll stay well. People don't know how important home is to their well-bein', but I do." She jabbed her finger down on the table. "Sandy's heart was broken, Talon. And folks with a broken heart need their home to recoup themselves, pull themselves up by the bootstraps, but she had her home torn out from under her."

Talon felt moisture in his eyes. He swallowed against a lump a couple of times before he could speak. His voice came out thick with barely veiled feelings. "If you could do that for her, Miss Gus, I know it would help her." He felt shame that he couldn't do it for her. The Navy never paid anyone that much, not even SEALs.

Patting his arm, she said, "Tut-tut, Talon. I may look old, gray-haired and wrinkled as all get-out, but I'm pretty smart when it comes to sizin' up people. This town has pulled together to help Sandy. But your comin' home is makin' the biggest difference. And it just so happened that months after you came back to us, that ranch suddenly comes up for sale again." She grinned and rubbed her hands together. "And I jumped at the chance like a duck jumps on a June bug. I want Sandy home. It will help heal her broken heart."

"Do you think you'll get the ranch?" Cat asked, hoping more than anything she would. She understood how much Sandy loved the ranch she'd been forced to give up. The best days of her life were spent there. Cat glanced over at Talon, and his eyes were suspiciously bright. The need to put her arms around his shoulders nearly tore her apart. Right now Talon needed a little TLC. She knew he was hurting, was disappointed in himself that he couldn't do as much for his mother.

"I'm hopin'," Gus said, finishing off her coffee. "When I find out, I'll let you two birds know."

"What do Val and Griff think about it?" Cat asked.

Pushing her chair away from the table, Gus smiled. "Griff is the one who's been doin' all the background investigation on the ranch and its state of disrepair. He's got an MBA from Harvard and I'm usin' it. Griff's the one who told me what to offer for it. And he's going to handle the negotiations." She slowly stood up, rubbing her hip. Casting a look over at Talon, she smiled down at him. "And if I get your ranch, Talon, I'm going to make sure that you and Griff spend a whole lotta time over there fixin' it up for Sandy. I don't want her movin' in until that place is spiffy lookin' again."

Talon could barely believe it. "I hope you get it, Miss Gus. I really do." For his mother. She would rally if she was home again, Talon realized. Who wouldn't? Grateful to the old woman, he rasped, "You really are a guardian angel, Miss Gus. I've heard others in town refer to you as that, but it's true. I know my mother would be happy. And I'm grateful to you."

"Yep," Gus said, patting his shoulder. "I've got a plan in motion. And just remember, you and Sandy are worth it."

"What a day," Cat said as she cut up some tomatoes for their dinner salad in the kitchen. The western sun was low on the horizon and they'd just driven back to the condo. Talon had been quiet on the ride in. She could feel many emotions going through him. The hope burning in his eyes nearly undid her. Hope for Sandy to have her home returned to her through Gus's goodness and kindness.

Talon pulled out a head of lettuce from the fridge and set it next to the cutting board where she was working. "Mind-blowing, to say the least," he muttered. Half the chicken breasts and rice were left from last night and he was going to warm them up in the oven. Cat stood with a red apron wrapped around her waist. As he walked by, he moved her hair aside and placed a quick kiss on her slender neck. "It's been a good day in lots of ways."

Her skin tingled in the wake of his mouth grazing her. Cat liked his ability to show how he felt toward her. "I imagine you're kind of shaken up by all of it?"

Talon opened the oven door. "Shocked," he said. Sliding the Pyrex into the oven, he shut the door and straightened. "When Mom told us about the Triple H and Miss Gus considering buying it, I didn't put much stock into it."

He came over and stood near to watch as she cut up the tomatoes. "Gus is wily, Talon. I'll bet you anything she's a lot further into this sale than she's letting on. She never does anything without studying it and getting the facts. Griff has done some smaller land acquisitions for her in the past. And he's always gotten what she wanted to buy." Smiling a little at him, feeling her body respond hotly to his nearness, she added, "I wouldn't even be surprised if she'd already bought the Triple H and is just waiting on the bank to clear the deal. Then I think she'll announce it to everyone."

"Why do you say that?" Talon pushed her hair away from the nape of her neck and moved his lips against her warm skin, inhaling her sweet, spicy scent. He wanted to love her. Right now. He felt her tense and then relax, a sigh issuing from her lips. She'd stopped what she was doing, focused on his mouth sliding across her neck, kissing her.

"Mmm," Cat murmured, feeling his arm slide around her waist, pulling her close to his body. She allowed the knife and tomato to sit on the cutting board. "You make it hard for me to think," she said, breathless. "Gus is a poker player, Talon. She keeps her cards close to her chest until a deal is done. That's why I said it."

"I think you're right. There was a glint in her eye when she was telling us about it. My gut tells me it's a done deal, too."

Cat leaned against him, closing her eyes, absorbing

his maleness, his mouth sending small kisses across her neck. "I can't think anymore," she said, and laughed. "And it's all your fault, Holt."

"And I've been wanting to do this all day," Talon growled, pulling her into his arms, turning her toward him. As she leaned against him, sliding her arms around his shoulders, Talon smiled down into her eyes. He could see so much in them. Cat didn't try to hide how she felt about him. And when her hips pressed against his, he groaned, feeling her belly against his arousal.

"Me, too," she whispered, leaning up, framing his face and sliding her lips against the line of his mouth. Cat wasn't disappointed as he pulled her tightly against him, his mouth curving hotly against hers, opening her lips, deepening their kiss until she felt her knees melting beneath her. The man knew how to kiss! His breath was moist, sensual against her face, his fingers tunneling through her hair, angling her just so to hold her captive, to plunder her mouth with unrestrained hunger. His other hand drifted to her hip, cupping her, crushing her against him, letting her know how hard he was, how much he wanted her.

As Talon eased his mouth from her wet lips, he opened his eyes, staring into hers. Cat's gaze was cloudy with arousal and he smiled a little. One kiss and it was like flipping a switch between them. They went from simmer to boiling in a heartbeat. He would bet his life she was damp right now and he moved his fingers, curving them around her thigh. Her breath hitched as his fingers grazed the denim across her entrance. She was wet and he smiled. Cat pushed against his hand, wanting more. The look in her eyes was the same as he'd seen just before she'd experienced her deepest pleasure.

He was trembling with need and positioned her to continue massaging the damp region. "I like what we have."

Cat found her voice husky as she moaned, wanting his fingers exactly where they were. "So do I." The act was so intimate, so arousing, her lower body burning beneath his fingers. She felt far away, taken to another place and time in his arms, the sensations building, scalding her, and she moaned, pressing her face against his shoulder.

"Hungry?" he rasped.

"As in food? Or as in going to bed with you?" She saw his eyes glitter with amusement, feeling his need of her, his erection obvious.

"Your call," he said, positioning her such that he could place his palm against her entrance. A cry caught in her throat, her eyes shuttering closed, her body sinking against his as he gave her pleasure.

"I want dessert first...." And she saw Talon give her that confident male smile of his, his eyes growing turbulent, sending fire of another kind singing through her veins. Tightness swept through her and she recognized it as an orgasm preparing to flood her. The way he rubbed his fingers against her, even through the denim, was making her ache with scorching fire heating her from the inside out.

"So do I," he growled, easing his hand from between her thighs. "You're so wet, so ready," he said, lifting her into his arms. "I've been thinking about loving you all day," Talon gruffly admitted to her as he mounted the stairs to her bedroom.

With a sigh, Cat laid her head against his. "Me, too...."

"A woman after my own heart," Talon said, pushing the door open with the toe of his boot.

This time, the evening light was cascading through the opened drapes into the bedroom. Cat had made the bed and he gently deposited her on it and sat down at her side, his arm across her. The smile on her lips sent a scalding fire down to his lower body. Her hair lay about her head, her eyes shining with love for him. Talon sat there, gently grazing her cheek, pushing some of the strands away from her temple, wondering how he knew what he saw in Cat's glistening eyes was love for him. How could he know? There wasn't any doubt when he held her gaze. Did she know it was love? Never in his life had Talon felt these powerful, almost obsessive feelings toward any woman. Every time he skimmed Cat's flesh, she responded. The sweet sounds in her throat spurred him on. She was incredibly sensitive, responsive to the briefest of his contacts. It fed him, his heart, his fractured soul, in a way no woman ever had.

"Tell me what you want," he rasped, his hand stilling beside her cheek.

Cat laughed softly and lifted her hands, sliding them down his arms. "You."

He grinned, his muscles leaping and tightening as her fingertips skimmed his arms beneath his shirtsleeves. "Anything in particular?"

She shook her head. "I loved everything we did last night, Talon." Her lips curved. "I still feel like I'm floating. I don't feel like I've come down, come back to my body."

"Good loving will gift you in that way," he assured her. Cat had lost her initial shyness from last night. Talon saw the glow in her face, the radiance that good sex gave when it was right. And, God, it had been so right last night. He moved his hand to her shoulder and grew serious. "Are you still sore?"

She shrugged. "A little. But it doesn't matter, Talon." Her voice dropped, becoming husky. "I like what we have. You make me feel so glad...so wonderful... The way you touched me in the kitchen...I want more of that...."

He grinned and nodded. "So do I. You're incredible. You really are." Her smile slipped and he saw moisture come to her eyes. "Hey," he murmured, leaning down and kissing her brow, "what's this all about?"

Cat grimaced. "Just—" and she stumbled, embarrassed "—me, I guess." She didn't have the courage to tell him that her exes tended not to say or give much. Talon brought his whole heart to her and so did she. "I feel what we have is like a beautiful flower garden, so colorful, brilliant...beautiful."

Talon kissed her temple and cheek, inhaling her scent. "I like the way you see us..." he said, because Cat was healing to him.

His mouth settled lightly upon hers and Cat gave a little moan of pleasure, wrapping her hands around his shoulders, drawing Talon against her. She felt him growl deep within his chest, the reverberation sent sweet ripples through her own body. She was in a heaven she never knew existed until now. Until Talon. His mouth plundered hers, fire tightening her breasts against his chest, nipples hardening, his hands gentle as he framed her face, lavishing her with his tongue, sending her lower body howling, like a starving wolf, for him to be within her once more.

Easing from her mouth, Talon rasped, "Let's get undressed." Before he took her with their clothes on.

Without hesitation, Cat sat up and divested herself of her clothes. Last night, she'd been wary about being seen naked by Talon. This morning, she'd felt bold. She'd felt her power as a woman sitting naked, his gaze burning with desire as he raked her body. Talon put her in touch with herself as a woman. Sex with Talon was addictive, Cat thought, as she watched him stand naked before her. The look in Talon's eyes for her made her heart race with anticipation. Those large, scarred hands of his made her ache to be touched by him. He had taken her to the edge of ecstasy. Her gaze dropped to his erection and, instantly, she felt her body contract with an eagerness that made her tremble inwardly. The man electrified her, made her body salivate, and she smiled, holding out her hand to him.

Talon sank his knee into the mattress next to her hip. All he wanted to do was give back to Cat. The shimmering smile in Cat's blue eyes melted his heart and made him grow even harder, if that was possible.

CHAPTER TWENTY

ALL TALON HAD to do was open her lips and Cat drowned in the strength and hunger of his mouth taking hers. It was so easy to surrender to him, to his roughened fingers skimming her slender neck, placing warm, wet kisses down the length of it, the fire skittering like small shocks directly to her tightening breasts. Her heart was wide-open to him and Cat felt fierce feelings for him flowing outward, being expressed in the way she kissed him, her fingers moving through his short, dark hair. Intuitively, she knew it was love. *Real love.* And as she moved to her side, pressing her hips against his, feeling him tense, a groan working its way out of him, she smiled and simply enjoyed how and where he touched her.

This time, there was ease between them, no anxiety or tension. Talon gave her the confidence to express herself, whether she felt very skilled at loving him or not. And as Cat moved her searching fingers down across his hard belly, wrapping her fingers around his erection pressing into her, she began to understand the power a woman had over her man. Talon growled her name, taking her mouth, plundering her lips, sweeping his tongue against hers as her fingers lingered around his shaft, feeling his steely warmth, his hardness. It excited

Cat and she arched wantonly against Talon, her nipples tangling in the soft hair across his chest.

Their breaths were uneven, and as Talon eased out of her exploring hand, settled his knees between her thighs, she saw the sexy look in his narrowing gray eyes. Her lips were wet, felt lush as she met and held his intense, burning stare. As Talon's large hands settled around her hips, Cat closed her eyes, wanting him in her. His fingers followed the crease of her thighs, moving toward her damp entrance, and her breath hitched with anticipation. She liked him touching her there, igniting that throbbing ache within her, heightening the scalding heat, feeling her entire being focused and centered around his exploring contact.

Cat was completely unprepared as she felt him move, his broad shoulders widening her thighs, his fingers curving beneath her thighs. The next moment, she felt him kissing the inside of her thigh. Her skin tautened and quivered as his tongue traced a lazy pattern across her flesh, moving much closer to her entrance. A groan tore out of her, fists clenching into the covers, back arching as his tongue went even lower. Her mind exploded as the sheer, raw pleasure tunneled through her. And when Talon kissed her entrance, his tongue finding, capturing that knot of nerves, she gasped and cried out. Mindless, writhing between his callused hands, feeling the sweet assault as his tongue dived inward, Cat felt paralyzed. Scorching heat roared wildly through her. Every mooring that held her functioning mind liquefied like hot wax. All she could do was sob and feel the raw fire arcing deeply into her, triggering her orgasm, which exploded with a power that sent her tumbling and fusing with the rippling contractions.

Talon felt the power of her pleasure. Her scent intoxicated him, pushed him so close to coming. He eased to his knees, watching the flush of orgasm sweep across her damp, quivering body. The look of rapture on her face, the burning arousal in her eyes as she held his hooded stare, made him feel good in ways he never had before. Her breath was coming in gasps, those ripe, full lips of hers parted, begging to be kissed by him again.

This time, Talon covered her body, his lips settling on one nipple, drawing it into his mouth. He felt Cat's hands fall across his shoulders, her hips lifting to receive him. There was no question she was ready, but he wanted to make his entrance smooth, without stress upon her. He suckled her deeply and he heard her gasp. Instantly, her fingers dug into his shoulders and she cried out his name. It was then he thrust into her, feeling her body begin to accommodate him. Talon sought and found her other nipple, suckling her more demandingly. Cat moaned and writhed as he thrust deeply into her. Moving in and out, coaxing her to participate, Talon felt the tension in her lower body melt and relax around him. Leaning upward, Talon captured her parted lips, taking her hungrily, feeling her response just as eager and needy as he was.

Talon could feel Cat's body building toward her release, heard it in her short, sharpened gasps. This time, he thrust powerfully into her, reaching that second knot of nerves deep within the muscled walls. He felt her shudder and whimper with pleasure. Her body was so reactive, so sensitive that Talon could feel her contracting and squeezing around him until he could barely think. He wanted to wait, wanted to please her first. Thrusting hard and quickly, Talon felt her starting to come apart in his arms, heard her keening cry tear out of her.

The heat, the tightness around him, was too much. Pressing his cheek against her hair, Talon groaned, feeling the explosive, scalding pleasure flowing out of him, filling her. Taking her. His body taut, Talon grabbed the covers on either side of Cat's head. His hips ground against her, the hot liquid shared between them. He felt his body melting like honey into hers. Felt her hands grip his hips, drawing him hard into her, her legs wrapping around his waist, prolonging the wild sensations unleashing and tunneling out of him. Talon gritted out her name, felt his entire body collapsing upon Cat, his weight against her softer, giving body beneath him. His nostrils flared and he drank in her scent, the fragrance of the sex shared between them.

Struggling, Talon pushed himself off Cat. He rolled off her, gathering her into his arms, tucking her tightly beside him, her cheek pressed into his shoulder. "Every time is even better," he rasped, kissing her temple, inhaling her fragrance. Just the way she made a sweet sound in her throat, straining against him, her arm sliding around him, Talon had never felt so fulfilled. So... happy. He could feel the beat of Cat's heart against his chest, her breathing uneven, nuzzling beneath his jaw. There was such innocence to Cat. Absorbing her on every level, Talon lay with his eyes closed, unable to conceive his life without her in it. So much had changed since he'd come home.

And as he felt her fingers move up his damp back, Talon tensed inwardly because he knew she could feel the ridges of the many scars across it. His heart contracted. Cat's fingers lingered lightly, tracing one scar that was nearly the full length of his back.

"What happened to you?" she whispered against his neck, feeling his pulse beneath her lips.

Talon held Cat a little tighter, not wanting to go there, but not wanting to lie to her, either. He thought all the grief, the terror, would avalanche him once again if he spoke. The soft movement of her fingers was surprisingly calming, not inciting the usual dark emotions. Talon kissed her temple, his voice rough with feeling, struggling to keep his emotions controlled. "I was tortured. But I'm fine now."

Cat suddenly tensed, her fingers going still on his back. He swallowed hard, not wanting to give it any more words. Any more explanations.

Cat nuzzled his neck, feeling Talon tense in her arms. She sensed his fear, heard it in his gravelly voice, his breathing going uneven. She eased back enough to look into his stormy expression. Tears jammed into hers as she saw the stark terror of that torture deep in the recesses, felt him wrestling to keep it all at bay. Her instincts told her not to push the topic. Her one question had seemed to rip a festering scar off his terrifying trauma. She comprehended on a level few would understand.

Wordlessly, Cat leaned up, softly pressing her mouth to his. She moved her hand lightly, caressingly, across his deeply scarred back. As she deepened the kiss, she felt overwhelming love for Talon, along with a fierceness to protect him. He responded powerfully, laying her on her back, curving his mouth against hers, almost desperately, and it made tears leak out of her tightly closed eyes.

Talon could taste the salt in her tears. Why was she crying for him? But she was and it strengthened his need for her. Her caressing fingers slid up his cheeks, into his hair, as if to soothe him, take away the nearly overwhelming pain he felt. Easing away, Talon stared down into her glistening eyes.

"I didn't mean to make you cry," he said, his voice hoarse.

Skimming his jaw, she whispered, "Tears are always good. Healing..."

Talon felt a fist of grief so huge he thought he might explode. He hadn't even cried for himself. Hadn't cried for the loss of Hayden. Yet, Cat could cry for him. It shook Talon to the bottom of his fractured soul. He closed his eyes, like a starving wolf, thirstily absorbing her every caress to his face, his shoulder. Did Cat know how healing her touch was to him? Somehow, it lessened his burden. Whatever they shared, whatever it was, Talon knew it was the only thing that could help him heal. *Cat's touch.* Her husky voice trembling with emotion. Blue eyes looking deep into his dark, wounded soul, bringing light, understanding and, most of all, her acceptance of him, no matter how damaged he was.

Talon forced himself to look down into her compassionate gaze. "I can't talk about it yet," he rasped.

"I know," she whispered, sliding her fingers through his hair. "It's all right, Talon. I'm here. We can heal one another over time. I know that...."

Talon buried his head against Cat's shoulder, holding her so tight he heard the air whoosh out of her. He clung to her as if she were the last anchor in his fragmented world. If he let go of her, he would be lost. Forever. Talon surrendered to Cat as he clung to her like a dying man. Her fingers moved gently across his shoulder, soothingly down his back, grazing his scars, lifting the pain and memory out of them as she did so. Tears leaked out of his eyes, no matter how hard Talon tried to force them back. They fell against her silky hair, the strands soaking them up.

And then his world turned upside down and all Talon could hear was the sobs tearing out of him, his entire body convulsing against hers. Cat held him with her woman's strength, with her softly whispered words, her hands moving in healing gestures across his back. Talon had never felt such shame, such helplessness, in his life. And yet, she absorbed everything with a calm sweetness that Talon couldn't believe.

Cat had suffered terribly herself. Somewhere in his shattered mind, Talon wondered if it made her stronger and far more capable to deal with him and his horror. Part of him was dying. A part that had already been dead, but now, it dissolved and left beneath her whispered words, her caresses and the warmth of her curved body against his. It was a miracle and Talon had no explanation for what had happened or why. As he lay in her arms in the aftermath of the storm that had rolled through him, that he'd finally given voice to, he felt cleaner. Hopeful.

Sliding his hand down her arm, Talon eased his grip on Cat. How could someone this soft and giving be so damned strong? Strong enough to hold him? Love him at his worst moment? And as Talon kissed her hair, inhaling Cat's sweet scent, he knew this was an act of love on her part. All these feelings he'd had within him since he'd met Cat were now brilliantly obvious to him. Talon loved Cat. He loved her just the way she was. She was perfect for him. She made him happier than he could ever recall.

Cat kissed Talon's hair, his neck and shoulder. "You're going to be okay now," she told him quietly. "We're all wounded. Every last one of us." She gave him a wry look and eased away enough to study him. "You and I have the physical scars to prove it." She caressed his damp cheek, the spent tears beneath her fingertips. "So many others have no physical proof of their wounds, but they're still there and they know it. They carry them around every day just like we do, Talon. That's the only difference...." Cat drowned in his raw devastation, in everything he'd endured.

He caught her hand, kissed her fingers and then wrapped it in his, pressing it against his heart. "How did you get so smart?"

The corners of her mouth turned faintly upward. "I learned in junior high when I had PE and would shower afterward, every girl in there saw the scars on my back." Her voice lowed with feeling. "At first, I lied. I told them a horse threw me and I landed in a barbed-wire fence. And then I hated myself for lying. I was ashamed of my scars, Talon. By the time I got to high school, I stopped lying to the girls who saw my back. I told them my father did it to me." She inhaled and added, "The moment I told the truth, I felt free. By that time, I knew I looked different to them. No one else had scars like me. But I found telling the truth made me feel better."

He frowned, moving his hand gently across her back, feeling her scars. "Someday, I'll tell you how I got mine."

"You're not there yet, Talon. I get it. I had my own journey with my scars." Cat tilted her head, becoming somber, a quaver in her voice. "I'll be here to listen when you're ready. Okay?"

Relief shuddered through Talon. He knew Cat would give him the time and space he needed to deal fully with his trauma. She wouldn't push. Wouldn't keep asking questions or stirring it up in him. Cat understood the long process it took to get to that point where he could give it voice. And Talon knew, without a doubt, she'd sit quietly and simply listen. She was strong enough to hold him and be there for him. Talon knew that with every cell of his being.

"Okay," he rasped, trying to smile but failing. Grazing her flushed cheek, her skin velvet and firm beneath his thumb, Talon felt a new kind of peace entering him. He eased away from her. He sat up and placed several pillows behind his back, leaning against the headboard. He gathered Cat into his arms, nestling her against him and holding her for a long, long time.

At some point, he realized the sun was no longer shining. Looking out the opened curtains, Talon could see dusk coming, the sky darkening. He pressed a kiss to her hair. "How did you get to be who you are?" he demanded huskily, smiling down into her eyes.

Cat shrugged, wrapped in his arms, content as never before. "I think our first eighteen years define us, don't you?"

Talon moved his thumb lightly across her eyebrow. "Yeah, that's part of it for sure."

"Why are you giving me that bug-under-a-microscope look?" Cat teased, giving him a playful smile.

"Because you're strong. Stronger than any man I know."

"And what? Men are always stronger than women in your world?"

Talon saw the feistiness in her eyes. "I'm rethinking it," he admitted.

"I like a man who is humble. That's a good sign."

He frowned. "Of late, I have been. Not before…" *Not before being tortured.* It had taken chunks out of his soul that were missing to this day. But, somehow, Cat was bringing those stolen pieces back to him. She accepted him for who he was right now, no questions asked.

"I've seen men cry before, Talon," she told him, sliding her fingers across the hard line of his jaw. "Trauma makes all of us cry sooner or later. There's no shame in it. Not ever." Cat narrowed her eyes on Talon. "Do you believe that?"

"I do now," he told her.

"And don't you feel better because you did cry?"

Nodding, he grimaced and muttered, "Yeah, oddly, I do."

Cat grinned. "You men are all alike. You think crying makes you look weak or something. When in reality, it shows you're strong. I don't get it. A man has a heart that feels just like a woman's heart does. God created tear ducts in both genders." She gave him an amused look.

Talon grazed her soft lower lip. "I did trust you, babe. I knew you'd hold me. My gut told me you had whatever it took to let me get it out of my system." He searched her eyes, saw tears come to them. Tipping her chin up, Talon kissed away the tears. He felt humbled as never before because Cat was entrusting her being with him. Utterly. Totally. Without any demands or borders. As she opened her eyes and smiled up at him, Talon took her mouth gently, breathing his life, his breath, into her. Claiming her forever.

CAT SAT AT the table much later as they ate a late evening meal. It was almost eight o'clock. She finished every bit of food on her plate. The quiet shared between them wasn't stilted or forced. So much had happened earlier in her bedroom with Talon that the aftereffect was a peace she'd never thought existed. But it did. With Talon.

She got up and brought over the coffee, filling their mugs after the meal. Talon looked thoughtful as he thanked her. The beard darkened his face and Cat smiled to herself as she sat down at his elbow. He no longer looked threatening. When she'd first discovered him on that icy, snow-covered road, he'd appeared more animal than human. This afternoon she'd discovered the human within him. And she loved him even more for being courageous enough to be vulnerable with her.

"What are you going to do if Gus is able to buy the Triple H?" Cat asked. She saw his eyebrows fall, and Talon stared down at the cup in his hands for a moment.

"Be happy. At least our home will be with someone who will care for it."

"Gus is doing it to help your mom. That's pretty humbling to me."

Talon nodded. "I've been thinking my way through it all. Gus is an astute businesswoman, but she's also fiercely loyal to the people around her. And I know my mother has been a friend to her ever since Gus came back to the Bar H when Val was sixteen. A lot of years of friendship shared between them."

"It's love," Cat said quietly, avoiding his eyes. She opened her hands around the cup. "I was always trying to figure out what love was, Talon. I finally got that my father did not love me. And I don't honestly remember my mother. I was so young when she died. I watched kids at school. I watched the wranglers at the ranch where my father was employed. I tried to piece together what love was."

"You never got a chance to experience it," Talon said gently, looking at the puzzlement in her expression.

Cat nodded, sadness moving through her. "When I met Sandy, after moving here seven years ago, I remember we had a long discussion about love one day. She'd just gone through a round of chemo and I'd driven her home afterward. She was feeling so miserable, but she wanted to talk about love with me. She told me about her first husband, Gardner, how he loved her so much that she couldn't give it words. And then Sandy birthed you. She told me about the special, maternal love she felt for you. And when Gardner died of a heart attack and she met Brad, how it was another kind of love." Cat hitched her shoulder. "I think love is a pretty rubber-band kind of experience. It's different for different people. Gus loves Sandy. Sometimes, I think she sees your mother as one of her grown children." Cat smiled softly. "Gus has a lot of children who aren't her blood kin, but she considers them her extended family. That's another kind of love, I suppose...."

Talon reached over and captured her hand. "It's something I wrestle with, too, Cat. When I joined the Navy and got into the SEALs, I was surrounded by women when we had downtime at Coronado. These women threw the word *love* around all the time. But when they used it, I didn't feel it. I didn't sense it."

Her fingers curved into his. "Well, in defense of those women, I can remember telling the first guy that showed any interest in me that I loved him." She snorted. "I didn't have a *clue* of what I was saying. I wasn't lying to him, I just didn't know the difference between my feelings." *Until now.* Cat knew what real love was, finally. And she loved Talon but wasn't going to admit it. They needed time together first. And it was way too soon to say anything.

"That's different," Talon said. "These women kept score on how many SEALs they took to bed. That was a lot different than your experience."

Cat's brows rose. "Are you serious? Women kept count?"

He saw her blush. Cat's innocence was showing again, but he didn't laugh. "It's a culture," he said. "SEALs are seen as the ultimate male to bed. It's a bragging right between them, I guess."

"Wow," she murmured, thinking about it. "Is that where you found out it wasn't love? It was…well…I guess, counting coup?"

He grinned a little. "Counting coup? That's one way of seeing it. But yeah, these women liked hanging out around SEALs and felt good if they could bed one or two of them."

"Sort of a game?" she wondered, frowning. She'd just gone to bed with Talon, and it was serious business. It wasn't about bragging she'd bedded an ex-SEAL. The thought rather horrified Cat.

"To be fair, it was a game both sides played," Talon admitted.

"But," she said, trying to grasp the whole idea, "if... if you go to bed with someone, shouldn't it be serious? I mean, something special between you and the other person?" And then she grimaced. "Not that I'm throwing stones. I thought the men in my life liked me...maybe loved me, but I was wrong."

"I think a lot of women confuse sex with love," Talon said. "Men see it differently. Sex is sex. The act doesn't need to have any emotional tie to it." And then he gave her a tender look. "With you, when I love you, my feelings are involved, Cat. It's me wanting to please you, make you happy. I like to see your smile afterward."

Nodding, she absorbed his husky words. "Thanks, I needed to hear that. Because I feel the same toward you, Talon. Just being with you lifts me. Makes me hopeful. Happy."

"It's the same for me, babe." He squeezed her fingers. "You make me happy."

Her throat tightened with emotions as she drowned in his warm gray eyes. She heard the feelings behind Talon's words. He meant them. And her heart did a little dance inside her chest. How badly she wanted to say she loved Talon, but she couldn't yet. But, until that time came, she could touch him, kiss him and love him when it felt right.

Cat reached for his hand, enclosing it between hers. "Gus loves your mom. I know that. And I think Gus wants to give Sandy her home back so she'll fight to stay alive. For you. For herself."

"Love is a strange thing, isn't it?"

She met his sober look. "Complex. Many layers. Like a torte cake."

Talon studied her in the low light, seeing the happiness banked in her eyes for him alone. "Whatever we have, I like it. And it suits us, Cat. That's all that matters."

CHAPTER TWENTY-ONE

"I DON'T WANT you to leave." Cat watched as Talon shrugged into his denim jacket, the morning cold, near freezing, in early July. Her body glowed from their recent lovemaking. He'd awakened her near dawn and the tenderness he'd shared with her still made her eyes moist. She stood near the door, waiting for Talon as he collected his baseball cap from the top of the sofa, heading her way, his smoldering gaze on her.

"I don't, either." He halted in front of her. There was such love shining in her drowsy blue eyes that Talon felt his body tighten with need for Cat once more. They'd spent an hour in bed with one another hours earlier, and he'd made love with her. Every time was better. He'd just showered, shaved and gotten ready to leave to go to work at the Bar H.

It was six o'clock. Cat wore her lavender silk robe around her tall, curvy body. Talon knew her body, held her heart, and he felt her warm gaze slide around his heart, holding him gently in her hands. *Beautiful hands. Loving hands.* His heart ached at the thought of separating from her this morning. She would be on duty at 3:00 p.m. with the fire department for a forty-eight-hour shift. He was going back to the ranch. Talon hated not being able to see Cat for two days. Worse, when she got off duty, she'd spend the next two off days at the ranch.

They'd both agreed they couldn't sleep with each other or even show their affection at the ranch. It wouldn't have been appropriate.

He slid his hand around her upturned face. When her lips softly parted, Talon groaned, leaned down and skimmed them, feeling her instant response, her arms sliding around his shoulders, pressing the length of herself against him. "No fair," he murmured, kissing her lips lightly. "Keep this up and I'll carry you upstairs and keep you prisoner in that bed."

"Mmm, I'd love nothing better," she whispered, savoring the taste, the strength of his mouth sliding against hers. She could smell the cleanliness of his skin, his male scent, and her womb contracted with need. "Bed versus work, huh?"

Talon absorbed her tall, firm body against his. He grinned and moved strands of hair away from her brow and temple. The change in Cat was heart-stopping. Her cheeks were flushed a pink color, her eyes danced with amusement. The past few days loving her were the best he'd ever shared with a woman. Groaning, Talon said, "You're the first woman to ever make me think twice about not going to work."

She moved her hips against his, feeling Talon becoming hard once more. Cat savored the power of herself as a woman to sway him. "Same here," she whispered against his mouth, reveling in his strength, his tenderness. "I find myself not wanting to go to work, either. All I can think about…feel about…is you, Talon."

"It's the same for me," he admitted thickly, resting his forehead against hers, closing his eyes. "I keep thinking this is all some kind of fevered dream."

"Better not be," Cat said with a short laugh, pulling away, grazing his cheek, watching his eyes turn predator-like upon her. Her breasts tightened beneath his heated look. "It's real. It's wonderful...."

"I don't know what it is, but I like it," he said, forcing himself to release Cat. Talon turned and picked up his baseball cap and settled it on his head. "Give me a call later. I'll have my cell on me." *Because I need to hear your voice. Listen to your breathy laughter. I'm starving for you already.* Talon felt drugged or maybe addicted to Cat. Oh, he knew he'd always been powerfully drawn to her and he'd thought it was just about sex, that was all. But there was so much more. He couldn't keep his hands off her as she wrapped her arms around herself, following him to the door. He saw the sadness in her expression because he was leaving. God, it felt like they were invisibly joined to one another, and to leave sent excruciating agony through him. Spinning from feelings that clamored so brightly within his heart, he cupped her cheek, kissed her gently and rasped, "Call me?"

"I promise," Cat whispered, leaning into his mouth one last time, one last kiss before he left. The cold air swept in from the morning and she lifted her hand. "Stay safe out there."

He halted, his hand on the doorknob, and gave her an intense look. "You'd better stay safe, too, babe. No heroics out there on your shift, okay?"

Cat grinned. "No worries. I'll see you in a couple of days." Her throat tightened as he nodded and turned away, walking down the sidewalk toward the garage where all vehicles were parked. Standing in the doorway, Cat shivered from the below-freezing air. The sky was a pale blue and to her right she could see the first rays of the sun touching the hill far above them. She absorbed Talon as he walked down toward the garage. There was no question of his confidence, his shoulders thrown back, the boneless way he walked in his cowboy boots. He looked rugged, like the West itself, like Wyoming was. Her heart beat with such fierce love for him.

Turning, she closed the door, the warmth sweeping through her as she padded across the living room and took the stairs. She'd already showered with Talon, finding new and beautiful ways to love him. Shaking her head, a faint smile on her mouth, Cat walked into her bedroom. Talon was stretching the boundaries of her love life in ways she never realized existed. Her lower body glowed with satisfaction.

Choosing a pair of jeans, a warm red sweater, thick socks and her boots, Cat swung into her morning routine. After getting dressed, she pulled on her firefighting boots and quickly laced them up. In early July, the weather didn't warm up until around noon. She didn't have to be at work until three. Just as she finished getting on her boots, her cell phone on the bed stand rang.

"Hello?"

"Cat? This is Cade Garner. I just wanted to let you know that the judge late yesterday afternoon denied Magee bail. Not only that, he slapped a million-dollar bail on him."

Relief fled through her. "Oh, that's great, Cade. Is there anything else I have to do?"

"Mandy Parker, our county prosecutor, wants to meet with you sometime in the coming two weeks," Cade said. "She's building a case against Magee and needs your help. She said it was a good thing that a year ago, when Magee slammed you into the wall, you went to the E.R. That is going to cinch the case against him. It shows a pattern of abuse toward you."

Cat closed her eyes and remembered that evening Magee had shoved her savagely. He'd cracked two of her ribs and she'd gone to the E.R., knowing he'd done some damage. There, after telling the doctor what had happened, X-rays were taken and photos of the massive bruising on her right side. All of that was turned over to the sheriff. Magee had spent thirty days in jail after admitting he'd done it. That was a year ago.

Opening her eyes, Cat went over to look out the window. "Can she put him away, Cade? Because frankly, I'm scared. If he gets out, I know he'll come after me." She felt fear just thinking about it. Magee was almost as big as Talon was and he had a short temper, to boot.

"No worries," Cade assured her. "He's going nowhere."

"But what if he makes bail? You said he has a fancy California attorney."

"Unless that attorney can convince a bail bondsman with enough money, Magee is going nowhere."

"Would you let me know if that happened? If Magee made bail?"

"In a heartbeat, Cat. Look, don't worry, okay? A million-dollar bail is a helluva lot, even for a California attorney to scare up."

"Why does Magee have an out-of-state attorney?" Her heart was picking up in beat.

"My take is that Magee works for the Garcia drug cartel that now owns Ace Trucking. And Magee is one of their drivers. Someone in the organization must have called this attorney over here to try and spring him until his trial date because they need every driver they have. Not everyone is going to truck drugs around a six-state area. Magee is important to their distribution systems, Cat."

"Ugh," she whispered. "Then drug money could spring him."

"It could, but I'm watching over this case, Cat. I'm not going to let you hang out there alone and uninformed. If that happens, I'll be calling you right away. Okay?"

Cat's mouth thinned. "Thanks, Cade."

"Go enjoy your day. It's beautiful out."

She clicked off her cell, frowning. Cat didn't feel safe. She didn't know why, but she didn't. How she wished Talon were here. He would protect her. He knew how to fight, how to defend her. She didn't. Pushing the cell into the back pocket of her jeans, Cat went to the closet and took out a dark green down vest and shrugged it over her red sweater. By noon, she'd be shedding the winter gear for light cotton. That was the way spring in the Tetons went. Freezing in the morning, warm in the afternoon. And then, as the sun went down, freezing temperatures once again.

The condo felt lifeless and empty as she hurried down the stairs. As she put the breakfast dishes in the dishwasher, her mind gnawed on Magee being in jail and a part of a drug cartel. Cat knew Cade and the sheriff's department were well aware of the intrusion into Teton County. She'd met deputy sheriff Shelby Kincaid at Mo's a week earlier. She was their chief tracker for the department. Cat remembered sitting with Shelby and her husband, Dakota Hunter. He was an ex-SEAL like Talon. Cat wondered if they knew one another.

Her mind went back to their conversation about

tracking two murderers and how they'd found them. Shelby had been drugged and captured by one of the criminals. The blonde deputy was even taller than Cat, and she had cringed when she'd heard the details of Shelby's capture. She would have died if not for Dakota tracking her with his wolf at his side. Shelby had come so close to death.

Shivering over those memories, Cat shut the dishwasher and turned it on. If Magee was out, he'd do the same thing to her and she knew it. She hadn't pressed charges the first time, afraid he'd want to get even. Cat knew he'd kill her. She leaned against the counter, her arms wrapped protectively across her chest. Cat didn't want to die. God, she'd just found Talon. Discovered what love...real love...was like. She'd never felt happier than right now. And it was because of Talon. While they were both deeply wounded by different circumstances, Cat had a connection with him, an understanding. She missed him so much. The condo was lifeless without his larger-than-life presence.

Damn. Turning, she picked up the washcloth and wiped down the stove. Cat remembered having lunch with Shelby a month earlier, just the two of them. Shelby was the only woman deputy, but she was a good one. Cat recalled their lunch conversation that day at Mo's. She had confessed to her deep love for Dakota. At the time, Cat remembered the shining look in Shelby's eyes, heard the softness in her voice every time she used Dakota's name. Cat had sat there wondering if she would ever find someone like that. Her eyes sparkled.

Well, Cat had found someone. And this morning, looking in the bathroom mirror, she had seen the new softness in her face, the luminous look in her eyes, and now she understood how Shelby felt. It was love. *Real love.*

After wiping down the counter, Cat rinsed off the washcloth beneath the faucet. Shelby and Dakota had been married in October last year. And she'd been invited. Everyone who knew the couple was happy for them. Dakota had joined the sheriff's department, part-time, as a tracker. So many people, tourists in particular, got lost in the Tetons, Yellowstone Park and the Wind River Range in Wyoming. Shelby and Dakota were usually very busy from June through October due to just that: tourists getting lost on trails, without a compass, extra food or water. It happened all the time.

She needed to go to the grocery store and made a list. Being back on the shift with the fire department, Cat's life became regimented. She had to make an appointment to get her truck in for an oil change. Maybe Sandy was available for lunch? Cat wanted to see her, to get back on her schedule so she wasn't left alone. She called Gwen Garner and gave her the shift schedule for the month. And then Cat called Sandy. Yes, she had no one coming over for lunch, so Cat would bring some food from Mo's and they'd enjoy an hour together.

CAT HURRIED BACK to her condo after having lunch with Sandy. It was one o'clock and she had to get ready for her shift that began at three. Her heart was full with happiness. Sandy's admittance that she looked at her like a daughter mingled with her observation that Talon loved her. Did he? He'd never said the words. Unlocking her front door, Cat stepped in. It was growing warm outside and she needed to swap out her cold clothes for her firefighting uniform.

"I've been waitin' for you, Cat."

She gasped as her most terrifying nightmare stood in front of her. Beau Magee appeared in the hall of her condo. Shock bolted through her and she froze. He was wearing a pair of Levi's, a dark gray shirt and work boots. His thumbs were hooked in his belt, his dark brown eyes narrowed upon her.

"What are you doing here?" she demanded, her breath raspy. Heart taking off at a gallop, Cat was confused. Beau was in jail! Why was he *here?*

"You and I have some unfinished business." He walked toward her, his gaze never leaving her stunned face. "And if you try to turn and run, I'll tackle you. So stay where you are."

Her throat ached with fear. His mouth curved in a frightening smile that didn't reach his eyes. Beau was over six feet tall and heavily muscled. His dark brown hair was short and recently washed. Cat took a step back because he got too close to her.

"How did you get out of jail?" she demanded. Every cell in her body screamed for her to run. To escape.

"I got bail," he said easily. "And I wanted to come and see you as soon as I got out."

Cat quivered inwardly. She had seen this look in Beau's eyes before. "Get out."

His smile increased as he slowly looked her up and down. "Now, is that polite, Cat? You know, when we hooked up, you were the sweetest girl I'd met. Now you got a sour look on your face." He reached out and tried to touch her cheek. She jerked away. How could she escape? She'd shut the door. She had no weapons. And she saw a hunting knife hanging off his belt. He'd always carried one on him.

"Polite? Who are you to talk? You just broke into my condo. I want you out of here, Beau. *Now!*" She jammed her index finger toward the door.

"Oh," he crooned, "that's not gonna happen, Cat. You and I? Well, we got some catching up to do. And you're going to give me a second chance to win back your hand."

TALON WAS RIDING his steel-gray horse down along the boundary fence between the Bar H and the Triple H ranch when his cell phone vibrated in his vest pocket. He pulled the gelding to a stop along the fence line. The sun was in the west, bright and warm. He pulled the phone out.

"Talon," he answered, thinking it was probably Val or Griff wanting something.

"Talon? This is Matt Sinclaire. From the fire department?"

He scowled. "Yes. What's wrong?" Suddenly, a bad feeling swept through Talon. Why would Cat's fire captain be calling him? His fingers tightened around the cell phone.

"Cat didn't show up for her shift. It's four o'clock now. I thought she might be running late. I tried calling her on her cell, but everything is going to message. Is she out there with you?"

His eyes narrowed. He tensed up. "No. I left her at six this morning. I haven't seen her." Something was wrong. Very wrong.

"Maybe she's with my mother. Did you call over there?"

"I did. I'd talked to Gwen first over at the quilt shop and she said it was Cat's turn to have lunch with Sandy.

And when I called her, she said Cat had left for her condo at one o'clock."

Son of a bitch! Talon twisted in the saddle. He picked up the reins and kicked the gelding into a gallop up a tall hill that would lead him back to the Bar H. "Something's wrong, Matt. Can you send someone over to her condo?"

Maybe Cat got sick? God, he hoped not. It wasn't like her to suddenly disappear off everyone's radar. He rode the horse hard, leaning forward as they flew across the hill, the wind making his eyes water.

"Yes, I'll send over one of my men right now."

"I'm calling Cade," Talon growled. "Keep me in the loop?"

"I will."

What the hell was going on? He punched in Cade's phone number and he answered right away.

"Hey, this is Talon. Matt Sinclaire just called me and said Cat didn't show up for work. What do you know about this?" His chest tightened.

"This morning at nine o'clock I called Cat because Beau Magee made bail. I got her voice mail, Talon. I'm assuming she got the message."

His heart squeezed with terror. "You called?"

"Yes. Do you know if she received it or not?"

He heard the sudden concern in Cade's voice. Talon remembered him telling Cat that if Magee made bail, she would be notified immediately. Oh, God, nine this morning? What had Cat been doing after he'd left? Hadn't she checked her cell phone? Had Magee gotten to her? "Can you get over to her condo? See if she's there? I'm out on the range. As soon as I can, I'm going to drive in to her condo."

"Yes," Cade answered hurriedly, "I'm on my way over there right now. By the way, I just tried her cell again and I got voice mail. She's not answering."

Talon came galloping into the barnyard, hauling back on his horse, bringing him to a skidding stop. Griff was in the barn working on the tractor. Leading his horse into it, Talon told him what was going on.

Griff scowled and slid out from beneath the tractor's engine. He got to his feet. "Cat's disappeared?"

"I don't know," Talon said. He quickly unsaddled his gelding and put him into a nearby box stall. "I'm going into town right now if that's all right with you."

"Sure," Griff murmured, frowning. "Could Cat be sick? At her condo and sleeping or something?"

"I hope so," Talon said. He pulled the chaps off and hung them in the tack room. "I'll call you when I find out anything."

TALON SAW A deputy sheriff's black Tahoe cruiser in front of Cat's condo. Her door was open and he saw a firefighter standing there with Cade Garner, a worried look on his face. Scowling, he parked behind the cruiser, got out and trotted up the sidewalk. Cade saw him.

"Hey, Talon, she's not here. We've searched the premises." Cade shook his head. "Cat's truck is gone. There was little sign of a struggle in her condo. I've got an APB out on Beau Magee."

Halting, Talon's heart plunged to his feet. The firefighter said goodbye and left. He saw another cruiser pulling up. "What else have you found?"

"Not much," Cade grumbled. "Come on in, but don't touch anything."

His heart was thrashing in his chest as he climbed

the stairs with Cade. Instantly, he saw some marks on the door and halted. Cade moved into the bedroom.

"Were these marks here before?"

"No, they weren't there this morning," Talon growled, suddenly anxious.

"Then Cat put up a struggle," Cade speculated, pointing to the black marks on the lower part of the bedroom door. "When was the last time you saw Cat?"

Rubbing his jaw, Talon looked around the bedroom. Everything was as it had been before. His heart ached with fear. "Six this morning. And she was fine when I left her." Happy. Kissing him. That soft look of love in her eyes. Talon rubbed his chest, feeling as if his heart were shredding, the pain nearly unbearable. "Would Magee kidnap her?" he demanded.

"I don't know. He's got a long list of criminal activity. But kidnapping isn't one of them."

"Magee's done this...." The words ground out of Talon's mouth.

Cade scowled. "Damn. I called her the moment I heard from the jail that Magee had made bail."

Turning, Talon cursed softly, looking around the quiet bedroom once more. "I don't know why she wasn't answering her phone."

"Sometime between nine o'clock, when Magee was released, and three, when Matt Sinclaire reported her not showing up for work, he made his way over here," Cade said, shaking his head. "Maybe the Garcia drug cartel is involved? "

Horror rifled through Talon. Two women, a forensics team, came to the door with their kits in hand. "Have you put out an APB on Cat's truck?" Because he wanted to wrap his hands around the bastard's neck and choke the information out of him.

"Yes, I've got my deputies watching for it. Magee left the jail on foot. It probably took him at least forty minutes to make it over here to Cat's apartment."

"Magee have an address? Did you send anyone over to see if he was home?"

"Already done it. His truck is in the driveway and the deputies searched his apartment. It appears that he didn't go home. Nothing's been disturbed. His landlady said she hadn't seen him, either."

Talon felt suddenly helpless. Cade was doing his job, no question. He looked around the quiet bedroom. Everything was as it had been this morning. The only difference was the bed was made. The bed where they had made love, talked for hours with one another and loved one another again.

"Have you canvassed this condo complex?" Talon demanded.

"We're doing that right now," Cade assured him. "Maybe somebody saw something."

Talon felt his whole world shattering around him. Tears pricked the backs of his eyes and he angrily forced them away. His hands fisted and unfisted as he stood there. Magee was in on this. He could taste it. And he wanted to kill the bastard. What had they done to Cat? Where was she?

CHAPTER TWENTY-TWO

Talon moved slowly through the condo, looking for anything else out of place. There hadn't been a struggle. Had Magee been waiting for Cat? The condo was two stories high and there were four in the squat, wooden building. Talon looked up at the condo above where Cat lived. He knew nothing about her neighbors. Anxiety twisted through him. He was a man of action, not waiting around like this. SEALs brought the fight to the enemy.

At the jail, Talon had quickly thumbed through Magee's extensive records. He still had sealed records from his childhood, so God only knew what he'd done at that time. His eyes traveling over the offenses, he noticed that Magee had gotten into drugs at eighteen. He'd been in and out of jail nearly every year since then.

His employment for the past two years was with Ace Trucking in Jackson Hole. He'd been clean since coming here. Talon noted that he was charged with assault against Cat. But he had only spent thirty days in jail for that crime. Talon's rage only mounted.

Cade joined him out on the sidewalk. "Deputy Shelby Kincaid just talked to an older woman, Molly Pritchard." He pointed up above Cat's condo to the second floor. "She saw Cat walking out of her condo with a man around one o'clock."

His heart jumped. "Do you have a photo of Magee? Could she identify him?"

"Shelby's with the woman right now and she's got her iPad with her and has Magee's photos on it. I'm sure she'll show it to Mrs. Pritchard." Cade looked at his watch. "Let's go up and talk with her."

Relief sizzled through Talon as they walked around the side of the wooden building and quickly mounted the stairs.

Molly Pritchard was in her sixties, gray hair, wearing large glasses on her small face. She invited Cade into her condo. Talon was introduced. He saw Shelby Kincaid in uniform, sitting at the kitchen table with a report she was writing out. Talon had seen her once, struck by the fact she was very tall, wore her blond hair in a ponytail and was beautiful. She looked up and nodded to them.

"Molly, why don't you sit down here with me?" Shelby invited. "Tell Cade and Talon what you saw."

Molly nodded and smoothed her apron across her dark green slacks. "Of course."

Talon sat, tense, his hands folded on the table.

Molly pushed her glasses up on her nose. "I was just telling Shelby here that I heard voices down below. Cat's a very quiet person, so naturally, that got my attention. I went to the front window." She pointed toward the opened drapes on the window that overlooked the sidewalk below. "At first, I thought Cat was in pain, but the yelling was between her and that man."

"Could you pick up any of the conversation, Mrs. Pritchard?" Cade asked.

Giving him a sad look, she shook her head. "I'm sorry, I didn't. It was all muffled."

"You're positive it was Cat's voice?" Talon asked tightly.

"Yes. Muffled or not, I know Cat's voice."

"What did you do?" Cade asked gently.

"Well…nothing." Molly appeared flustered. "I guess now, I should have called her on her cell. Asked if everything was all right." She gave the two men an apologetic look. "I'm really sorry…."

Cade reached out and patted her hand. "You couldn't know. It's all right."

"What happened next?" Talon asked, trying to keep the tightness out of his voice. He could tell Molly was deeply shaken by the unfolding events.

"Well, I heard more yelling and went to the window over there to look out it. I saw Cat walk out with a man." She frowned and pointed down at Shelby's iPad in the center of the table. "That's the man who was with her."

"Magee," Shelby said.

"Were they still yelling at one another?" Cade asked.

"No. He had his hand on her arm and they were walking out of her condo as if nothing was wrong."

"Where did they go?" Talon demanded.

"Down the sidewalk to the garage where we all park our cars."

Shelby looked up from the report she was writing. "Molly said Cat was driving her truck and they took off down the street." She pointed north.

"What was Cat wearing?" Talon asked her.

"She was in a pair of jeans, a red sweater and had her backpack over her right shoulder."

"Did you get a look at Cat's face?" Cade asked.

"Yes."

"Did she look injured?"

"No. But she didn't look happy. I just thought it was because she'd had a fight with that fellow in her condo. I didn't think much of it."

Wiping his mouth, Talon looked over at Cade. Some relief moved through him. Magee had taken her. And if she wasn't injured, it was a good sign. He desperately wanted to speak to Cade but didn't want to do that in front of Molly, who seemed very rattled and was wringing her hands.

Shelby smiled a little at Molly and slid the report over to her. "Molly, if you could just read this over? It's what you've told me. As you read it, if anything else comes to mind, tell me?"

"Of course, dear." She pulled the report over to her.

Cade glanced at Shelby. "We're going back to the department. If you get anything else, will you call me on the radio?"

"You bet," Shelby murmured.

Talon held his tongue until they were out of Molly Pritchard's condo. "So, Magee has kidnapped her."

"I think so," Cade agreed, walking around the building and heading for his cruiser.

"What now?"

"I'm heading over to Ace Trucking. I'm going to talk to the manager, a guy named Keith Jenkins. We know he works for the Garcia cartel, although his hands are clean." Cade opened the cruiser and gave Talon a dark look. "You need to wait to hear from us, Talon."

"I want to go with you to talk with Jenkins."

"You can't. You're not law enforcement and I can't risk it."

Anger spilled through Talon. "I feel damned helpless, Cade. I want to do something to find Cat."

He placed his hand on Talon's shoulder. "I know you do. But you're a civilian."

Talon wanted to go over to Ace Trucking and move into SEAL stealth mode. He was good at watching and waiting. "Magee hurt Cat before. Don't you think he's going to again?"

Cade grimaced. "It's possible. But remember, he just got bail. My gut tells me the Garcia cartel anted up the bail money. Why would Magee screw them like that by kidnapping Cat? They aren't going to be happy about this, either."

"Magee has been stalking her," Talon ground out. "That's plenty of reason for him to do this." And what would he do to Cat? A cold, icy feeling drowned him and Talon knew he couldn't just quietly stand by and do nothing as Cade moved this investigation forward.

"I know." Cade gave him a concerned look. "I'll keep you in the loop, Talon, but you can't go with me."

"Has my mother been told what's going on?" He even worried that she might be in Magee's gun sights. He knew Cat was over there a number of times each week.

Cade shook his head. "No. Why don't you go over and see if she might know anything." He touched the cell on his belt. "If I hear *anything,* Talon, you'll be the first to know."

"Okay," Talon said, resigned.

"Turn in here," Beau told Cat, pointing to a cabin hidden by tall Douglas firs on all sides.

The dirt road, if it could even be called that, was nearly invisible. Cat drove up the steep, winding road, the shadows of the trees darkening the area. Her pulse leaped as she saw a two-story cabin up ahead. "You own this?"

Beau smiled a little. "No. It belonged to Curt Downing. Probably still does, but he's dead."

Cat frowned. Curt Downing had been murdered on a trail riding his horse nearly a year ago. Shelby Kincaid had been kidnapped by an escaped convict and Curt had been riding on the same trail. The criminal had shot Curt off his horse. The man was a powerful kingpin around the valley and had owned Ace Trucking. Shortly after his death, it was bought up by someone else and that was who Magee worked for.

"And you have permission to be here?" she demanded, giving him a measured look. She saw the slight smile that always hovered on Beau's thin lips. She'd learned too late that smile was false, to put her at ease, that it was all a lie. Magee was a stalker. He was a predator. And now, she was his prey.

Beau shrugged. "Doesn't matter. No one's been in here to this cabin since Downing died. I just happen to know where the key is at and we can make ourselves at home in it. No one will find us."

Terror filtered through Cat. So far, Beau had been his usual self, thoughtful, smiling and his voice soft. The hard glitter in his dark brown eyes warned her differently, however. She could feel the locked tension in Magee. She put nothing past him. Unsettled, she said, "You won't get away with this, Beau. Why blow your chances? You got bail. Once the bail bondsman knows what you've done, you're in so much more trouble."

He reached out, settling his hand on her shoulder, his fingers moving slowly across her sweater. "You're worth it, Cat."

A chill filled her. She pulled her shoulder away and snarled, "Don't touch me!"

Magee grinned and removed his hand. "I see I'm going to have to sweet-talk you all over again. You liked me before, Cat. I'm going to get you to like me again."

Sandy had warned her about Magee. And she shivered inwardly, wishing Talon was here. They *had* to be looking for her. When she didn't show up for her shift at the fire department, she knew Matt Sinclaire would have called Talon, asking if he knew where she was.

Her throat grew dry as they crawled up the unused road. They'd find her truck gone. They'd put it together. Glancing around through the thick forest, she figured they were at eight thousand feet above Jackson Lake. What should she do? If she fought Magee, he'd explode into a rage, just as he'd done before. She couldn't stand the thought of his slimy hands on her, either. He always carried that damn knife on him. Dread filled Cat. There were many ways to die. She remembered thinking she was going to die when her raging father came after her with a belt and she'd tried to run away from him. She could never outrun him.

Cutting him a glance, she saw Beau with that sickening smile curving his mouth. He'd always tried to get her in bed and she'd always refused. His kisses, what few there had been, were sloppy and wet. Nothing like when Talon kissed her. Her heart squeezed with fear she'd never see him again. Never feel his hands caressing her, loving her. Never see that burning warmth he held for her in his gray eyes, or hear it in his voice. She wanted to cry. Swallowing several times, Cat looked at her options.

If she leaped out of the truck and ran, Magee would

come after her. And more than likely, he'd catch her. She had no weapon with which to defend herself. If she played weak and let him take her into that cabin up ahead, she'd encounter a different set of horrors. She knew what he was capable of.

Biting down on her lower lip, Cat's mind raced with possibilities. The urge to run was powerful. She was strong and she was in good shape. But Beau was a man and he had a lot more muscle. He was in good shape, she knew, because he hiked in the Tetons every chance he got. He also worked out regularly at a local gym. He would do everything in his power to catch her. And then what? If, on the other hand, she played meek and seemed to go along with his mind games, she could wait for an opening to escape. If she appeared subdued, he might lower his guard. And then, after knowing the layout of the cabin, Cat would have a better idea of how to defend herself. A kitchen always had knives in its drawer. A pair of scissors. She cringed, the thought of using a weapon against Beau sickening. She was a paramedic. She saved lives, she didn't take them.

Yet, as she guided the truck up a long curve, Cat knew her life was on the line. Kill or be killed. It would be her choice. She never wanted Magee to touch her again. Not ever. She'd have to fight for herself.

CHAPTER TWENTY-THREE

TALON WASN'T WAITING around. He was going to find Cat. His mother's information about Beau using a friend's cabin up at Jackson Lake was a definite lead. A thin one, but one worth checking out. He headed to the courthouse, to the Records Office. Within minutes, he was poring over deeds on the cabins. Luckily, a deed showed the longitude and latitude of every dwelling, plus the name of the owner. He sat at a desk with the huge book open and his notebook nearby. Careful attention to detail might yield information that would find Cat.

There were twenty-five cabins around the entire lake. It was a daunting task, some of the gumshoe work that Cade had told him would have to be done. The only other kind of break they might get, he'd told Talon earlier, was for an eyewitness to have seen Cat's truck. But what were the odds? His mind kept leaping to her being harmed by Magee. He'd done it once before. He'd do it again. Talon wished he'd been able to show Cat how to defend herself, but there hadn't been time.

He loved her. God, how he loved her. Rubbing his jaw, he closed his eyes for a moment, wishing he'd told her that. Even his mother knew! And he hadn't said those words to Cat. Now it could be too late. He whispered a curse, turning the page, moving to the next entry. But his heart, his aching, bleeding heart, was completely focused on Cat. She deserved none of what was happening to her. Who the hell had posted bail on that bastard? Right now, Cade had four other deputies with him and they were interviewing every employee at Ace Trucking. Would they find anything? More than anything, Talon hated his helplessness, not being able to do something to save Cat.

"Beau, you don't have to do this." Cat stood inside the cabin. She watched him lock the door. Her heart was pounding with dread. The cabin was huge, with two floors. It hadn't been used in a long time. There were white sheets hanging over all the furniture. Dust lay thick on the cedar floor and everywhere else.

Shrugging, Beau turned and gave her a little smile. "I need to convince you we have something good between us, Cat." He walked over to her, looking into her eyes.

"Do I have your word you won't try to escape? I don't really want to have to tie you up. If you give me your word, you have the freedom of the cabin. All I ask is that you don't try to go out that door." He pointed to it.

Feeling his sincerity, Cat looked down at her feet. "Yeah, okay. I give you my word." Anything was better than being handcuffed or tied up. She'd never be able to escape if he did that. Better to lie and let Beau think she was staying. When she looked up, she saw hope burning in Magee's eyes. His nose was badly swollen, his left eye black and purple. Cat forced a slight smile. "Really, I will stay here, Beau."

He grinned, rubbing his hands. "Thanks for giving me a chance, Cat. I'm not as bad as you think." He looked around the cabin. "Sure is dusty, isn't it?" He took off his jacket and hung it over one of the barstools at the granite island. "Why don't you make yourself at home? I'll get things cleaned up so this looks like a proper place to live."

Relief surged through her. At least he wasn't coming at her. He seemed happy. "I need to go to the bathroom."

"Go right ahead."

Cat located it off the main living room. Would there be anything in there she could use as a weapon? Or was Beau going to follow her in there? Mouth dry, she risked a look over her shoulder. He was pulling off sheets and piling them on the floor. Her heart wouldn't stop beating hard. In the bathroom, she shut the door. There was no lock on it. Luckily, there was electricity to the cabin even if no one had used it in a long time. Cat tried to keep her movements quiet. She didn't have to go to the bathroom—it was just an excuse. The first thing Magee did was to take her cell phone off her. She opened several drawers. In one, she found a seven-inch pair of scissors. Just knowing they were there was enough right now. She didn't want Magee to find them on her or things could get rugged between them in a helluva hurry. She had to know the layout of the cabin, had to know exits points, places she could escape out of.

Flushing the toilet, Cat tried to collect herself. Tried to calm down. As she opened the door, she saw no one around. Once she moved out into the hall, she saw Beau with an armful of white sheets coming her way.

"Are you hungry?" he asked as he walked past her toward the other end of the hall.

"A little," she lied as Beau approached a washer and dryer.

"Make yourself comfortable," Beau called over his shoulder.

Cat's mouth quirked. Did Magee think she was willingly going to stay here? She walked out into the main room, scanning the area for her truck keys. Had Beau put them in his pocket? As she moved from place to place, Cat didn't find them.

Should she run away? Risking a glance, she saw Beau stuffing the sheets down into the washer. Cat gulped. It was now or never. She raced silently for the door, unlocked it and quietly stepped out. Her truck would be of no help since she had no keys. Looking around, she saw the entire cabin was surrounded by thick forest. Vaguely, she knew where she was. Her heart started pounding as she turned and raced off the porch, heading into the woods. She didn't know if Magee was a tracker or not. Most likely not. Cat knew she didn't dare use the road, because it would be the first place Magee would think to go. Her breath came in explosions as she leaped into the woods, a slight slant to the hill where the cabin was located. Adrenaline surged into her bloodstream and terror made her run as hard and fast as she could.

She had to get far enough away, blend into the dark, shadows and light caused by the sunlight, and disappear. The pine needles on the ground were brown and dry. They covered a lot of black rocks and she stumbled all too often. She had to get far enough away and do it quietly. And Cat knew if Magee found her, he'd explode into a rage and kill her. This time, she had no illusions. This time, she'd die.

BEAU WALKED OUT into the living room. "Cat? Where are you?"

No returning answer.

Cursing, he couldn't see her anywhere. She'd walked down the hall into the main room. Was she upstairs? He quickly took the cedar stairs, his boots thunking against the wood. On the second floor, he opened each of bedroom doors, calling her name. Why would she leave him? Cat knew he was going to treat her right. He didn't want to scare her. He just wanted an opportunity to show her he loved her. That she could learn to love him. At the same time, as he tore each door open and didn't find her, his rage mounted.

By the time he quickly went down the stairs, Beau knew she'd run away. Jerking the door open, he stepped out. He yelled her name. His voice was quickly soaked up by the forest around him. He fished the keys out of his pocket, made a quick run around the huge cabin. He peered into the woods, trying to see if he saw her. Anger burned through him.

He ran back to the truck. Cat would run down that two-mile road to the main highway to get help. Most likely, hitch a ride back into Jackson Hole. Mouth thinning, Beau cursed and climbed into the truck. He'd find her and bring her back here. And then he'd beat the shit out of her and teach her that she couldn't run away from him ever again.

TALON'S GAZE HALTED on one land entry: Downing. His ·heart thudded. His instincts screamed at him. Downing had owned the Triple H. He was dead now. After running his hand over the entry and then moving to the computer that had all the updated information, Talon typed in the property number. On the computer screen, he saw that the taxes on the cabin were paid and up-to-date. Further, it had Downing's name on it, but it was in legal limbo since he had been murdered. Talon had no idea if Downing had a will or if he had family who would inherit the cabin. There were no other names on the ownership of this land. Could Magee have used *that* cabin?

Once he jotted down the GPS, Talon quickly left the room and headed out of the courthouse. It was now nearly five o'clock. He pulled out his cell phone and dialed Cade Garner.

"Garner here."

"Cade, it's Talon. I've found the location of Downing's cabin. It's at Jackson Lake. I'm heading out there right now. Do you have anything yet?"

"Negative. So far all the employees we've interviewed don't have a clue about a cabin."

Talon heard the frustration in his voice. "Okay, I'm heading out there to see if I can find anything. I want to give you the GPS coordinates just in case."

"Go ahead...."

By the time Talon reached his truck, he'd ended the call to Cade. His heart was aching with dread. With hope. He climbed inside the truck, and Zeke whined hello. Talon gave him a pat on the head. It would take forty-five minutes to drive up there. Glancing at the sun, he was glad it was early summer. There would be more light available for a longer period of time.

Talon opened his glove box and took out a Glock 18, his pistol choice. It would stop a grizzly and it would stop a human. After putting bullets in the chamber, the safety left off, he set it on the seat beside him within easy reach. He had a permit to carry the firearm and would use it if necessary.

As he drove out of town, he couldn't stop thinking

about worst-case scenarios. He wished he had a drone, eyes in the sky, to try to locate Cat's truck. He wished he had his teammates, because SEALs always worked together. He had none of those things available to him. Except Zeke, who was a weapon of another kind. All he had were his wits, his knowledge and, more than anything, he needed some luck. As he drove out of town, he kept his eye out for Cat's truck. There was every chance that Magee hadn't taken her to that particular cabin. He looked down at his GPS unit and, once out of Jackson Hole, pushed his truck, breaking the speed limit going up the hill that would take him that much closer to Jackson Lake.

Inwardly, Talon could feel Cat. It was that invisible connection between them. He could feel her panic, anxiety, and he wiped his mouth, trying to remain detached. If he let his emotions go, they would do nothing but distract him and he could miss something. God, he loved her.

By the time he located the road, which was barely visible, Talon pulled off to the side, got out and checked what he thought were fresh tire tracks. He put the work leash on Zeke and the dog jumped out the door, his ears up, alert. It was nearly six o'clock, the thick woods making everything darker as the sun was in the west. He moved to the dirt and pine needles, which were mixed and disturbed. Kneeling down, he studied the tracks. It was wide, denoting it was probably a large vehicle. And the tread was fresh. Glancing up, he saw the road lead upward.

The cabin was sure to sit at nine thousand feet and they were at seven thousand right now. Slowly standing, Talon oriented his hearing. There was a blue jay faintly calling, but otherwise, he heard nothing else. Mouth tightening, Talon opened the door to his truck, and Zeke jumped in. He left the leash on him and climbed into the vehicle.

Not knowing what to expect, he crawled along the narrow one-lane dirt road. There was no place to turn around, the woods crowding right up to it. He kept the butt of the Glock toward his thigh in case he needed it in a hurry.

Now in SEAL mode, Talon saw the huge cedar two-story cabin come into view around the long curve. He halted the truck, turned off the engine and got out. Talon let Zeke out, holding the leash. Sliding the Glock into his rear waistband of his Levi's, he moved quickly and quietly on the side of the road, his gaze focused entirely on the cabin. Breathing harder because of the altitude, Talon moved silently. Zeke remained at his side, panting, waiting for a command.

Near the door, Talon stopped and studied the soft, fine dirt. He gave Zeke a hand command to sit. The dog did so. There were tracks. Fresh ones. Moving around them, not wanting to disturb them, Talon cased the cabin. He looked into the windows along the one side but saw nothing. The cabin was dark. And quiet. It appeared no one was at it right now. Going to the main door, he drew the Glock. To his surprise, the doorknob twisted and the door opened. His heart rate amped up as he moved into his crouch, opening the door and swinging in, the Glock raised.

Talon needed to clear every room on the first floor. He unleashed Zeke and gave him the signal to "seek." The Belgian Malinois instantly moved like a silent shadow. Zeke went to the bathroom, shot out of it and ran down the hall, his claws clacking on the wooden floor. Talon watched, gun drawn, following the dog's progress. Zeke reappeared, galloping toward him, panting. The dog shot past Talon. Frowning, Talon turned. Zeke moved toward the living room and stopped at a couch, whining, tail wagging.

Talon's heart thudded. There, hung over a chair was a denim vest. Talon thought it was Cat's. But he couldn't relax, couldn't check it out until they'd completely cleared the entire cabin to make sure no one was here. Otherwise, he could be surprised and possibly shot by Magee. As soon as he gave Zeke the command, the dog bolted up the stairs. Talon followed, quickly making it to the second floor.

To his surprise, all four doors were wide-open. Zeke took the first door on the right, disappearing inside. If the dog met any resistance, he would immediately attack whoever was in there. Talon knew he wouldn't attack Cat, because she was a known quantity to his assault dog. Zeke dashed out of the door, spun to the left and dived into the second room on the right. Talon remained crouched, Glock aimed. Within a minute, Zeke had cleared the four rooms. There was no one in the cabin.

Hurrying downstairs, Zeke as his side, Talon tucked the Glock in his waistband and went over to the vest.

Zeke whined, looking up at him, tail wagging excitedly. Talon knew he could pick up Cat's scent on the garment. His heart soared as he recognized the vest. It was Cat's. His fingers curved around the soft material. Instinctively, he pressed it to his nose, inhaling her scent. There was no question it was Cat's vest. So where was she?

Her truck was not here. Neither was Magee's. Talon

knelt down on the concrete slab that was the entry into
the cabin. The shade made it tougher to see the tracks,
but he noticed two sets. One was much larger than the
other. Bending down, he peered at the second set of
tracks. His heart thudded. Cat wore special boots that
firefighters used while on duty. The boot had a steel
plate throughout the bottom. The reason, she had told
him, was that if they stepped into burned, charred
wood, no nails or metal could jam up into their foot
by accident.

Talon clearly remembered that her boot had a particular kind of tread. And as he studied the deep, fresh
print in the disturbed soil, he knew it was Cat's boot.
Getting to his feet, he scowled. The larger boot track,
which he assumed was Magee's, moved out to the road
and disappeared. Cat's boot tracks, instead, moved
around the end of the cabin.

He put the vest to Zeke's nose. "Smell," he ordered
the dog.

Zeke sniffed it with his long, black nose.

Talon pointed to Cat's track. "Smell."

Zeke stuck his nose along where Talon had his finger. Talon wanted him to get a good scent on Cat. The
dog whined and lifted his head, his brown eyes spar-
kling with excitement.

"Yeah, it's Cat," he told the dog.

Zeke's tail pumped with renewed excitement.

What the hell? Talon scowled as he continued to follow the prints. Had Cat escaped? He halted, turning and
looking for Magee's tracks along with hers.

There were no other tracks.

Lifting his chin, he saw how Cat's tracks moved into
the woods, heading in a southerly direction. That would

be toward the highway two miles below them. The area was rough, rocky, and the pine needles dry and slippery. The shadows were deep, the gloom setting in because the sun was on the other side of the mountains.

His mind spun with possibilities.

Following her trail a little farther, Talon could tell she was running, the stride between each track much longer than if a person were walking somewhere. His hope amped up. Cat had escaped! He tried to still his excitement. She might be wounded. Squinting his eyes, looking for blood droplets or anything else to suggest Cat was hurt, Talon continued to follow the tracks for a little farther.

No, she's okay. She's all right. More relief poured through him. His heart ached with hope. With dread. He needed to call Cade and give him the intel. Halting, Talon drew out his cell phone. It had two bars, not much. It was enough to connect with him.

"She's running toward the highway from what I can tell," Talon told him.

"But you didn't see her truck? Magee?"

"No."

"If Cat ran, then he's probably hunting for her," Cade said, worry in his tone.

Talon's mouth thinned. "Yeah, my thoughts, too." He craned his neck, trying to look through the gloom of the forest. "What do you want to do?"

"Cat's trying to reach the road," Cade said. "Trying to get help or get a ride back to Jackson Hole. We have to assume Magee took her cell phone, so she can't call us. Why don't you continue to track her? Use your dog. He'll find her even faster. I'm going to get into the cruiser right now and head your direction. I'm bringing Shelby with me because she's a tracker. We'll try to watch for Cat's truck on the way up. I don't know how smart Magee is. We don't know if he's trolling the highway thinking she's trying to reach it or not. He might be guessing she's going to end up on that highway sooner or later. And then grab her."

Talon held on to his fear. "I was thinking along the same lines. He's got her truck."

"Yeah," Cade growled. "I'm going to call the sheriff up north in the bordering county and get him involved in this. If Magee doesn't have her, he could also be using the truck to escape and leave the area."

It was a manhunt. Talon nodded. "I'm going back to my truck to get my gear and then I'll start tracking her. I'll be in touch."

"Right," Cade agreed.

Talon shoved the cell into his pocket, turned on his heel and ran back to where his truck was parked. As a SEAL, he always carried a rucksack. And it was something he'd never be without. He quickly checked for things he knew he'd need. Among them, a flashlight because as the sun set around eight he'd need it to keep hunting for her tracks. There were four bottles of water in his rucksack, along with protein bars. That would keep him going for a long time. Also, first-aid items, which Talon hoped he wouldn't have to use any of. He threw the bag over his shoulders, belted up and kept the Glock in his right hand.

As he trotted past the cabin, Talon halted. Zeke stood at his side, his eyes on the forest ahead of them. Should he loose the dog and have him follow the track? Zeke had no armored protection, which an assault dog always wore. And he had an injured shoulder. Did he want to risk his dog like that? What if Magee found Cat? Talon knew Zeke could swiftly follow her trail, find her and keep her safe. And if Magee had her, Zeke would instantly pick up on the fact Cat was afraid and he'd attack the man who had her. If he gave Zeke the signal.

Talon was torn. He couldn't keep up with Zeke when he was on a scent. Almost always, he remained with him on the leash. Zeke would find her. He knew he would. And that would let Cat know he was nearby, coming to rescue her. Further, with grizzly always a danger, Zeke would protect Cat from any possible attack. He leaned down, his hands on his dog's head, looking into his eyes.

"Zeke, find Cat. Seek." He put his finger into her boot track.

The dog instantly woofed the scent. His tail wagged strongly and Zeke looked up at him, his huge brown eyes glinting with excitement.

Talon unsnapped the leash. "Seek," he ordered his dog.

Instantly, Zeke shot off into the forest, running hard and following the fresh scent. Talon watched him disappear among the trees. He felt some relief. Zeke would find Cat. Now he had to move as fast as he could and, eventually, catch up. Talon trotted alongside Cat's tracks, watching as she angled down the long slope. He'd grown up in this area and he knew the land well. This particular hill was long and gentle, so she could make good time, gravity pushing her.

There was one fly in the ointment, besides Magee. This whole area was rife with grizzly bears. Each bear had a territory and would often cover twenty to thirty miles a day, looking for food. It was early July and the bears had just come out of hibernation and they were hungry. Both Cat and Zeke were easy prey.

Talon felt urgency thrumming through him. Many of the rocks were hidden beneath a six-inch layer of dried pine needles. He tripped often. And he could see where Cat had tripped, the needles and dirt torn up where she had fallen. It wasn't easy going although, on the surface, it appeared to be.

And where was Magee? Slowly driving up and down the road below this area? Talon hoped he'd left the area. He knew Cat was smart and, if nothing else, she could flag down a motorist and get help. All she needed was a cell phone. Cat could then call him. Call Cade. God, he hoped she was able to make it down to the highway.

CAT SKIDDED TO a halt as the slope of the hill ended and another hill rose up in front of her. Lungs burning, she leaned over, hands on her thighs, trying to catch her breath. The woods were silent, thick and gloomy. How long had she run? She wasn't sure if Magee was following her or not. Straightening, her heart bounding in her chest, she turned toward the hill. She was thirsty, her mouth dry. Slowly, she turned, trying to get her bearings. In a forest, it was impossible unless the sun was up. And it was getting darker and darker.

Cat felt panic as she tried to remember where she'd been and where she needed to go. But all the trees looked the same. The only thing different was the slope and change of the land. Standing in the V between the hills, she wiped the sweat off her brow. Her breath came in huge gulps. Even though her body was acclimated to high altitude, the run had been swift and hard.

Turning, she decided to start climbing the second

hill, praying that on the downward slope, she'd hear car traffic, maybe see the highway. The trees were thick and it was impossible to see more than fifty feet in any direction. Scrambling, the pine needles slippery, she used her hands and feet to start scaling the steeper slope. What spurred her on to scramble and grab at the earth was the fact that Magee could be on her trail. Following her. And he had a knife. She had nothing.

A huge, rocky promontory jutted out above her. The ground was a lot rockier and tougher to climb. Cat's boots kept slipping on the layer of pine needles hiding a lot more rocks. Just as she straightened to grab at a bush sticking out between the rocks, Cat twisted her knee. With a cry, she went down. She rolled several feet, grabbing for her right knee. *No! Oh, God, no!* Groaning, she sat up, her hair littered with pine needles. There was no pain in her right knee as she quickly pushed and prodded against it with her fingers. And yet, her knee had given out beneath her. What was going on?

Panicked, Cat slowly got her left leg under her. When she tried to push up on her right knee to stand, she felt it give out beneath her. *Damn!* She went down, grunting as she hit the ground. The rocks hidden beneath the pine needles were bruising. Gasping for breath, Cat sat up, frowning. Once more she felt, poked and prodded around the injured knee. What the hell was going on?

Again, she stood up, this time, putting all her weight on her left leg. Arms out to keep herself upright, Cat tested her right leg. Her knee felt like it was loose, sliding around. And then it hit her: she'd torn the meniscus, a cartilage that existed between the knee joints. With a small cry of terror, Cat sat back down. Blinking back tears, she held on to her right knee. A torn meniscus meant it would start swelling immediately. And she wouldn't be able to use the joint at all. She couldn't even put weight on it or she'd fall. Terror wound through her as she sat in the gloom, halfway up the steep hill.

Cat had nothing on her she could wrap her leg with in order to stabilize it. Nothing. She wasn't wearing a belt around her trousers, either. Closing her eyes for a moment, she felt a sob work its way up her tightening throat. Tears burned behind her lids. Oh, God, she was in real trouble now. If she tried to use her leg, she would only damage it more. She couldn't hobble out of here on one leg.

Lifting her chin, she choked back a sob. If Magee was following her, he'd find her. And there was nothing she could do about it. Wiping the tears off her cheeks, Cat looked around again, trying to find anything she could use to wrap around her injured knee. If she was going in the right direction, she estimated a half a mile of walking over this hill before she found the highway. *If* she was going in the right direction. She couldn't stop shivering as the temperature dropped. All she had was her sweater. It would get down below freezing tonight and Cat had another thing to worry about: hypothermia. People died out here in these mountains because they froze to death, not wearing the correct apparel. Her fingers were cold and she rubbed her hands against her arms.

There was a sudden sound that caught her attention. Jerking her head to the left, she looked down in the cut where she'd been. Fear jammed in her throat. Her eyes widened. A huge, lumbering black shape appeared out of the gloom. Her heart began to pound with dread.

An enormous grizzly bear!

Cat held very still, knowing bears had lousy eyesight. Everything was in their nose. The cinnamon-colored grizzly was moving slowly, stopping, digging into the pine needles, tearing up rocks and dirt. He was looking for grubs and worms for a meal. Cat was paralyzed. She was a hundred feet away from the bruin. He hadn't seen her, his massive head down, his nose following scents of grubs hidden beneath the rocks.

She tried to swallow, her heart racing, the adrenaline flooding her. If she didn't move or make a sound, the bear might not realize how near she was. Unable to tell which direction the wind was blowing, Cat worried. Because if the direction flowed toward that bear's nose, he'd scent her and come after her. And she had no way to defend herself against an eight-hundred-pound grizzly.

Her mind spun. If the bear discovered her, she'd have to roll into a ball and play dead. That was the only way to potentially survive the attack. Cat had once been life-flighted into an area in the Tetons where a backpacker had encountered a grizzly. She remembered all too clearly how the man's back and neck had been savagely bitten into. He'd lost a lot of blood and barely survived, paralyzed from the waist down.

The grizzly was hunting for food, hungry and focused on the cut where he was digging. Cat saw his five-inch-long claws as he lifted his one arm and dug savagely into the ground. Dirt and pine needles flew in a cloud around the front of the bear. She watched, mesmerized, as the bear delicately turned the large rock over, snuffling and eagerly eating the grubs he'd just found beneath it.

Cat could hear him chomping his jaws, saw the flash

of those huge fangs. She was out in the open, nothing to hide her. She couldn't get up and run. Trying to outrun a grizzly would be impossible for her or anyone. She still wished she had two good knees at this point. There was a broken limb near her hand. It had fallen off the nearest tree. Slowly, Cat moved her hand, her fingers meeting the gray bark and curving around the end of it. Bears had one Achilles' heel: their sensitive, large nose. And if the grizzly discovered her, Cat was going to try to strike the bear's nose. Often, a bear would back off, hurt and angry, with a bleeding nose. It was the only defense she had.

As she sat there, barely breathing, her heart turned to Talon. Cat had a terrible feeling she wasn't going to survive. If Magee didn't find her, the bear probably would. Either way, she was dead....

CHAPTER TWENTY-FOUR

CAT'S THROAT ACHED with tension. She could barely breathe as she sat frozen on the side of the rocky hill. The grizzly was within fifty feet of her, still not aware of her presence above him. He was focused on digging up rocks to find food. The woods were gloomy, the day growing grayish. Cat knew there would be light until around eight o'clock. She didn't dare look at the watch on her right wrist, but figured it was around seven. Her heart was doing a fast pound in her chest. It was so loud she wondered why the grizzly hadn't heard it yet.

She had never been this close to a grizzly before. His reddish-brown coat was thick and he looked fluffy. But the massive size of the bruin made her feel shaky with dread and fear.

Suddenly, there was a screaming of a blue jay's warning echoing nearby in the woods.

The grizzly jerked up its head, looking in that direction.

Cat's breath jammed. The sound came from the other hill.

Oh, God...

The grizzly's ears flicked as his head was turned away from her, intent on the warning cry of the noisy bird. And then Cat saw the blue jay burst out from beneath the cover of the tree where it was and fly directly at the grizzly. And as it swooped over the bear, it flew right to where Cat was sitting.

Cat tensed, the bear following the low flight of the screaming jay. Her heart tripled in rate as she saw its small, dark eyes study her. The grizzly halted, watching her. What did he see? Adrenaline poured through her. She had no way to escape. Everything in her world started slowing down to frames, just like a movie.

The grizzly woofed once. He stood up on his hind legs, nearly eight feet tall.

Cat was transfixed, not breathing.

The bear woofed again, turning directly toward her, his massive front paws hanging like human hands in front of him. He lifted his nose to the air, testing it.

She was a dead woman. The bear had picked up her scent. Cat felt her whole world anchor to a heart-thudding stop. *I'm going to die....*

A low, snarling growl filled her ears. She blinked once as she saw something small and dark racing out of the darkening line of the woods. Straight at the grizzly.

Cat gasped. Zeke!

The Belgian Malinois hurtled like a rocket toward the grizzly. The bear heard the dog's warning growl and twisted its head in that direction, momentarily distracted. Cat gripped the limb, pulling it up, unsure of what would happen next. In shock over Zeke's appearance, she realized Talon had to be nearby. *Talon!* Tears stung her eyes as she watched Zeke hurtle his seventy-five-pound body against a grizzly that probably weighed around eight hundred pounds. Zeke opened his mouth, lips curled back, and leaped.

Her eyes widened enormously as the Malinois launched itself at the bear. Her breath exploded while

Zeke aimed for the bear's neck. Everything was in slow motion. Zeke's powerful, fawn-colored body sailed through the air. His lips were lifted away from his muzzle, long fangs sinking into the bear's thick neck.

The grizzly wasn't expecting the attack from behind. It roared and jerked away, coming down off his hind legs. Zeke's teeth sank deep into the bear's neck, his long legs straddling the shoulders of the enraged bruin.

Cat tried to get up, but her knee collapsed beneath her as she watched the dog hang on, the grizzly roaring, trying to swipe at him with his long claws. The dog had perfectly situated himself on the bear's back. As the grizzly whirled around in circles, trying to shake Zeke off, the dog clung stubbornly, only his teeth holding him on. Cat saw Zeke yanked from one side to the other. His growls and snarls were as loud as the grizzly's roars. The entire area shook with the two animals combating one another.

Cat sat tensely, worried for Zeke. It was such a mismatch but the dog was a trained combat assault dog and he did not give up one inch as the grizzly moved around in a circle, trying to shake him off.

Finally, the bear slung Zeke off. Cat cried out, watching him being hurled through the air at least twenty feet. To her shock, she watched the grizzly turn and charge after the dog. Screaming, Cat tried to get the bear's angry attention.

The grizzly jerked to a halt, saliva dripping out of its opened mouth. It turned toward her, breathing hard.

Zeke had landed with a thud, rolling several times. Without missing a beat, he leaped to his feet, whirled around and snarled. He charged the bear as it started to go up the hill toward Cat.

Cat screamed and tried to get up as the grizzly growled, taking huge, galloping strides toward her. Zeke came out of nowhere, lunging again. He jumped up, jaws snapping shut once more on the back of the bear's neck.

Cat threw up her hands as the bear was little more than twenty feet away from biting her. She lifted her legs, arms flying across her face.

The grizzly turned, swiping at Zeke. He missed.

The snarling of the dog, the roaring of the bear surrounded Cat.

Suddenly, she heard the booming sound of a gun being fired at close range. The grizzly turned around with surprising speed and grace. Zeke was hurled off again, landing ten feet away from Cat. The startled grizzly whirled toward the sound.

Out of the woods, Cat saw Talon running toward them. He had a pistol in his hands. He fired a second shot.

The grizzly woofed and suddenly whipped to the left, running down the slope, heading for the V where he had been hunting grubs earlier.

Zeke came to Cat's side, his tongue hanging out of his mouth, panting hard, his eyes locked on the fleeing grizzly as he guarded her.

Cat gulped, watching Talon move with silent speed. She saw his darkly shadowed face, the intense concentration on it, his gun sight fixed on the bear, which quickly disappeared into the dark woods.

Relief sped through Cat. Talon turned his attention to her, to his dog, who stood like a protector at her side. She reached out, touching Zeke's fur. The hackles on his neck and shoulders were standing straight up. The dog was still growling, watching where the grizzly had run and hidden. He was panting heavily, his sides heaving from exertion.

With ease Talon took the hill to reach Cat. His eyes were narrowed, his mouth thinned as he made it to her side.

"Are you all right?" he gasped, dropping to one knee.

"My right knee. I can't walk…." She was shaking with fear. Talon was here. He and Zeke had saved her from being killed by the grizzly. Tears splattered down Cat's face. She saw Talon's face go from hard to anxious. He reached out, sliding his arms around her, holding her hard against him.

Cat sobbed once, burying her head against his shoulder, never so glad to see Talon as right now. He was breathing hard, his chest rising and falling sharply. He was sweaty, but she didn't care. "I was so scared, so scared," she muffled against his shoulder.

"Makes two of us, babe. Are you okay? Any wounds?" Talon squeezed her gently and eased away, anxiously looking down into her taut, pale face. Cat's eyes were filled with terror. With relief. Talon quickly glanced over at Zeke. He seemed to be no worse for wear, panting heavily, fully alert and in combat mode.

Sniffing, Cat clung to his dark gaze. "I never told you I love you, Talon. I—I thought it was too soon and, God, after Magee kidnapped me, it was the one thing I regretted the most." She touched his unshaven jaw, saw the fierceness in his eyes, the glittering of hate for Magee and the anxiety for her.

"It's all right," Talon rasped, moving strands of her hair away from her face. "I love you, too, Cat." Talon turned, looking in the direction of where the grizzly had fled. He gave Zeke a signal and pointed to a spot from which he wanted the dog to guard them. Zeke immediately leaped to his feet, moved ten feet down the hill and sat down, eyes on where the bear had disappeared. The dog would be his warning alarm in case the grizzly decided to come back. Turning his attention back to Cat, he said, "Where's Magee?"

Sniffing, her hand trembling as she tried to wipe the tears off her face, she whispered unsteadily, "I—I don't know. He went back to the laundry room and I escaped. I ran into the woods, Talon. I didn't have the keys to my truck and I didn't dare use that road or he would've found me."

He nodded. "You did the right thing." He saw her hand rubbing over her right knee. "Can you walk?"

Shaking her head, Cat said, "I think I tore my meniscus. When I try to put weight on it, my whole knee collapses under me."

"Pain?" he asked, gently feeling the joint. Cat was shaking now, wrapping her arms around herself. She'd come so damned close to death. First, by Magee and then a grizzly bear. If not for Zeke, she would have been attacked by the bear before Talon had ever gotten close enough to save her. Talon's heart was pounding with dread. With terror.

"A little pain. It's starting to swell now," she whispered, her voice unsteady.

"Okay, hold on. I'm going to call Cade," he said, and pulled his cell phone out of his back pocket.

Cat sat there, her gaze pinned on where the grizzly had run into the dark forest. Zeke was down below them, his black ears pricked up, watching the same area. A sense of safety blanketed Cat as she listened to Talon speaking to the sheriff's deputy. Safe. She was safe. Or was she? Where was Magee? Cat instinctively looked around the hillside that was now quiet once more. She didn't see anything. Besides, if someone was around, she reasoned, Zeke would hear or see them first long before she did.

Talon's hand on her shoulder comforted her as he spoke to Cade. She felt his alertness. He never stopped looking around. Probably his military training at the forefront. Her emotions were in chaos. One second, she felt terror. The next, shattering relief. The grizzly had been twenty feet away from her, charging her, its mouth open. Cat could see those fangs, see the saliva dripping off of them, the tiny, angry eyes focused on her. She closed her eyes, feeling incredibly grateful to have survived the confrontation.

Talon finished the call and stuffed his cell back into his pocket. He returned his attention to Cat. She looked paler, if that was possible, shock in her eyes. "The highway is just over this hill," he told her. Shrugging off his rucksack, he opened it up. "First things first, I'm going to wrap your knee and get it stabilized."

"Where's Magee?"

"I don't know. Cade said they've got three sheriff's cruisers out looking for him. They know he's got your pickup." He pulled a pair of flat, short pieces of aluminum from his pack. Next, he located a roll of duct tape.

"What are you doing with those?" she asked.

Talon grinned a little. "This is called combat medicine." He held up the two flat pieces of aluminum in his hand. "Splints. And once I position them on either side of your injured knee, I'll use the duct tape to hold it all in place. Help me?"

Cat nodded, her hands shaky as she placed the two flat pieces of metal on either side of her leg. She watched as Talon drew out a hunting knife from the pack. He quickly wrapped the silver duct tape around and around until it provided her new stability.

"Not fancy," he grunted, dropping the tape back into his rucksack, "but it works."

"You've done this a few times," she said, catching his gaze. When Talon gave her that cocky grin of his, Cat felt sheets of warmth curling through her, chasing some of her shock away. Just the way he dealt with her, his confidence and quiet ability to handle the situation leached off some of the terror.

"A few," Talon murmured, running his fingers lightly across the makeshift splint, testing to see that her knee had the support it needed. He lifted his head. "Are you thirsty?"

Groaning, Cat nodded. "Dying of thirst."

Talon pulled out a pint of water and handed it to her. "Drink up."

He watched Cat. When she lifted the plastic bottle to her lips, it exposed the slender curve of her throat. A throat he'd kissed, where he'd felt her pulse beneath his lips. He struggled with his own shock of almost losing her. Who would have counted on a grizzly being part of all of this? Talon knew in the spring, the bears were starving, covering many miles in search of food. Cat happened to be at the wrong place at the wrong time. Talon glanced over his shoulder, checking on Zeke. His dog had saved Cat. He looked closely at Zeke but couldn't find any evidence that the bear had wounded him. His fawn-colored coat was smooth and shining in the low light. The dog was panting heavily, but hell, he'd just taken on an eight-hundred-pound pissed-off grizzly bear. And lived to tell about it. Zeke had been absolutely fearless.

Cat emptied the entire bottle. She whispered her thanks to Talon, wiping her mouth with the back of her hand. "Zeke was incredible," she told Talon. "He saved me."

Tucking the empty bottle into his pack, Talon nodded. "He's a combat assault dog. He'll take on anything or anyone without any fear."

Cat felt tears coming into her eyes again, her emotions seesawing through her. "He's a hero. I was never so scared, Talon. God, he attacked that bear like it was nothing."

Nodding, Talon closed his bag and shrugged it over his shoulders. "Zeke's good at what he does." He studied her for a moment, his heart bursting with so many feelings. Sliding his fingers across her cheek, he said, "He just saved the woman I love…." and he leaned forward, his mouth searching, finding hers.

Cat moaned softly, lifting her hands, sliding them around Talon's neck as his mouth pressed gently across hers. It was a soft, tender kiss. Not sexual. Just…loving. When Talon eased from her lips, she saw the glitter in his gray eyes. "I love you so much it hurts…" she choked, her chest tight.

He gave her a faint smile and caressed her pale cheek. "Love shouldn't hurt, babe. Come on, I'm going to help you to your feet. We need to get up and over this hill and down to the highway below. Cade is sending an ambulance our way."

Cat wanted to tell Talon, as he helped her to stand, that her pain was the anguish of thinking she was going to die, never to see him again. She compressed her lips, taking all the weight on her left leg and allowing Talon to slide his arm around her waist. She leaned heavily against him, suddenly feeling weak.

"Okay?" he asked huskily, kissing her tangled hair.

"Okay," she said. As he positioned her hand around his waist, Talon was solid and made it easy for her to limp forward. "This isn't going to be fast," she warned him, feeling pain begin in earnest in her knee.

"It's all right," he soothed. "Take your time." Talon looked over his shoulder and called Zeke, who leaped and swiftly closed the gap between them. Talon pointed toward the hill and gave the dog an order to guard. That meant Zeke would move out in front of them, making sure there were no bears, no humans, anywhere around them as they walked slowly up the hill.

Cat was grateful for Talon's patience and strength. As they finally crested the rocky hill, she spotted the highway below. There were no vehicles waiting for them but she knew they were deep into the Grand Teton National Park and it would take time for the ambulance to arrive.

Talon looked around.

Cat felt him shift into a different mode. "What are you doing?" she asked in a whisper.

Talon looked down at her. "Sensing if there's any enemy around. In this case, Magee. I don't feel anything and Zeke doesn't, either." He moved his chin in the direction of where his dog was operating about twenty feet in front of them, farther down the hill, trotting back and forth, always alert, always looking around.

"I wish I knew where Magee was," Cat muttered, feeling raw and vulnerable.

"Cade called the sheriff in the county above ours and

gave them info on your truck and Magee. He thinks he might be slipping away, making a run for it."

"God, I hope he's gone from this area," she said as she looked down the hill.

"Did he hurt you?" His breath jammed in his throat for a moment.

"No. He's crazy. He never touched me, thank God. He said he wanted to win me back, that I'd get to like him again as we stayed at that cabin." She shook her head, her voice bitter. "Like I'd *ever* want that bastard anywhere near me."

"I'm glad he thought he could trust you." Talon grunted as he helped her down a rocky expanse. "You ran out of the cabin when he was distracted?"

Compressing her lips, clinging tightly to Talon, she said, "Yes. But I was torn. He had a knife, Talon. And I knew he could use it on me if I ran. I wasn't sure if I shouldn't stay and try to talk sense into him or run."

"It was smarter to run," Talon said. They were halfway down the hill when he saw Cade Garner drive up and park below them on the berm of the highway. "There's Cade," he said.

More relief sped through Cat. "I'm so afraid Magee is out here lurking around somewhere...."

"Zeke would pick him up in a heartbeat," Talon assured her, watching as she carefully lifted her injured knee to hop another foot down the hill.

"You're safe, Cat."

Breathing hard, winded by the run and the adrenaline starting to leave her system, she groaned, "Not until they find Magee. I'm afraid to go back to the condo. Somehow, he got in. He was waiting for me when I unlocked the door and walked in."

Scowling, Talon said, "You're going to the hospital first."

Cade emerged from the black Tahoe cruiser and he quickly took to the hill, reaching them in no time.

"How are you, Cat?" he asked.

"I'm alive. That's what counts."

"Let's stop," Talon said, looking over at Cade. "Let's put our hands like a seat beneath her butt. We can carry her down to the cruiser a lot faster."

"Good idea." Cade smiled at Cat. "Ready for a short ride?"

She nodded. "Thanks…"

In no time, Cat was sitting in the backseat of the cruiser, waiting for the ambulance to arrive. She kept her right leg straight, protecting the swelling knee. Talon stood near the open door, never far away. He had given Zeke water earlier, the dog lapping it eagerly out of his cupped palms. Cat was amazed at the calm of the dog and his master. If she'd leaped on a grizzly's back, she sure would be shaken up even now. But Zeke was calm, attentive, his dark brown gaze moving up to check on her occasionally. Talon seemed unruffled, focused and intent, as he and Cade talked.

The ambulance rolled up, parking behind the cruiser. Just as Talon helped Cat stand, Cade's radio came alive. Another sheriff's deputy reported that they'd spotted Magee in her truck.

Talon listened as he allowed Cat to lean against him. The two fire department paramedics came up with a gurney. As he helped her sit down on it, he said, "I'm going with Cade. We need to get Magee. He's left the truck on the side of the road and disappeared into the woods. Zeke will find the son of a bitch in a hurry."

Cat nodded and lay down. "Please, be careful? Both of you. He has a knife."

Talon grimaced and placed a kiss on her brow. "I have a combat assault dog. Zeke will find him and take him down."

"But—"

"Hush," Talon whispered roughly, taking her hand. "I want you out of here, Cat. Safe. At the hospital." Talon saw a second cruiser pull up behind the ambulance. "I'll come and see you as soon as I can. I promise." And his gaze locked on to hers. He felt Cat's cold, damp fingers on his. Trying to not sound so gruff, he added, "I love you, Cat. Let these guys take you to the E.R. and then home."

CAT'S TRUCK WAS pulled off the road and partially hidden. Shelby Kincaid, who had been driving toward the Yellowstone southern entrance, spotted it with her sharp eyes. As a tracker, she was used to looking for small but telling details. Magee had driven off and put the gray truck into the woods and almost succeeded in camouflaging it. The truck had a flat tire and no spare, so Magee had abandoned it. Shelby was waiting beside the road for them when they pulled up.

"Hey," she called, lifting her hand toward Talon. "I see you brought the serious firepower. Your dog."

Nodding, Talon had Zeke on a leash. "Yeah, he'll make short work of this. Let's get over to the truck. Zeke needs to pick up Magee's scent and then I'll unleash him."

Cade walked beside Shelby and they followed Talon and Zeke to the truck. Talon opened the door, pointing to the driver's side of the seat. Zeke leaped up, his front paws on the floorboards, sniffing loudly. He whined and began wagging his tail in excitement.

"Okay, he's got the scent," Talon told them. He called Zeke down and the dog instantly put his nose to the ground, moved quickly around the pickup, straining at the leash, on the scent.

"I'm going to let him go," Talon told them over his shoulder. "Get ready to follow him...."

"But he'll outrun us by a mile," Shelby said.

Talon grinned darkly. "Oh, you'll hear him, no problem. He'll find Magee and take him down. The screams will tell us what direction to go. Ready?"

Cade nodded, drawing his pistol. He glanced over at Shelby, who did the same. "Let him go."

"Seek," Talon ordered his dog. He unsnapped the leash and Zeke leaped forward, moving at top speed, whipping in and around the stands of pine trees, swiftly disappearing.

"Let's go," Talon growled, pulling the Glock from his waistband, digging his toes into the dirt and pine needles.

Talon moved at top speed, brush whipping past him, swatting at his legs and hips, the pistol held high and ready. He was used to working with his combat dog and could hear Zeke's explosive breath somewhere out in front of him. He followed the sound without ever seeing his dog. Cade and Shelby were hot on his heels, crashing through the brush right behind him.

There was a low, snarling growl and Talon knew Zeke had spotted Magee. He couldn't see anything, the darkness starting to fall around them. The temperature was dropping rapidly, near freezing as he lunged in the direction of the growl. Zeke would not make a sound when he found his victim. He would growl only at the last second, getting the human's attention, throwing him off guard just before he lunged.

A man's startled scream split the air. Talon moved quickly toward the sound. He heard Zeke's guttural growl, Magee's yelp of panic. In moments, Talon came upon them. Zeke had a hold of Magee's left arm, having dragged him down to the ground. The man was striking at Zeke, but the dog refused to release his arm. Zeke was snarling and growling, hauling back on his rear legs, forcing Magee to stay on the ground.

Talon quickly came around Magee, looking for the knife he carried, which he saw in a sheath on his belt. "Stay down or I'll let my dog rip your throat out," he snarled at the man, pulling a pair of flex cuffs from his back pocket.

Terrorized, Magee stopped struggling.

"Zeke, sit!" Talon ordered. Zeke released Magee's arm and sat down nearby. Talon quickly pushed Magee on his belly, jerking his arms behind him. Cade came around and helped him cuff Magee from behind.

"Wow," Shelby said, impressed as she put her pistol away. "That's some serious tracking Zeke did."

Talon smiled grimly and stood up. He and Cade hauled Magee to his feet. His left arm was bleeding where Zeke had bitten and held on to him. "Maybe you ought to get a dog for the department."

Cade read Magee his Miranda rights as they pushed him toward where the cruisers were parked.

Shelby nodded and gave Zeke a proud look. "He's really something special." And her green eyes danced with mirth. "And so is his owner."

Talon felt proud of Zeke, who now obediently walked

at his side. Panting heavily, the dog kept his eyes on Magee, always alert, always guarding. Talon reached down and ruffled Zeke's fur. "Good boy!" Later, he would tussle with Zeke, give him the ball he loved to be rewarded with for doing a good job. Right now, all Talon wanted was to get back to Jackson Hole to the hospital and be with Cat.

As they walked out of the woods, Talon's heart and soul were oriented to Cat. She'd been so frightened. Helpless with a knee injury that had made her a target of the grizzly. Thank God for Zeke. Even though he had a shoulder injury that would never improve, his dog had responded magnificently to the bear. Talon patted Zeke's head, more than grateful to his dog. Zeke had saved him and his team so many times in the past. Now, even though he was no longer in the military, he was still saving lives. A fierce love for Zeke rose in Talon and he caressed the dog's ears.

"Shelby," Cade called after they got Magee into the backseat of his cruiser. "Would you take Talon and Zeke to the hospital?"

"Will do," she called.

Talon opened the rear of the cruiser and Zeke leaped in. Right now, he had to call his mother and let her know what had happened. And then put a call in to the McPhersons. Talon knew they would be worried sick. At least these calls he'd make would have a happy ending. All he wanted was to be at Cat's side, be there for her. He loved her, and Talon was going to make sure she knew it in every way possible.

CHAPTER TWENTY-FIVE

TALON WATCHED CAT come out from beneath the anesthesia after her knee operation. He stood by her bed in the private room at the hospital, his hand around her cooler one. "Welcome back to the real world," he teased, giving her a tender smile. She'd undergone a one-hour operation to repair the torn meniscus in her right knee.

"Hey," she mumbled, feeling his warm, strong fingers around hers. "Are you okay?"

"Never better," Talon promised, leaning down, lightly kissing her lips. This was all he wanted: Cat. As he eased away, he could see her trying to smile, the corners of her mouth lifting slightly. He held her eyes, the pupils large, rimmed with blue. "Cat? I love you. Just hold on to that, okay?"

She heard the thickening of his voice, the barely withheld emotions behind his words. "I love you, too, Talon." She frowned, closed her eyes and then felt more of the drug leaving her, her thoughts more lucid. Obviously, he was anxious, though his face remained unreadable. She knew he cared. His hand was wrapped around hers and the way he looked at her told Cat everything. "Did they find Magee?"

Talon straightened and smiled. "Zeke found him. Cade Garner brought him over here earlier while you were in surgery to get his arm medically taken care of.

Now Magee's in jail without bail." He saw the relief come to Cat's wan face.

"Is Zeke okay?"

"He's a happy dog. He got to take down a bad guy."

Cat managed a half smile. "Ugh, I feel so dopey...."

"Jordana McPherson was just in here to check on you. She said the orthopedic surgeon, Dr. Lyons, did a good job on your knee. Said it would take about an hour for you to feel normal after coming out from under the anesthesia. Can I get you anything?"

Cat felt the dressing around her right leg. "No...I'm okay. Just glad to wake up and see you here. Glad Zeke's okay, too." Her heart opened wide to Talon. He loved her. He was here. "Guess it's your turn to take care of me for a while," she teased, her voice hoarse sounding.

"I wouldn't want it to be any other way, babe." Already Talon could see her eyes beginning to clear and he drew in a deep sigh of relief. "Gus, Griff and Val sat out in the surgery lobby holding space for you during your operation. The doctor told them your surgery was a success and you were fine. They just left to drive back to the ranch once you were in recovery."

Nodding, Cat said, "That was so nice of them. And Sandy? Did you call her?"

"I did. We were all worried about you, Cat. Matt and Casey Sinclaire were in the surgery lounge when I arrived. They were holding guard for you, too, until I could make it back here to be with you."

Smiling softly, Cat whispered, "I have the best friends."

"They're like family to you," Talon told her gently. And, indeed, they really were. "Matt said you'll be getting six weeks of medical leave because of your knee injury. Told me to tell you to call him when you felt up to it. Casey wanted to know if she could be of help at your condo, if you needed anything cleaned or errands run."

"They're wonderful friends."

Talon grazed her cheek, seeing a tinge of pink coming back to them. "I told them we were living together and thanked them but that I'd be doing the cleaning of the house and any other errands you might need run." Because, unless Cat said differently, Talon was not leaving her side again. He'd nearly lost her.

"I like the sound of that," Cat admitted softly.

The door opened. Jordana peeked in. "Hey, you're awake!" She walked in, hands in her lab coat, the stethoscope around her neck. "Welcome back to the world of the living, Cat." She nodded hello to Talon and then walked over to Cat. "How's that knee feeling? Any pain?"

Cat was grateful when Jordana brought the bed up into a slightly sitting position for her. "It's a bit cranky, but no real pain."

"Good," Jordana murmured. "Dr. Lyons will be by shortly."

"The surgery didn't take long," Cat said, moving her hand over the light pink blanket over her knee.

"It doesn't. The good news is, once you feel like your old self again, you'll be discharged from the hospital. You can go home."

"That's great. I hate hospitals." And then Cat gave Jordana an apologetic look. "Not the people. Just being in a hospital."

Patting her hand, Jordana grinned. "I understand. In the meantime, no work for six weeks. Dr. Lyons and I can go over what you can and can't do."

"Six weeks," Cat muttered. "God, I won't know what to do with myself."

Talon grinned. He knew Cat wouldn't sit around—she was too restless and active. "Can she ride a horse, Jordana?"

Jordana laughed. "I'm sure after a week or so, Dr. Lyons will approve four legs for her to get around with."

"I'm feeling better already," Cat murmured.

"I'm going to get the crutches for you. I'll be right back."

Cat pushed her fingers through her hair. It felt dirty. "I'm going to have to take a shower when you get me home."

"Let's be sure to ask Dr. Lyons if that dressing around your knee is waterproof."

"Good idea," Cat muttered, realizing her mind still wasn't firing on all cylinders.

"Miss Gus wants to talk to us about something she said that was important," Talon said. "I told her once we got you stabilized that we'd drop over to the ranch and see her. That okay with you?"

"Sure," she murmured. Cat moved her right leg a little, testing it. She absorbed Talon's quiet presence. "Are you really okay?" He looked fine.

"I am now. Magee is in custody. And he's not getting out again."

"Whoever put up his bail might try it again."

"Cade said that the manager over at Ace Trucking, Jenkins, had put up the bail. That fancy California lawyer admitted it to Cade."

"Is it drug money?"

"Cade thinks so. Can't prove it. But Magee is in jail and won't be set free again. His trial will be in three months and you'll be one of the people testifying against him."

Suddenly, Cat was worried. "But if Magee is part of a drug ring, will that set them against me, Talon?"

He shook his head. "I don't think so and neither does Cade. Right now, ATF and the FBI are telling the sheriff's department that Garcia's trying to remain low-key. Magee was a loose cannon in their organization. Cade doesn't think they realized Magee was the sick bastard that he is, that he was obsessed with you. Otherwise, Cade says they probably wouldn't have hired him. They don't want their people causing waves or catching the attention of law enforcement." He saw some of her worry recede.

"All I want to do," Cat whispered, reaching out for his hand, "is go home, sleep with you in our bed."

"You'll get that," Talon promised her thickly, holding her fingers. "And Zeke will be downstairs being our guard dog. He's our first line of defense if anyone thinks they'll come through either condo door, so stop worrying."

IT WAS MIDNIGHT before Talon drove Cat to her condo. Zeke was in the rear seat, panting happily as Talon pulled into the driveway. Tapped into his SEAL training, he stayed alert as he held the door open for Cat, looking up and down the quiet, well-lit street. Above, the stars glimmered. It was chilly, near freezing. Zeke leaped out of the truck and stood by Talon's side, watching Cat's slow, awkward progress.

"Good thing I don't have to use these crutches long," she growled unhappily, hobbling slowly up the concrete driveway.

Talon grinned and shut the doors. "No, I don't think you're going to be friends with them." He gave Zeke orders to remain at Cat's side while he took the keys out of his pocket and opened the door to her condo and swung it open. Turning on the light, he went inside and cleared the place. Talon trusted no one. Magee worked for a drug cartel that was trying to get a toehold in the town. It was enough to put him on guard. The condo was empty and by the time Talon came out to the front door, Cat was hobbling up the two steps. He could see she was exhausted. It had been one hell of a day.

Zeke patiently stood behind her as she made slow progress into the condo. Once Cat was in, the dog leaped across the threshold and then sat nearby, watching her. Talon closed the door and was grateful that Zeke was with them. The dog didn't seem to be favoring his injured shoulder even after finding and taking Magee down. Still, tomorrow, Talon would take him to the vet to make sure.

"I'm whipped," Cat said.

"I bet." Talon took the crutches. "Hold on, I'm carrying you upstairs to the bathroom so you can have that shower."

Cat was going to protest but saw the very male smile lurking at the corners of his mouth. A mouth she wanted kissing her, loving her, once more. She'd come so close to losing her life, losing Talon. "Okay, I'm ready for a ride."

Talon deposited her in the bathroom. "Want some help undressing?" he said, and gave her a teasing look.

Cat sat down on the chair. "Yes." Talon shrugged out of his jacket and hat, setting them outside the bathroom. Zeke watched her from the doorway. He had saved her life, too. Tears burned in Cat's eyes and she felt suddenly emotional. As Talon came in and knelt down in front of her, gently easing off one of her boots, she whispered, "I'm going to cry…."

He put the boot aside. "You've been through a lot," Talon said, seeing the moisture in her eyes. "Want me to hold you?" Because he wanted to. Needed to. He saw her nod once, fighting to keep from crying. Talon stood and gently helped her stand. He wrapped his arms around Cat. He felt her arms slide around his waist, pressing her face against his shoulder and neck. "It's going to be all right, babe," he rasped, kissing her temple, easing his hand across her back. "I know you've been through hell…."

Cat let her tears flow. She wasn't one to cry often, but when she did, it felt like a flood. And Talon held her gently in his arms, grazing her hair, whispering words of comfort to her. Finally, the tears passed and Cat eased back just enough to look up at Talon. His stormy gray eyes were brighter than usual. Was he crying, too? Cat wasn't sure because she saw the tears disappear as quickly as she'd seen them. His mouth was tight, as if he were holding back a barrage of feelings.

Lifting her hand, she muttered thickly, "Thanks… I needed to get that out of my system."

"I always want to hold you when you cry," Talon told her, his voice low and thick with feelings. Grazing her wet cheek, he looked deeply into her exhausted eyes. "Come on, let's get you that shower and then I want to hold you all night…."

CAT DROWSILY AWOKE the next morning, the sun peeking around the edges of the drawn curtain. She rubbed her eyes, slowly rolling from her side to her back. Feeling the pinch of her injured knee, she grimaced. There wasn't much pain, just a lot of swelling from the surgery.

She heard a dog whining nearby.

As she opened her eyes, Cat saw Zeke sitting expectedly at the side of her bed. When she smiled at him, he thumped his tail and started to pant.

"Hey, big guy," she murmured, putting out her hand and petting his head. "How are you this morning?"

Zeke whined, the tail thumping even harder and faster.

Cat smiled and slowly sat up, being careful with her knee. Where was Talon? And what time was it? Groggy, she looked up at the clock on the dresser opposite her bed. It was ten o'clock? Gasping, Cat couldn't believe she'd slept ten hours. Looking around, she didn't see or hear Talon. The condo was quiet. Was Talon gone? If so, where had he gone? Cat saw her crutches leaning against the wall within her reach. There was a hand-scrawled note on the bed stand next to the crutches. "Babe, left to go to the bakery in town to get you some of your favorite cinnamon rolls. Be back soon. Love, T."

Cat held the paper, feeling her heart swell with a fierce love. She set the paper down on the surface and brought the crutches over. She wore a pink knee-length cotton nightgown and carefully got out of bed. First, the bathroom and then she'd get dressed. Just in time for Talon to return with those delicious cinnamon rolls.

Zeke followed her to the door of the bathroom.

"No, you can stay outside," she told him with a smile. "I don't need guard dogging in here...."

Cat had just struggled into a pair of loose white linen

slacks, put on her new knee brace and hobbled downstairs when Talon arrived. She smiled at the bottom of the stairs.

"Cinnamon rolls?"

Talon grinned, a sack of groceries in his hand. "You're up. Yeah, got your favorites." He saw she'd brushed her hair and it lay like an ebony cloak around her shoulders. Cat's eyes were clear and her smile went straight to his heart. As Talon shut the door, Zeke came up, whining and wagging his tail hello at him.

Patting his dog, he took the sack to the granite island. He walked over to Cat, who was walking without the aid of the crutches but with the serious knee brace on instead. Resting his hands on the shoulders of her dark yellow tee, Talon leaned down, claiming her smiling mouth. Holding her last night had been a special hell all its own. The only comfortable position for Cat's knee was on a pillow between her legs to keep the knee in a position that didn't cause her aggravation. She lay on her left side with the pillow and he'd slid in behind her, curving his body around hers. It had been sweet to slide his arm beneath her neck and wrap his other arm around her waist and hold her against him. He didn't know who had fallen asleep first.

Cat moaned softly, putting her arms around Talon's broad shoulders as he kissed her long and deeply. Her breasts were pressed to his chest, the black T-shirt fitting him like a second skin, emphasizing his breadth and power. Threading her fingers into his hair, she kissed him hungrily, feeling his moist breath along her cheek, inhaling his special scent that drove heat quickly into her lower body. She could feel Talon being careful with her, not wanting to cause her knee any pain. As he eased from her mouth, she whispered, "That's even better than a cinnamon roll."

His mouth moved into a faint smile and Talon released her. He kept his arm beneath her elbow as she walked slowly to the stool and sat down. "I like kissing you." He moved around the island and took the groceries out of the bag. Pushing the white sack toward her, he said, "And, trust me, last night I wanted to do a whole lot more than just hold you."

Groaning, Cat opened the sack and inhaled the scent of cinnamon. The huge rolls were thickly slathered with white frosting, making her mouth water. "I know," she lamented. "The doctor said it would be at least a week before I can start bending that knee again."

"And you'll be getting physical therapy for it," Talon reminded her, putting the boxes and cans into the cabinets above the sink. He pulled out two iron skillets and put half a pound of bacon in one of them to fry. "Hungry?"

"For you." Cat saw him cast her a warning look over his shoulder.

"Don't be a tease."

"Since when is being honest being a tease?" Incredible happiness threaded through her. Talon was dressed in jeans and a black T-shirt that made her salivate. She had run her hands over this man's body, felt his muscles tighten beneath her fingertips as she'd explored him. She had felt his love for her in so many different ways. Cat knew she'd been given a second chance. No longer was she going to self-censor anything about her feelings toward Talon. Every day was precious. A gift.

Talon took eggs over to the skillet. As he looked at

Cat, he noticed her cheeks were flushed. He felt himself hardening with need of her. "Want some breakfast?"

"Coffee?"

Talon moved to the counter and poured her a cup, sliding it into her hands. "Anything else?" A wicked look came to her face.

"You?"

Shaking his head, Talon muttered, "I'm in such a hurt locker. I'm going to count each of those seven days," he promised her with a growl, returning to the stove.

Laughing, Cat pulled a chunk off the cinnamon roll and savored it. "You look kind of nice in my kitchen. I'd like to wake up every morning and see you in there."

Talon grinned and broke half-a-dozen eggs into the heated skillet. "My cooking abilities are limited," he warned her. "However, my ability to love you isn't."

Cat sighed and gave him a warm smile. She pulled out a roll and set it on top of the sack. "Want a bite?"

"Of you, yeah."

She snorted. "Is this going to be the limit of our conversations? That we have to keep a distance and can't do much about it?"

"Most likely," Talon murmured, smiling.

She watched him cook up the eggs. Talon placed slices of bread into the toaster and put the butter and strawberry jam on the island in front of her. "You're really good at multitasking."

"A SEAL habit," Talon informed her. He put the eggs on a plate and set them on the island. In no time, he had plates and flatware for them. He found some pink linen napkins in another drawer and added them. "Can you divvy up the eggs?"

Cat nodded and gave him four while she took two.

He brought over the bacon in a small plastic bowl lined with paper towels. She took them and he came around the island and sat down next to her.

Zeke came closer, looking up at Cat, thumping his tail.

"Uh-oh," Cat murmured, picking up a piece of bacon. "I've got a beggar over here. What do I do?"

Talon looked around Cat and saw his dog. "A dog always knows who to hit on," he muttered casually, grinning.

Cat gave him a dark look. "What? You're saying he thinks I'm easy?"

Talon's mouth pulled into a full grin. "Something like that. He knows something sweet when he sees it."

"Well," Cat pouted, tearing the bacon in two, "he *did* save my life. Don't you think he deserves some kind of a reward?"

"When you put it that way," Talon agreed, "yes."

Zeke daintily took the proffered bacon from Cat's hand, his eyes glistening with happiness. Cat smiled. "Thank you, Zeke. You saved me. You're such a good friend to have." She patted the dog's broad head.

Zeke quickly finished off the bacon and looked pleadingly up at her again.

"No," Cat said, "lie down, Zeke," and she pointed toward the floor.

The dog whined.

"Zeke." Talon's voice was firm.

Zeke instantly went over toward the stairs and lay down.

"You're tough," Cat said, grinning over at him.

"And you're such a marshmallow, Ms. Edwin."

Sliding her hand across his shoulders, she laughed. "But you love me anyway?"

Talon turned and cupped her cheek. "Yes," he rasped, kissing her lightly on the nose, "I love you anyway."

Heat moved through Talon as he saw her expression turn somber. No doubt, she was cycling emotionally from nearly dying. He caught her hand, kissed her palm and allowed her to take it back. "I have a feeling you're not only going to spoil my dog, but you're going to spoil me, too."

Cat nodded, her voice strained. "You both saved me. Why wouldn't I?"

Talon put his fork down and turned on the stool, cupping her face. "Babe, you saved my life first. Remember? And I'm going to take the rest of my life and spoil you rotten. Okay?"

Tears stung Cat's eyes. She heard the barely held emotions in his voice. "Okay, can we agree we'll do our best to spoil one another so long as we live?"

He leaned down and brushed her mouth, feeling her warmth, the lushness that was only her. "You got it," he whispered against her lips.

CAT WAS RESTING on the couch in the early afternoon when her cell phone rang. She picked it up from the coffee table and answered it.

"Cat?"

"Hey, Miss Gus. How are you?"

"I should be asking *you* that!"

Cat grinned and slowly sat up, maneuvering her knee into a comfortable position. "I'm fine. Happy to be alive. Happy to have Talon here with me. Life doesn't get much better than that."

"That's true. Listen, I just got done talkin' with Sandy. Val, Griff and me want to go up to visit her tomorrow afternoon at one o'clock. Do you think you and Talon can make it? Are you able to walk at all?"

"Sure, we can make it. What's up?"

"Oh, not much," Gus hedged. "But it'll give us a chance to not only see Sandy, but to see how you're doing."

"I'm okay. I was never so grateful as yesterday when Zeke charged that grizzly that was coming after me."

"Talon told us about it. That dog's a real hero, but so is Talon. And you should be proud of yourself, Cat. You escaped and ran. Good for you!"

Wryly, Cat muttered, "Yeah, but in escaping, I took that hill the wrong way and screwed up my knee but good."

"Val was talkin' with Jordana today. They met over at the grocery store earlier. She said that you're on six weeks' medical leave from the fire department because of it?"

"Yeah," Cat said glumly. "I'll go crazy not working."

"Well, Jordana said that in a week, you'll be up to doing light ranch work. Are you interested? Work for us full-time for the next five weeks? It'll keep you busy and out of trouble."

Laughing, Cat said, "I'd love to, Miss Gus. Count me in. It will give me something to look forward to."

"Well," Gus said, "I've got a very special project in mind and I think it's a perfect fit for you. Won't cause you a lot of knee pain or anything. How about we talk more tomorrow when we visit Sandy?"

"Great," Cat said, relieved. "Whatever it is, I can do."

"Oh, I know. You're a real handy gal to have around.

By any chance do you feel like comin' out here for dinner tonight? We really miss you and Talon. I'm makin' my world-famous spaghetti and meatballs. I've already made the French bread and it's risin' right now. There'll be plenty for the two of you."

Cat felt such love for Gus. "Talon's out in the garage. Can I call you back and let you know? I love your spaghetti and, besides that, it will get him out of making me dinner tonight."

Gus laughed heartily. "I'll betcha he'll be more than ready to run you down here for dinner, then."

"I think so," Cat said, "but I'll call you back in about ten minutes."

"Sounds good. Oh, did I tell you? My strawberries are ripe? I'm makin' strawberry shortcake for dessert."

Groaning, Cat muttered, "Well, even if Talon doesn't want to come, I'll be there one way or another!"

Cat sat on the couch after the call, feeling such hope. There was soft music playing from the radio in the corner and Zeke was lying at her feet. Every time she moved, his head would pop up like the guard dog he was. She petted him. "Strawberry shortcake, Zeke. I'm hungry already." She slowly stood, carefully putting weight on her injured knee. The brace was state-of-art and allowed Cat to walk without much of a limp as she headed to the side door that led to the garage. Zeke got up and followed at her side. "I don't know if Talon wants to bring you down there or not. You'll probably be expecting Miss Gus to feed you a meatball or something…."

She smiled and the dog barked softly as if he understood.

CHAPTER TWENTY-SIX

BY THE TIME Cat arrived with Talon at his mother's house at one o'clock the next day, everyone was waiting for them. Val and Griff had come out to meet them once they parked, wanting to know if she needed help. Cat wasn't used to this kind of concern and care from so many and used Talon's hand to move slowly to Sandy's apartment. The sun was high overhead. It was a perfect day.

Once inside, Sandy, who had been sitting in one of the two overstuffed chairs, got up and came to greet Cat.

"How are you doing?" she asked, giving Cat a gentle hug of hello.

"Much better," Cat assured her. She released Talon's hand and watched as the woman hugged her son. It did Cat's heart good to see the look of love on both their faces. Family was everything. For a moment, her heart grieved because her own family had been so much less than what she saw shared between Sandy and Talon. She turned to find Miss Gus sitting in a chair.

"Hey, Miss Gus. How are you?" Cat slowly walked over and smiled at the silver-haired woman. She was all dressed up in a bright red short-sleeved blouse with ruffles around the neck. Usually, Miss Gus was in rancher mode with work clothes. She had on a pair of white slacks, too.

"I'm fine, Cat." Gus reached up and squeezed her

hand, staring at the brace on her knee. "We were glad you three could come to dinner last night. How's the knee today?"

"I'm doing better," Cat joked. "The brace really helps me be able to walk. Hate those crutches they gave me." Cat saw a beat-up leather briefcase leaning against the chair where Gus sat.

"Well, it all turned out okay. Have a seat," Gus said, pointing at the couch. "I want you, Sandy and Talon to sit over there."

Cat grinned and nodded. Miss Gus, being the elder, had the say. "Sitting sounds good," she said.

"Grab a cookie there," Gus said, pointing at the tray of cookies on the coffee table next to the couch. "Val is makin' us coffee."

Cat was happy to sit down. She chose the end of the couch where she could rest her knee against the arm and keep it out of the way of people walking. Ordinarily, Cat would be up, in the kitchen, helping Val, who was setting a bunch of mugs on a tray and filling them with fresh, hot coffee. The noise and laughter in the room warmed her as nothing else could. Griff was slapping Talon on the shoulder. They were joking and laughing about something. Sandy was looking much healthier. She went over to help Val in the small kitchen. The window curtains were all drawn aside, allowing in lots of light and slats of sun. It made Cat feel good that Sandy was coming back so strongly after the chemo treatment.

Talon leaned down and kissed Miss Gus on her fuzzy crown of silver hair. Cat grinned as she saw Gus blush. Talon scooped up some cookies and Miss Gus told him to sit at the other end of the small couch, leaving room for Sandy to sit between them.

"Want one?" Talon asked, handing Cat a cookie before he sat down.

She grinned and took it. "Thanks." He gave her that look that made her go weak with need. He'd taken off his black baseball cap and set it on the lamp table next to where he sat down.

The air was festive and Cat saw Miss Gus watching the proceedings. She always reminded Cat of a hawk sitting high on a tree watching the land that she flew over. Miss Gus had a sparkle in her eyes today and Cat sensed something was going on but wasn't sure what it was.

Val brought over the tray and set it down on the coffee table. She handed Miss Gus the first mug, then as Sandy sat down on the couch, she handed her the next one.

"Coffee, Sandy?" Cat asked, grinning. She used to drink coffee but, with chemo treatment, it hadn't tasted good to her any longer.

Sandy nodded. "First cup, Cat." She held it up. "Progress."

Laughing, Cat said, "For sure. That's great!" Val handed Cat her cup and Cat thanked her.

Griff and Val brought two wooden chairs from the table and sat down on either side of Miss Gus. Soon, everyone was settled in a more or less circle of chairs and the couch.

"Well," Miss Gus said, "I gotta tell all of you, this is a day to celebrate. Cat, we're glad to have you among us. You gave us all a scare the other day."

Cat felt heat crawl up her neck. "I'm glad to be here, too, Miss Gus." And she looked down the couch toward Talon, who had a serious look on his face. "Thanks to Talon and Zeke, I'm sitting here with all of you."

Gus snorted. "Good thing! I had a surprise I was gonna spring on Sandy, here, and when we heard what happened to you, I held off."

Cat grinned over at the elder. "I love surprises." She looked at Sandy. "Did you know about this?"

Sandy shrugged. "No. Nothing."

Gus chortled and hauled the beat-up, scarred leather briefcase and set it in her lap. "That's what a surprise is supposed to be! A surprise."

Val leaned over and helped Gus get the straps loosened so the briefcase could be opened. Gus pushed the top back and thanked her granddaughter.

"Now," Gus said, peering intently at Sandy, "this has been a surprise that's taken a lot of twists and turns. We had last-minute upsets with Cat being kidnapped. Just thank the good Lord that things worked out all right," and she gave a nod to Talon.

Talon said, "Zeke did the hard work, Miss Gus."

"Yes, that dog is mighty special," Gus agreed. Her hands were shaky and she peered down into the brief-case, hunting through the sheaves of paper.

"Gus? The originals are in this one," Val said, pointing to it.

"Oh, okay. Thanks."

Gus pulled out a lot of paper. Val took the briefcase off her lap and set it next to her chair. Settling the papers in her lap, Gus looked over at Sandy. "Now, you know your ranch, the Triple H, has gone through five owners since you were forced to sell it. Right?"

Sandy became serious. "Yes, that's right, Gus."

"Well, what you didn't know is that I've had my eye on your ranch for a long time. Every time it came up for sale, I wanted to get a chance to put a bid in on it. Four of those times, I found out too late it was for sale."

Gus looked around at the intent expressions on the faces of her loved ones. "The last time, the owner came to me, telling me he was gonna sell it and move back East. He was tired of playin' cowboy."

The group laughed.

Gus smiled like a wolf. "I asked him what he wanted for it. And it was way too much. I went over to check it out and I told him I'd buy it, but at a lower price."

Sandy gasped, her eyes widening. "You bought it, Miss Gus?"

Holding up her thin hand, Gus said, "Now, Sandy, let me finish tellin' the story, will you?"

Sandy smiled and looked over at Talon. His whole focus was on Miss Gus. "Fair enough," she murmured with a smile.

"Now, what I'm gonna tell you is private." She placed her hands over the pile of papers in her lap. "For most my life, I moved from Jackson Hole over to Cheyenne. I met and married my husband, who inherited his father's five-thousand-acre cattle ranch. We worked hard, expanded it and by the time he'd died, our ranch had fifty thousand acres to it. Between us, we had one of the best ranches in Wyoming. Might not have been the largest, but it was one of the most productive." Gus gave Val a warm look.

"I moved back to the Bar H when Val was sixteen. My daughter, Cheryl, had married Buck, who was an abuser. When I realized what was goin' on, I sold the ranch and came home to protect my daughter and granddaughter from the likes of him."

Val reached out, sliding her hand along Gus's small

shoulder. "You were like a fierce mama wolf. My father never laid a hand on us from the moment you moved back into the house with us."

Gus nodded, her thin, reedy voice cracking. "Yes, that's right."

Val smiled at her grandmother. "But you gave up so much to come and protect us, Gus, when we couldn't even protect ourselves. You sold a ranch that you and your husband had worked so many decades to expand and make a prime business model."

Griff nodded and shared a look with his wife, Val. "Gus, you sacrificed your entire way of life to be with Val and her mother. There's not many people I know who walk away from their life to do that."

Gus snorted. "Oh, stop! I wanted to do it." She patted Val's arm. "I've never regretted a moment of that decision." Looking at the three people on the couch, she said, "Bottom line was when I came back to the Bar H, I had a lot of money in the bank from the sale of our ranch. Griff here has an MBA from Harvard and he's been helpin' me to invest it wisely and make more money." She patted his cheek. "And so when the Triple H came up for sale again, I asked him to go over and deduce just what it was worth. The ranch was goin' downhill because the owners, past and present, didn't know how to be ranchers. When Griff came back with a bottom line, I had him drive me over to the guy who wanted to sell it. Griff went through the list of why the ranch wasn't worth what he thought it was."

Gus grinned, a sparkle in her eyes that she shared with Griff. "Now, I always thought I was a real horse trader, but you know what? Griff here is brutal when it comes to bargaining. And when he bargains, he's got his facts straight and in order." She rubbed her hands and cackled. "By the time Griff gave the owner the presentation, the guy agreed on the sum that I wanted to pay for it, not what he'd asked for originally." Gus beamed at Griff. "I've got one heck of a horse trader for a son-in-law!" She patted Griff's broad shoulder.

Griff blushed.

"So," Gus said, "that leads us to these papers." She picked them up in her hands. "Sandy, I saw you give up everything that meant anything to you. We were all aware, because you were our ranch neighbor, that you'd lost two husbands that you loved. And with Talon gone and in black ops, you were on your own with the cancer. I know we all pitched in to help you, but darlin' girl, I saw the light of life go outta your eyes when you had to sell your home to pay off those damnable medical bills." She slapped her hand on her knee. "It made me angry that if a person got sick, they had to sell their home to pay the damned bills. That isn't right. You and Bradley had always been good neighbors to my daughter, Cheryl, and my granddaughter, Val. I wanted to do something to thank you for being the kindhearted person you've always been."

She gave the papers to Griff. "Give 'em copies?"

Nodding, Griff took the papers and handed a stapled group to Sandy and to Talon. Lastly, he leaned across and handed the last group to Cat.

Sandy frowned, looking at the papers. "Gus...this is a deed...."

"Yep, sure is, Sandy." She gave her a huge grin, looked at Val and Griff and then focused on her. "I've bought the Triple H back for you, Sandy. For you and your son, Talon. Now, before you say anything, I have just one request. The Triple H is five hundred acres of prime grazing land for cattle. I'd like you to agree to *lease* me two hundred acres that I could run our herd on each summer for the next twenty years. After that, the lease expires. What do you say?"

Sandy stared down at the deed in her hands. The top paper had her name and Talon's name on it. Tears came to her eyes and she looked up at Gus, who was frowning and staring at her with great seriousness in her wrinkled expression. "Miss Gus…this…this is a shock…."

Talon rapidly read the first page of the deed. His heart thudded in his chest. Lifting his chin, he stared at the elder. "You really did this?"

"Sandy, the ranch is yours again," Gus said gently. "You have your home back." And then she looked over at Talon. "And your son has his family's ranch back, as it should be, to be passed on to him and his family." She smiled over at Cat. "And it wasn't lost on me that Talon and Cat are more than likely to get married sooner rather than later. So, Cat has a family ranch to marry into. She never had much of a life as a child. Not even what I'd call a halfway decent family. Now she has everything back that was taken from her when she was so young."

Cat felt tears jam into her eyes. Miss Gus's stern face blurred for a moment. She heard Sandy sob and press her hands to her face, weeping. Talon leaned over, sliding his arm around his mother, drawing her into his arms, holding her, his eyes bright with unshed tears.

"Miss Gus, you really are a guardian angel," Talon rasped. "Thank you…."

"Humph, I ain't no angel, Talon Holt!" She waggled her finger at him. "Now, you're a hired wrangler on our ranch and you need to keep workin' for us to make money to get your ranch back on its feet." She turned to Cat. "And you, young lady, you got a fork in the road starin' at you. I know you love Talon, and I betcha there's a marriage comin' soon. Val, Griff and I thought you might like a little weddin' present that was money instead of goods."

Val pulled out a check from the briefcase and stood up, leaning across the coffee table and handing it to Cat. "Gus didn't know you were going to hurt your knee. She felt this check for a hundred thousand dollars would be like a dowry for you and Talon. A little something to help get the Triple H back on its feet."

Gasping, Cat took the check. She gave Gus a look of disbelief and then turned, looking over at Talon. He seemed utterly stunned.

"That's a nice dowry," Talon finally admitted, his voice thick and unsteady. "Thank you, Miss Gus."

"Have ya asked her to marry you yet, Talon?"

"Er...no, ma'am, I haven't." Talon grinned a little at the feisty old woman. "But it's going to happen very shortly."

"Better," Gus mumbled, eyeing him. "You two were meant for each other. Even a blind fool could see that."

Cat wiped her eyes, staring down at the check. "Miss Gus...this is just too much...."

"Well," Gus said, "look at it this way. I talked to Jordana McPherson. She's a doctor. And she told me yesterday that it would be doubtful you'd ever be able to do firefighting again with that kind of knee injury. The way I look at it, Cat, you have some choices starin' you in the face. You can either remain in the fire department as a paramedic, which may or may not be good for that knee of yours. Or—" and she raised her eyebrows "—with that money, you could choose to get married to Talon here, stay at the ranch and not only be part owner, but be a full-time wrangler. Jordana said that being a wrangler was a lot less stressful on that knee of yours. And—" she wriggled her silver brows "—she also hinted that if you wanted a part-time job at the hospital, they have an opening for someone who's a paramedic."

Shock rolled through Cat. She put her hand on Sandy's shoulder as Sandy sobbed against her son. They were good tears. Tears of happiness, not sadness. Talon's eyes were moist and she loved him so much in that moment as he held his frail mother in his arms. Gus had just given them all a better life with her incredible generosity. As she looked over at Val, Griff and Gus, who were all smiling and who also had tears in their eyes, Cat had never felt so happy. Or so hopeful.

She slowly stood up, set the check on the coffee table and walked over to Miss Gus. Leaning down, Cat kissed the woman's cheek and whispered, "You *are* the best guardian angel in the world, Miss Gus."

She squeezed her gently and added, "I love you so much. I never knew my grandparents on either side of my family but if you don't mind, I'm going to adopt you as my grandmother?"

Gus pursed her lips and studied Cat. "I wouldn't have it any other way, child." She patted Cat's cheek. "I've had my eye on you for a long time. And that's why I wanted you workin' at the Bar H. You're special, Cat. You're responsible and you're loyal. I think Talon's getting one heck of a wife and partner at his side."

Cat smiled tearfully and pressed one last kiss on Gus's wrinkled forehead. "You are incredible, Miss Gus.

Thanks for letting me have you as my grandmother. That's worth more than any amount of money...."

"I'M STILL IN SHOCK," Cat admitted, lying in Talon's arms on her couch in her condo. Night had fallen and she was exhausted by the day's unexpected events.

He kissed her hair. "You? So am I. I don't know if my mother will ever get out from under the shock." And then he smiled.

"So much has happened," Cat whispered, her arm around his waist, content to be held by him. "And then Gus tells your mom that she's hired a group of men to repair not only the inside of your ranch house, but put on a new roof, new and improved double windows... Wow!"

"And tomorrow," Talon said, "we can all go home." He eased her away, studying her in the soft light from the kitchen. "And I haven't even officially asked you to be my wife. My partner. Will you?" Because he couldn't conceive of anything more right in his life. Searching Cat's shadowed eyes, which suddenly grew moist, her lips parting, Talon leaned down, kissing her slowly, deeply and with all the tenderness he had. Her mouth was soft and he could taste the salt of her tears as they silently ran down her cheeks. Sliding his hand across her jaw, he wanted to convey, with everything in his heart, what he held for her alone.

They'd come so close to losing each other. He knew it would take him time to deal with the ramifications of what had almost happened.

As he moved his mouth across hers, cherishing her scent, her tears and love he could feel radiating from her heart to his, Talon had never felt so grateful. Cat was here, in his arms. He would marry her. And he would love her. Now he knew what love was. What it felt like. How it breathed new life and breath into his shattered, grieving heart. Cat had replaced his loss of Hayden with new, beautiful promises of life to come. Her love was helping to heal his tortured past, helping him to realize how much good was left in his life. When she had come into his life, when she had looked down at him, sick and dying, Talon had not known how important Cat was going to become to him.

Time and space had shown him love. And Cat loved him without reservation, without games or manipulation. She was loyal in ways he'd never seen in a woman before. But it was her love that melded that loyalty to his grieving, broken heart. She was healing him by simply being with him, never mind the great sex they shared. As Talon eased from her wet, lush lips, he studied her slowly opening lashes. Her eyes were a deep blue with gold in their depths. That was her love reflected in them for him and he knew it.

"Well?" Talon asked her huskily, sliding his fingers through her hair at her temple. "Want to marry me? Be my best friend? My partner? Share our happy and our sad days together?" He saw her face soften with love for him.

"I can't even think of life without you in it, Talon," she whispered, leaning her cheek into his palm.

"You sure this is what you want?" Because Talon knew she was a career woman, no question.

Nodding, Cat sat up and faced him, their knees touching, her hand on his thigh. "The moment I saw you out in that blizzard, Talon, I felt my heart burst open. It surprised the hell out of me. I'd never felt like that be-

fore toward any man. There was just something about
you...." Cat gave him a smile and then looked over at
Zeke, who lay nearby, his head lifted, watching them
intently. "And Zeke, here, touched my heart, as well."

Tears burned in his eyes. One day, Talon would tell
her about Hayden, the brotherhood, the love they'd
shared as friends. Cat would keep the secret and by
telling her, it would ease some of his horrific shock and
trauma, too. Talon knew that about Cat. She wasn't a
paramedic for nothing. She was a healer, pure and simple. Now she was infusing him with life once again.

"You know, that morning you found me out on the
highway? I'd given up, Cat. I fell and I was lying there,
feeling what little energy I had left flowing out of me.
Zeke knew it. He was lying by my side, trying to warm
me, trying to give me his strength, but I'd already given
up." He picked up her hand, pressing a kiss to the inside
of her palm. Her fingers were long and tapered. Fingers
that had the ability to lift him out of a special hell that
had taken him down and was on its way to killing him
that cold, snowy morning. His voice thickened. "Someday, babe, I'm going to tell you the rest of the story...
when I'm ready...and you're going to understand just
how much you brought me back from the edge of that
grave I was ready to lay in."

Cat held his hand, hearing the rawness in his low
tone, seeing the terror banked deep in his eyes. "I sensed
it, Talon. I knew...."

Nodding, he stared at her in the gathering silence.
"You're healing me, Cat. You have from the start." Talon
shook his head, giving her a wry look. "I never knew
what love was. I really didn't. Until you came along.
Until you showed me every day in so many small and

large ways. I honestly don't feel I can breathe a full breath unless you're there beside me. You taught me so much about loving another person. That it's real, that it really exists…"

She smiled. "Your mom loves you, Talon. Your father, Gardner, loved you. You know what love is. Maybe, as a SEAL, you lost that? Maybe you've come home, reclaimed it."

He slid his fingers through her hair, gently settling it on her shoulder. "You *showed* me love, Cat. And what's amazing about it is you had nothing growing up. You, least of all, knew what love was."

"You can't steal love out of a heart, Talon," Cat whispered, giving him a warm look. "It's always there. I might not have known family love like you did, but when I became a paramedic and could help others, I understood what love was. And I could love that person who was injured and traumatized. I saw what love could do to equalize the situation, to ease their pain and fear."

"You eased mine," Talon admitted, his voice a rasp. Her eyes were soft with moisture, her lips curved gently with compassion. "I think I'm the luckiest damned bastard on this planet to love you, Cat. You feed me hope, babe. Hope I thought was torn from me and would never come again."

Cat slid her arms around his shoulders, seeing the ravages of things that had happened to him, bad things, which he'd never given voice to. "That's what love is all about, Talon. It feeds us, helps us survive, gives us hope and, best of all, dreams for the future."

Talon framed her face with his hands, drowning in the tender look of her eyes. "You not only saved my life, you saved my soul, babe. I'll never forget what you've

done, Cat. I'm going to wake up every morning looking for ways to love you."

Tears fell from her eyes as she stared at Talon. "I
want to be your wife, Talon. I want to be an equal partner at your side." Cat grazed his cheek, the stubble making her fingertips tingle. "Life is never easy, but the love
we have is so beautiful and strong, that we'll take it all
in stride. Okay?"

"Okay," Talon managed, pressing his brow to hers,
grateful beyond any words he could say. "I don't know
who's going to be happier. Us or my mother."

Laughing softly, Cat eased back and smiled. "She
knew we loved one another long before either of us
did," she confided. "And I think that not only having
her home back, but us living there, being married, is
going to give her a strength, a return of a dream she
thought had died a long time ago."

"You're a dream catcher. You know that?" Talon
kissed her smiling mouth and drowned in her shimmering gaze. "You've not only infused me with my
dreams, but you gave my mother back her dreams, too."

"Your mom isn't out of the woods yet. I want to be
there for her, too. With my knee out of commission,
hanging around the house, painting the rooms and stuff,
I think will be good for Sandy. Maybe after a while,
we can plan a winter wedding. That would give Sandy
time and space to adjust. She could help pick out the
wedding dress, the flowers. I know that would fulfill a
dream she's wanted for you for so long."

"I like the way you dream." Talon gently turned her
around so her head lay on his shoulder, his arms coming around her. "Are you okay with my mother in the
same house?"

"Totally. It's a big house, Talon. And Sandy isn't going to be the mother-in-law from hell with me. We've had a seven-year friendship and we respect one another." She shook her head and moved aside to meet his gaze. "Like Miss Gus said earlier, we're going to be one big, happy family."

"I think so, too," Talon admitted, meeting her smile. "You're an easy keeper, babe." He held Cat close. In the next few summer months, all their lives were going to change for the better.

Zeke rose up on his feet and came over, laying his head on Talon's thigh, looking up at them. He whined, his big, whiplike tail wagging back and forth.

Cat smiled and petted Zeke's black head. "You need to repair that white picket fence, Talon. He needs a place to call his own, too."

Gus had mentioned the fence around the main ranch house was partly down, badly needing sanding and a new coat of paint. "It will be one of the first things I fix over there," Talon promised her. Kissing her brow, he murmured, "I remember reading that real estate magazine, the photo you had circled, and you had drawn in a white picket fence around it." Talon watched her eyes go soft. "You are going to get your wish, babe. And Zeke can hang out with me as I repair and paint it. And it can be his yard that he'll share with you."

Cat nuzzled her face into the crook of his shoulder, contentment flowing through her. "That sounds wonderful," she said, and sighed.

Zeke whined and his tail wagged even more enthusiastically than before.

* * * * *